The Clapham Common Caper

By

Michael Fitzalan

Copyright © 2019 by Michael Fitzalan

Set in 1959, this Jo Murphy Mystery introduces Doctor Josephine
Murphy a pathologist and General Practitioner who lived in Clapham.
This is her adventure as told by her mentor and friend Richard Regan.

Dedication

To mothers and fathers, brothers, sisters, husbands, wives, sons and
daughters.

Contents

Chapter 1 - The Man - Mars the Bringer of War

"Are you coming in?" asked the handsome, young man as the heavy main door of No 1, Wetherby Gardens, swung open.

He was always willing to help a beautiful blonde woman, well-dressed and her hair coiffured exquisitely. If he had not been running five minutes late to meet friends for supper, he might have stayed to flirt with her, perhaps, but he was going to meet a young girl who was new to the group.

It was only down the road at the Hereford Arms, pre-dinner drinks, but he could not afford to be too late, making a good impression was normally a guarantee of a later date.

'A brunette in the hand was worth a blonde on the steps,' he mused.

Jo had been studying the buzzers for each flat. She smiled, her disarming smile, acknowledging his gallantry and good looks. He was fair-haired and handsome, perhaps a Guardsman, tall, elegant and thin, dressed in a light grey, single-breasted, suit, Jo reckoned it was from Gieves and Hawkes, a red and blue striped tie and white shirt hid behind a navy-blue cashmere jumper.

"Yes, please, I'm visiting the top flat, worse luck," she explained, giving him eye contact, hoping he would believe her.

"Be my guest," he announced, stepping backwards and drawing the door open.

He gave her an appreciative smile as she was very good looking, stunning in fact, and the camel skirt and jacket ensemble looked reassuringly expensive. She was a bit older than his usual type but definitely attractive. With the endearing hopefulness of youth, he thought he might well see her again.

Perhaps, he conjectured, he might get to know her better if things did not work out with the girl at the pub. At his age, life was full of infinite possibilities.

"Thank you," she replied, slipping past him with ease, a rush of joy ran through her, she could not believe her good fortune. A closed gate had swung open.

As Jo started to shuffle up the carpeted staircase, she heard the door slam shut behind him, which meant she could increase her pace. There was no longer any need for pretence. She wondered why Jenny Strong should buy the top floor flat, it was not for the views; the other stucco apartment buildings blocked any vista of the capital. The brass runners and wine-red carpet became a blur as she bounded up the four flights. There was no room for a lift in the stairwell.

Jenny had good legs and Jo could see why if she was trundling up and down these stairs every day. Grabbing the bannister, she hauled herself up, taking two steps at a time. Jo was tall and athletic, which stood her in good stead for the climb.

She had no idea how she would get into Jenny's apartment or what she would find there. All she knew was that Jenny Strong had secrets hidden in there. Her train was at this moment hurtling towards King's Cross St Pancras. Jo had very little time to search the flat for answers. She had to act fast.

For some strange reason, she thought of her brother at the monastery in Nunraw. Thoughts of stations triggered memories. It was from St. Pancras Station that Father Stephen had left to join the silent Cistercian order at Sancta Maria Abbey. It was a fleeting thought.

Silence was also required at Wetherby Gardens; she did not want to alert the neighbours to her presence. Jo rested halfway up the stairs; already she was glowing, her heart thumping in her chest. Cigarette smoking had shrunk her lung capacity, so she was panting. She was tall, a size ten, statuesque but she was not used to exercise. She 'caught her breath'.

She simply had to give up smoking, she told herself.

Taking a deep breath, she walked up the two remaining floors to the flat. At the top, she rested. Her heart rate was returning to normal, but adrenaline kept her pulse rate racing. She wanted to remain calm and she tried her best to quell her panting.

Discipline was needed.

Pulling herself together on the landing at the top of the stairs, she looked down. It was a very, very long way down. Wondering how she might pick the lock, she suddenly thought that the neighbour might have a spare key. Just as she was turning to ask, she noticed the door was ever so slightly ajar; it was not flush with the wall. Not only that, but the lock looked like it had been forced open.

'Burglars,' she immediately thought.

There were scars on the white gloss paintwork, which she might have dismissed as carelessness with keys, if the door had been closed. Her heart stopped. This was a complication she had not foreseen.

Hesitating, only briefly, Jo determined to approach them with her charm. There was no going back, she had to be brave, she decided. Perhaps, a woman might be able to talk her way out of a situation. Hopefully, her Irish charm would help to diffuse any charged atmosphere she might encounter.

On second thoughts, it would perhaps be better to call the police and let them deal with it. There were already two detectives in hospital, she remembered so she dismissed the idea. Leaving it up to the police might complicate things; the burglar might get away before they arrived. It was time for action, 'time and tide, wait for no man,' she intoned in her head. There was no choice; she had to go in alone. Jenny would be home soon. Jo steeled herself to open the door.

Not for the first time, in this caper, she was unaware of what lay behind the door. One thing she did know; she had to find out who was there, how they got in and what they were doing there in the first place. It was clearly not Jenny. Why would anyone break into her flat?

Her heart hammering, she pushed the door open, conscious that she should do it slowly and gently so the hinges did not creak, she stepped through the doorway and only half closed the door behind her, making sure the door would not blow shut and give her away.

She had been expecting to be greeted by a large room overlooking the street. Instead, she was confronted by a blank wall and, to her right, yet another staircase leading up from this second landing.

Inwardly sighing, she tiptoed up the stairs. As Jo emerged out of the stairwell, she froze.

Her head was only just visible above the last step, but she could see that the burglar had drawn the heavy claret drapes and he had turned on all the lights and lamps in the room.

Her heart was pounding now, she felt sick, she had come so far and now there was yet another obstacle. She realised she had no choice but to go on.

It was definitely a man, big, broad and fighting fit. Her luck, it seemed, had changed. Fortune's fickle wheel had turned full circle. He had removed his gloves and his head was bowed as he shuffled some papers, skimming each leaf as he searched for something. His hands worked frantically through the piles of letters. Next to his pigskin gloves, was a heavy handled commando knife, which Jo immediately realised was not for letter opening.

It had a blackened steel blade and a ribbed handle. It was about a foot long, the blade being six inches. The sight of it made Jo's heart stop. Opening another draw, he took out another pile of papers and scanned each of those.

The burglar was wearing a balaclava, not one of those open-faced woollen ones that everyone used to wear to keep warm in winter, but a menacing black mask with two holes for the eyes and a slit for the mouth.

Jo wished she had been dressed for flying; her camel Pierre Balmain skirt-suit was not ideal for fight or flight. She noticed her green silk blouse was clinging to her skin. If there had been time, she would have taken off her jacket, it would restrict her movement, being pursued down the stairs with that drop worried her and she wanted to keep cool physically as well as mentally.

She drank in the situation.

On the desk there were piles of papers a green shaded desk lamp burning brightly and a black Bakelite telephone. The phone might be of use, the lamp might make a weapon, or the paper might offer a distraction if she showered him in it, she might be able to escape or maybe she could pretend that she could find the document for him, had been told by Jenny to help him locate it.

Thoughts flooded her head.

It was as if he smelt her approach, despite her soft tread on the carpeted stairs, he sensed her presence.

There was no escape at that stage. Jo continued up the stairs. The burglar appraised her as she entered the large drawing room. They were matched in height, he was six foot; Jo was tall, too, five foot nine. She was strong and her fencing gave her agility and stamina, but she doubted that she could match him in strength, not with his bulging muscles and boxer's pose.

Being on the fifth floor of No. 1 Wetherby Gardens meant the window could not provide escape. She could bolt down the stairs, but he would follow, hurling himself on top her, she did not doubt that for a second. Even worse, he could bundle her over the bannisters, and she would not survive the plunge to the bottom.

He put down the papers.

Jo was ready for a fight. She had two brothers; she had fought with them enough times, physically and mentally. The knife was a worry. At first, Jo thought he was reaching for the black leather gloves. Then, she saw his left hand grasp the black, ribbed, handle of a knife. Suddenly, the odds were not so even.

She flicked, her long blonde hair away from her face, trying to see what colour her assailant's eyes were, trying to see if she recognised them. They stared at her, ice blue like her own, but his burned with anger while hers darted left and right, desperately searching the room for something with which she could defend herself. A knife-wielding thug threatened her on the other side of the desktop.

Talking was no longer an option, yet that was her forte. He wanted her out of the way, and she wanted to have answers. Their eyes locked over the sea of the desk for a full minute. He had the power; he had the strength. He was militarily fit.

She was determined to stand her ground.

Perhaps, he was a former soldier or a physical training instructor. He was all muscle. That was clear. She was relatively fit, and her long limbs might allow her to outrun him, but he was beefy, he could crush her easily with his strength. There had to be a way for her to save the situation, she reasoned.

She was right; he was might. She had to prevail.

"One of the Tweed twins?" she announced from the relative safety of the other side of the room. "Breaking and entering is hardly your forte, I thought that was extortion and murder."

He was surprised to hear her posh voice, cut glass Kensington.

"Doctor Nora Josephine Murphy, I presume," the man hissed, his lips curled into a grotesque smile behind the mask.

"My friends call me Jo, but you can call me Doctor Murphy," she replied dryly, taking a step towards the desk.

The mouth became a pair of pouting lips twisting into a bigger smile, he was finding all this entertaining. Jo was just another problem that he had to solve. He had been successful so far that night.

She heard a snort. Jo knew he was evaluating the situation, deciding when to pounce. It was like being in the room with a cobra.

"I don't see any of your friends here, I dealt with Regan outside and you sent Stephens to take him to hospital. How did you get in here anyway?" he drawled in his south London accent, his eyes never leaving her face.

Jo smiled knowingly, provoking him.

"I recognise the voice and you're left-handed, Derek Tweed, I assume," Jo asserted proudly, moving a step towards him, playing grandmother's footsteps. She had only met Tweed once before, but she had managed to pierce his disguise. She was bluffing about recognising his voice, but he did not know that.

"You should have stuck to doctoring love," he advised, the mouth forming itself into a dismissive smile that showed his teeth, "no one asked you to stick your nose in."

"Doctoring those files seems to be your purpose. What are you doing, destroying evidence?" she asked, taking another pace closer to the desk.

"Mind your own business," he warned, the mouth was, now, a sneer.

"Jenny wanted some incriminating information destroyed before we could get a warrant and so she sent for her tame assassin," she goaded him, moving yet another step towards the desk that she hoped would form a protective barrier against her attacker.

"That's my twin," he explained.

"That's what he says about you, he's pointed the finger of suspicion at you, anything to escape a life sentence, Regan tells me."

"I'm not falling for that one. I just clear up after him, normally," he said and, then, paused, "but this time I'm prepared to make an exception, on medical grounds."

"Oh really, what medical grounds are they?"

"I don't like doctors who think they are detectives."

He lifted up the receiver. Jo thought he was going to call someone for instructions and was about to tease him about that fact and his inability to make up his own mind, when he smashed the receiver down on the desk.

The earpiece split, the cover flew into the air, landing on the floor, and a silver disk fell out like a dislocated eye, the internal receiver, hanging from coloured electrical wires. He tore it off. Raising, what was left of the receiver, he smashed the mouthpiece on the leather tabletop. Again, the Bakelite cracked, splitting open like a walnut, the microphone cover flew off, joining its double on the floor. Tweed tore that grey disk from the electrical flex. Again, he stared at her with his cold blue eyes. Again, Jo stared back at him.

Neither of them was prepared to blink.

"So, my assumptions were right," Jo beamed, hoping to rile him further.

She hoped that his anger would be his Achilles heel.

Chapter 2 - i - Josephine Spills the Beans

That was her story, which she related to me, at Lyons' Corner House, in The Strand. It was a rainy Saturday morning and the traffic was light. I had travelled up from Maple Road, Penge, in my gunship grey Morris Minor, 1000 Series and she travelled up from the west side of Clapham in the Brown and beige Rolls Royce, Silver Cloud Mk 1, a car I wished I could drive just once.

We parked in Craven Passage, which we had agreed to do so over the telephone. I arrived early and waited for her, carrying an umbrella big enough to cover us both. I had only been there for a few minutes when I saw the familiar brown beast with its iconic radiator grill and Spirit of Ecstasy. She parked expertly, as if the car were a Mini, parallel to the pavement, only half an inch from the kerb. From there, we walked through the drizzle and mist to the restaurant opposite Charing Cross Station.

She had just come back from holiday at the Hotel Nixe Palace in Palma de Mallorca, so she was looking in rude health. Jo put her gloved hand in the crook of my arm, and we strode at her pace, she was leading, again. It was the 10th June 1960. We had wrapped up the Clapham Common case on 17th December.

Jo was pregnant but she did not show yet, it was a bit parky anyway and she was wearing her green thick wool overcoat over a tan skirt suit from Jaeger, I wore a sombre suit, my de-mob suit, in slate grey from Burton, a chain of gentleman's outfitters popular at the time.

So, why was she telling me about her fight in a flat?

It's because I am a copper. My name is Richard Regan; people called me Dick. In the fifties, it was an acceptable nickname.

So why am I telling the story, now? The safety of years, which means most of the protagonists are dead, now. I was only 27 when I made Detective Inspector.

At that age you never consider you might want to look back at any stage of your life, even adventures like the ones we had.

Of course, when I realised those 'halcyon days were over', another one of Jo's expressions, I wanted to write about Jo. Wanting to do something and actually doing something are to entirely different matters. Anyway, after typing so many reports, sitting at an Olivetti in the sixties and seventies, the appetite for, and the effort of, typing our story lasted less than a week.

After that, rheumatism and the Rotary Club kept me away from the keys. Then, the years moved by too rapidly and now I feel its time to tell the tale. As a result, I am dictating this to my grandson, Rory. He's my stenographer, a speed-typing journalist. He deserves a mention. He calls me Ricky or Rick In those days, I was known as Dick to Jo and no one giggled at the name.

Back at the Lyons 'tea-house', Jo, finally, got to tell me the conclusion or what she called, the 'denouement', of our investigation. After the Clapham Caper, the Criminal Investigation Department had arrested the last of the Tweed twins and I had been transferred to Division when I was promoted.

Our meeting was the first chance to hear the story from the horse's mouth. Being in hospital with a head wound, people had fed me snippets of information but the best person to tell the story was Jo. She was a wonderful raconteur and although I love my wife deeply, I was a little bit in love with her, if I am truthful. Unrequited love, I am afraid, the worst kind.

Since our adventure, she had been working hard at her surgery and helping her husband to build up their pub portfolio so a Saturday lunch was the only time we could make for each other.

The children had gone to the Royal Automobile Club, in Pall Mall, for a swim with the Swiss nanny while George had a steam bath. He practically lived in the sauna at the Royal Automobile Club when he was not working.

After the pleasantries, Jo took me back to that night, telling me about facing Derek Tweed and his knife.

"You must have been petrified," I exclaimed, looking in awe at this elegant lady who had tangled with and survived an encounter with one of the Tweed twins, two notorious thugs in their day.

Jo was three months pregnant, but she did not look it, good tailoring, and her height, and her slimness, all helped. She turned quite a few heads in the restaurant, she did wherever she went, blonde and blue eyed, rich and refined, intelligent and witty, a heady combination.

The rumble of trolleys laden with cakes, the click of waitresses laying heavy cutlery and the clash and clack of tables being cleared, along with the noise of other people talking, became a background sound as we talked about that night; the night when the caper came to its conclusion.

"I didn't have time to be frightened," she drawled in her cut glass Kensington voice. she was in no hurry.

Jo was certainly a dichotomy. She told me that she had been born in the East End and yet she sounded like a posh resident of Mayfair, more Buckingham Palace than Bow Bells.

"How come you talk even more posh than Queen and yet you told me you were cockney?" I asked.

I knew her well enough by now to ask such a question.

"I think you have fallen into the trap of preconception, surely you should be more interested in inspection, that's my perception?" she replied cleverly, offering me a Senior Service cigarette. "Will you join me?"

"No, thanks, I thought you were giving up?"

"As Mark Twain opined, giving up smoking is easy…"

"… I've done it a thousand times."

"I've taught you well, my dear boy," she said sounding like a Duchess, it always confused me.

"Well you could knock me down with a feather, you say you were born in a pub in the East End, sounds like you were born with a silver spoon in your mouth," I confessed, putting my hand up to decline the cigarette, " I thought you were really wanting to give up, I reckon that's the third one since you arrived."

"Cutting down, darling, cutting down."

"Not from where I am standing," I quipped, it was an old 'in -joke'.

She had expanded my sense of humour and my sense of fun.

We both laughed, hers was carefree and tinkled like crystal, mine was repressed Hendon. I knew that she called everyone darling; I was not going to get my hopes up. It still made me feel special despite myself. Logic and the heart are never related, sadly.

"How's the toddler?" she asked, in those days infant mortality was high, it wasn't the halcyon days that everyone imagines.

No one believed what Super Mac told us that: 'we had never had it so good'. There was still a lot of poverty and poor health around. We still had barefoot children, childhood diseases and malnutrition. You would not believe the statistics if you read them.

Post-war Britain was in a sorry state and I can safely say, things remained pretty grim until the swinging sixties changed everyone's perception.

"He's on fine form, now, after suffering the whooping cough, my wife Susie is exhausted, after six weeks of it," I confessed.

"Pertussis is very nasty, you got off lightly. It can last ten weeks, I'm glad he's better. Make sure you give him plenty of milk and fish to build up his stamina."

"Thanks, I will. How are your brood?"

"All well, Heidi is looking after them during the week and on Saturdays when they go swimming, George officially has charge of them today, but all he's doing is driving the darlings to swimming, leaving Heidi to supervise them in the pool while he slopes off for a sauna, no doubt, and next week, he'll be taking me to the obstetricians for a view on number four."

"Have you thought of any names?" I ventured, hoping she might want to call the baby Richard, after me.

"Deidre or Fiona if it's a girl, Anton if it's a boy."

"After Anton Fox?"

I bridled at the name; I was sure he had impressed her. He was charming and better looking than me. Since I had met him, he had become my nemesis. I could not believe what Jo was doing, naming her son, not after me but after Anton.

"No, after St. Anton where the baby was conceived. We were there in April," she chortled.

"What were you doing there?" I asked, my face crimson, no longer with suppressed anger but with embarrassment.

"Apart from the obvious?" Jo asked, she could not be embarrassed but she adored teasing people in a gentle way.

"A long way to go to conceive," I managed to say, then regretted it; maybe she was at some clinic for mental or physical problems.

"Some people will go to any lengths, but we were ski-ing, it's George's latest passion."

"You two are a couple of dynamos, aren't you? Fast cars, flying, horse racing, and now ski-ing," I noted.

I was feeling more than a modicum of jealousy not about the ski-ing or owning a horse but definitely the flying and driving. I had only been in a plane once and that was flying from one airfield to another. After my initial fear, I had loved the experience. Having survived one flight, I felt sure the next would be easier. It seemed a lot less bother than taking the train from South Norwood.

As for the cars, I was a petrol-head through and through; we called them motoring enthusiasts in those days. I wanted to order a Mini as soon as they were launched in late August 1959, four months before I had met Jo. I had to save for another year and only finally managed to buy one in September 1960. It was a bit cramped inside, but it was nippy and easy to park. I loved it.

"How's Susie?" Jo asked, she always asked after her and it always made me feel slightly disloyal.

I never told her if I was meeting Jo, I wanted to avoid her getting jealous or upset.

"She's fine, a little worn down by looking after the baby after the illness but she's in good spirits otherwise."

"It's hard work."

"It's the spirit of the age, we all have to work so hard."

"Work hard and play hard," she laughed, flicking ash from her cigarette.

"Fight hard, too, by the sound of things," I added, reminding her of her description of the struggle with the man in black.

"Yes, I learnt to fight from the Quiet Man," she joked.

She was referring to the film with John Wayne set on the West Coast of Ireland. Her husband's cousin, Joe Melotte, had been the stand in for Big John.

The fight scenes were obviously choreographed to make the star shine and not violent in any shape or form.

In fact, Jo reminded me of a blonde version of Maureen O'Hara, full mouth, generous lips a straight long nose and a high brow, but Jo's hair was a lot longer, it reached down her back, and it was blonder.

"Well you didn't fight fair, like him," I complained.

"I was fighting for my life," she protested.

That's what they all say," I quipped, of course it was an expression that Jo had taught me.

I think she felt guilty about fighting but she had no choice; it was her life in danger, literally. Tweed would have dispatched her if he could. That had been his instructions.

"Not in line with the Hippocratic Oath, kicking someone below the belt and leaving him with a burnt hand, is it?" I announced, smiling to show I was teasing.

We had been through many awful and gruelling experiences together, so I was entitled.

"I had to guarantee my getaway, George called an ambulance and the police on my instructions, remember, you were not there, were you?" she remonstrated before smiling sweetly to show that, firstly, she forgave me, and secondly she could tease me back.

 I always felt slightly heady in her presence. I had to keep my wits about me, anticipating her wit and wordplay. That hurt, her last comment reminded me of how I had let her down. I had promised to protect her, no matter what happened. My spectacular failure haunted me. She had to fight her way out of a situation on her own and I felt bad about that. Jo could be disarming as well as charming.

"Okay, I'll do the fighting next time, or Sergeant Stephens will," I assured her.

"Well, I think our roles are flexible, it was me who found out about the crime ring in the first place and it was George who tracked us down when we were in trouble and Detective Sergeant Stephens who saved my life. We all had a role to play even if they were muddled up."

"I suppose you're right," I admitted.

It was never easy to argue with Jo, she was used to getting her own way and beside all that, she was generally right.

"How is Sergeant Stephens?"

"Terry? He's well, fully recovered from our adventures. He's a bit bored, now, though."

"Still a dab hand with a revolver?"

"Does Jo Murphy smoke too many Senior Service cigarettes?"

We both laughed uproariously. It was good to be in her company again. She was such great fun.

"Stephens knows how to handle a gun and got us out of a few scrapes besides," she noted.

"He was a good detective sergeant, one of the best, I miss him, now he's gone to provide his services to the Diplomatic Protection Division, I miss him and my old office. They were all good people, great colleagues," I confessed.

"Onward and upward," Jo reminded me and, as usual, brought me back to my senses.

Those magical moments with the dear doctor made the mundane minutiae of everyday life seem more tolerable. Even now, I borrow expressions like those from Jo.

She was a font of knowledge, well-read and able to quote from Shakespeare, Shaw, Twain and Wilde. She had an encyclopaedic knowledge of art and medical matters, too. To me, she was a wonderfully extraordinary woman.

Maybe it would be best if I start at the beginning of this caper.

I know it was a long time ago, but the story is worth telling.

Still women are not equal, despite their so-called liberation, still women are deemed to be inferior to men in some societies. Still women do all the work and get all the blame.

The world that I lived in has changed for the better in so many ways but still, almost sixty years later, some things have sadly remained stubbornly the same. Our story is rather like 'Waverley', the book by Walter Scott.

One of the most baffling is that despite all their efforts for recognition and all their contribution to society, women are still not valued adequately. People like Jo are never celebrated properly, and the fairer sex is not appreciated or respected enough. When I say fairer, I have to say I mean fair in the true sense of the word. It should be a level playing field and it's not. That's not fair.

It was ever thus.

Maybe this book in some way will make amends for the injustice.

Chapter 3 – Cedars Road – When I Met Jo

It all began on a freezing night in December.

"Battersea, 7990," Jo announced into the black Bakelite receiver, she twiddled her finger around the brown cord cable.

"Doctor Murphy?" I asked; my voice was hard and dry like gravel, I was tired and so were my men, it had been a long shift.

"Speaking," she replied putting on her best telephone manner but there was caution in her voice; this was obviously not a social call.

"I am sorry to disturb you on a Sunday night, but I understand you are the duty pathologist, on-call today," I stammered.

"Yes, of course, you're right, and you are?"

"Detective Inspector Regan, Richard Regan, I am afraid we'll need your services tonight."

"Of course, Inspector, can you give me the address, please?" she asked.

Picking up a pencil and a sheaf of A5 paper piled neatly next to the telephone, she stood poised to take down the details. Fitzpatrick Brothers, Haymarket London SW1, was written in embossed navy blueprint on the top of each sheet. Her husband had branched out into owning pubs just like his father-in-law but had added a wine merchant to his portfolio.

His business was smaller and not as successful as his fathers-in-law, but it was still a good business, good enough to buy two racehorses, Babette and Prince Paladin and have three holidays a year.

Jo pulled her weight with her practice.

"Flat 49c, Thornton Place, 48-52 Clapham Common North Side. It's at the top of Cedars Road."

"Thank you, Inspector, the large mansion block, I know it," she asserted.

"Really?" I replied, surprised.

"I live on the West Side. I can be there in fifteen minutes," Jo explained, helpfully.

"Good, my men would appreciate that. By the way it's the one on the left as you turn into Cedars Road."

"I know it."

"Good, a constable will escort you from the front drive."

"I'll be there as soon as I can," she promised, "goodbye Inspector Regan."

"I look forward to seeing you soon, goodbye," I added, knowing that my voice had not softened during the call. Besides, I had to remain professional much as I hated to disturb anyone's Sunday night.

I was a copper; I'd signed up to ungodly hours at inhospitable venues. As a General Practitioner, so had she but it did not occur to me. My men were expecting a long delay, they were used to waiting ages for the doctor who signed the death certificate to arrive. They were normally based in Surrey and it could take up to an hour for them to drive up or if they were local, they made us wait while they finished their meal. From experience, I was already doubting Jo's word, but in all the time I knew her she was always earlier than I expected and never once late. She was a lady.

Frankly, I have to confess, I was intrigued by the fact that the duty pathologist should be a woman. It piqued my interest, nothing more, I imagined a Miss Marple type, what I actually got was pure glamour, a veritable blonde beauty, long blonde hair, blue eyes, tall and womanly.

Jo had hung up when she heard the click of disconnection. Standing in the dining room, looking at black marble mantle clock in the middle of the mahogany mantle-piece, she saw it was ten o'clock. George was not yet home as he was out inspecting the pubs, checking the takings, and chatting to the manager, but the children were upstairs at the top of the house in bed in their rooms.

Catherina and Georgina were a year apart in age, the eldest, Catherina was seven years old, Georgina was six, both had been born in August; a day and a year apart.

Their Swiss nanny slept in the bedroom between them on the top floor. She was in charge and was used to taking over when Jo was on call. It happened every three weeks. Their only boy Patrick was four and he was on the second floor, sleeping next to his parent's room, in the Blue Room, the nursery.

Jo's medical bag was out in the hallway; standing on a hexagonal Moroccan table and beside it was a standard lamp, with a pale green shade, that guided her to the double doors at the front of the house. A fire burnt in the grate, a copper guard encased an exquisite glossy green tiled Art Nouveau fireplace, an Arabic design, surrounded by mahogany boxing. Flame danced around the coals.

She warmed herself by the fire for a moment as she checked her bag, stethoscope, auriscope, blood-pressure kit and pathologist paraphernalia, including blank Death Certificates. There was a spacious coat cupboard under the stairs, opposite the fire, from which she chose a green, three-quarter-length, wool coat.

Dressed and equipped for her mission, she walked to the wide door, turned the delicate door handle, a brass teardrop, and slipped into the gap between the sets of doors, carrying her bag. It was icy cold. She pulled the inner door quietly behind her using the substantial brass handle in the centre of the door beneath the art nouveau glass.

Before putting her case down to turn the locks, one above the other that released the left-hand side of the double doors that led onto Wakehurst Road, she buttoned her coat with her left hand. Grabbing her case, she steeled out into the night air, putting the bag on the first of two stone steps. She turned around and inserted both sets of keys to turn the locks in order to close the door behind her as soundlessly as smoke. Leaving the house was like leaving Fort Knox.

Outside in Wakehurst Road her car stood under a lamppost, an Atlantic Marlin and strato, two-tone blue, 1942, Nash 600 Ambassador 6, the 'Slipstream sedan'; it was aerodynamic and sleek, a beautiful expression of modern design.

Her father, John Rickard Murphy, had shipped it over from America for Jo to drive while she was a student at the Royal College of Surgeons in Dublin. There was no alternative; car production in England had been halted by the war, yet in America, the smaller car producers had continued production whilst their larger competitors produced trucks and tanks.

That meant that anyone with enough money could pick up an American classic, and have it shipped over to England. The Nash was a 1940s 'American beauty'. It was all aerodynamic, curved lines and bulky beauty. It was the future of motoring, stylish and sophisticated. It was a car that could cruise in comfort on highways and speed effortlessly through the cityscape. It was the epitome of futuristic, streamline design. It was something our transatlantic cousins were so supremely competent in designing at that time.

The brown leather seats were cold, and the windows had condensation on them, but she was wrapped up warm. Jo started the engine and the windscreen wipers came on with a flick of a switch, clearing the evening dew from the outside of the windscreen. Wiping the inside of the glass with a chamois cloth cleared her enough space in the large windscreen to drive safely, the efficient heater was already clearing the condensation at the bottom. Tossing the cloth onto the dashboard, she selected drive using the stalk on the steering column.

Checking the road was clear, by looking over her left shoulder, she drove left onto the West Side and filtered onto the South Circular Road, racing towards Battersea Rise. Being left hand drive, she sat close to the line down the middle of the road that separated traffic bound for Battersea Rise and traffic headed for Clapham Common, Northside.

She kept to the left-hand Lane. Then, she turned right onto the A3, heading to Clapham Old Town, slipping into the left-hand lane just after Elspeth Road. The Northside boasted a church and several large houses built or bought by friends of the Clapham Sect, those fine individuals who worked so hard for the abolition of slavery.

At the top of Cedars Road, a Victorian developer had created two stunning apartment blocks. They were constructed using beige brick. All the flanking buildings had been made with London redbrick. The roof was modelled on some chateau and would have looked more at home on a Parisian boulevard. The buildings loomed over their terraced house neighbours. It was an imposing sight. Jo turned left at the lights, and sharp left into the walled gravel driveway, white and beige predominated. The perimeter walls were three-foot-high and topped with white stone flagstones. The drive at the front had two cars, one at each end. She drove into the large space left by a white Ford Zephyr Mark III and an Austin Wolseley, police car.

They were the only two cars in the car park and the good doctor had not encountered any other cars on her journey. Jo thought that George's Rolls would have looked quite at home in front of the edifice, the courtesy car of a chic Cannes hotel. The Nash looked like it belonged to a visiting American film star, perhaps a successful writer like Scott Fitzgerald who favoured holidaying in the south of France with Zelda. Maintaining the French flavour, each apartment had three French windows accompanied by a white decorated stone balcony. The building was completely out of place in a south London winter.

Jo flicked the switch to douse the lights, extracted the key and grabbed her medical bag from the passenger seat. Habit meant she locked the door despite having spotted a uniformed constable at the bottom of the steps at number forty-nine, one of the entrances located in the middle of the apartment building.

He had not expected the pathologist to arrive in such an ostentatious car, but he had gone to greet the passenger anyhow, bored of standing by the dark double doors at the top of the stone staircase, he ran down the steps. Jo was not the passenger; she was the driver; her car was left hand drive. Walking to the sloping back of the vehicle, she looked up at the impressive building with admiration.

There were three different doors to choose from but the one on the far right was the only one with a policeman positioned outside, so Jo headed for that one. Within ten minutes of my phone call, Jo had parked the car and was introducing herself to the policeman who I had promised would be posted inside the entrance to the car park, which was on Cedars Road.

He looked cold, even in his storm-cape and she felt sorry of him.

"Good evening Constable," she sighed, trying to invest as much sympathy as she could muster into the remark.

"Good evening, Doctor Murphy, Inspector Regan said I should expect you, but I was expecting the usual wait for the duty pathologist."

She smiled; he was clearly grateful that she had arrived promptly. "I tried to get here as soon as I could. I think we're the only people out and about at this ungodly hour."

In those days, ten fifteen on a Sunday was an ungodly hour when Monday was around the corner.

He smiled indulgently at her; they only had time for brief pleasantries.

"Forty-nine, flat C for Charlie; you'll find it on the first floor, Doctor."

"Thank you, officer."

"Follow me, doctor," he added, walking briskly ahead of her.

He was glad because he could warm himself a little by standing in the hall, now that she had arrived. It was damp and chilly outside; the common parts were dry and relatively warm.

Of course, he had to patrol outside occasionally but he could spend the majority of his time inside, which was a relief with the damp cold air penetrating his uniform. No one was about.

He trotted up the stone steps, ahead of her, informed me of her arrival through the intercom on the wall and opened the door, pushing aside the left-hand leaf of the wide, heavy gloss black, double doors. Above them was a white stone façade with carved flower patterns clinging to a large arch window that topped the ornate doorway.

Jo told me, much later, that it reminded her of the entrance to a Georgian mansion house. It seemed incongruous to her that someone should kill himself or herself in such a plush place. She admitted that it was this fact that had made her suspicious in the first place.

She was, also, a fan of Sherlock Holmes. He, as you know, started any supposition with the maxim: 'When you have eliminated all of which is impossible, then whatever remains, however improbable, must be the truth'.

Jo bounded up the stairs remembering the races she used to have with the other students, at the Rotunda in Dublin, to deliver a baby. The first one to reach the round delivery room always delivered the baby; the runners up had to wait around the hospital until they had a delivery.

Doctors had to perform a dozen deliveries before they could leave the Rotunda, escape midwifery duties, and go home. A dozen times she ensured she reached the delivery room, first.

The Rotunda was the first lying-in-hospital in the world, but the doctors did most of the lying around on daybeds, on call, twenty-four hours until they had filled their quota.

Jo had wanted to go to bed, not hang around a hospital dayroom, in the middle of Dublin, waiting to deliver a baby, so simply, she ran faster.

The apartment block hallway had beautiful Moroccan style floor with cream, grey and green tiles and above them loomed a wide, winding staircase with a heavy mahogany handrail and thick pile, tan carpet.

The flower theme was continued on the black painted wrought iron balustrade. Some sort of iron, Russian Ivy curled up two trellis poles at every step. The bottom of the stairs had not been smoothed flat with plaster but instead mirrored the steps above, meaning the outline of the steps was picked out from below; she had never seen that before.

Jo liked that; it was unusual.

The brown bannister rail was so highly polished that her gloves slid along them as she ran. The ceilings were high, more like the ones at the 'Georges V' in Paris than the terraced houses of Clapham and Battersea borders. It was incongruous in a working-class area, just like the dozen or so remaining Georgian mansions that were dotted around the common.

She knew the 'Cinq' because George had taken her to the famous hotel one summer perhaps because it was the best hotel in Paris, at that time, or perhaps because the hotel shared his name. With his ego, it was hard to tell, she had explained to me once.

She was reading 'Down and Out in Paris and London', by George Orwell, at the time and she was convinced Eric Blair had got a job as a 'plongeur', washing up dishes in the kitchen of the august hotel while in Paris.

Jo hurtled up the stairs, swinging her free arm but keeping the medical bag, a brown, leather, Gladstone, level.

At the top of each flight of stairs was a wide landing, beyond which was an arched window like a fanlight on a Georgian doorway and below that was another door. The top half was made of glass, the bottom-half was wood. Rectangular windows, on either side, flanked these doors, which allowed light to flood into the landings. As an extra barrier, they also kept the wintry weather of the stairwell away from the apartments.

As I have already told you, she kept on wondering why someone had committed suicide at this residence. It was a nagging feeling that played havoc with her feminine intuition. She had seen lots of death, but this was her first suicide, she had expected the person to be destitute and unhappy.

The opulent surroundings did not fit into her preconception of a suffering soul. It was a mixture of Georgian grandeur and fin-de-siècle opulence. If she had been going to a party at the flat, she would have adored the place. Pushing the door open, she arrived. What an entrance. I had never seen such a stunning woman. She was tall. She was blonde. She was beautiful.

I stood in the open doorway, holding my brown trilby, I had lost one already, wearing my demob suit, and a beige trench coat as well as a hangdog expression. The truth was I needed sleep and had not got it. My first baby, Brian, was teething and I was working longer and longer hours without a break. Another early start coupled with a late night was exactly what the doctor would not have ordered.

When I was younger, I was considered a handsome man and Jo was amazingly attractive. Her Guerlain perfume oozed into the room; her hair was perfectly styled. her clothes were expensive and top quality and her downright animal vitality struck me immediately.

My heart leapt.

It was plain for my officers to see that Jo was a beauty. There was no denying it. She had shoulder length, golden blonde hair, bright blue eyes, a high forehead and high cheekbones, a generous mouth, a straight nose and a heart shaped face. As ever, she was impeccably dressed but what was less obvious that night, in her professional persona, was that her striking looks were accompanied by a quick wit and intelligence that made her such a magnetic personality.

We smiled at each other. It was an acknowledgment of our good looks and prowess, and a salute to our sacrifice in public service and to show we had good teeth. I gasped and I think I heard an intake of breath from Jo, but it could have been just a sigh of relief at reaching her destination and being able to start the process of examining the body. We held each other's gaze for a fraction of a second longer than was normal or necessary.

I felt my nostrils flare.

It was clear to me there was an animal attraction and only conventions stopped us acting further or succumbing to our impulses. I think one or other of the two policemen in the flat noticed a slight frisson between us, but we all shrugged it off. There was work to do and convention to adhere to, the caveman in me had to be put back into the darkness.

A 'coup de foudre' in the apartment of a suicide in Battersea during the depths of winter was bound to be short lived. I put my hat into my left hand so I could shake hands with her. She had a firm grip; I was relieved, confidence can prove to be a powerful aphrodisiac as well as a reassurance. I spoke first, welcoming her; I was beholden to do so.

"Good Evening, again, Doctor, thank you for coming so quickly, I'm impressed you made it here so quickly, normally fifteen minutes is an hour in medical circles." I noted dryly, remembering that I had spent long evenings waiting for doctors to finish their meals before deigning to come and relieve my hard-pressed men, and I, from our duties.

Protecting the bodies at the crime scene was one of the most unnerving and depressing duties a policeman could perform. We all wanted to be out of there as soon as possible. It was refreshing to meet a doctor who actually arrived when they said they would.

"Good evening, inspector; I suppose you could say it was fortunate that I live locally" she replied. Typically, she ignored my barbed comment about her fellow physicians.

She always felt that if you did not have anything nice to say about anyone, then it was best to say nothing at all. It was one of the reasons that she was better than me.

Jo accepted people for who they were not what they were, and she realised that you cannot generalise with people and professions. She knew that people are good and bad no matter what they do. In time she turned me into a less cynical copper and a better person.

"Indeed," I observed coldly.

"I would never, ever, keep the constabulary waiting if it was at all avoidable," she insisted.

She smiled at me and I was immediately charmed by her. She seemed to respect us unlike most of the male doctors that I had met. I had no idea at that time that her father, John Rickard Murphy, was a retired copper. He had been in the Royal Irish Constabulary. Rumour had it that he was taken off an IRA hit list only because he was stepping out with Kitty, Jo's mother, and Kitty's family was well respected. Maybe he had been a policeman in another country, maybe he had carried a gun and maybe he was keeping the Black and Tans from the Irish and the Irish from the Black and Tans, but he was still an officer of the law and as a result she knew that my men and me commanded respect.

Our work involved sacrifices.

I was beginning to like the personality of this doctor as much as her striking looks. She was stunning and charming, too. It was a heady combination. I have never believed in love at first sight, lust perhaps, that was an animal reaction, but falling for someone within in a few minutes of having met them, that was ridiculous. It just did not make any sense. It certainly did not make sense to a man who was happily married. I dismissed the whole idea as fantasy brought on by lack of sleep.

"Let me introduce you to P.C. Watkins and Sergeant Stephens, they responded to the call and contacted me," I explained.

"Good evening gentlemen," she said smiling at both men, they returned her greeting with slight nods and small smiles, "What have we got Inspector Regan?"

"Suicide, from what I can gather, a gas fire left on, carbon monoxide poisoning, we suspect. We've opened the windows," I informed her, moving to one side to let her proceed, gesturing with a flamboyant arc of my arm that the room was hers.

"Thank you, inspector," she responded, taking in the scene.

The flat was sparsely decorated, a brown leather chesterfield armchair and matching sofa faced the fireplace; behind the sofa there was a low table and a Garrad Radiogram. I nodded towards it.

"Ray Charles on the turntable and The BBC World Service on the radio, it was switched on when we arrived, the radio was on quite loudly. His name was Robert Harris," I elucidated, "he lived alone, no fiancé or girlfriend as far as we know, his family are from Manchester, he has a sister in Australia, that's all we know."

"The suicide note?" she asked.

"Not as far as I can see, my men have searched the flat," I assured her looking deep into those beautiful blue eyes.

She held my gaze.

"Interesting."

What was interesting; the information or me? I was not sure and, then, she looked away, looking at the body curled up on the floor. I put it down to the usual eye contact good-looking people share.

It was, merely, the recognition that we were different, the mutual admiration of our more beautiful facial features, acknowledging the incredible way that we had been shaped and formed.

"Psychology is your field, too?" I asked.

"A little," she admitted, "we all do some psychology at medical school and it's a personal interest."

"Really," I said dryly, unimpressed, it sounded sarcastic, but she did not flinch.

"It's just strange," she noted.

"In my experience, there is no pattern to this crime," I insisted.

"Crime?"

"Isn't it a crime to take a life, either yours or someone else's?" I answered acidly.

"You're right," agreed Jo, she had signed the Hippocratic oath and she was a Catholic, of course she should agree with me, she should, shouldn't she?

I think after that comment, she viewed me in a new light.

I was no longer just a cynical copper. She told me later, she felt I was less of a hard-bitten detective and, clearly, a philosopher as well as an investigator. Of course, she might have been saying all that to make me like her but one thing I admired about Jo was she was always honest with me. Praise from highly intelligent people is hard-won and yet she praised me that night.

It meant an awful lot to me.

We walked together towards the body and stopped, standing over him. The corpse was lying close to the gas fire, slumped on the carpet. He looked a sorry sight, poor chap.

His left hand showed the lines of his palm, it seemed to be reaching out for the fireplace, his curled fingers stretching out for the source of his demise. His right arm lay across his chest, that fist was clenched. His face seemed serene. His body was curled up as if he were trying to snuggle up in bed. He had been wearing grey flannel trousers, a brown belt and a white cotton shirt covered by a burgundy cardigan. Jo noticed that his shoes were off and his black wool socks had been darned on the right big toe.

It baffled her that he would have taken his shoes off before committing suicide but there they were next to the fireplace. Everything else was fastidiously positioned but the shoes were on their laces and looked as if they had been tossed there, in a careless last act of defiance. It did not add up. A voice was nagging her, and she always listened to her intuition.

Taking in the scene, she also noted the incongruity. There was a pair of huge, red marble columns on either side of the wall, separating the drawing room and kitchen at the far end of which was a small French window overlooking the back of the building.

The drawing room itself was massive, with high ceilings and three, double door, French windows overlooking Clapham Common. Each led on to a stone balcony with some expensive, flower-motif stonework on the perimeter edge, echoing the ivy pattern of the staircase and topped by a heavy stone slab.

It was a substantial piece of architecture and engineering. Any of those French windows would have afforded a means to commit suicide but on professional reflection, Jo decided a fall from that height would not guarantee instant death.

The highly decorated ceilings and wooden floors, carpeted in rugs, made the room look luxurious. The owner of this flat was clearly a man of means despite the fact that the apartment building was located on the south side of the river.

On the vast, grey marble mantelpiece, there were dozens of invitations. He was clearly a sociable and popular individual, which did not preclude suicide but made it more doubtful. There was also a silver framed photograph of the deceased who appeared to be enjoying an afternoon with friends. He was smiling broadly.

You never knew with suicides; the person seems to have a normal happy life. The whole atmosphere of the flat, the invitations and the picture did not suggest someone of a suicidal nature.

Her intuition told her that no matter what happened, this was no ordinary suicide. All her textbook experience had profiled the suicidal male. Normally, they were younger or older and not of the same social standing, to put it bluntly. Jo put her medical bag on the table behind the sofa and walking around the furniture, she bent to examine the dead man before speaking.

"Well, I would say he looks very healthy, his cheeks are rosy, the classic sign of gas poisoning. A blood test will confirm the amount of carboxyhaemoglobin in the blood," she said.

"Yes, Doctor, the autopsy will give us most of what we need to proceed, you've confirmed my suspicions," I asserted. I was young enough to want to sound competent, old enough to be professional, I was tired enough to believe we would all be home soon

"Good, I'll examine the body and, then, we'll do the paperwork," she announced.

"I appreciate your thoroughness."

I did but I also wanted to get home to bed in London Road, Penge, with 'Baby Brian' in a cot and my wife sleeping next to me. We were all tired and a busy week awaited us all. I, for one, wanted that long Sunday night to be over.

As Jo crouched to examine the body, she took hold of his right hand, it was cold, and it had no pulse. The coolness of a cadaver always filled her with dread.

She knew beyond doubt that he was dead, but she still went through the procedures. It was a routine, almost a ritual but it calmed her down and helped her to be both detached and methodical at the same time. She had been trained to an extremely high standard and she would leave nothing to chance: 'check and double check'; that had been drilled into her.

Only a thorough examination would yield certainty. All avenues had to be explored. These mantras provided her with security.

After a thorough inspection, she was satisfied with her diagnosis. I shifted uncomfortably on one leg, I had not expected her to take so long and I was relieved to find she was finally finished.

"How long have you been here, Inspector?" she asked.

"The incident was reported at eight fifteen, he was meant to meet a friend for supper, the friend phoned us at about eight forty-five, apparently Robert Harris was a stickler for punctuality, normally arriving early. We also had a call from the occupant in the flat below who smelt gas, so a beat bobby called it in about nine fifteen."

"I see."

"We're at Lavender Hill so we were around here pretty sharpish. Otherwise he could have been here for days," I explained.

"That would not have been ideal for any of us, I'm glad you were able to act so quickly," she noted, sounding relieved.

Jo examined the body, probing with her fingers, starting with the head, looking carefully and gently feeling around the skull before checking the eyelids, the nose and the mouth She turned his head and moved it from side to side before gently laying it down on the carpet again. Moving on to the torso and limbs, she, examined the flesh on his arms, she, also, checked the back of his hands, the palms and his fingernails. I was beginning to feel impatient at her thoroughness and I could sense my officers fidgeting in the background. Unperturbed, Jo completed her work, stood up, and returned to her case on the table.

"What do you think doctor?" I asked, hoping she would quickly write out the death certificate and let us all get home to our beds. We all had a long journey home after we had finished at the flat.

"Well, I would say he died between two and three hours before you arrived," she asserted.

"Really, how so, Doctor?" I was a young copper and dead bodies were not a currency I was familiar with as yet.

Despite my weariness, I was fascinated by the fact that doctors could work out the rough time of death and I wanted to know how they knew. Mr Robert Harris might have died a lot later than we thought.

His body was telling us the time of death.

"Primary flaccidity is still there; rigor mortis is just setting into the eyelids, but it has not advanced to the mouth or the neck."

"Keep going, I'll let you know when you've lost me," I assured her, and I fixed my eyes on her to show I meant it.

My men could tolerate a few more minutes. It appeared that what seemed a cut and dried case had suddenly become more interesting.

"Obviously, the mortuary will give a more accurate time. They'll measure glycogen levels among other things. We'll have a much clearer idea of the exact time of death once they have finished."

Efficiently, she packed her medical bag again while talking. She was aware that my men and I were keen to get back to the station, file our reports and finish our shift.

"Right, we'll leave that to the boffins at the morgue," I decided, we had been hanging around here for a long time. It was time to leave. I was about to signal that to my officers when Jo interrupted.

"One other factor is the ambient temperature," Jo continued, "when conditions are warm, the onset and pace of rigor mortis are sped up, providing an ideal environment for the metabolic processes that cause decay."

"Go on," I urged.

"It's very warm in here so I would have expected him to be further along the process," she noted.

I acknowledged her point by raising a quizzical eyebrow; I suspected there was more than just the time of death on her mind.

"Yes, the building is warm, some form of central boiler system feeding radiators in all the flats, providing them with background heating; there's hardly any need for fires according to the caretaker, we have not been idle since we arrived. You're saying he might have died at a later hour than we thought. So, we only just missed him."

"It's likely, but there's one other thing I noticed, Inspector."

"Really what's that?" I asked.

"A bruising around the neck," she said.

"Go on, I'm listening intently," I assured her.

"There is chance that some sort of struggle, or even a fight, preceded the gas poisoning."

"You mean there's a possibility it wasn't suicide after all."

"Only, a possibility, the pathologist at the morgue will know more, of course. A full coroner's examination would reveal any blows to the head and a more detailed look at the neck may yield the answers."

"Sergeant, have a look, will you?" I said to Stephens who was only too pleased to be given something to do, he was as anxious as I to be home, but he also hated standing around doing nothing.

"Just ask the pathologist to look out for signs that this was not suicide. They are generally very good at spotting inconsistencies," Jo suggested, helpfully.

"Not necessarily, junior pathologists sometimes miss details," Stephens argued.

He was an old hand. He had seen it all. Clearly, by implication, he was letting her know that sometimes police officers can fail to spot clues and he was suggesting that it could happen to anyone even at an autopsy.

"You have a point," she admitted readily, Jo smiled.

Nora Josephine Murphy liked Sergeant Stephens's no-nonsense approach. It was frustrating to admit but the bruises were so small and on the wrong side of the body, we had not suspected a southpaw.

Both Sergeant Stephens and I had examined the body for any signs of foul play, and we had both concluded that any injuries were due to the fall. We did not see any reason to suspect anything but suicide. That was what the murderer had wanted of course. The left-handed assassin has an advantage in avoiding detection.

"Everyone makes mistakes; to me it looked like a straightforward suicide," I explained, "the position of the body, the tap on the gas fire turned on. That's why the windows were open. Even we missed the evidence that you spotted."

I was candid as well as philosophical that night, which was a change for me, but I felt immediately that I could trust this beautiful, tall, elegant woman with my life.

"That's because you were waiting for me to do the examination and you did not want to disturb the body," she assured me, "I cannot see any obvious contusions to the cranium, but I can feel a few bumps and lumps on the skull. I would say this man fought before dying; there are traces of blood under his fingernails."

"Isn't it just dirt?" I asked, even the cleanest of people had dirty fingernails with all the soot from the chimneys, that's why everyone wore gloves.

"They look like dirt," she acknowledged, "but I have swabbed them, and it looks more like blood. A more thorough examination will show whether this is from an assailant or from his scratching an old cut."

"In that case, I'll see you at the autopsy, it will take place at the Battersea mortuary, tomorrow, at ten," I insisted.

Jo was about to object but my brown eyes bored into her and made all protestation useless. She could go willingly, or she could be forced to go by subpoena. The former was preferable.

I needed her help and although she wanted to refuse to give it for the sake of her patients, she knew resistance or defiance was useless. On reflection, I think we knew, even then, that our paths had become irreversibly interwoven.

I was certainly 'star crossed'.

"Of course, Inspector, I'll complete the death certificate as far as I am able, you and your men can be on your way. I should be able to move some appointments from my morning surgery to the afternoon. It will take some juggling in the waiting room, but I can manage, I think."

"Thank you, that would be helpful. We've found his driving licence you can copy the details from there," I suggested, handing over the document.

"That's perfect, thank you."

"So, you think there could have been a murder?" I asked incredulously, it seemed like a simple suicide to me.

"There is evidence for that," she said seriously.

"As you've just outlined,' I admitted, I was tired and felt foolish, I should have spotted something.

"I would say the pathologist is likely to discover there's been a murder on Cedar's Road."

"Thank you for your diagnosis," I responded.

I smiled at our use of each other's terminology. Jo picked up on the joke and smiled back. She dared to quote the Bard and see my response.

"Who worse than a physician, would this report become?" she announced.

I recognised the quote immediately. My father had been a fan of Shakespeare and he tried to instil in me the same affection.

"These are troubled times, scarce a day goes by when a king does not lose his crown," I replied.

I could not help reddening being aware of my poor knowledge of Shakespeare; it was the only quote I knew; it was my father's favourite expression.

"Trouble comes not in single spies but in battalions," Jo added, handing over the certificate and bowing.

"Thank you, doctor," I said, taking the certificate, "Until tomorrow?"

"Until tomorrow, goodbye" she answered, "Tomorrow and tomorrow, and tomorrow, creeps in this petty pace, from day to day."

As she spoke, she swept from the room.

Both of the officers looked at each other but kept their thoughts to themselves. It was no ordinary day; it was no ordinary suicide and she was no ordinary pathologist.

Chapter 4 – The Autopsy and Normality

i

Thinking about things, overnight, it seemed to me that the man, whom I suspected of suicide, had in fact been killed. I was sure that, the visit to the coroner would confirm this especially with Jo there, too. I was disturbed to know that a murder had been committed in 'My Manor'. I had not slept well; Brian was up in the night and I could not stop thinking about poor Robert Harris lying dead in front of his fireplace with all the invitations.

When we met the following morning, it was a miserable Monday, a thick blanket of big-bellied, cumulus clouds floated across the sky, their grey, sombre shapes threatening rain.

Jo told me she was worried about the fact that a murder could have been committed less than a ten-minute-walk from her home. She had moved to a poor area to set herself up as a General Practitioner, but she had never dreamt that her family might be in danger from a marauding murderer.

We were both unsettled when we met in Falcon Road. Jo was waiting for me in an American Nash. Stepping out of her car as she saw the police car arrive at the kerb, she walked to meet me. I jumped out of the passenger seat and slammed the door before my driver could make any comment about my keenness to greet her.

She was of course smoking, so she needed to transfer the cigarette from her right hand to her left hand. She shook my hand firmly, she gave me eye contact, her blue eyes sparkling as she smiled, her teeth were white and perfect.

I later found out her secret was Euthymol, smokers' toothpaste. You hardly ever see it these days.

Her smile brightened up my day, it was only a shame we were visiting the mortuary. Our second meeting confirmed my initial feeling. She was an extraordinary woman, bright, charming and wonderful to behold. She was not perfect; there was an endearing dark mole on the nape of her neck.

After dropping me off, Sergeant Stephens was driving on to investigate a burglary near Battersea Park Road, at one of the Victorian mansion blocks. Showing off to her, I thought, he pulled away from the kerb slightly more dramatically than necessary, waving at Jo in a very unprofessional manner.

She even waved back.

A police driver should always keep both hands firmly on the wheel and drive a police car with decorum when not responding to an incident.

As I scowled after him, I heard a 19 bus as it pulled up by the side of the road, a whole crowd of people would be exploding from the platform at the back at any moment so I urged Jo towards our appointment, guiding her along the pavement, walking on the outside as any gentleman should.

The Coroner's Office on Falcon Road was near Clapham Junction Station, in the direction of Little India, a collection of streets named after provinces in India.

On the other side of the road was the network of old railwayman's cottages, Mantua Street, Heaver Street, Natal Road, Musjid Street and Kamballa Road, all of which have, now, disappeared, bulldozed to make way for tower blocks, vertical slums taking the place of horizontal ones.

It was an old-fashioned working-class community with 'two up and two down houses', which had been deemed slums and were going to be cleared. They did not look too bad to me. The houses were in good nick, the masonry was in good order and their paintwork was clean and when I arrived ten minutes before eight, I saw a teenage girl being sent out to scrub the steps; the windows on most of the properties were clean. The area was proud and poor, not dingy and dirty. It was a typical south London working class area.

People took pride in their homes and their appearance and took care of their possessions in those days, in Battersea that is.

The people of Lambeth and Wandsworth were clean and looked sharp, always smartly turned out, even if the clothes were 'make do and mend', or 'hand-me-downs'. They lived in spotless homes; the only people who thought they were anything but 'home sweet home' were the town planners and their friends the architects. They had to justify their jobs and the architects had to make money.

There was no litter on the street and people looked after their shopfronts and cleaned their windows and the facades on their properties, rented or owned. There might have been a bit of peeling paintwork on the poorer people's properties and lots of the houses needed a lick of paint, but they were scrubbed inside and out.

Of course, the areas around Jack Barclays service centre, the candle factory and the flourmill had their fair share of villains and miscreants, too. From my time on the beat, I knew people, in the area, were generally happy.

There were no gardens, but these people worked so hard and travelled so far to work that they had no time for gardening. A back yard was all they needed, a small outside space, to hang the washing out on a summer's day. They had space for walking and playing; the park was only ten or fifteen minutes walk away.

They left home in the dark and returned after dark, six days a week. The lucky few might have an allotment. They worked hard and lived by the sweat of their brow; they washed in their sculleries using boiled water from the kettle, a tin basin and soap. The toilet was outside. It was basic but plenty of properties like that survived elsewhere with updated interiors.

It was a community that looked after itself and people cared about one another.

There were some rogues, but we knew who they were. The others, the normal people, greeted their neighbours and sent one of their children to the pub for a jug of beer each night to help with the drudgery of washing, ironing and polishing shoes. We all took pride in our appearance, scrubbed collars, starched shirts, pressed suits and polished shoes for men; brushed coats, scrubbed and starched, pressed, dresses, with polished, shiny, high heels, for women. My shoes were the first things that Jo noticed the morning. I take pride in my shoes, a habit instilled in me by my father; you could see your face in mine.

My Dad was a copper; I wanted to be like him. National Service had helped me perfect my polishing techniques. Jo had commented on how well turned out I was, my wife had ensured I looked the part when I left the house, pressed trousers with razor sharp creases and a crisp ironed and starched white shirt. Any stains were sponged out of my jacket and it was regularly dry-cleaned.

Jo was wearing her light green coat and brown high heels. She looked immaculate. Her smoking added to her film star glamour. Naturally, I was grateful that she admired my shiny shoes. Praise from someone looking so smart made me proud of myself. The black brogues were almost brand new.

They were expensive looking but mercifully fairly cheap. Even on an inspector's salary good quality footwear was dear. I used to get them from a cobbler's outfit near Brick Lane, Blackman's Shoes, in Cheshire Street. They were an investment and paid back the trip to the East End. They were definitely more comfortable than Bobby's boots.

Blackman's was one of those thin narrow shops that had not changed since Victorian times, all tongue and groove wood on three walls and just a front window displaying its wares next to a wooden framed half-glass door. The shopkeeper stacked up boxes to the ceiling, buying in bulk and passing the saving on to the customer.

Even his window display was simply brown shoeboxes topped by a pair of a particular style: brogue, banks and capped, lace up and slip on. Mr. Blackman specialised in selling good quality Northamptonshire shoes, cheaply, even though they had leather soles as well as leather uppers. You, still, cannot beat a well-made English shoe in my humble opinion.

When we came out after visiting the coroner's office, I stood admiring the colour and curves of her Nash. I love four things, women, cigarettes and alcohol, not necessarily in that order, and, above all, cars. I love their shape, their size and the smell of their leather seats, the design and the engineering. I know that Mark Twain opined: 'A woman is a woman, but a cigar is a good smoke' but I think a woman is a person, fascinating and awe-inspiring. Cigarettes are perfect cylinders of pleasure and cars are the epitome of man's ingenuity, gorgeous expressions of freedom and engineering prowess.

That particular American motorcar was a real beauty as shiny as my shoes and of similar high quality.

It seemed to epitomise Jo, modern, beautiful and powerful.

The roof was light blue, like a stratus sky in summer, and the bodywork was the colour of a marlin fish, that rich, dark, deep blue of a fathomless ocean. It looked incongruous under the grey curtain of cloud, the white wall tyres, the sleek lines, all at sea in the wilderness of two-up-two-down, Victorian houses built for the railway workers.

"Thank you for all your invaluable help, I announced, tearing my eyes away from the beautiful mass of metal. It was not difficult Jo's eyes were twice as magnetic. I could have stared into them all day and her body was more beautiful, I could tell, even though it was shrouded in green. Her arms and legs were thin, and she was tall and willowy. "So, what do you think, doctor?"

"I think we should have a cigarette," she replied, perhaps noticing the way I admired her turn of ankle, "would you care for one of mine?"

She ostentatiously offered her packet to me sliding the packet open.

"Senior Service? Yes please," I replied gratefully, noticing the distinctive white box and blue, tall ship, emblem and writing, an expensive cigarette was a treat.

I smoked Wild Woodbine; if it was good enough for the men in the trenches, it was good enough for me. It was a pleasant tobacco; I smoked the filter-tipped ones, which made them less strong.

Having a non-filter was 'bliss' as she said, often. Over the years, her expressions and vocabulary became mine. I thanked her.

"Pleasure," she intoned, pushing the box from below to reveal the white sticks of tobacco. I helped myself; she lit my cigarette with her gas lighter before I could rummage in my raincoat for my petrol lighter.

"Thank you for showing me what you found, it means that this is more of a murder enquiry than a simple suicide," I observed, to fill the silence, two addicts indulging in their tobacco fixation. I had read a bit of Freud in the library when I was at Hendon.

"I'm just glad the coroner corroborated my diagnosis, it's important to make sure in cases like this," she responded, drawing smoke into her lungs.

Smoking was an alluring ritual, I am afraid to say, the parting of the lips, the sharp intake of breath.

It made Jo look magnificent, like a Hollywood idol.

Sadly, we glamorised smoking in those days, not fully realising their terrible toxicity. We understood that they damaged the lungs but so did the smog and working in the candle factories and coal fired industries.

"Thanks to you, we now know, for sure, the murderer was left-handed or, at least, used his left hand to commit the murder," I asserted.

"That should narrow things down, once you rounded up the possible suspects who might have been responsible. Then, we might be able to sleep soundly in our beds," she added, it did not sound like she held out much hope of anyone finding the killer.

She was wily enough to realise what we were up against. It seemed Robert Harris had no enemies, there was nothing obviously missing from the flat and no forced entry. He either knew the perpetrator or the murderer was convincing enough to gain entry.

That was a worrying feature in itself. Without a motive, it would be impossible to establish why the murder was committed and, if it was not someone the victim knew, then it could have been a complete stranger and we could be looking at some sort of psychotic on the loose.

"You've been very thorough, this vital evidence could easily have been missed," I assured her, exhaling slowly and smiling. "I'm grateful."

"I thought you and your men seemed keen to get home that night, but I suspected something was not quite right. I had to check. I'm sure pathology would have picked up the evidence all the same but maybe this has speeded things along. So, what happens, now?" Jo asked.

Leaning against the car, she had folded her arms: her left hand supported the other elbow, her right hand holding her cigarette close to her generous mouth, held between her index and middle finger.

"The case will be investigated by the New Scotland Yard," I explained. "They had their fingerprint people at the flat first thing, they'll look for treads on the floor from unfamiliar shoes."

"I know, an officer called around and asked Mrs. Haines, who works at the surgery, for the pair of shoes I was wearing last night," Jo noted.

"We ensured the flat was disturbed as little as possible. This is now a murder enquiry and you've ensured we have a lead before the trail goes cold."

"Once they've finished their forensic tests?" Jo asked, making a point.

She knew more about police procedure than I gave her credit for, I should have known better.

"I am sure they will let me know their findings in due course," I replied, regretting the assumptions I had made.

"So, you won't be involved?" she gasped.

"No."

"Why not?"

"I'm afraid it's no longer in my hands," I answered, trying not to show how disappointed I was.

"But you found the body, won't you be involved in the investigation?" she asked, sounding as if she sympathised with my situation.

I suppose she had a point; it did seem a little unjust that we did all the work to discover the fact the man had been murdered and yet we had to hand over the case to the Criminal Investigation Division.

"No, I'm based at Battersea, it's no longer my concern. CID will handle the case; they'll use my report to establish their premise and work from there. Don't worry, I know the investigating officer, I'm sure they'll keep me informed and if they do, I'll let you know."

I looked at her and she seemed crestfallen at my words, I paused to let her speak but she just looked at me, urging me to continue with those beautiful enquiring eyes of hers. "Most murder cases are easy to solve. It's generally someone the victim knows. There are few unpremeditated murders in this day and age. The experts will know how to go about it."

"That's reassuring," she said, I could almost taste the irony in the wind.

"The Criminal Investigation Department are at the flat, now. They'll deal with the details; you'll read about it in the Evening paper."

"Let's hope so, Inspector," she responded, letting me know that she was not convinced.

"Don't worry," I assured her, feebly.

I, already, knew she felt strongly that I should have been given the case, but I did not know that she thought that she should have been given free rein to snoop as much as she liked.

Jo was beginning to get a taste for police work and her scientific mind was ideally suited to the sort of analysis we were undertaking. She was unusual in the fact that she was also an amazing artist; she had drawn the lines of the victim's hand while the autopsy was being performed.

It was, in fact, something she had done since she had passed her examination because part of her practical examination had been to do exactly that, draw the fissure of a hand and she practised her drawing skills at every available opportunity. Her drawing of the suspects proved invaluable as we built up the case.

"I expect they are the best qualified to deal with the inquiry," Jo nobly acquiesced.

"Indeed, they are. However, if you want to talk about the case, you'll find me at Lavender Hill," I continued, rules were rules, but I wanted her to know that she could see me at any time.

She was married and I was married, the case would be solved, and we would most probably never see each other again after meeting that day. It made me feel depressed. That's what I felt at the time.

We were kindred spirits, both good-looking, we shared the confederacy of good-looking people, we had both had our share of unwanted advances; it was the curse of being pleasing to look at. I was attracted to her and I wondered if she was attracted to me, nonetheless.

Again, I have to reiterate that as much as we appreciated our mutual situation, we understood the conventions of the time, marriage was sacred; she was married, and I was married. We would never cheat on our spouses.

Marriage vows were not there to be broken. Yet, I could not help admiring her beauty, intelligence and wit. Perhaps, the passing of time has intensified my recall of my feelings just as much as it might have blurred some of the facts.

I cannot remember pining for Jo like a lovesick teenager but equally I can remember being drawn to her physically as well as spiritually.

Who knows? Maybe, if I could have abandoned my self-control, I would have told her how I felt, even at our second meeting.

It would have been foolish, but she was compassionate and intelligent. All I did know was that Jo was a doctor who was my best medicine. There were codes and rules for everyone in those days and for the sake of society we followed them. That was one, maybe the only good thing about that time. You knew where you stood and understood the rules were designed for everyone.

Of course, there were exceptions, what we used to call 'bounders' and 'crooks. Generally, we avoided the company of cads and tried to arrest the criminals, if we could. I used to joke that the Lavender Hill police knew every nook and cranny and every crook and nanny in Battersea. On the whole, most people were decent, no matter what they did for a living.

Even the criminals avoided viciousness, barring a few notable and notorious exceptions, the Kray brothers for example. They were two nasty pieces of work. Jo interrupted my confused thoughts.

"If I do think of something, can I rely on you to take it to the other investigators?" she asked cryptically.

"It's my duty to help the C.I.D. in any way that I can, of course you can. I owe you a favour; you helped us detect a murder where we would have dismissed the incident as suicide."

"It was just luck really," she said modestly.

"We'll keep you abreast of developments, never you fear."

"Thank you, Inspector, I appreciate it."

"I have to thank you, we'll look more carefully before we jump to conclusions, my officers and I, but that's off the record," I conceded.

"Strictly off the record," she laughed, unlocking the car door.

"I look forward to our working together again and thanks for the cigarette."

"Pleasure, if there's nothing else inspector? I have a waiting room full of patients."

"You've been most helpful, let me get the door for you," I offered, opening the left-hand driver's door for her.

"Thank you."

She slipped into her seat and I closed the door gently behind her, doffing my trilby in salute. We smiled at each other as kindred spirits.

We were both attracted to each other, I was sure of it, even, back then, there was a frisson in the air.

Perhaps, if we had met much earlier in our lives, we may have at least become sweethearts, might even have married. Sadly, life was not about 'ifs'; it was about getting on and doing the job.

She knew that and I knew that.

I liked her, I fancied her, too, and I wanted to think that she reciprocated the feelings, but even if she had, there was nothing either of us would or could do.

I told myself it was sheer lust and it would fade in a day or two. We were not suited, anyhow. She was a highly intelligent and charismatic doctor; I was a process driven, shy, investigative plodder.

The psychologists, these days, would classify her as a hunter brain; they would classify me as a farmer brain. I was quite happy with my routine and peeling back the layers to find the truth, she craved excitement.

She wanted to hunt down the killers.

We were young and naïve; I was too green to know that our roles were reversed. As a hunter, if she had been interested, she would have been clubbing me over the head and taking me back to her cave, I suppose.

Neither of us would endanger our burgeoning friendship by revealing our feelings. It's different, now. Then, there was a code of conduct to adhere to. Now, people say what they like and do as they fancy. It seems all too casual to me; wives and husbands have to work at marriage all the time.

Friendship was all we had to offer each other and, in the weeks, to come we would need all the friends we could get.

ii

Jo went back to her routine, if you could call it such. Her days were more varied than mine. I had to liaise with the other detectives, write up reports and carry on with my usual job, keeping my officers on their mettle and boosting their morale, protecting the law-abiding citizens on my patch, plus look after the misses and the nipper. It was exhausting.

On the other hand, Jo's first job, every morning, was filling the cream coloured coal Aga. Before that she had to rake out the ashes. She had to use a zinc bucket and a small coal shovel that she placed next to the warming oven on the right.

First of all, she opened the bottom left hand door, where modern Agas have their thermostats and hers had the bottom of the furnace where the ash collected. From the back of the range, she took a tool, which was basically a thin iron bar with a hook on one end and a two-prong fork at the other, then, she squatted down and using this combined riddling tool and plug lifter, she raked out the ashes.

First, she inserted the pronged end of the riddling tool into the slot above the ash pan and engaged it around the pivot on which the grate rested. She raised the shaft of the tool and jiggled it about, moving the floor to one side until all the ashes fell to the bottom of the grate.

Taking the small hand shovel out of the bucket, she shovelled the still warm white ash into it, turning the gleaming zinc a matt beige colour. Taking the ash out through the scullery, she went out into the garden and emptied the bucket onto the compost heap in the brick planter nearest the carport. Rushing back inside, she took care not to slip on the frosty concrete floor of the yard that covered the small area around the side door. On her return to the warmth of the kitchen, she shivered before checking the thermostat in the top middle of the Aga. It was located between the two lids of the hob just under the handrail.

The thermostat had three sections, black silver and red, from left to right, black was too cold and red was dangerously hot, the silver section was ideal. The mercury in the thermometer was bang in the middle; there was enough coal in the furnace to maintain the heat in the ovens. The Temperature, being exactly where it should be, allowed her to raise one of the hobs covers to let more heat into the room. The warmth had already evaporated the moisture on the inside of the window, but she still felt cold. Owning a stove like that, in the days of coal, was like looking after a patient on the ward.

Finally, she went down the two flights of steps into the cellar. The cellar was deep and despite being just shy of six foot, she could stand up easily. In the first part of the cellar, there was a cast iron furnace dating back to when the house was built. It was in the corner opposite the bottom of the stairs. It looked like something from a cowboy film, a slender cylinder with a smokestack that had a dogleg that led into the ceiling, then, into one of the chimneys. The rest of the wall was taken up with wine racks filled with wine bottles. On the opposite wall to the stove were shelves for medicines and chemicals to make medicines. On the wall, next to the staircase was the electricity and gas meter.

Beyond the main room, there was a second cellar, slightly smaller, sitting under the kitchen. That was where the coal was kept. The anthracite formed a pile on the roadside of the building, spilling in a tarry cone like a slagheap, from the coalhole that formed its apex. Directly opposite, there were three tin hods lined up neatly against the wall and a large spade leaning against the plaster.

Jo collected the shovel and a hod, which after six attacks at the coke pile, she had filled three quarters full of fuel, ready to go in the top of the Aga. Lifting the hod was not easy; it was heavy and cumbersome. Jo took hold of the handle at the top and the other at the bottom, struggling from the cellar to the staircase.

Upstairs, she lifted both hobs covers and, secondly, using the hooked end of the tool, she locked it into a small bar sunk into the top of the circular hob. With that attached, she could lift the hot hob out of the stove and drag it along, so it sat on top of the simmering hob.

Lifting the hob, and slipping it to the right, she picked up the hod and emptied the smooth, black nuggets into the open furnace, put the hod down, replaced the hot hob and closed the two hob covers.

After taking the hod back into the coal cellar, she went upstairs again and washed her hands, hanging her overall on the hook on the back of the scullery door. Then, she went back upstairs to get ready for her day. The children and the au pair were still sleeping. Her surgery opened early.

Arriving at six thirty, Mrs. Haines had already scrubbed the two steps up to the doorway on Wakehurst Road. She was tidying and sweeping the surgery waiting room as Jo filled the Aga. They were a good team.

Outside, the hedge at the front of the house had been kept trimmed by a man who cut back the foliage all along the common and the white paint stripe that ran across the side wall, at waist height, had been freshly painted so the surgery looked clean and shipshape

Mrs. Haines had polished the stained-glass window on the first landing inside and out, using a small stepladder to get to the street side of the window. The art nouveau lead and glass took an age to clean but with her care and labour the glass gleamed like new and the lead seemed blacker and more solid than ever.

Jo had made a pot of tea and they shared a cup of Darjeeling. Mrs Haines had a sweet tooth and had two sugars. George had already left to prepare for his Harley Street clinics, at his Uncle Henry's practice at number 186. He had taken it over when Henry had retired. Jo had wanted to be a vet and had been persuaded that humans would benefit more from her contribution to medical science. She had also gathered that animals have a variety of different bodies and complications whereas with humans the only difference was gender, the stomachs and organs were all the same.

George had wanted to be a specialist ever since his uncle had arrived at the Glebe in his Rolls Royce Silver Ghost and told him that life as a London doctor was agreeable and would make a good career choice. Becoming wealthy was an attractive ambition. From that day, George was determined to become a doctor, as he knew it would make him a wealthy man. It had of course. His second ambition was to have a car like his Uncle Henry, a Rolls Royce. Fortunately, his pub business and wine importers had flourished along with his clinics so he could afford the price tag.

The added ability of the vehicle to, inconspicuously, transport a ton of coins and cash made the car the only viable option for him.

Both Jo and he had worked hard at medical college and afterwards, their motivation was different; she was to heal the sick, he wanted to do better than her father, in a shorter time and with less business acumen. He wanted his car for the kudos it gave him, she wanted hers for the freedom and independence it offered her.

- v - The Surgery

Jo opened the surgery at seven thirty and the receptionist, Barbara Kirmode, opened the front door and led a procession of patients into the hall where a fire was already glowing orange in hearth of the dark brown, rectangular wooden fireplace with the Moroccan green tiles. It really was reminiscent of the style shown by the great pre-Raphaelite, Lord Leighton and his magnificent house near Holland Park.

The house where Jo had her surgery had been built as a swansong of a local developer who had done extremely well. It was the epitome of taste and style. A great house opened up to the public with pleasure not through necessity. Of course, all patients were encouraged to wipe their feet before treading on the Persian rug that had been laid to protect the parquet floor.

They were able to check themselves in the long hall mirror opposite the door where Jo religiously brushed her hair each morning, first thing, trying to tame her long flyaway mane There were four doors: one immediately to the left, the study and that was the waiting room where the patients were led.

There were two doors, dead ahead, the door to the left was the surgery, the drawing room on the bell system and to the right the dining room, which was where Jo kept her private phone, her grand piano and the green e suite, it was used as a sitting room. The fourth door on the far right led into the kitchen. They were all two-inch, thick pine and they were stained such a deep mahogany that they appeared almost black.

Mrs Haines had diligently polished the brass plates above the door handles, along with their Mexican-hat-shaped matching doorknob, that morning. It was a daily ritual. She came in five days a week and cleaned the house in sections.

Her use of potions and proprietary brands ensured the house sparkled. Mrs. Haines was a fantastic asset to the family. She worked tirelessly and kept the three reception rooms, the kitchen, the scullery, the larder, seven bedrooms, the bathroom and the loos spotlessly clean. It was hard work, but she took on the huge task with enthusiasm and fortitude.

The receptionist, Barbara Kirmode, known as Bubs, would answer the door during surgery hours and seat the patients on some old pub chairs that had green cushions on the seat while she updated her records and collected notes from the filing cabinet. She would take the first patient in, knocking on the door before opening it and announcing the patient's name and delivering the file. A quick glance at Jo would allow her to check if there was anything else needed before closing the door. Bubs had worked for military intelligence during the war and had a wicked sense of humour. She would keep the fire going in the small hearth in the corner of the room.

The study had two sash windows that looked out onto the front garden and the common beyond, a low bookcase, full of classic novels, in one corner and the seating in an L shape in the other.

Her desk was next to the door, opposite the windows and beside the fire. She kept her back to the fire because London winters were cruel and draughty gusts of wind would be brought in by the patients arriving and leaving.

The reception door was always kept open so Bubs could hear the patient closing the door as they left. Some went straight out into the street in a hurry, some came in to say thank you before they left. Most days, Bubs would, listen for the patient to come out, take the new one in and lead the previous patient to the door allowing them to talk about the next steps if they so wished.

I remember Jo telling me years later about her surgery and its efficient yet relaxed atmosphere. I saw the surgery once. You walked into the room and it was amazing. There was a huge free-standing set of bookshelves on the wall to the right of the door, it was the first thing you noticed, five tiers high and reaching the picture rail. It was over seven-foot-tall and must have been twelve-foot-wide and a foot deep. It was filled with medical books and journals; old textbooks, which looked like they had been bound by Victorians, they were made of dark claret and dark forest green leather and vellum paper. The textbooks were all hard back, too and the medical journals had wine red covers.

The next thing you noticed was the mantelpiece.

Due to the fact that the builder of this house had been a successful developer in the area, he had spared no expense in design and materials. It was his home and reflected the decades he had grafted and the years of experience he had gained as a master builder and craftsman.

It was stunning, looking like a Regency, John Nash, original, you can see similar ones in The Pavilion in Brighton. The wooden mantel had been painted white; it had a circular mirror in the centre and a triptych design, the leaves, on either side of the round looking glass, were decorated with Nash style urns complete with the decorative oval patterns around them.

The house was a tasteful nod to previous styles, Robert Adam, John Nash and George Aitchison.

Each room seemed to have a particular theme and feel, homage to a particular era or architectural style. The house celebrated and copied various styles and fashions, bringing them into an amalgam of taste and beauty. In the grate, a fire burnt to take the chill off the morning, the coals glowing satisfyingly thanks to Mrs Haines. Moisture had already started to settle on the windowpanes demonstrating how cold it was outside.

The wallpaper complimented the room; it was a classical pattern with green throughout a real regency effect, which would have been more at home in a Georgian house than an Edwardian one. Jo had only added a deep red, junior Wilton carpet that ran throughout the house except in the hall. George had bought it at an auction of fittings from a cruise ship that was being refitted in Liverpool docks.

The whole house was as special and as unique as any stately home. The builder, whose house it became, had insisted on the finest materials, the best quality designers of the time giving each feature a light touch. The picture rail and the beautiful circular design on the ceiling celebrated designers of fine Georgian homes and highlighted the plasterers' skills. It really was exquisite and the chandelier that hung from that ceiling centrepiece was incredible. It was three tiers of teardrop crystals and it sent a warm glow into the room. Three standard lamps with pale green shades, one in each of the corners of the room, adjacent to the door, made the room seem warm and welcoming even on the greyest day.

Opposite the fireplace on one of the longer walls was a servant's bell, which allowed Jo to summon Mrs. Haines who would bring some more hot water for Jo to wash her hands with between patients or even to prepare for an examination.

The bell consisted of a long-braided flex with a bulbous enamel end with a button at its base.

Clasping the spherical object, allowed the application of a thumb against the base button, which would trigger the window on the kitchen display to be blocked by a red flag.

Mrs Haines would hear a click, look up at the cabinet above the doorway, and know that it was time to take the kettle off the simmer plate and boil some water on the hot plate of the Aga.

Underneath this bell-button, standing against the wall, was a Victorian glass cabinet stocked with some Scott's Emulsion and Pulmo Bailly for coughs, in bottles lined up like soldiers on parade, on the top glass, shelf, while packets of Aspirin, Disprin and Alka Seltzer were stacked neatly on the middle shelf.

There was magnesium sulphate paste, merbromin, iodine, plasters, antiseptic cream, bandages, white spirit and a kidney dish containing a pair of surgical scissors, jostling for position on the bottom shelf

Jo's desk was leather topped and lived in the recess of the large bay windows; the main frame looked east, the one to the left looked to the Northside of the common and the one to the right to the Southside.

Behind the desk was Jo's chair, a simple bentwood frame with armrests and, in front, were two chairs from one of her father's pubs, again, bentwood but with a green cushion on each seat.

Often husbands and wives would come as a couple to consultations or children would dangle their legs from the second seat when they sat next to their mothers to hear the grown-ups discuss their symptoms.

On the desk were two piles of the patients' notes, conveniently placed by Jo's right arm so she could readily access them. On the far side, nearest the patient, sat a white marble cigarette box, a green onyx table lighter and an elegant green stone ashtray. No one could be in any doubt that Jo's favourite colour was green.

Jo would not be behind the desk when you went in, she would be striding across the room to greet you with a warm, firm handshake.

Then, she would offer you a chair and once you were seated, she would offer you a cigarette unless you were a child, of course, which would mean you had to settle for a friendly smile and a conversation about how you were feeling.

It was through making her patients feel valued that she gained her reputation.

Everything was designed to put the patient at their ease. A patient who feels relaxed is far more likely to confide in their physician. That was the idea and it worked, she had a fabulous reputation as a thorough and caring doctor. I know that simply because I had checked locally, Sergeant Stephens also backed up my research by making his own enquiries.

She came out with glowing references.

One time, she told me much later, she had a syphilitic patient who claimed he had contracted the disease from a toilet seat. Syphilis can only be contracted in one way.

Jo coolly offered him a second cigarette and when he accepted it and lit it, she said, "You'll have to tell me the name of that toilet seat, we caught you before you infected anyone else."

"I don't know what you mean,' he complained, enjoying the cigarette yet squirming at the details of his infidelity.

"We have to make sure that said seat does not infect anyone as well," she joked.

"Of course, your right doctor," he conceded and gave her the name of the woman and her address so Jo could write to her and find out who had infected her in the first place.

She advised the adulterer to have his wife come in for a check up, too. He could not refuse; his wife's address and telephone number were in the records. He knew he would have to tell his wife or Jo would.

Everyone who came to the surgery received the utmost care and attention, a thorough examination and a sympathetic ear. Sometimes couples could not get their babies to sleep. Jo sympathised, Georgina her second born had also hardly slept so much so that Jo had gone to see Martin Walsh, the other GP in that area, to ask for advice.

Of course, there was nothing anyone could do but as with everything, the young Georgina ended up sleeping, soundly.

It was all just a passing phase, unpleasant but mercifully temporary though it did not seem so at the time. That was another one of Jo's expressions: "Don't worry, everything is passing."

She was a wise woman; even the worst times pass by, eventually.

On other occasions people came to the surgery just to talk; they would smoke a cigarette and discuss bereavement, their general tiredness, their lack of sleep or their boredom at the drudgery of life. They discussed personal problems and they asked for advice, she presented the options. She was as much a psychologist as a medical practitioner. She healed the body and the mind.

Jo was still on the General Practitioners' rota for duty pathologist at weekends, but that was to be the extent of her involvement in police matters. Every three weeks she was on call at weekends to attend any incidents that needed a pathologist present.

However, there was no reason for us to see each other and we returned to our normal lives. Mine was keeping crime off the streets hers was healing her patients.

It was a time when public service was respected much more. So, what about me at this time; was I pining over Jo, hoping to see her? To be truthful, no, I was not.

I was married and very much in love with my wife, Susie and my baby boy, Brian. I did not think of Jo once after the first week.

I had bought a two-bedroom, garden flat that formed part of an old Victorian house at the top end of Maple Road in Penge. Coincidently Jo's father, J.R. Murphy owned the London Tavern halfway up the street, conspicuous because it was on the corner.

I could not get away from her, or her family, so it seemed, but I was busy with so many cases, my head was spinning.

Being a policeman has never been easy and most of our work back then was preventing crime by getting to know the community and the rotten apples in the barrel.

There was a lot more crime than everyone thinks in those days and a fair few fights in pubs every night. It was in the period when they were packed with people every evening and some people could drink easily eight pints in a session without food.

We also had more than our fair share of domestic violence.

If you went to the Falcon on a Friday or Saturday night, there was bound to be a fight. Broken bottles, smashed glasses, table and chairs would be involved, just like a fight at a saloon bar in a 'Western' film. It was never like the fight scenes in The Quiet Man or Fort Apache. There was no choreography, no studio stuntmen, no pulled punches.

These fights were vicious.

A lot of the time it was a domestic argument between a man and a woman that would spark it off.

Often the woman would get in first, smashing her husband's half-pint, brown bottle that had contained his 'light and bitter'. Watching her like a hawk, he would, then, end up smashing the top off her cut glass 'port and lemon' sherry copita, or her half-pint glass. Then, they would both plant the broken receptacles into each other's faces or bodies. Inevitably, there was jostling involved, a jogged elbow and a spilt drink, an elbow carelessly withdrawn, hitting someone in the ribs, someone nudging someone else in the melee. All of which would need a violent and senseless response like a punch in the stomach or a fist in the face.

After that, it was considered a free for all; all hell would break loose. Chairs tables, glasses and bottles all became weapons as the whole public bar joined in the fray.

Then, when they heard the sirens, everyone would scarper, the bar staff would sweep up the mess. We would arrive, log the complaint and the miscreants would drift back into the pub with bandages and slings like they were coming back from the trenches.

Those seriously injured would take the bus or walk to the Bolingbroke Hospital, Accident and Emergency Department. None of the staff would snitch on their customers, so we could make no arrests.

Battersea and Clapham were working class areas, full of decent people putting bread on the table for their families, but there were bad boys amongst them.

Burglary was rife, people did keep their back doors unlocked but only because they had nothing to nick or a relative was looking after the baby. It was quieter in southeast London where I had settled or so it seemed to me while I lived there. Maybe, I had failed to notice what was going on. I was seldom home with all the work I had on my plate and we never went out.

It seemed all right but, in London, you never knew what was lying just beneath the surface. We lived in Maple Road because Susie's mother and grandmother lived on the street.

You might have whole families, three our four generations, uncles and aunts, living in the streets around south London and the East End in those days. North and west London was more fluid.

Battersea was no exception, and if they happened to be a family of villains, they, more often or not, kept up the family tradition. We knew the names and faces of all the burglars and villains but that did not mean we could always catch them at it and catching them in the act was the only way we would get a conviction.

Still, we were aware of the rascals and rogues, mainly. Generally, we knew who to ask and who to search and whose lock-up to rummage through.

Car theft became a huge problem, as well. There were no steering column locks and cars were easily hot-wired, National Service had ensured there were lots of lorry drivers but also lots of mechanics and those boys were able to pass on the techniques to anyone willing to learn or they could set up on their own.

The locks on the cars were generally easy to pick if you had a good set of heavy tools and knew what you were doing.

The cars were only stolen to order, most villains would have struggled to pay for the petrol, so they had to be off-loaded quickly, the cars were re-sprayed, and a new set of plates put on. It was a lucrative trade for the specialists, and we did not have the manpower to stop it, but we never told the public. Every day there was another list of crimes to investigate and hopefully solve.

It took a lot of footwork and perseverance but above all it all took time.

I hardly saw Susie and the baby with the workload and Sergeant Stephens complained that he never had enough time to play football with his two sons, Ben and Tim, aged seven and nine.

It was a tough time; England was rebuilding itself still and stolen goods and drugs were the meat and drink of organised crime. Then, there was the local crime, burglary, domestic disputes, drugs, fighting, petty theft, you name it and we had it in spades.

Chapter 5 – Breakfast and Bacon - Venus, the Bringer of Peace

When the surgery closed at lunchtime, Mrs Haines went home for the day, Bubs took her dog, Remus, out for a walk, often taking Jo's dog Ching along if the Swiss nanny had not had time to walk him, and Jo had a respite. There was a thump as a package landed on the tiled floor beyond the inner door. Sunlight had briefly permeated the gap between the inner and outer doorways. It was the letterbox opening and closing.

Jo was in the hall brushing her long locks in the mirror. Combing out the problems and processes of the morning surgery. She had backcombed her golden mane by leaning forward and had stood up straight to brush out the wisps, so it fell away from her face. The brush was the colour of sand and it complimented her honey hair.

Out of the corner of her eye, she had seen the flash of light before the letterbox snapped shut; she had heard the sound of the package landing on the floor. That made sense, light travelled faster than sound, it was nothing to worry about. Jo had been concerned about the murder and her nerves were on edge, she could smell danger in the air, she was after all investigating a murder, her female intuition was something she listened out for, it told her she was in peril and it had not failed her so far.

Placing her comb into the bristles of her long-handled brush, she left her grooming kit on the ledge of the fireplace, the wooden one in the front hall, with the Moorish tiling that seemed to proffer a tribute to Lord Leighton and his house in Kensington. Striding over to the cream-coloured front door, she turned the small brass handle. There was a reassuring click and the door opened smoothly.

Pulling the door fully open, to the right, she looked at the package on the terracotta coloured tiled floor, rectangles arranged to look like arrowheads.

The brown parcel lay in front of the double-doors that led out into Wakehurst Road. Swiftly, she bent at the knees to pick up the brown paper parcel; it was rectangular. It was heavy but she suspected what it was. The handwriting and postmark were familiar. Her mother's script was beautiful, italic letters joined in the continuous cursive style and a green Irish stamp confirmed to Jo that she was holding a present from Bromley, her parents' home in Ireland.

Grasping the thin package and returning to hall, she closed the door and walked through the hall. The hallway fire had died down and she wanted to hurry back to the true warmth of the Aga. There were four doors that lead off the hall, they were huge heavy, thick, pine doors, stained dark brown to look like mahogany, she chose the one on the far right, which led into the kitchen. She turned the palm-sized brass oval knob with her free hand and pushed the door open, finding herself in a tiny hallway.

There was a change from the dark colours of the hall; all was cream, the skirting board, the half-rail and the wall. She pushed open the kitchen door, which was also painted cream the little corridor had been designed to separate the kitchen area from the main house, trapping sounds and smells in its dark recesses. She found herself in a white tiled room and the heat from the Aga hit her as she stepped into the kitchen.

The Aga was coal fired and emanated a constant heat that took the chill from most days. The kitchen was the only room that did not have condensation on the inside of the windows every morning. It was the days before central heating in every house and the heavy cast iron radiators in the drawing room, dining room and two main bedrooms were linked to the now defunct boiler downstairs. Electric heaters took the chill off the rooms in the morning. The white rectangular tiles, arranged portrait style, stretched from skirting board to ceiling.

Above the kitchen door was a brown, boxed panel, a servant's bell system, about the size of a big, board game box. All the various rooms were labelled to alert staff to where they were required. Each name stood above a beige box that was blank until the bell rang.

A red rectangle would tumble into the box when assistance in that room was needed. In each room, there hung a brown cord with a teardrop enamel or wooden handle at the end with a button in the base, just like in the surgery.

The button was pressed to summon someone to that room, the servants had gone but the system remained. Jo liked to keep the old character of the house and added to rather than removed things, leaving the original features in one piece even if they were no longer functioning or were no longer needed. In the dining room that Jo had turned into the sitting room, there was a defunct radiator connected to the old boiler. Its cane cover and the marble top looked so exquisite she left it in place. At one point the house had been lit and heated by town gas. The gas outlets, on either side of the fireplaces had been capped and the supply disconnected but the features had not been removed. That was at floor level.

On the walls, there were white china ovals that had housed the lighting. They were bevelled around the edges and had not been removed as they added to the old-world charm of the place. There was a black hole in the middle where the jet used to protrude out of, but it looked as if it were a small round black gem in the white porcelain.

Jo walked through into the large kitchen, her shoes changing tune as they moved from parquet to linoleum; it became a deeper tone. The cream, wooden, dresser was immediately to her right, as she walked in, running perpendicular to the hallway. There were Spode and Wedgewood plates standing up and china Stilton cheese pots, Christmas presents from Guinness on the shelves.

There were two drawers below and four cupboards that ran along the length of the wall until they reached the cellar door. That was one wall. The next wall housed the high window, which let in light and provided privacy because it was set high up in the wall.

She passed the large sash window, the frame and ledge picked out in cream.

Below the four huge panes, which let light flood into the room, was an old, dark wood, Edwardian dining table that had been pushed against the wall underneath. The door to the cellar was between the dresser and the kitchen window. It was painted in cream like the old wooden dresser, as were the doors at each end of the room.

Opening the door at the far end of the room, she left behind the warmth of the kitchen and strode into cool scullery. She closed the door quickly behind her to keep the warmth in the house. Small, square terracotta tiles replaced the red linoleum, sea of the kitchen floor.

When walking over the tiles, her high heels click-clacked like wheels on a railway track. The, ceiling to skirting board, white tiles were square in the scullery. The doors and window frames were all painted matt white. The terracotta floor tiles were about the same size of those on the wall, it was all designed to keep the area cool.

The house's design was a close to perfection as anyone could get. This top builder, who had been working in the area for over twenty years, had learnt much about what made the perfect home. The house had been designed to be the most luxurious home possible. Everything about it was first class.

The specifications and materials were top-notch, the best that Edwardian England could offer, when England was at its industrial and commercial peak. Since, then, Jo and George had put every single modern convenience that could be thought of into the house after they moved in.

To her left was a huge American style double sink, a Dainty Maid, wood laminated and painted white, on top of which was a fully functioning American dishwasher that took up most of space on the draining board and would have cast a shadow over the scullery had it not been for a rectangular sash window, painted white to match the tiles, overlooking the back garden, that allowed light to flood into the room.

To her right was a massive American Kelvinator fridge, in cream and ahead of her, slightly to the left, was a Hotpoint washing machine, only available in one colour, white.

In America, domestic fridges were cream and industrial ones were white. Strangely enough, British white goods only came in white in those days, it was typical of the Americans to offer a different colour, but it came at a price.

Fortunately, two hard working, young urban professionals could afford all these labour-saving devices, few others could. I certainly couldn't on a police inspector's salary. She ignored all these necessities of modern life. Instead, she pulled open the larder door to the right and walked into the cool room. The heavy black slate shelf felt cold to touch as her hand brushed the surface. The room was about four-foot-wide, three-foot-deep and it had a high ceiling, there were eight feet between the ceiling and the ground.

Opening the package, peeling back the wrapping paper, she revealed greaseproof paper around an almost oval object. Jo bent down, there was a wine rack underneath and on top of that were two heavy pans specifically designed for use on the hob. Selecting the one on the left, she placed it on the slate and straightened as she did so.

The pan had a layer of lard at the bottom; it was beef dripping that had hardened when it cooled. It was a whitish, cream solidified crescent of fat. Taking two rashers from inside the paper, she placed them on the pan, folded the rest back into the package and left the dark larder, the cool scullery and returned to the warmth of the kitchen.

Before putting the pan on the stove, she flipped the bacon onto a third plate, on the dresser. Raising the hob lid, she placed the pan on the hot hob, waiting for the lard to heat and after a few minutes the lard became clear like clarified butter. Once the fat started to sizzle, it would be time for the bacon rashers to fry.

Meanwhile, there was a box of half a dozen eggs, a loaf of fresh unsliced bread and two larges white, china plates waiting on the red Formica surface of the cream dresser. Using a bread knife, Jo sliced two pieces off a bloomer loaf and cutting off the crusts on the breadboard, she cut a square in the middle of the doughy doorstep.

She put these on the plate before moving the plate onto the Aga, in the space between each hob, to warm it. She fried the bacon from the spare plate when the fat was hot enough by flipping the rashers four or five times to ensure they were cooked on both sides but not too crispy. Moving them onto the plate once they were done.

Casually, she placed the two squares and one of the pieces of bread in the pan and fried them both on each side, popping them on the plate. She flipped the bacon back on to the pan and crisped the rashers, at the same time; she took the second slice of bread, frying it on both sides. Once the bacon was cooked, she used the slice to serve the bacon, flipping it back onto the clean plate at the top.

Taking both the fried slices with the square holes from the plate, she placed them in the piping hot beef dripping, cracking an egg into each hole. Ensuring there was the briefest time for the egg to fry, she flipped the fried slices so the egg cooked on the other side but only for the briefest of moments; allowing the albumen to change from clear to white and to solidify slightly before flipping the bread a third time and then a fourth.

Satisfied that the egg had cooked enough, though not too much, so that the yolk was still soft, she slipped the metal spade of the slice under each one in turn and placed one beside the other on the plate with the bacon. A quick sprinkle of salt and a twist of pepper and everything had been made ready. Lastly, she took the squares of fried bread and put them on top of the egg to protect them from getting cold.

The idea of the dish was to keep the egg-yolk as runny as possible. The rich fried bread was as crispy as physically attainable. That way, there was a complete contrast, soft egg with crisp bread. The egg-in-the-hole, it should have been called egg in the square space, was a deliciously rich breakfast treat that Jo had seen cooked in an American film. George adored the dish. It was especially delicious with two rashers of bacon from Bromley.

Within five minutes, there was a hot pan, cooling between the two hob covers and a plate with two rashers of bacon and two egg-in-the-holes sitting on the kitchen table. She had time between morning and afternoon surgery to cook her husband a quick and nutritious, hot, midday meal. George looked at his Longines 1947 watch, a gift from Jo so he would not be late for dates. It was precisely one o'clock; he had fifteen minutes to eat his lunch. He sat at the table

"Bacon" he announced appreciatively, as he sat at the table.

"It arrived from Bromley in the post ten minutes ago," she replied, proudly admiring the plate before George.

It looked delicious. She never ate lunch, herself; there was no time.

"From your mother in Wicklow?" he commented unnecessarily, cutting into the crispy fat of the meat.

"She sent it from Kilpedder at five yesterday afternoon."

"The postal service is good."

"Not that good, it missed the morning post," Jo joked, smiling indulgently at him.

"Good enough," responded George, without smiling, "bacon is better for lunch when I am more awake."

"Enjoy your food, it will give you strength."

Jo never ate the bacon that her mother sent from Ireland, she saved it all for George to eat. Meat was still rationed even though some goods were no longer under restriction, but meat was still rare and expensive. Her mother sent it to her out of love and she gave every last rasher to George out of love.

"The weather this weekend should be good for your golf," Jo ventured as she watched George cutting up the bacon.

"Remind me where are you off to tomorrow?" George asked, managing to put a large piece of bacon and fried bread on the end of his fork. He would have enjoyed it more with black pudding, as well.

"I'm going to visit Birmingham, this weekend" she replied, "Peg has offered to help me with this mystery on Cedar's Road."

There was a brief pause while George thought about dissuading her, and then, he decided to choose his words carefully instead.

"That's kind of her. I suppose you won't rest until you know the killer's inside and justice has been done," he announced, wiping his mouth with a white linen napkin, he had taken from the drawer of the dining room table where he sat. He was enjoying his meal too much to spoil it with an altercation.

"I have to do what I can. I was there, that poor man, murdered. I have to do whatever I can to help find the culprit and Peg has some information, which Inspector Regan might find useful. I have to see her," Jo explained, leaning against the rail of the Aga, her arms folded. There was a carton of Senior Service in the cupboard above the dresser that she had brought from a weekend away in Amsterdam and she wondered whether she should breach it and have a quick cigarette.

"Well, I wish you were coming to France with me," George replied petulantly. "I'll miss you."

"Don't worry George, I'll make it up to you, we'll have a lovely evening on Sunday, whether you win or lose," Jo joked,

She decided to leave the cigarettes until the evening unless of course one of her afternoon patients wanted a cigarette and she might join them in a smoke while they were discussing their symptoms with her.

"Astonishing, good luck to you both," he added before cutting into his egg and watching the yolk spread over the fried bread and ooze over the bacon.

Chapter 6 - A Ton to Birmingham – Mercury - Winged Messenger

Jo eased the brown two-tone Rolls off the roundabout, onto the slip road and into the inside lane of the motorway. George, ever-the-generous-and-thoughtful-husband, had leant the car to her as he was flying to Le Touquet for a weekend of golf.

He viewed the Rolls as a workhorse, carrying currency from his pubs to the night safe of the bank. For pleasure, he favoured a sports car, which he had kept in the garage at 88. His clubs sat in the passenger seat of his preferred, third automobile, a small 1948 MG TC Midget sports car, which he was driving to Lydd Airport.

He had bought the car within months of their arrival in 1952 and was loathe to get rid of it. The MG was his first and favourite car; he had driven it down from Calais to Grasse and onto the French and Italian Riviera where the met Harold Clowes. It was easier to manoeuvre onto the plane as well.

George and his prized wooden golf clubs were flying with Silver City Airways, which ran a car carrying air ferry, using Bristol Freighters, which flew from Kent to the Pas-de-Calais. Remarkably enough, it was one of the busiest airports in England; a quarter of a million people used it each year. Needless to say, on my wages, I was not one of them.

The Swiss nanny was looking after the three children, leaving Jo free to complete her investigation. She should have been resting after her busy week, but she was determined to get to the bottom of the mysterious death in Cedars Road.

Jo had woken at five thirty and left the house at six before the children woke. They knew she was going away and were quite used to their parents disappearing to Paris or to Amsterdam for the weekend. If it was not that, it was going to a party on Friday or Saturday evening.

One of Jo's daughters would always want to powder Jo's back when she wore her Balmain gown. If there was no ball or party to attend, they might go to the Alexandria, a pub in Clapham Old Town, which somehow managed to get hold of excellent Irish beef.

Their friends would eat out and then return to 88 West Side, for dancing and drinking into the small hours. They were a very social couple. Jo was a great cook, but she seldom had dinner parties, they were too busy otherwise. The Friday night before her trip to the Midlands was a rare evening at home and an early night as George had to be up early to drive to the airport.

Jo loved the Rolls. The speed and luxury and the ease of driving made eating up the miles an absolute pleasure. The five litre, six-cylinder, motor was as smooth as silk. The Silver Cloud was supremely comfortable, thick wool carpet, fat leather seats and walnut throughout, the smell, look and feel of opulence. White wall tyres gave it an American glamour.

It took about forty-five minutes to an hour to clear London. The journey to Watford where the M1 began, meant driving down Cedars Road, crossing Chelsea Bridge, negotiating Knightsbridge, passing Paddington, finding Finchley Road, brushing by Barnet and Bushey before, finally, reaching the new black top motorway. It was the first of its kind in England. It was easy to negotiate the first part of her journey on a Saturday morning. Traffic in those days was light at the weekends and early mornings.

The first section of the M1 had only been opened recently, on Monday 2nd of November 1959, by the Minister of Transport, Ernest Marples, less than two weeks before Jo tried it out on Saturday 14th. It lacked many features of a modern motorway, namely, no central reservation, no crash barriers, no lighting and no speed limits.

The road was like a taut, black ribbon, its freshly laid tarmac providing an immaculately flat road that stretched for miles and miles. The clock mounted in the middle of the dashboard showed it was just after seven. Jo pressed her foot down, the Rolls cleaved through the early morning mist, hitting sixty miles and hour.

Rather than easing off, she pressed on to seventy, settling down into a comfortable cruising speed. In a mile, less than a minute, she pushed the car on to eighty. After half a mile she was up to ninety and still she could not hear the engine.

The brute power appealed to her. As Watford became a speck in Jo's rear view mirror, she sped up to a hundred miles an hour. She cruised at that speed for as long as the motorway allowed. The road was clear except for a truck sitting in the inside lane, Jo did not slow as she checked her rear-view mirror and gradually moved from the inside lane across the middle one to the outside lane well before she drew level with the leviathan.

She gave the lorry a wide berth.

All she could hear was the ticking of the clock. Keeping a weather eye on her rear-view mirror, she saw the lorry as it disappeared as quickly as it had appeared. There was no sound coming from the engine, it was so smooth at speed.

Only the swift progress that she made, eating up the miles, reminded her of the fact she was driving and not sitting in a stationary car. George had bought the Rolls because it was a lot less conspicuous than a security van and could carry a ton of weight.

All the cash from his pubs, particularly The Lord Rodney's Head, could be transported in the boot of the car without a problem and without attracting attention to its cargo. Who would use a car as a security van? George always took a friend to collect the takings and deposit them in the bank's night safe.

Jo had no idea that this sedate saloon could be so much fun to drive. Sadly, the motorway was too short to really enjoy the experience for long, it petered out at Rugby.

The rest of the journey was conducted at half the speed. She felt elated at having done one hundred miles an hour; she loved the idea that she could travel a mile in 36 seconds on the ground. It was similar, in a way, to when she was flying a light aircraft.

Jo was sufficiently aware of current affairs to know about bikers doing a ton-up on that same motorway. It had been widely reported in the press. Birmingham was 120 miles away so she could have done the journey in much less than the three and a half hours it actually took her if the motorway had been a bit longer.

Admittedly, a good hour was used getting across London, the traffic was not a problem; it was the sheer size of the city. The metropolis spread over miles and miles.

The advantage of living in south London was you were close to the roads that led to the south east coast and to the continent of Europe but going north, taking the ferry to Ireland, for instance, involved traversing the city. Although, the motorway had been speedy, the subsequent roads were narrow and twisting, filled with frustration and delays; Jo was stuck behind various slow moving vehicles, including a bright scarlet Messerschmitt KR200 three-wheeler, 'bubble car', a tractor and a slow moving horsebox trailer attached to a muddy 1948, Land Rover.

Arriving in Birmingham, she parked in Shadwell Street, directly outside St. Chad's Cathedral, which was the first Catholic Cathedral erected in the country since the Protestant Reformation. Completed in1841, it was designed by Pugin, who was also responsible for the Palaces of Westminster and the iconic clock tower of Big Ben. Jo was fond of his style of architecture and she even knew his first two names were Augustus Welby. Jo had read a book about him and his architectural style in the library at Bromley, the house she stayed in during the Second World War.

Having completed her arduous journey, she stepped out of the car, closing and locking the aluminium alloy doors. Jo was wearing an ocelot fur coat, that had belonged to her mother in her younger days, and she was carrying a brown leather clutch bag in which she kept her cigarettes and her silver 1957, Ronson, Varaframe, gas lighter and her tan, Italian leather purse. Her father had bought the leather goods for her when she had first gone to Rome by train when she was in her early twenties; the lighter was her own, he smoked cigars so he only ever used matches and took a dim view of lighters especially gas ones.

Jo sat on a bench and put her bag on her lap. The wind ruffled her hair, but the coolness revived her after her long drive. Slipping off her black silk, gloves and snapping open the bag with her free hand, she fished the car keys from the pocket of her fur and dipping into her handbag, she swapped them for a packet of Senior Service. She pushed the bottom of the packet up to reveal sixteen cigarettes, non-filter, they looked like over-grown, white birthday cake candles. Extracting one and closing the box, she returned the pack to her handbag, keeping the keys company, exchanging it for her lighter. The mechanism clicked, the flint sparked, and a small flame danced on the top of the open jaws of the lighter. Touching the end of the cigarette with the fire, she breathed in and the noxious, toxic fumes filled her lungs.

A rush of nicotine went straight to the receptors in her brain. She knew the science behind the toxic ritual, but she enjoyed the feeling of light-headedness it gave her so much that she could not stop.

The first cigarette of the day was the best. It was a delicious narcotic hit from a most addictive drug, which left the head spinning and the heart racing. She exhaled luxuriantly; the smoke blowing through her nose and slightly parted lips. Jo enjoyed smoking, knowing full well that it was bad for her health. Logic told her to give up smoking, all her medical knowledge and tracts of research proved smoking was bad for her, but she enjoyed it so much.

Perfectly aware that she was lying to herself, Jo pretended that she only smoked spasmodically on her own and generally only smoked on social occasions. She often smoked in the car when she felt like it but rarely on long journeys where she needed to concentrate on her driving skills. This was the first and last, she would have for that day, or so she told herself at the time. To be fair, a packet of twenty would last her a fortnight, usually. These were not normal times though. There was a murderer on the loose.

When she finished the cigarette she rose, walked to the edge of the pavement and tossed the butt down a drain and went into the cathedral. It was home to the relics of St Chad and was designated a 'Minor Basilica' by Pope Pius XII. It was a beautiful building. Before making the sign of the cross, she dipped her fingers, middle and index, into the cold Holy water, scooping it from the stoup in the Narthex. Praying for the soul of Robert Harris, the poor man murdered in Cedar's Road, she lit a candle and focused her thoughts on her prayers, it was a five-minute-meditation. She had already said the Rosary on the way up in the car while driving through the streets of London. For all I knew, she might have said a few Hail Marys while she was driving at a hundred.

As a teenager, growing up in County Wicklow, she had read in the newspaper about the night in November 1940 when an incendiary bomb came through the Cathedral roof, bounced on the floor and exploded when it hit the central heating pipes. The pipes burst and the water extinguished the fire, thus saving the Cathedral from destruction.

Although, many other buildings, in that fine city, had been destroyed by the firebombing that night, the church had been saved. It was considered a miracle at the time and provided the devastated people of that fine city with some vestige of hope and comfort.

Call it a coincidence, fate, or an act of God, the church had survived, and it was a beautiful building.

She looked at her Longines Conquest Ladies watch as she stepped back out into the winter sunshine. Someone was waiting for her, standing on the steps looking at the Rolls and wondering where Jo was. Peggy Donaldson was wearing a beige wool coat that came down to her knees, she wore tan stockings and black court shoes. To protect her brown curly hair from the wind, she wore a blue parachute silk scarf. Jo with her flyaway hair wore nothing. Peg was about five foot four and cuddly.

Typically, she had arrived ten minutes early for their appointment. Jo always hated being late, George adored it, so it seemed. It was one of the many needless frustrations her husband created in her life.

"Hello Peg, darling," Jo called, "you're early."

"Hello, Jo, darling," replied Peg, the two old friends hugged affectionately, so are you my love."

Doctor Peg O'Brien was a Medical Practitioner as well. She worked as a doctor in the Accident and Emergency department of the nearby hospital. Her lawyer husband, Roderick, was in the Cayman Islands writing the constitution for the newly independent state.

Their Constitution Day had been 4th July 1959, over four months before but Roderick still needed to tie up some loose ends; dot an 'i' and cross a 't' or two. He was hoping to be back in England for Christmas to celebrate with his family and see in the year, 1960, in England. Roderick had introduced Jo and George to Calypso music. He had bought over Harry Belafonte's album 'Calypso' when he was on leave. They had one boy, Patrick Donaldson, who was only a baby, and he was being looked after by his aunt who had two children of her own.

Peg and Jo had known each other well for over a decade and were more like sisters than friends. They walked as they talked, going back to the Rolls. They caught up on each other's work lives, the children and their own extended family. Jo asked after Patrick as she unlocked the passenger door for her friend and Peggy confirmed that her son was thriving at a nursery near the hospital. Once Peg was installed in her seat, Jo walked around the front of the car, running her hand over the Spirit of Ecstasy on her way to the driver's door.

It was like a talisman that would bring her luck when touched.

"I'm going to drive around the town, and you can tell me everything," Jo announced, opening the driver's door.

"Of course, as you said on the phone, I'll fill you in, it's quite a coincidence," Peg responded, "how was the trip up?"

"Very smooth, thank you, darling," Jo replied before ducking her head to climb into her seat.

Jo was not going to boast about doing a hundred miles an hour. She had done it for her on quiet satisfaction, not to brag about it. Jo loved speed, flying, ski-ing, driving big fast cars. She was a great driver despite being taught by George. Her husband was a bit of a bully behind the wheel. He was less patient and intuitive when he was driving the car.

The city of Birmingham was a building site at that time, December 1959 and although it was a Saturday, the streets were bustling with builders and the roads had a fair few trucks delivering raw materials to all the different sites. During the Second World War it had been a major manufacturing centre, and therefore an obvious target for German bombing.

More than two thousand people died.

The government was still implementing its post-war building programme. Between the end of the war and nineteen-fifty-four, more than thirty thousand council houses were built but a survey in 1954 showed that twenty per cent of the houses in Birmingham were still unfit for human habitation so the council building programme had continued unabated.

The bombing, the depravation, the squalor, dating back to Victorian times, and the ruined homes and shops, all the woes were to be forgotten in the forward sweep of progress that would reshape the city and the inhabitants' lives. Birmingham was going to be renewed in a forward-thinking modernist building programme. Despite its problems, Peg loved the city, it had a great community of wonderful people, but everyone admitted that the housing conditions were dire, which did not bode well for the health of the residents of the city. Birmingham had the largest Irish immigrant community next to Liverpool and London; it was like being at home. Most of her patients, at the Birmingham General Hospital, were Irish as were a large proportion of the staff.

"Spill the beans," Jo demanded putting on a creditable American accent, trying to sound like a hard-bitten Chicago gangster. They had both been brought up on the Hollywood gangster movies.

"Okay, sweat heart," Peggy replied, sounding like James Cagney playing a violent hoodlum, she actually sounded alarmingly convincing in her role.

Jo negotiated another roundabout and pulled into a side road. Reaching under the dashboard, she pulled the handbrake on and put the gear selector in park. Switching off the engine, she looked at the clock; it was ten-forty. She had done well, getting there in just over three and a half hours, ensuring she had said her prayers in the car and lighting a candle at the church all before midday.

"Now," Jo said seriously, turning to Peg, "Tell me again what you found."

"After your call last week, I was surprised that we had a very similar case, a man coming in with carbon monoxide poisoning," Peggy declared,

Jo looked askance, was it too much of a coincidence to mean nothing? She had to rule out the obvious. After all Sherlock Holmes was her mentor, he and Dr Watson had kept her company through many a rainy afternoon in Bromley.

"I would imagine there are a stream of them from what I can gather about living conditions in some rented accommodation. It was the same in Dublin," Jo noted dryly.

"You're right but our man, Charles Wood had bruises around his neck like your cadaver and there was a blow to the head," remonstrated Peg, "he reckoned it was a hammer of some sort. A friend saved him, and he was able to tell me that his attacker was left-handed."

Jo took in all this information; it certainly chimed with her victim.

"So, like our 'so called' suicide, your patient had been strangled, hit on the head and then gassed," Jo confirmed, shaking her head in disbelief.

"Exactly, quite a coincidence, wouldn't you say?" Peg agreed.

"Cigarette, darling, I could use one?" Jo asked, realising that she was breaking her rationing yet again.

"No thank you, Jo, they're bad for you, didn't you know?"

"Darling, I live in London, the pollution there will kill me long before the cigarettes do," Jo replied.

She had promised herself she would not smoke more than her quota each day and yet this case encouraged her to smoke more. Jo worried that soon she would be regularly smoking when driving the car if she was not too careful. She dreaded filling the ashtray in case George decided to replace the car as a result.

As a concession, she wound down the window before lighting up another Senior Service. That action let in the damp, chill November wind laced with the pollution form the smokestacks and chimneys of the city, not to mention the leaded fuel from all the transport. This was one of her thinking cigarettes. She would normally eschew smoking more than one cigarette a day.

Since the murder her intake of cigarettes per week had risen considerably. In her routine existence, she rationed her intake of her one and only luxury purchase but on special occasions she relented and smoked more. Jo confessed that cigarettes and cold cream were her two vices; Senior Service and Pomeroy were her only indulgences. The cream was necessary because she had dry skin. She could make her cream last a month and twenty cigarettes last a week, just not this particular week.

These were mitigating circumstances as far as she was concerned. Taking a long luxuriant drag on her cigarette, she drew on the decorated end where the brand's emblem of a sailing ship was printed in blue on the white cigarette paper.

They were the most expensive and luxurious brand of cigarette in the country, unless you included those that were hand made, in Haymarket, by Fribourg & Treyer. The nicotine coursed through her bloodstream, the nicotine receptors in her brain made her feel high for the second time that day but the effect was more subdued.

"You have a point," Peg admitted, "but my drug is tea, so strong you can stand a spoon in it, I'm dying for a cuppa, now."

"Yes, with two sugars and you know sugar is a poison and affects the liver and kidneys, plus it plays havoc with your insulin levels," Jo warned, "sugar is as much a poison as tobacco and it will kill more people one day."

"Don't tell Coca Cola!" Peg teased.

She knew about Jo's pet theory, but she was not impressed by it, not least because she liked two sugars in her tea and had a sweet tooth. What it did to her liver, she did not care.

"Precisely, or Pepsi! Now, back to the case in point."

"Well, I think you'll be interested in this information," Peg assured her eking out the suspense.

"Come on stop teasing, cut to the chase," Jo cajoled her in a good-natured manner.

"It's relatively simple, these murders and attempted murder are connected, I'm sure there are more than just our two cases. There could be a serial killer or a gang behind it."

"And it could have remained undetected but for one thing," Jo noted mischievously.

She took a valedictory drag on her cigarette,

"Exactly, we talk to each other, we discuss things properly, not in a superficial way!" Peg joked.

It was one of their 'in-jokes', a comment on modern conversation and people's inability to engage in a deep and meaningful way.

"It's only the fact that I know you so well and mentioned all the details to you that has allowed us to see this connection," Joe agreed, "if you hadn't picked up on the similarity, we would both still be at square one."

"What about the police? They haven't made any progress, have they?" asked Peg as a matter of course.

"Not in London, no, and the police here, what do they think?"

"We naturally reported it, but the victim refused to tell the police what had happened," explained Peg.

"How did you know, then?" Jo asked.

"I only found out all the details by quizzing the nurses; our particular patient was found unconscious by his best friend just before the gas entered his bloodstream. His friend turned off the gas and administered the kiss of life."

"That was fortunate," Jo sighed.

"Luckily, his friend had called around to see him; his motorbike was there so he broke down the door when there was no reply."

"That was extremely lucky."

"Charles Wood was slumped by the gas fire, but his injuries were consistent with your victim."

There was a long silence between them.

"That's incredible," Jo, gasped, she meant it in the literal sense of the word; she could not believe it.

"Sadly, the Metropolitan Police and the West Midlands Police don't necessarily share information, it's not like the Garda back home; each region polices their own area," Peg elucidated, she had spoken to a sergeant who regularly attended the Casualty Department in a professional capacity and he had pointed out the disparity between police forces.

"You think we should tell our respective inspectors the coincidence. Your patient…"

"Charles Wood," Peg reminded her.

"Sorry, Charles Wood was too scared to talk to the police, but he might talk to me," Jo suggested.

"We should definitely tell our inspectors and then that's the end of it, it's all we can do."

"I want to try and talk to Charles Wood, if I can," Jo insisted,

"Jo this is dangerous work, the people who tried to kill him might try to do you in, as well," Peg warned.

"To dig I am unable, to beg I am too proud; I have no choice Peg, you know that, we signed the same oath, you and I."

"I hate to be accused of Hippocratic hypocrisy, but you don't need to do this, you could leave it to the police," Peg pleaded.

"I can't and I shan't," replied Jo.

"We signed an oath to save life where and when we could, not to endanger ourselves by investigating the taking of a life. Let the professionals handle it."

"I could, but there are only two problems, they would not get as far as I can."

"Do you know that?"

"And I would be unable to sleep, knowing that I had not done my utmost to see this through. I cannot sleep knowing there is a murderer at large, you can understand that, surely?"

"I understand; a woman has to do what a woman has to do," said Peg, smiling indulgently at her friend, "now, let's go somewhere and get a cup of tea."

"A splendid idea," Joe confirmed; they always agreed on the important things.

"I'd love to know how you think you're going to track down this Charles Wood," Peg admitted.

"Where did he work?" Jo asked.

"I wrote down the address the nurse remembered, it was some big company that invests in shares for wealthy clients, here it is," Peg proudly announced, producing a neatly folded piece of notepaper from her overcoat pocket.

"Well done," Jo commented admiringly.

Jo would take the information to Regan and then she would be rid of the investigation and return to full time general practice. Pathology was an interesting branch of medicine but investigating a murder on the back of that was not a suitable vocation for a wife and mother of three young children who was also trying to build up her medial practice.

Carefully, unfolding the scrap of paper on which she had made copious notes, Jo waited, with her pen poised.

"Global Portfolio, he tried to get the nurse to invest!" she declared.

"You are a marvel, Peg."

"He told her that he worked down the road so it's not far from the hospital. The nurse also told me that the friend, Bert Cousins, the man who found him, plays pool at the warehouses in Fazeley Street. I'll show you where it is, I've brought you a map."

"I'll drop you off and we'll compare notes later, thank you Peg."

"Have a cup of tea first."

"I intend to, I'm parched. All this detective work has left me with a dry mouth," Jo exclaimed.

Jo pushed the butt of the cigarette into the ashtray underneath the dashboard, before turning the ignition key.

"You'll be replacing the car once the ashtray is full, won't you, Jo?" quipped Peg as she sat back in her seat and prepared to direct Jo to the nearest café. They both laughed. The Rolls purred into life and a cursory glance over her shoulder allowed Jo to check the road was clear, to indicate and to pull out. She was going to need more than just tea and cigarettes to get her through the day

Chapter 7 - The Pool Room Blues

The Poolroom was accessed by two fire doors, one pinned open against the brick wall, and the other closed. The wide stone staircase of the warehouse led down to the area where tobacco barrels, cases of gin and whiskey or boxes of fine wine had been stored in-Bond.

The Bonded Warehouse had not been used since the end of the war; the business had moved to a more secure site outside of town; an enterprising entrepreneur had filled the ground floor with full size pool tables. He had set up a bar in the far corner to allow the members to quench their thirst.

Jo parked the Rolls in a side street, folded her fur coat so the lining was showing and placed it reverently in the carpeted boot, swapping it for her pea-green wool coat, which lay next to her overnight bag.

She closed the boot and locked the car up before fishing in her pocket for something to protect her hair from the wind that whispered between the warehouses. Draping a green chiffon scarf around her golden locks and tying a bow under her chin, she strode confidently around the corner to the entrance and walked down the steps as if she owned the place.

That was Jo, fearless in the face of adversity.

She had struggled to establish herself. She had learnt that the only thing to fear was fear itself. If she wanted something, moving mountains was on her agenda, if fear ever bothered her, I never, ever saw her flinch from danger. There are people who mask their doubts and fears people who seize the day.

All those clichés: fortune favours the brave, he who dares wins, nothing ventured nothing gained, summed up her attitude. She was determined to find the murderer.

Jo stepped into a cloud of cigarette smoke, but the hall was much warmer than outside. Her eyes adjusted to the dim light. She was a beauty amongst the beasts. Her height, five foot nine, her natural blonde hair and her blue eyes made her seem more Nordic than Celtic. Jo was good looking and she knew it. Confidence, she knew was half the battle. If she wanted to find out what had happened, she would have to pretend to be fearless. She was not intimidated. She had been born in a pub.

A fug of cigarette smoke obscured the light that was coming from the green shaded table lights, moving up to the ceiling like wisps of morning mist. Four bare light bulbs provided the only other light in the room. The click clack of balls being hit and striking the others in the pockets, echoed through the room. It was like a tournament. Eight tables of 'eight ball' pool, all played with intensity. These were high-stakes games, bet on by other members of the club, their rent money for a week could be won on a single game, a player ruined by his loss.

The floor was occupied by people who would not have looked out of place in one of J. R. Murphy's, East End, docklands pubs: they were strong and tall, men whose muscles were hewn through hard graft and long hours lifting and carrying. This was a bastion of masculinity. There was the odour of cigarette smoke and the stench of sweat, it was no place for a lady and Jo knew it.

Alerted to her presence, the first table played a shot and stopped. The pool cues slammed onto the stone floor. A wave of activity saw all cues on their handles and all players staring at the interloper.

Some of the crowd muttered about the disturbance but most just stared at Jo. She untied her scarf and shook her hair, slipping the scarf into her coat pocket. Dipping her hand in her other pocket, she rummaged around and, suddenly, in her right hand she held a Senior Service, which she slipped between her lips.

She smiled at the nearest pool player.

"Have you got a light, please?" she asked, raising her eyebrow.

The man smiled, admitting to himself that whoever she was, she had nerve.

Moving the cue from his right hand to left and resting it on his left shoulder, he approached her, struck a match on the back of his denim overalls and raised his hand to the cigarette end.

She inhaled deeply and turned her head, deliberately avoiding blowing smoke in his face. She thanked him and folded her arms, casually holding the cigarette in her right hand, challenging the man to fill the silence.

"What are you doing here?" he asked barely disguising his contempt. "This is a men's club."

"I want a game of pool, are you man enough to take me on?" Jo retorted. She was not afraid, she could take care of herself she stood smoking her cigarette slowly and deliberately, demonstrating how she enjoyed inhaling and signalling clearly that she was in no hurry to go anywhere.

"You sound a bit posh to be hanging out here, what's the story here?" the man asked, suspicion in his voice, "Buck House is due south."

"I'm a doctor, I've just written a Death Certificate for a man not dissimilar to you," she informed him, looking him up and down as if sizing him up for a coffin or wondering how long he had to live, "I need distraction."

"And you want to play pool?" he asked, eyeing her with a mixture of admiration and incredulity.

"I do play pool, I've been playing it for years and ten shillings says you won't beat me," she announced full of bravado, loudly, so everyone could hear her challenge, before taking a further drag on her cigarette and giving him a steely look with her bright blue eyes.

"Ten shillings is too much for me, who the hell do you think you are?" he growled.

"Ten shillings if you win, a brandy for me, if I win," she said ignoring his jibe.

His opponent, Maurice piped up from behind the table, "Go on Bert, you could do with the cash, take her on, it will be a short game. Then, we can get back to our game!"

"Bert, I'm Jo," she said, knowing that he would not be able to refuse a game, it was easy money for him, "now we know each other we can play; what do you think?"

"I think you have more money than sense. Can you give her your cue, Maurice, put some chalk on it for her, would you?"

The whole pool hall formed a sweaty perimeter around the table, leaving a cue's length for the players, thirty-three spectators for an early evening game was a record for that club. Jo threw the butt of her cigarette on the floor and stood on it with one of her high heels.

"Can someone take my coat?" she asked

The barman came over, there was no business, now that everyone was gathered around the pool table; he locked the till and sauntered over to watch the match. He took her coat. Bert was gallant and gave her first break.

Maurice set the frame and the balls on the table. He had been losing their game and was glad the stranger had interrupted; he had been in danger of losing two shillings. Bert should have tossed for who broke. Then, he might have had more of a chance.

Jo hit the first red ball into the far side right pocket and followed with every single other ball until the table was clear. The room erupted in a tumult of applause. All the men admired how she played.

"Let's get you that brandy and you can tell me why you really came here," said Bert, now a defeated man.

He had lost the money from Maurice but not too much face, the way Jo had cleared the table was a sight to be admired. All that practising by herself in the billiard room at Bromley House, in Kilpedder, had finally paid dividends.

"Thank you, Bert" Jo acknowledged with a smile.

A brandy might be just the thing to bring her blood pressure down. It was gruelling being the only woman in the room; she could only imagine half of what they were all thinking. The barman followed them to the bar folding her coat so that the silky, green lining was showing and placing it carefully on the bar stool next to her on her right.

"What can I get you?" he asked as he lifted the hatch across the bar top and stepped through.

"Bert?" Jo asked.

"It's my round," Bert protested sitting on the stool to her left.

"Bert, I need information, the pool game was just so I could get to talk to you without making it obvious. Have a drink and put your pride in your top pocket for later."

"Why talk to me?" he asked innocently.

He watched as she turned to her coat and fished around for her cigarettes and change. She had left her wallet locked in the glove box of the car.

"Because, you know everyone and everything, so I have been reliably informed. Would you like a cigarette?"

"I've got some roll-ups," Bert replied as he emptied his trouser pockets of matches, papers and Old Holborn tobacco.

"Indulge me, try one of these," persisted Jo, offering the pack to him, "What will you have?"

"Light and Mild thanks," he replied, taking one of the proffered cigarettes and lighting Jo's with a match before lighting his own.

While they had been talking, the bar man had poured the half pint of beer, which was in fact three quarters full and placed the half pint bottle of pale ale next to it.

"Can I have a brandy and soda, please?" Jo added.

A brandy, in a highball glass, without ice arrived seconds later followed by a soda water bottle. Jo raised her glass and sloshed some soda onto the caramel coloured liquid.

"So, you know, Charles Wood?" she asked, putting some coins on the bar and pushing them away from her.

Bert looked intrigued; she had obviously palmed the coins when she rummaged in her pocket for her Senior Service.

"Who wants to know?" he almost spat; he was still suspicious.

"Just me, I live in London and someone was attacked in a similar way; I thought it was suicide at first, but I, now, think it was a murder."

"So, what's it got to do with Charlie?" he asked.

"The attacks were similar, identical in my opinion," she expanded, wondering how he was implicated.

"So, you say," he protested.

"If they were connected, it means we have someone who is murdering indiscriminately," Jo argued, trying to read his thoughts, her icy blue eyes never left his face as he looked down at the polished wood bar top.

"It's not my business," he protested, not looking up at her.

"They have to be stopped. It was a miracle Charles Wood survived. His friend in London was not so lucky and the technique is obviously being perfected."

"If they were connected," he observed, staring up at her for the first time before looking down into his glass, again. She wondered what fascinated him so much in the woodwork. "It's a coincidence that's all."

"You my be right, but that's why I'm here, I've gone to check if they were connected."

"And if they weren't, you can go home," he sneered, taking a long draught from his pint, followed by a draw on his cigarette.

Nervously, he flicked his cigarette into the square china ashtray at Jo's elbow.

"I need to know," she insisted, making him look up, suddenly.

She locked her beautiful, blue eyes on his brown ones, willing him to realise resistance was useless.

"You need to know nothing, leave it to the police," he hissed, "they're the best people to deal with it. Go home."

"So, you won't help me?" she complained.

Jo's disappointment showed on her face, he was not sure if it was an act. He only saw a woman who was getting in way over her head and was in imminent danger.

"I am helping you; go home," he asserted, taking another puff on his cigarette and swallowing more beer before continuing, "finish your drink, go home and forget about all of this."

"It sounds like a warning to me."

"Just some friendly advice from me. Trust me, you definitely do not want to get involved with these people."

"So, I was right."

"If that's what you want to hear, so be it. Now finish your fag, drink your brandy and get lost."

"If I could."

He snorted with disdain.

"If, if, I'll give you if," he answered, "my Old Dad said, if your auntie had balls, she'd be your uncle. If you were meant to be a detective, you wouldn't have spent all that time at medical school."

"Saving peoples lives is the same thing, someone is trying to murder friends of yours."

"Concentrate on what you do best, pet. Don't mess with these characters. Stay alive."

With that, he drained his glass and left her at the bar. The owner placed another brandy on the counter.

"On the house," he said smiling.

"I'm fine with the one drink, thank you," Joe laughed, "are you trying to get me drunk?"

"Go on, I put my money on you, and you've made me a fortune," he urged and left the drink there.

"I'm feeling a bit giddy already, I've forgotten to eat, never drink on an empty stomach," she advised.

"Never share a drink with strangers," he countered.

"Especially, bar men, you never know what they might slip into your drink," she joked.

"You are dead right, so easy for someone to slip in a Mickey Finn, I would imagine," he mentioned, as sudden steely tone to his voice.

He watched her as sudden realisation played across her face.

"Chloral hydrate?" she said, suddenly realising she had been duped.

"Something like that, but don't worry Josephine Murphy, I'll catch you when you fall."

"I didn't tell you my name," she noted, frowning like a puzzled child.

"You're surprisingly lucid, of course your tall, maybe I should have used a few more drops," he said, rapidly removing the two glasses from the bar.

"That's all right, I'm fighting it."

"Well, you might be a demon with a pool cue but, this time, you've been well and truly snookered, love."

"I am feeling a bit giddy, I must admit."

With that she put her elbows on the wooden counter, folded her arms and slumped forward, onto the bar, her hair spilling over the polished surface.

Chapter 8 – Driving Drugged

i

Jo woke up in a small square room with no windows, above her head was a planking roof, exposed rafters ran along the ceiling and a dusty cement floor was at her feet; it was just like the cellar in her house. It was possible to stand up, but she was tied to a bentwood chair by some heavy ship's rope.

There was a square table under a single sixty-watt bulb suspended from a brown cord and shrouded by a green, metal, cone shaped shade. At the table sat a man in a white shirt, a navy three-piece, pinstripe suit and black brogues; next to him on the third chair sat a man in a once white, lab coat that covered charcoal grey trousers, he was wearing black wellington boots, glasses and a frown. All his clothes could have done with a wash and a layer of dust seemed to have settled on him, he might have lived in the cellar stock room.

"Good afternoon Doctor Murphy," he hissed with a hint of a mid-central European accent. "It is imperative you get home to your children. You must rush, put your foot down."

"Of course," she acquiesced.

"How fast were you going to get here in the first place?" he persisted.

"Very fast," Jo said, trying to remember more of the trip up to Birmingham and failing.

"You must go faster."

"Faster?"

"Put your foot down."

"Foot down," she slurred drowsily.

"Faster," he implored.

"Faster," she agreed.

"Put your foot right down."

"Right down," she mumbled, dribbling from the corner of her mouth, her face slack, her body limp.

The professor turned around to talk to the man in the suit.

"Bray, is the car outside?"

"Yes, professor."

"Help me get the doctor to her car and help me with the key words."

"Key words," Jo muttered.

"Faster, doctor, it's an emergency, faster," the professor pronounced slowly and deliberately so she would not mishear them.

"Faster, doctor," Bray parroted, moving around the table.

"Faster," Jo repeated.

"Put your foot down," Bray whispered.

"Put your foot down," urged the professor.

"Put your foot down," Jo mumbled.

The two men hauled the limp body out of the chair and, supported by both of them, she staggered to the doorway. Taking her right hand, the professor led her up the wooden staircase to the door that led out into the street. Bray held her other hand and pushed her up the stairs. Like a malfunctioning robot, she stomped up the stairs. They stood on the landing at the top and the professor pushed open the door that led into a small courtyard. A chill wind whipped around the small space. A pale sky hung like a grey curtain above their head. Crossing to a black metal gate, the two men supported her. Bray pulled open the gate and she stumbled through it, managing to stay on her feet only because the professor had supported her.

Bray rushed ahead and opened the door of the Rolls, slipping the key in the ignition, and turning on the engine before helping his accomplice to settle Jo into the driving seat. He turned the key and started the engine. Physically pulling her right leg onto the brake, he selected drive from the stalk gear lever.

Before he closed the driver's door, he flicked the switch to work the headlights.

"You must go, doctor, it's an emergency, quickly" the professor whispered in her ear before turning the steering wheel a half turn anticlockwise and slipping out of the passenger seat, whispering to her before closing that door. "Go straight, you'll find the way."

"Straight on," she mumbled in affirmation.

The men watched as she eased her foot off the break and the car slipped silently and slowly from the kerb and pulled out to the left and into the empty road.

"There's a dead end at the bottom of the hill, a wall around a graveyard," the professor announced, looking briefly at Bray before his eyes were drawn back to the Rolls.

"It's the end of the road for Jo, then," Bray quipped, putting his arm on the professor's shoulder. "She'll end up in the dead centre of Witton."

The car swerved to the right and was corrected once again so it sat in the middle of the road. The speed increased. They watched the white lines disappearing under the centre of the car, more rapidly as the car built up speed. Bray smiled at the professor and they returned behind the metal gate, which clanged shut. The car sped down Farley Road.

ii

Her bloodstream was pumped full of a cocktail of Benzedrine and alcohol. She was as high as a kite. Every sense was alert due to the upper, the amphetamine and her sense of reality deadened by the alcohol, the depressant. Jo's foot was on the accelerator, her body was upright, her chin held high. She stared through the windscreen. Her eyes were trying to focus through the fug, which she thought was mist. Jo squinted through the fog in her mind.

She needed to get back to London. The clock on the dashboard ticked and the houses flashed by.

Time was flying by and she thought she could fly.

She was flying.

She remembered what he had said.

"You're on the motorway, put your foot down."

But who was he? It did not matter, the children counted, she must get back to them.

Still the clock ticked; still the buildings flashed by.

"Put your foot down!"

She crossed a junction without realising. Luckily, there was scant traffic on the side roads. The car shot past Brookvale Park Road towards The Ridgeway. She glanced down; the speedometer read sixty. The clock read midnight. Miraculously, there were no cars on that road so late, that night.

"Faster."

The headlights shone; the buildings of the next street flashed by. She was going faster, just as they asked her. Tick, tick, the dashboard clock told her time was running out. She was on her way back to the children.

Her head cleared as adrenaline filled her system. She marvelled at how alert she was, at how smoothly the car was driving. The car could easily reach a hundred if Jo pressed down a bit more on the accelerator and it was so important to get home. She flew past all the side streets, it was just like piloting a plane, and she was coming into land, heading downhill.

"Put your foot down."

Ahead was the dead end; on the other side of the wall was the cemetery. Still the buildings flashed by; still the clock ticked; still the car raced down the road towards it.

"Faster, faster," he had urged. "You have to get back to London, quickly, go faster, the children are in danger."

She was trying to comply. The wall grew closer, she could hear the tick, so clearly; she could see the wall so clearly. Everything was so bright; every sound was enhanced, and the smell of leather was so strong.

"Faster," he had exclaimed encouragingly.

She felt she could see over the wall. Once she was through the wall, the road would be straight. She would be home in no time.

"Faster," he insisted in her head.

Not long now, she would be at the wall and through. The wall would not stop her getting home, it would not stop her getting back to her children; it would not stop her getting back to George. Once she was through the wall it would be a short trip. The wall, the wall, the wall, it was coming closer and closer and closer.

A wall!

What had he said? "Put your foot down!"

A wall!

"Faster, Jo, go faster!"

A brick wall!

"Put your foot down."

She did.

She stamped her foot down.

There was a screech; the hydraulic brakes bit.

The servo-assisted drums locked. The car ground to a halt. The sudden cessation of motion meant the bodywork lurched forward; the chrome bumper hit the wall with a clang.

She heard it and thought of the quote: "Therefore, send not to know for whom the bell tolls, it tolls for thee."

"Faster, Jo, go faster," the words were repeating in her head.

The car had stopped the bumper just brushing the brickwork.

"Put your foot down," urged the strangers' voices over and over again.

Jo slumped over the steering wheel, which she had used to brace herself.

'Who was he?' she wondered.

Suddenly, her mind was clear, she felt alert, awake; the Benzedrine was working. The amphetamine was beating the depressant influence of the alcohol in her system. It was beginning to have its proper euphoria inducing effect.

Benzedrine had been given to RAF pilots to keep them awake on night-time bombing missions. After the war, it had become one of the earliest synthetic stimulants to be exploited by the criminal underworld.

The drug had made her high.

However, the alcohol was still making her feel fuggy, just as the professor had intended. Jo could not remember how she had got into the car, how before that she had been slipped the Benzedrine capsules; had been plied with alcohol and had been hypnotised to drive at breakneck speed, through two junctions, driving towards the wall.

As a doctor, she knew that the alcohol was a depressant and that the Benzedrine was a stimulant. The drugs fought inside her body and fought inside her head.

Still slumped forward, she somehow took the keys from the ignition. Very slowly, Jo sat upright and stared ahead at the wall.

She could have been killed; she should have been killed; she would have been killed. Thanks to her quick thinking and engineering, she survived. Thoughts of her mother, her children, her father, her brothers and sisters and of course George had somehow entered her addled brain a split second before it would have been too late.

Any other car would have smashed into the wall and the engine block would have been forced into the passenger compartment; a mobile object meeting a stationary object at speed would have had the force equivalent to an elephant hitting a tree trunk. The wall would be a ruin, the car would be a ruin and Jo would be a ruin.

Neither would have survived the impact.

The only thing that saved her life was the servo-assisted brakes and the sudden realisation that the wall was an immobile obstacle. The Birmingham police confirmed all this to me after their accident investigation team had carried out all their tests.

Shaken, Jo still had the presence of mind to slip the keys from the ignition, and hide them under the passenger seat, before she staggered from the driver's seat, opened the back door and lay across the bench seat at the back of the car. She curled up on the cool leather and waited for sleep to sweep over her. It did not take long; she had only just closed her eyes when she found herself in the arms of Morpheus.

Chapter 9 - The Proposal

i

Outside, it was a typical drizzly December day. The five-storey redbrick building, the headquarters of Gately, Macaulay and Robinson Holdings, was a 1930s office block. GMR had interests around the world. Bray sat on a black leather armchair, in the huge Managing Director's office, facing a massive black desk and the tabletop was bordered by gold leaf detailing.

"Are you insane?" asked James Bannister, sitting behind his desk as Arthur Bray sat down opposite him.

Bannister looked tense, the meeting had not gone well, before they had even exchanged niceties at the door, Bray had dropped his bombshell.

"Certainly, you could argue that, but we think you will be quite happy with the performance your company makes when it is listed," Arthur Bray replied

"You're asking me to promote Matthew Andrews to the post?"

"Of course," Bray responded casually, he located his gold, Colibri, Stormgard, lighter in his waistcoat and fumbled for his box of Benson and Hedges cigarettes, which he extracted from the inside pocket of his light grey, suit jacket.

"Would you care for a smoke?" he asked.

Bray chose the brand because they were the favourite fag of George VI and has a Royal Warrant.

He had to lean forward out of the heavily padded, low slung chair in order to place his smoking paraphernalia on the desk. Bray hovered, crouched forward, waiting to leap forward or sit down, again.

"Thank you, but Mary McAllister is far more qualified and more suitable for the job, she's been doing the same role in Hong Kong for five years; Andrews is a blow in, hardly been with us a year. The shareholders won't like it," Bannister argued, leaning forward on his elbows.

"You'll have to sell the idea to them, then, unless you want to be looking for a job next year with a worthless reference and a ruined share portfolio," Bray warned, proffering the pack and, once the cigarette was taken, snapping his lighter into life.

"Is that a threat?" Bannister asked, taking the light proffered and inhaling deeply as he gave Bray a steely stare.

He leant back afterwards, drawing on his cigarette while he appraised Bray. He was a comical character but what he said was not funny. His suit did not fit him. He wore cheap shoes, which seemed at odds with the rest of his clothes. He was short and tubby, an overweight Napoleon. A harmless character yet his whole being emanated evil.

"More of a promise, I would say, my colleagues would prefer if you were taken out of the picture all together but bankrupting you will suffice."

"What?" Bannister cried incredulously.

"You may have read about such matters, there has been a spate of poor unfortunates poisoning themselves with gas."

"You don't expect me to believe you were responsible for all those deaths, do you?" asserted Bannister.

"Believe what you wish, dear boy. All I can tell you is that all those victims were single men, except your friend Tim, what was his name?"

"Dunmore."

"Yes, unfortunate accident in his car, poor, Tim Dunmore. I feel sorry for the widow; he had children just like you."

"So, I'm going to meet with a fatal accident on my way to one of the factories?" asked Banister.

"I sincerely hope not."

"Good, in that case, Mary gets the job."

"You miss my point; we cannot allow women into these high-ranking posts and we'll have to pay them the same as men."

"That will never happen."

"I should hope not; what we're doing here is saving the establishment; we can't have competent women coming on board, making us look slipshod and amateurish," Bray argued.

"So, you and your friends are petrified that the rise of women in the workforce will threaten your cosy jobs, is that it?"

"In a nutshell, yes," Bray admitted, smiling sheepishly. You must see we cannot let them loose in the boardroom or in management."

"The world would be a far more pleasant and productive place, judging by Mary's record in Hong Kong, even her rivals adore her, and her sales figures are impressive, too"

Bannister flicked the ash that had grown on his cigarette towards the ashtray in frustration at his inability to convince Bray of the efficacy of her appointment. A cylinder of ash landed like a fat, grey caterpillar on the side of the desk.

"That's precisely what we want to avoid. Up until now, we have only targeted the men who have suggested promoting women, if the women are in post, we will have to execute them."

"Did I hear you right?"

Bray smiled; he was used to this reaction.

"I never said a word, dear boy. Remember Europe is being built out of the ashes of war. Remind me when rationing ended if you would?"

"You know as well as I do, 4th July 1954."

"Precisely, over nine years after war; do we want to measure our progress in decades?"

"But women will help the process or rebuilding as they helped in the war effort," Bannister argued.

"Not in our world."

"You know women are just as competent and diligent in their roles. They are as good as men, if not more so," protested Bannister, stubbing his cigarette out violently in the ashtray.

"Yes, yes, of course but we don't want an equal world and a fair workplace for women. We want them to have children not careers. We'll never be safe once the women take over."

"You're serious," Bannister interjected.

"Deadly."

"And if I don't comply with your wishes?"

"I cannot hold back my colleagues, they will take the action that they see fit."

"Who are they?" Bannister asked, getting redder in the face.

"Never you mind, suffice to say, you and Mary will not be on their Christmas card list and that, my dear boy, is not good news."

"You're all mad."

Bray leant forward and stubbed out his cigarette in the round gleaming, glass ashtray that stood in the corner of the desk. Bannister was only halfway through his.

"Without a shadow of a doubt, however, we have the power to prevail, so don't you worry about us," Bray sighed unimpressed. "Now what's your answer?"

"I would be mad not to promote Mary."

"Wrong answer. You'll have until I finish my second cigarette to come up with the right one," announced Bray, extracting a cigarette from packet and lighting it.

Bray returned the pack to his inside jacket pocket and the lighter to his waistcoat, inhaled greedily on his cigarette before staring back at Bannister with cold, calculating eyes. Releasing the smoke from behind his teeth, he blew the smoke away from his victim's face and into the corner of the spacious room.

His gaze never left Bannister's.

"Okay, I know what happened to Robert," Bannister replied.

"And Charles."

"Charles Wood, you didn't?"

"He survived this time, but the warning worked. I want everyone to realise we are serious."

"You win, who would you like appointed in her place?"

"My man of course."

"I suppose Andrews will do a reasonable job."

"Then, it's all agreed Matthew Andrews gets the job," Bray confirmed.

"One thing, can Mary be his assistant?" Bannister asked, hopefully.

"Why of course, she can do all the hard work and he can get the credit; we have never, ever, objected to that."

"It was ever thus," admitted Bannister, smiling grimly and sitting back in his chair.

"You made the right choice," Bray soothed.

Both of them knew that a life had been saved that day.

ii

Jo was preparing her surgery for the morning clinic when she heard a truck rounding the corner. It pulled up with a squeak rather than a screech of brakes. Looking out of the surgery over the hedge she saw the burgundy roof of the collier.

The coal truck had five tons of hard coal on board. This Anthracite generated the highest heat of all the fossil fuels available, and its relatively low sulphur content made it a comparatively clean-burning fuel.

The Government tried to ignore the Great London Smog of 1952, but the first Clean Air Act was eventually introduced in 1956, following the Beaver Committee Report.

The Act aimed to control domestic sources of smoke pollution by introducing smokeless zones. In these areas, smokeless fuels had to be burnt.

The Clean Air Act focused on reducing smoke pollution, but the measures taken actually helped to reduce sulphur dioxide levels at the same time. Air pollution in cities dramatically reduced.

Jo lived in a smokeless zone and had to use the right coal.

After reversing from the cul-de-sac marked by the wall of the RAOB Club. The Royal Antediluvian Order of Buffaloes was one of the largest fraternal organisations in the United Kingdom at that time. The honourable order was founded in 1822 and was, generally, known as 'The Buffs' to its members. Their motto was: 'No man is at all times wise', or in Latin: 'Nemo Mortalium Omnibus Horis Sapit'. It had the maxim of 'Justice, Truth and Philanthropy'; it was loosely modelled on and fairly similar to, but not associated with, the Freemasons.

They had purchased a huge Georgian mansion overlooking the west side of Clapham Common.

There were many examples of fine houses sold when running servants became prohibitive and heating bills became extortionate after the First World War. Worthy associations and political parties bought these cavernous spaces and ran them as members clubs, complete with bars and ball rooms for events.

The truck reversed back along the slip road and, then, turned right into Wakehurst Road, pulling up on the left-hand side of the road opposite the kitchen window. Directly under the kitchen window was a black square at pavement level.

This square was the coalhole cover, which opened outwards from hinges in the top. Jumping out onto the road, the coalman, in the passenger seat, hopped onto the pavement, carrying what looked like a wooden broom handle. Casually, slamming his door shut, he walked over to the wall under the kitchen window.

Using a special hook on the end of a wooden pole, he pulled open the cover to the coalhole, which opened from the bottom. It has a cantilever hinge and opened up upwards as well as outwards, revealing a coal slide at forty-five degrees that lead down from the street into the cellar at a suitably steep angle for the coke to shoot down.

When the black steal square was horizontal, looking like an open beak, he went to the back of the truck. Already, the driver had leapt down from the cab, strolled to the back and climbed up on to the flatbed where charcoal grey sacks of coal stood leaning against each other.

It was the dray's first delivery and Jo had ordered twenty bags. The driver manoeuvred the sack onto his mate's back and watched him stagger under the weight towards the coalhole. Kneeling down, he slipped the massive sack from his shoulder and laid it flat on the ground, over the hole.

After he ripped open the top, he stepped to the bottom of the sack. Lifting it gingerly at first, he raised the two seams to his waist emptying the coal into the cellar.

It slipped from the sack and slid down the slide with a satisfying rumble, like thunder. At the bottom, the coke spread in a mound on top of the coal hill that crept up the blackened interior wall. Starting as a small pile it grew and grew into an impressive mound.

Coke, as a fuel for hot water and cooking, was common back then.

Repeating the process nineteen times more, laying the full sack onto the empty, the coalman completed his delivery, making it all seem straightforward, not the backbreaking task it truly was.

When he was finished, he folded and bundled up the peanut hessian sacks, and handed them to the driver who stowed them while his mate sauntered back to the cab. The driver had left the delivery note clipboard on his seat and the coalman slipped off his gloves, tossed them expertly onto the passenger seat and picked up the paperwork and marched to the front door.

Jo always tipped, roughly the cost of a pint of beer each.

She knew these men worked hard and deserved a drink at the end of the day. They were delivering heat to her family. She handed over the coins, two shillings, and signed the white top copy, which was presented to her with a genuine thank you. Once she signed with the black pencil, she received a cheery cheerio; her receipt was ripped from the pile of delivery notes and handed over, leaving the pink and yellow carbon copies on the stack.

The coalman waved and joined his mate. A pint was nine pence and half a penny; they had started their collection for an early afternoon session at the pub. Delivering coal was thirsty work. Jo wished them both a good day, waving to the driver as he walked around to the cab once he had secured the load and moments later Jo heard the engine starting up.

It was a cold winter's day, dampness in the air and the mouldy smell of mulch from the carpet of leaves on the common wafted across to her. The wind was Arctic, blowing from the sea. It was going to be a cold winter. She shivered as she shut the inner door; at least, she had enough coal for the next month.

Chapter 10 – Follow - Me Follow

(Down to the hollow and there we will wallow in glorious mud!)

i

On a cold and frosty morning, before dawn, a car coughed into life, its headlights flicked on at the touch of a switch and the full beam cut through the morning mist that was swirling in the twilight.

The motor chugging with the choke fully out, the engine sounded as if it were about to stall, but John Rickard Murphy drove his Rover P5 out of the garage at Fernbank. He stopped the car and wound down the driver and passenger windows to clear them of condensation. It was cold but he wore a camel coat and pigskin gloves, a brown trilby hat and a cream silk scarf. Assiduously, he wiped the windscreen with a chamois cloth, there was no frost on the window, but moisture had collected on the windscreen. Frances Cahill, his stock taker and fellow director, walked out of the kitchen door.

"Bridget has cooked you some chicken to have for your lunch," she said swinging a wicker basket in her right hand.

With her left hand, she pushed the button on the unlocked boot and lifted it, before popping the basket onto the thin carpet lying on the floor of the boot.

Underneath, the Irish linen tablecloth was a whole roasted chicken, three boiled eggs in their shells and nestled in the bottom a fresh baked cottage loaf and a butter dish filled with Kerrygold butter brought over on the Liverpool steamer by a friend of Bridget's.

She had also provided boiled broad beans from the kitchen garden to compliment the chicken. Bridget has been Kitty and John's cook for ten years.

She was a jolly character, an excellent cook and a wonderful woman. Her speciality was French cuisine, but she was also capable of roasting chicken to perfection and cooking vegetables al dente.

Frances had joined the company in 1940 at the height of the Battle of Britain, during the Blitz. Her aunt had been working in the Mount Pleasant post office where John Rickard, or J.R., used to carry out various transactions. He and the aunt had a grand rapport and she had mentioned her niece, Frances, who was looking for a job.

He agreed to employ her.

Frances was from Cork, she talked quickly, and her mental arithmetic was legendary; she could do a stock take in the time it would take two men to complete the same task, she would be right, and they would be out by at least a pound. She would find their error for them and leave them red faced and amazed. Frances was a no-nonsense, warm and witty woman who was fiercely loyal to the family and adored them all despite their faults or because of them.

They performed their daily pantomime. She loaded the boot with whatever needed taking up to the office. While she did so, he climbed out and held the driver's door open for her.

"I was going to have lunch with the Blooms," J.R. grumbled, feeling disconcerted and looking daggers at Frances, like a sulky schoolboy.

He had been looking forward to some delicious kosher food, the rude waiters and a chat with his old friend, Mr. Bloom. As he stood holding the door handle as she walked around to the driver's door. He made little attempt to disguise his disappointment and would have complained had she not explained.

"You are having lunch with them tomorrow, Mr Murphy," Frances corrected him as she watched the old man walking around to the front of the car, opening the passenger door with relief spreading over his features.

He sat heavily in his seat, he was overweight, but he moved elegantly most of the time, all his movements were choreographed to show the minimum of effort, he had mastered them all except for sitting down, he was too old and bulky to perform the act elegantly.

Sighing, he reached over and shut the door as soundlessly as he could.

"Oh, it's Tuesday today, I was a day ahead again, I must be getting old or stupid one or the other," he noted, he had never been the same since his mild stroke the previous year.

"Or both," Frances suggested.

"Yes," he admitted, "but there's a third thing, too, I'm getting impatient with my children, too, where is Michael?"

"Here he is," she assured him, looking in her driver's side mirror as Michael slammed the kitchen door and walked down the side alley that ran down between the house and the garage.

Michael appeared at Frances's shoulder. He was as equally elegantly dressed as his father, a sombre grey, double-breasted suit, Church's shoes, pressed shirt, claret tie and camel coat. On his head he wore a smart Bates trilby. She wound down the window and he leant in greeting them both with a cheery good morning and a beaming smile.

"What time did you come in from The French House last night?" asked J.R. leaning forward to catch his eye.

"I'm not sure," replied Michael, smiling at the driver, "Frances, was its quarter to, or quarter past?"

"I'll give you quarter to, or quarter past, you stop out," J.R. seethed.

Michael jumped into the back seat and grinned mischievously, at Frances, in the rear-view mirror. J.R., eagle eyed as ever spotted him but decided to say nothing.

"You stay in the back seat and make sure you don't do any backseat driving," Frances commanded and when Frances commanded, Michael, Doctor John, the other scion, and J.R. obeyed.

The French House was a pub in Soho, officially named the York Minster but receiving its nickname, or moniker, due to its Belgian owner, Victor, who handed the pub down to his son Gaston.

They may have been Belgian, but they had French names and after de Gaulle's visit during the war, the idea that it was a haven for the French seemed to be secured. Gaston and Victor called everyone either 'madame', or 'monsieur', 'cherie', or 'cher', depending on their frequency of visiting and, frankly, their age or attractiveness.

Michael was definitely 'cher'. He was a regular and spent most of his free time there when he was not visiting prisoners in jail or the sick in hospital.

Generally, you could find him in the bar talking to people, telling jokes and desperately persuading prostitutes to look for other professions.

Frances eased the Rover onto the Cheam Road. She was a good driver, J.R. had taught her how to handle his car at any rate. There was a pre-selector gearbox, like an old Routemaster bus and an accelerator and brake. It was different to both a manual and automatic, but she had taken to the experience like a duck to water. The rest, he had assured her was confidence and experience. Like anything she learnt, Frances had a propensity to learn quickly.

The dark blue Vauxhall, PA, Cresta, parked opposite the house, started its engine. Inside sat two men who were both dressed in grey trilby hats, navy raincoats and charcoal suits. They looked uncomfortable in all three. They were in no rush; they waited for the car that they would be following to gather a pace before following.

"Is that the target vehicle?" asked the driver.

"What are you on about, you've been watching too many films, that's the car we should be following, yes, a claret, Rover P5, registration: JRM6. There can't be many of them around, can there?" his passenger moaned, waving his hand in the driver's face as a signal to proceed, which was not very helpful.

The man behind the wheel shot his twin a glance of annoyance, waving a hand in the driver's face was a habit of his younger brother. He thought he was in charge and being the indulgent eldest, he let his brother believe that.

"I would reckon maybe six, at least," suggested the driver as he eased his car onto the main road and accelerated in pursuit.

"They won't all be blooming Rovers will they smart Alec? Use your noggin, this must be the only one driving so early in the morning, the barristers don't get up until eight."

"So where are we headed?"

"If they are creatures of habit, which most people are, and, if our information is correct, six o'clock mass at St. Anselm's next to Tooting Bec tube, followed by a drive along the south bank to Number 1, Mile End Road, at the end of Whitechapel."

"What's that then?"

"What do you think?" the driver sighed.

"An office. What sort of orifice?"

"I'll shut your orifice if you don't watch out!"

"Is it an 'ouse?"

"A pub, you dolt, work it out, I told you that mug Murphy was a publican."

"I could do with a pint."

"They won't be open at eight will they numbskull."

"I can wait an hour or two."

"We'll go to the café, there's Truman's brewery in Brick Lane, nearby, there's bound to be a few cafes around there."

"You are a bit of a know it all, aren't you?"

"Bray sent me a very comprehensive dossier on the family and the area, you know how detailed he can be," he complained.

"A very comprehensive dossier, la-di-dah, when did you get so fancy? Remember you work for them, you're not one of them. When do we put the frighteners on them, that's all I need to know, sunny Jim?"

Frances drove the P5 expertly, it was a 1958, three litres, straight six with an overhead intake valve and side exhaust valves, which meant that it was very powerful and very quick, especially in Frances's hands. Changing gear was taken care of by the automatic transmission, she just had to select the gear and it even had Burman power steering, unusual in those days in English cars.

The brakes were 'Girling' drums, which took a bit of getting used to, but Frances had their measure, even in wet weather. The Rolls could stop on a sixpence; the Rover took more time. Ironically, in October 1959, disc brakes were employed on the same model, for the first time. J.R.'s company had bought the car a year too soon. However, if Jo had been driving that Rover, with the drums, she would have crashed through the wall and would not have been able stop before hitting it.

The Tweed twins were surprised at how quickly and expertly Frances drove. She clipped along at a breath-taking pace, like a getaway driver. They almost lost her at two roundabouts and at three sets of traffic lights. Going through a red light was risky but the Tweeds did it, the likelihood of being caught that early in the morning was infinitesimal. They were unsure if she was racing for a train or training for a race.

The Ford followed J.R., Michael and Frances, from Epsom to Tooting Bec, waited the forty five minutes while the party attended morning mass at St Anselm's Church, a twenty five minute service, and followed their car through Balham, Clapham Old Town, Stockwell, Kennington, Elephant and Castle, along the Old Kent Road, across Tower Bridge and through the Minories, Aldgate and on to the Whitechapel Road.

At the junction of Mile End, the two cars made it through the traffic lights together before turning off and parking in Cambridge Heath Road. The Tweeds stopped a few yards further along on the opposite side of the road to the Rover. Watching as the trio entered the side door that led up to the offices, the two men said nothing. The navy raincoats bought themselves a bacon sandwich from a café on Whitechapel Road and waited for the pub on Mile End road to open.

It was a popular pub not least because J.R. bottled his own Guinness imported in casks straight from Dublin. The bottling line was in the vast cellar. It was rumoured to be less bitter than the Guinness that they had been pumping out from Guinness in Park Royal since 1938. The word on the street was that it was 'a taste of sweet, creamy Guinness from home'. Whether or not that was true. They shifted a lot of crates, but they also shifted an inordinate amount of draught to the Irish community in the East End. Luckily, they had Frances to take the stock in all the pubs. Sometimes it shifted so fast, it was difficult to count it all.

ii

The following Sunday, George parked the Rolls, outside The Atheneum Club, and stared up at the, one hundred and twenty-four-foot, Duke of York Column. Seeing the back of Prince Frederick, Duke of York, the second eldest son of King George III, he admired the ingenuity of the cylindrical tower and the bronze statue at the top. He wondered why the prince was facing towards the Mall Galleries when the better view was behind him.

Being inquisitive he knew the designer was Benjamin Dean Wyatt. He wondered when they would open up the staircase and allow people up; they would get a wonderful view of Admiralty Arch and Horseguards. When it was originally unveiled, the public had access to the viewing platform at the top.

Taking Catherina's hand, he led the six-year-old from the passenger seat next to him, closed the door and opened up the back door to allow

Georgina and Patrick to propel themselves off the leather upholstery and to the carpeted edge where their father lifted them down onto the road. She was five, born a day and a year after Catherina; he was three and a half.

All the cars were parked at forty-five degrees to the pavement, in bays helpfully marked out by Westminster Council.

"Now, you three, best behaviour on the pavement, hold hands tightly," George demanded, his Irish brogue making his request less stern, before grabbing his eldest daughter's hand, "I don't want to stop coming, here do I?"

"No, daddy," Catherina agreed readily, smiling at her father.

She looked forward to her weekly swim at the RAC club.

"I wouldn't mind too much," Georgina muttered mutinously. She grabbed her sister's hand and skipped alongside her.

George was not in the least bit surprised. Georgia, as he called her, had always known her mind. She could be stubborn if the situation demanded it. She could be witty and precocious, too, if there was a good reason like sweets or money, or chocolate of some kind as a reward for being that way.

"Are you swimming with us today?" asked Patrick hopefully.

"After my massage," promised George, having no intention of setting foot in the pool. This was his time, a massage, sauna and then a pint of milk. "I've arranged a swimming lesson for you."

"Thank you, daddy," they all chorused in unison.

Good manners cost nothing, and Jo and George insisted on their children showing gratitude for all they had. They had been to Majorca for their holidays in August, flying via Madrid, as everyone did. There were no direct flights to the island. They were desperate to learn to swim properly, although Georgina would have been as content with a book. However, for the sake of the other two, she had decided to comply with the consensus, even at her young age, she knew her mind.

The pavement on Pall Mall was wide and despite the fact that the trio had a combined age of fourteen, they made swift progress, helped by their father's long strides and the skipping girls forcing the youngest boy to run along behind, barely managing to keep hold of Georgina's hand.

They passed The Reform Club, The Traveller's Club and George could already, see light blue flag of the Royal Automobile Club, flapping in the wind.

Above him, the smog had not yet settled over London but given time, he knew that it would. People would be lighting fires, it was allowed at weekends, and a cosy fire was a Sunday treat.

In his mind, already, he was walking through the revolving doors and walking down the spiral staircase to the pool to drop off the little ones before his indulgent sauna and massage, so when a man stood in front of him, George felt perturbed. He stopped and the children sensing a slackening of the rope that bound them, stopped, too. All eight eyes stared at the smartly dressed stranger. A black trench coat and grey trilby, s sombre grey suit and shiny black shoes impressed them all.

"Excuse me Doctor," said Tweed.

"Good morning," George replied, racking his brain, it would not have been the first time a grateful patient had stopped him in the street and thanked him for saving their sight or providing excellent treatment, he was a specialist and a perfectionist in his professional life. "Can I help you?"

"It is I who can help you. Perhaps we should talk in the club?"

"What's it about."

"Your family, of course, I wouldn't be bothering you on a Sunday morning if it were not of vital importance."

"I'm with the children today."

"Yes, but for how much longer?"

"You can reach me at 186 Harley Street, I'm there at six thirty, my clinics start at seven," George explained, not listening to what Tweed was really saying.

"Very well, I thought we could do things the easy way," Tweed muttered despondently.

He had been instructed to be menacing nothing more.

"If it's the easy way you want, I should take that; the club only allows members," George persisted.

"Really?"

"Check their policy with the doorman if you do not believe me. I could invite you to lunch but you would have to hang around for three hours and sadly I have a reservation elsewhere with the family."

"It's like that, then?"

"I can see you during the week. Thank you, Mr.?"

"Tweed."

"Have a good day, Mr. Tweed."

"Oh, I intend to doctor."

Mr. Frank Tweed crossed the road and headed towards Jermyn Street. He looked like a man in a hurry hurrying to report back to Bray, already fishing in his coat pocket for a penny to make a phone call from the phone box just behind St. James's Church in Piccadilly.

"Who was that man, daddy?" Georgina asked, "I didn't like the way he looked at you."

"I don't know, come on little ones, the pool awaits," George jovially responded.

As he watched the man move along Pall Mall, he noticed him consulting his watch.

It was not on the left hand as it should have been, but it was strapped to his right wrist and the face was placed over the radius and ulna where a pulse would be taken. George had only ever come across three cases of such an affected way of wearing a watch, on all occasions, they had been left-handed pugilists, boxers brought up on the streets, they had been from the Repton Club in London's East End. All of the patients that George had seen from that place had been treated for damage to their eyes from a fist. That was a bad omen. George wondered what he might want with him. He decided he would discuss the incident with Jo but not before he relaxed. He was not going to let a stranger, and a puzzling event, upset his equilibrium.

'Was Tweed, a similar south-paw, who made his living with his hands?' he wondered.

His message had been anything but cryptic; he wanted to cause someone harm and George immediately connected him to the Murder on Cedars Road.

Chapter 11 - Mass Paranoia

At mass, meanwhile, Jo waited for the woman to walk past her before going out into the aisle, the smell of incense and candle wax filled her nose even though there was no thurible in sight. Perhaps it was a lingering smell from Benediction, the evening before. There were four rows of candles burning brightly in the small side chapel at the Holy Ghost Catholic Church in Nightingale Square.

The tranquillity of the church helped her feel calm and the total immersion in the rhythm of the service was comforting. It was her only chance in a busy week to be still: to think about her spirit, to reflect on her blessings and forget all her worries. It was a rare opportunity to nurture the soul.

She walked towards the altar where the other members of the congregation were filing up the aisle; others came back down the gap in the pews, following a minutely choreographed display that was practised every Sunday. Jo followed as if mesmerised. Her footsteps matched those of the person ahead, left foot forward, right foot forward, stop. It was as if the two of them were practising a dance step. They repeated the movement as the flow preceded them.

A line of people processed towards the altar and, on the other side of the aisle another line proceeded to move away from the altar and back to their pews to pray, kneeling as they did so.

Once past the church pews, Jo was able to walk to the right, step forwards towards the altar, waiting for a kneeling parishioner to cross herself and exit stage left.

As the figure passed her, she knelt down and waited for the priest. He was working his way down the line. She closed her eyes and prayed while the priest approached.

She heard the whispered exchange next to her, felt the sudden movement of the departure of the person, her eyelids flickered open and she was ready.

The host was offered to her.

"Corpus Christi," the priest intoned in a hushed voice as if sharing a secret.

"Amen," she whispered back before opening her mouth and pushing her tongue forward to receive the body of Christ.

The host was placed on her tongue; it felt warm and hard like a piece of card; she closed her mouth over the flat white disc. Immediately, it cleaved to the top of her mouth, wet paper sticking to the bottom of a glass.

Her tongue rolled over the roof of her mouth to cement the wafer there while she let it dissolve, slowly. Crossing herself, she rose from her kneeling position, feeling a presence at the right shoulder, she moved off to the left to make way for another celebrant.

Her eyes on the floor, she walked back to her pew. A man stood up and let her into place; she knelt and prayed, she felt elated, grateful for everything she had, her soul soared, and her heart filled with rapture. This was the communion. This was communing with the life essence that provides the will to live, the life to love and the life of love. She was at one with the universe.

At the end of the service, the priest intoned, "Ite missa est."

The congregation bowed their heads for the blessing, which was also given in Latin. As she left the church, following the priest out of the door, she saw Anthony Bray sitting on a pew.

Of course, she did not recognise him from Birmingham, she had been drugged too deeply. He was staring at her with a look that emanated evil and she shuddered as she passed him.

Jo was sensitive to moods and feelings. She told me once that she had visited a room at Mile Hill House, her husband's family home, which she was convinced was haunted.

Every time she opened the door, the door would close, and she would feel a cold draught.

I scoffed at her story until one time my brother took his children there and they could not sleep. They felt the same presence.

Yet the next night, he put the two boys in the opposite room, a mirror image of the other and they slept like logs. Jo was intuitive, spiritual and right about the room. There was a rumour that someone had been shot in that room during the Irish Civil War.

Chapter 12 - i - Car Crash

After the Sunday mass was over, Jo had intended to make up some more medicines for the Trinity pharmacy. She climbed into the driver's seat of the 1942, Nash, 600 Ambassador 6, Slipstream Sedan parked in Nightingale Square. It was a four door with the back door opening forwards, not on at the back just like the old classic cars from the movies but that was all that was old-fashioned about her; she was sleek and elegant. Jo had always loved cars; they represented freedom and new adventures.

An independent woman needed her own personal transport and J.R. Murphy recognised this, buying her a, 1933, Austin Twelve to learn on. The Austin Twelve was the biggest car the company produced, he wanted her to be safe in an accident and have room for all her friends to sit in comfort. Once she qualified for medical college by passing her entrance exams, he decided to indulge his youngest daughter by buying her a brand-new car. The Nash was the best available and the most modern design.

Jo admired her lines and her American opulence; the Americans loved their cars and it showed. Her Nash was like an old friend; her father bought it for her when she passed her examinations into The Royal College of Surgeons.

She had been the only person to own a car apart from the Dean, his was a pre-war Austin; hers was a sleek two-tone beauty, a navy-blue body and a midnight blue roof with white-wall tyres.

The Nash was one of the last cars to come off the production line before the American factory turned its focus to wartime production. It had been impossible to buy a car from England or Europe due to all factories being used to help the war effort or had been bombed in air raids.

The only way to get a car was to have it shipped from America to Ireland. The 600 Nash was so named due to it being able to complete six hundred miles on one tank of petrol. It came in useful when she was visiting George in Mayo. The huge bumper at the front wrapped around the front of the chassis like a chrome smile, the football-sized headlamps guarded the five chrome horizontal lines that adorned the radiator.

The engine cowling started off like a fireman's helmet with the Nash badge, a Chevrolet style affair in red black and silver, on the front before sweeping back and widening to meet the sloping windscreen divided into two sections, which made it look like the cockpit of a streamlined plane. At the back, the boot swept down to the rear bumper like a beetle's back, just as shiny and sleek; they termed it a fastback.

The whole car was the epitome of post-war American exuberance. The world was going to be a far better place, technology and design was going to transform everyone's life. This car was the future, sleek and streamlined, opulent and well equipped, it was made with the best materials, which would last for decades to come.

Easing herself into the leather bench seat, she was confronted by the wonderful smell of quality hide and a chrome dashboard with two gauges that looked like clocks on either side of the speedometer that went up to 120 mph, the numbers of each decade of speed were picked out in white.

She had grown fond of her comfortable and stylish car and its sophisticated switches and dials. Above those, was a beautiful dashboard cover in dark brown, polished wood like the hull or a nineteen thirties racing yacht. The white steering wheel was thin and elegant.

Just like the Rolls the gear lever was mounted on the steering column behind the steering wheel, unlike the Rolls, she was a three-speed manual with overdrive.

The six-cylinder purred into life when she turned the ignition, the 2.8 litre engine ticked over laconically, humming beautifully. Easing out from the pavement, she passed three parked cars, south London was changing; cars were becoming more commonplace. There were a number of cars in garages, but the streets were still fairly car free.

She weaved through the backstreets, turning on to Endlesham Road; she drove across Nightingale Lane then turned left into Thurleigh Road and right into Wroughton Road.

She was four minutes away from home.

She slowed as she approached Roseneath Road, braked, took the left turn into the road and pushed the accelerator again. As she appeared around that corner, the driver of a green Bedford truck with a canvas-covered flatbed, parked outside number thirty-eight, reversed backwards for the count of ten and then stopped.

The driver revved the engine, engaged first and drove the truck towards the junction of Ballingdon Road and Roseneath. She suddenly saw the headlamps blazing as she passed the junction. Out of the corner of her right eye, she saw a flash of movement.

That was the last thing she remembered.

The truck, a seven-ton Bedford S Type RL truck thudded into the side of the car, the passenger's door was crushed, the windscreen split and cracked as if hit by a stone, her passenger window shattered, the doors rumpled like a concertina.

Still the truck rolled on, its six-cylinder, 4.9 litre, monster of an engine providing the power; it was accelerating not breaking, sweeping the car against the pavement like a snowplough.

The car hit the kerb.

The right-hand-side of the car was lifted into the air. All four wheels of the truck were still spinning; the RL was four-wheel drive. A man ran out of his house, climbed up onto the cab of the truck and tore the driver's door open, pulling the driver from the seat. The truck engine stalled as the driver's foot was removed from the accelerator; the truck gave one final lurch as the engine died, buffeting the car for the last time, the car swayed on its chassis for the last time.

Jo would have been thrown across the car, slipping across the bench seat, if she had not held on to the steering wheel so tightly, when the car was hit. Perhaps, if it had been in an ordinary car, she could have been killed. Thankfully, the American car was built like a tank.

Her head hit the driver's door, but the panel was padded on the inside, which cushioned the contact. It made her release the steering wheel and she slid across the seat.

The chassis had absorbed most of momentum of the impact and the subsequent battering of the car merely bounced her on the bench like a rag doll. She had curled into a ball as soon as she realised that she was travelling across the bench seat, protecting her arms and legs and minimising the chance of injury to her organs. Through the smashed window she heard the engine of the truck choking and dying, she felt the car being released from the constant battering, then, settling into a stationary wreck.

"What are you doing?" a man's voice asked.

"I thought I was braking," replied another voice.

"Really?" asked the first voice. She heard footsteps. "Where are you going, hey, come back, hey you can't leave the scene of an accident. What are you doing? Come back."

The man chased after the driver.

"Stop!" he called at the top of his lungs before running down the street after him.

He gave up on the corner of Broomwood Road when it was clear a middle-aged man was not going to catch up with a fit man in his thirties. Returning to the car, he found Jo in a foetal position; she was lying amongst the crystals of smashed glass on the leather bench seat. He poked his head through the smashed passenger window, realising that it was best not to move her. Another neighbour told him she had phoned for an ambulance and the police were on their way, too.

"Help's on its way," he assured her kindly. "The driver's run off but the police will catch him."

He waited with her, reassuring her that everything would be all right. Jo lay still and it must have been only five minutes later when she heard the ambulance arriving. Just then, the man who had challenged the driver opened the passenger door. The chill wind revived her, but she was still shaken. Her body had gone into shock and she felt cold and vulnerable. There was a throbbing pain in her left wrist.

In those days, ambulances arrived promptly and this one had driven from the Ambulance station on Battersea Rise on the corner of Auckland Road, which was less than five minutes slow drive away. With its blue light flashing and bell siren sounding, the ambulance only took four minutes from the first phone call to arrive at the scene of the road traffic accident.

The 1957 Austin LD Wandsworth ambulance parked behind the wreckage of the car. The ambulance men stepped out from the front and approached the Nash. Just as they reached the passenger door, a police car arrived.

It was a black 1956 Wolseley 6/90, which was a controversial car even at the time; it could barely reach 96 mph for a start and was unpopular with the police. Its designer Gerald Palmer was sacked and replaced by Alec Issigonis, designer of the Mini. If Jo had been in the front seat of that Wolseley, it would have been curtains for her.

The police sergeant switched off the flashing blue lights using a black, flick switch on the grey striped Formica instrument panel. The blue lights, which were mounted on the large chrome mesh 'cheese-cutter' grille, went dark.

Pulling on the hand brake control under the dash to the side of the steering column, he moved the column mounted gear lever to neutral. The leather trimmed front seats were mounted closely together, which would have stopped Jo on her trajectory from one side of the car to the other.

The second assassination attempt had failed only because the bench seat allowed her body to slide out of harm's way, rather than be buffeted against the interior. That, and the fact that the Tweed twins had not taken into account the car was left hand drive. The truck struck the passenger door and not the driver's door. If it had hit her on that side, she would have been seriously if not fatally injured.

The first thing the mobile patrol did was close off all the roads leading to the accident spot. That meant closing the far end of Ballingdon Road and the bottom and top of Roseneath Road. While Jo was treated in the back of the ambulance, the police organised a tow truck, ironically from Cedars Autos, in Cedars Mews, which would take the two vehicles to the nearest scrap yard.

After, having her bruises checked, and a cut bandaged, Jo sat in the back of the Wolseley to give her details to the policeman. She was still feeling shaken and confused. A beat bobby arrived at direct traffic and oversee the towing away. The policeman who had taken her statement, then, drove her off to her local General Practitioner who had readily offered to open his surgery to see his old friend after her accident. It was a short drive from Broomwood Road to Battersea Rise.

ii

It was still Sunday and George was not back from Pall Mall and he was still looking after the children, but it was, he who had organised the appointment at their friend's surgery as soon as the call had come through from the house. The nanny had answered the phone to the police and immediately contacted the RAC. George had been located in the Turkish bath and organised everything from a telephone in the stairwell above the pool. The children were still swimming so he showered and went down to get them changed before telling them the bad news.

Jo sat in the front room of a house that wrapped itself around Lavender Sweep and Battersea Rise. Doctor Walsh had established the surgery, on Battersea Rise, about the same time as Jo had set up hers on Clapham Common. Even the number of the house was similar, his was number eight; hers was 88.

It was simply furnished with a desk, two chairs, one on either side of the leather topped bureau, and an examination bed. There was also a desk light, plain lining paper walls in cream, a net curtain and a beige blind rolled up at the top of the wide window. The surgery was kept warm by a two-bar electric heater. There was an optician's Snellen chart on the wall adjacent to the treatment table.

Jo sat on the cushioned seat of the examination table, which was covered in red plastic. Her feet dangled over the edge. Doctor Martin Walsh stood in front of her. He was of medium height and slight build; his thick brown hair was slicked back over his high forehead. The sideburns were greying slightly.

Like her, he was Irish, he was from Cork; like her, he had established a practice in south London; like her, he was an exceptional and thorough doctor with a charming bedside manner. They had become firm friends, Anne, his wife, and he spent frequent evenings together with Jo and George, chatting, smoking, drinking and dancing.

Martin was amusing company and could always muster an amusing anecdote or a topical joke. On the occasion of Jo's visit, he was looking serious, peering over his glasses, he knew she had just had a miraculous escape.

"Jo you've had a nasty bash in that American car of yours; you were lucky it was made so solid or you might not be here," he explained, making some notes in his book, to conclude his examination.

Jo sat up on his examining couch; her silk, cream camisole covered her modesty a matching pair of French knickers unintentionally showed off her long legs. Her brassiere, corset, skirt and stockings had been draped over the screen in the corner where she had striped before her examination, which she found difficult with her injured hand. After the examination, she had slipped only her basic underwear back on. Climbing back into the other accoutrements seemed too much trouble.

Martin discovered that she had bruises on her arms, a lump above her temple but apart from that she seemed unscathed. She had suspected a fractured left wrist; such was the pain but was relieved to find that on manipulation the wrist could be moved without pain and it was just a sprain.

Martin wore his stethoscope around his neck and a pen in one hand, his notebook in the other; the other instruments that he used to examine her were spread on his desk: sphygmomanometer, auriscope, nasal speculum, ophthalmoscope and percussion hammer.

"My lovely car, gone," Jo complained.

"It might have been you," Martin exclaimed.

"I'm fine, I just need a cigarette and a brandy," she insisted.

Martin put down his notebook and fishing in his suit jacket, he silently proffered his cigarette case and when Jo had taken one, a Player's Navy Cut, the only other brand she would ever consider smoking, he lit her cigarette with a silver Zippo, petrol lighter, the only one he found reliable when out walking. He used to take a stroll on to the common to think at least twice a day.

"It's time to give up the investigation, Jo," he insisted.

"So, they have got to you have they, Martin?" Jo replied, drawing on her cigarette, it had been a hard day.

"No one's got to me Jo, you're not in a film noir, this isn't some melodrama, that's twice you have cheated death."

"I'm a cat with nine lives."

"Seriously, those drugs would have weakened a horse and you managed to stop before they wiped you out. Now, they've rammed you with a three-ton truck."

"I know; I'm still feeling it."

"Do you think they'll give up?"

"I shouldn't think so."

"They might be successful next time, third time lucky. Think of the children, Jo; I would never do anything to jeopardise Madeline and John."

"I'm thinking of all the children and all the parents, too. These people have murdered three people that we know of. Those people had parents; they were somebody's children."

"Let the police deal with the situation. You should be concentrating on your job," he insisted.

"They are the very people who have asked me to help them and, frankly, this is the second attempt at my life, I don't feel like letting it go."

"These men are dangerous, their attempts on your life cannot be ignored; they mean business. I got a call from George at the RAC before you arrived; they've threatened George and the children as well. They've also talked to Anne and me, it's a rum business."

"They seem to have influence everywhere but that doesn't mean they cannot be stopped."

"What would you like me to do?" he asked, still feeling reluctant to get involved but she left him no choice, they were old friends, they had arrived in the early fifties and were fellow General Practitioners.

"Strap up my wrist, give me a prescription for some Benzadrine and reassure Anne that all will be well."

"I can do all those things. Anything else?"

"Thank you, Martin, you are an amazingly good person. I think we can have this case sewn up soon."

"You're lucky you weren't sewn up today. I still want you to have that wrist x-rayed."

Martin indicated a chair next to the examination couch. Jo slipped off and sat down, putting he elbow on the couch and laying her arm flat. Martin unfurled some gauze.

"It's fine, don't worry."

"I do worry, this is a dangerous game you are playing."

"We're winning though," Jo assured him.

She was always confident about our abilities. That was one of the reasons I loved her so much.

"You and Regan?" Martin asked.

"That's right," Jo bridled, she had absolute faith and a will of iron.

"Is the Benzedrine to keep you awake?"

"If you say so."

"I must remind you about the dangers of mixing them with alcohol; you are aware of the high you can get."

"I think that is the combination that led me to almost crash the car. They plied me with booze and a cocktail of hallucinogens."

Martin was about to say something but when he saw the expression on Jo's face, he changed his mind. He knew how determined and fearless Jo could be.

"It sounds to me as if they want to get warn you off."

"Or get rid of me altogether."

"There's nothing I can say to dissuade you is there? It's so dangerous, Jo, two attempts to injure you."

"That's because I'm close to the truth and nothing you will say will matter a jot."

"Maybe you should see this through to the end, after all," Martin conceded, he looked at her over the top of his bifocals, trying to look disapproving but at the same time realising it was an empty gesture.

"Thanks, Martin."

She smiled.

"Let me know if you need anything. Anne and I will do what we can."

"Thank you, I know Madeleine and John will be fine, they aren't monsters, they wouldn't target children."

"Their track record is not good; didn't you say Peg had found a victim in Birmingham."

"Yes, that's right."

"They seem to be all over the country, and I fear you've only discovered the tip of the iceberg."

"I can't sit by and watch them get away with this."

"I don't like bullies either, but you have to watch out for yourself."

"I will, don't you worry."

"I know you want to do all you can to save life, but it does not include putting your life in danger. You have three children and a loving husband, and they all rely on you and need you to survive."

"Regan's put some men on our door, they've tried to twice, I doubt whether they will try again with the police guarding us," Jo assured him.

"They say lightning never strikes twice but it already has, you've had two narrow escapes and they have threatened your father and his business."

"My father supports my stance," Jo insisted.

"It was ever thus," Martin noted dryly. "You know the adage of the third light, one, raise rifle, two, take aim, three, fire."

"We're not in the trenches but I take your point, I'll keep my head down."

Martin left the examining room and Jo dressed again, slowly; her wrist strapped up to support the sprain. Anne came through with a cup of tea.

iii - Josephine

Bray sat in the corner of the saloon bar of 'The Woodman' in Battersea, High Street, nursing a gin and tonic; the Tweed twins had a light and bitter each. It was seven thirty on a Sunday evening and there were few people in that area, most of the customers had gone home after their midday drinks to have roasts or walk in the park.

The public bar was full, as usual, the cigarette smoke curling over the screens and crawling along the ceiling above Bray's head. He did not notice, the big extractor above his head set in the window.

"Nora Josephine Murphy seems indestructible," Bray complained.

"She's a slippery one," Derek complained, leaning forward and flicking ash into the ashtray in the middle of the table.

"My file tells you she was born in the pub where Dick Turpin famously shot his partner in crime," Bray announced pointedly, suspecting the twins had not sufficiently digested the research Bray had carried out on their victim and the context he had set it in, "The stables behind the Old Red Lion, on Whitechapel High Street, was where the local constables grabbed Turpin's accomplice."

"Not a blooming history lesson," Derek complained.

His twin grimaced but said nothing.

"Turpin decided to shoot one of them with his pistol," Bray continued undaunted, crushing the filter of his cigarette into the ashtray as he warmed to his tale, "He had one shot to free his friend, Mathew King. There was a tremendous crack and the pistol smoked. The ball lodged in his associate's heart and King died instantly. Running through the back door and into the inn, Turpin threw himself through the front window and escaped. That had been in May 1737 and two years later, he was caught and executed in York."

"Blimey, I thought Turpin was luckier than that, he started life as butcher don't you know," Frank interjected, "our dad was a butcher wasn't he Derek."

"In more ways the one, my son, in more ways than one," Derek muttered menacingly.

Obviously, since that time, the pub had grown and the street had spread on either side, running up to Mile End Gate to the East and Aldgate to the West. As time went on, it had been absorbed by the great spread of Greater London so much so that, opposite the pub, a hospital was built in 1757. It was well known to anyone who visited the East End. The Tweed twins knew it from going to boxing matches at the Repton Club, in Cheshire Street, and being treated there for their bruises and cuts.

"So why wasn't she born in the London?" asked Frank, stirring himself from his disinterest and rewarding his question with a swig of the malty bitter brew in his glass.

"You're right to ask, the Royal London Hospital was across the road but Nora Josephine Murphy was born in one of the rooms above the pub, as there were no maternity wards there in 1922," Bray explained patiently, he secretly enjoyed showing off his knowledge, "Her birth on the 14th July, Bastille Day, was recorded at, her aunt's pub, The Three Jolly Weavers, 94 Lever Street, London E1. John Rickard did not want anyone to know that he was living at the pub for some reason."

"I knew he was dodgy," asserted Frank, looking please with himself, he suspected everyone was as crooked as he.

Whichever pub she was delivered in, she had been born within the sound of Bow Bells and so she automatically became a cockney. That was ironic because she sounded posher than the queen. She spoke with what we used to call Received Pronunciation or, as we used to say in those days, a plum in her mouth.

Bray continued.

"Her father, John Rickard Murphy, 'J.R.' to his friends, had been in the Royal Irish Constabulary'. The Old Red Lion, in Whitechapel, was the first pub he bought."

"Where did he get the money, a bank job?" quipped Frank.

"He had received his pension as a lump sum," Bray continued, ignoring Frank's interruption, trying to hide the fact that he felt uncomfortable in their company, "he stayed with his sister at the Three Jolly Weavers, in The City, and worked his way up to manager at The Falcon, a pub in Clapham Junction."

"We know the Falcon," boasted Derek, "My first pint was in there, I must have been fourteen, no one cared back, then."

"His wife, who was Catherine Conlon from Clare, was known as Kitty, had five children, John, Michael, Moira, Stephen and Nora, in that order," elucidated the twins' teacher.

"Those Irish breed like blooming rabbits," moaned Frank.

"They were all healthy and tall like their father. Kitty and JR had a thriving pub because they looked after their staff and their customers. They were very close friends with a local celebrity, Maurice Bloom, whose kosher restaurant, Bloom's, was around the corner in Brick Lane. In those days people were famous for what they did in their community, not what they made like nowadays. The tailors, many of whom were Jewish, who worked nearby, locked up their workshops and popped into Murphy's for a double scotch on the way home for their evening meal. They called him 'The Irish Jew'; it was a compliment and he took it as such, the local community had accepted him," Bray further expounded, he had done extensive research on the family and he wanted the Tweeds to know it.

"We know about 'Old Bloomy', we've had a bit of kosher nosh in our time, haven't we frank?" Derek bragged, Frank nodded, "Been to a few pubs where the tailors went, too, 'Double Gold' was all they asked for."

"What's a double gold?" asked Bray. He was uncomfortable when he was not the font of all knowledge. Anxiously, he lit another cigarette.

"What, you don't know? 'A double gold', is a double scotch, gold watch is cockney rhyming slang for a scotch, it's a constant cry up East," Frank said, enjoying passing his knowledge on to the know-it-all.

"Anyway," Bray persisted, "Kitty, the dutiful wife, flirted with the customers, provided them with gefilte fish and pickled herrings and looked after her children while John looked after the stock and kept an eagle eye on all staff."

"He'd have to," sighed Frank, knowingly.

"He was making sure they did not take too much from the till, or the cellar, and protecting his cut of the profits as proprietor," Bray ploughed on, "John Rickard paid his staff well but he was a martinet, he expected everything to be shipshape in his hostelry, every day, he checked the tops of doors for dust and mirrors and glasses for smear every single day. In those days there were lots of mirrors in pubs, on the walls and on the partition between the saloon and public bar."

"Sounds like a right sergeant major what about bloody Nora?" Derek quipped. 'Bloody Nora' was a popular profanity after the war.

"After thirty-seven different moves, Jo was evacuated to a new home, far away from the bombs, in Ireland. It was called Bromley House, it had twelve bedrooms and was just outside the village of Kilpedder."

"Sounds like it was in the bogs to me."

"J.R. had bought it at the end of the Irish Civil War," Bray continued unabashed."

"A la-di-da doctor whose sticking her nose in our business," complained Derek.

"The house had belonged to the Duke of Wellington's family; it was sold when Ireland broke free from Great Britain," Bray said, "there were sad memories for them because one of Wellesley sons had died in the garages experimenting with engines. They were glad to sell it. Jo's siblings were packed off to boarding school near Dublin."

Eventually, it was time for JR to return to London, so he bought, Fernbank in Cheam, a big house in the London suburbs, he made sure he had a cook and a driver, who lived in, and a cleaner who visited twice a week. Good food and fine wine were part and parcel of their life at weekends. Bray thought he had the twins spellbound but he was wrong. They only listened to him in the hope he would buy them another pint.

"When the war had broken out JR had bought whiskey in bond, which made him some money when peace came back to London. The bombs had given him a fair few insurance pay-outs and the post-war road widening schemes had allowed him to sell other pubs at a good price, he had kept some whisky in bond during the war and the price had risen afterwards so that gave him more income. Business acumen and luck kept the Murphy family wealthy."

Bray had done his homework.

Later, Jo told me that she had lived there throughout the war with her mother, Kitty. Every night she slept in a different one of the twelve bedrooms to keep the beds aired and she played billiards every day on her own in the billiard room until she could clear the table efficiently. It was a skill that she never lost. There was school for her, but she frequently missed the bus into Dublin and, when she did catch the bus, she played truant and went to the cinema where Joseph Locke played the organ and sang.

"She loved to watch films like: "All This and Heaven, Too". When the nuns found out what she was doing, they approved, it was after all a religious film or so they thought," Bray continued, having overheard a conversation.

"Well, that's funny, blooming penguins," Derek added.

"After the war, they moved to Rockmount in Dublin so Jo could attend the Royal Colleges of Surgeons while John Rickard Murphy worked in Ireland and England. In London, J.R. continued building a business buying, turning around and selling pubs.

While Jo was in Ireland, J.R. started his Irish company, buying Dublin pubs such as McDade's, The Finglas Inn and The Bottom of the Hill. It was long hours and hard work but, in the end, there were sufficient rewards in the hard graft. Mr. Murphy could afford the finer things in life.

The business thrived and grew with the increasing number of builders, dockers, road makers and tailors needing food and drink after work. Customers found a crowd and a warm atmosphere plus beer kept in good condition.

It was a basic formula, but it worked effectively. The docklands pubs were busy, too; it was where the dockers traded their purloined goods. The Irish workmen were moving into the East End and hankered after a good pint of Guinness as they built the new roads and houses after the war. JR's surviving pubs were therefore packed with drinkers.

As with all cities, the demographic changes and the Irish moved into other areas and during the eighties the pubs were sold. There was little market for black beer among the new arrivals in the area. Curry houses replaced kosher restaurants and halal supermarkets and sari shops replaced the pubs.

The dockers were stopped from taking their bunts, (the goods that they managed to pilfer and sell,) by the introduction of sealed container ships and went on strike. The shippers were fed up with losing greater chunks of each shipment as the workers' percentage crept up and were not going to bring back open shipments.

Containers remained and the companies just switched to less volatile docks like Bristol, Liverpool, Southampton and Tilbury and the docks closed down, waiting decades before they were finally redeveloped. Life is all about change. A new community thrived where once Bloom and Murphy made their mark.

Bray finished his gin and went up to the bar to replenish their glasses. They were given fresh ones.

When Bray returned with a tray, two half pint bottles of light ale, two-pint glasses three-quarters filled with bitter form the pump and a highball glass containing a double gin and tonic and a slice of lemon, there was no ice, they all had a cigarette to celebrate.

The fug in the bar was part of the atmosphere and it seemed to bother no one least of all the members of staff who were smoking behind the bar.

"Tell us about George," Frank pleaded, hoping the story might last and Bray would have to get another round in.

"I haven't finished telling you about Jo," he protested but looking at their faces, he decided he should tell them about George, nonetheless.

"He's the next one we want to lean on," insisted Derek, he had picked up on his brother's thought waves as twins often do and he fancied a third pint, they only lived across the road in Trott Street. Weaving back to his mother's house, pie-eyed, and sleeping in on Monday morning seemed like the ideal end to a disastrous weekend.

"George Patrick Joseph Fitzpatrick was born, on 21st July 1921, in a Glebe, which was one of five hundred such edifices built by the Church of Ireland in the reign of George III,: Bray began, recalling all the facts he had so painstakingly assembled when Sebastian Hepher and Jenny Strong had asked him to create a dossier on Jo and her family, "the birth certificate recorded the event as happening at The Neale nearby, not in the first floor room at Mile Hill House, there was a possibility therefore that he might have been born slightly prematurely like his brother but not so seriously so."

"Where's he, we could put the 'frighteners' on him," suggested Derek.

"I don't think so, he lives in the Glebe, still. Can I carry on?" hissed Bray before returning to his dull monotone, "The parsonage of some fifty acres was built during the Napoleonic period in 1813; it was located between Lough Corrib and Lough Mask, in County Mayo. It was the parochial house of the grey, sombre stone, Church of Ireland, chapel, which was about halfway between Mile Hill and The Neale."

"I didn't want a frigging history of Ireland," complained Frank menacingly, taking a drag from his cigarette and washing his comments down with some beer.

"All right, Frankie boy, calm down," soothed Derek.

"It's context, it's important," insisted Bray tetchily, "George's father, Patrick Fitzpatrick, was also a sergeant in the R.I.C., just like Mr. Murphy but he had been in a three-man patrol in Cork city. The Irish Republican Army drove by in a car, shooting his two colleagues. The shock of seeing his two friends, on either side, being gunned down haunted him until his dying day."

"Sounds like a lucky escape," sighed Derek.

"Yes, quite right," Bray sarcastically agreed. Marrying Elizabeth Melotte, he settled in Mayo. The Civil War in The Irish Free State led to the founding of the Republic."

"Less history, Mr Bray," moaned Frank.

"It's still important," argued Bray, "Elizabeth's father had been a wool merchant and had bought up supplies of local wool before the outbreak of the First World War."

"Blimey, the price of raw wool must have rocketed with both sides needing blankets and uniforms," asserted Derek, diffusing the tension.

"Indeed," acknowledged Bray briefly, "Patrick's father-in-law made a fortune, and, with the proceeds, he bought the Glebe from the English landowners and administration as they sold off their properties cheaply to the local population when they extricated themselves from the island after Irish independence. Patrick and Elizabeth had two children, Henry and George."

"Georgy porgy's the one we want," Derek decided.

"Only, we'll make Gorgy porgy cry, not the girls he kissed," Frank agreed.

Bray wondered whether they had a point.

From my point of view, I gleaned all I could from my doctor, Jo. Like her, George was the youngest. He was the most handsome of the family. She was the prettiest in hers. George was born big and bumptious, his brother Henry had weak eyesight and had been born prematurely so he was frail. Apparently. Patrick read the newspapers, recovering from his experience. The shooting had affected him greatly. He had known his colleagues well, they were friends, both of them good people, and he often wondered why fate had spared him the bullet. Contemplation and piano playing filled his days. He was grateful for his good fortune.

The Glebe was a wonderful dowry and provided a good income. Lilly Melotte rented the fields, drew water from the well in the stable yard, washed the clothes, tidied the house, tended the chickens, pigs and peacocks, cooked and cleaned, wearing herself out in the process. She was a good wife, a loving aunt, daughter, mother and sister but more than that she worked tirelessly to balance the books, bring in an income from the farm and to look after her three boys.

Inevitably, she died young, over work and caring for others took its toll, leaving Patrick and Henry to look after themselves while George went to the Royal College of Surgeons in Dublin and then on to London to carve his career in England. The big draughty house built into the side of a hill was damp and cold but there were trees to provide wood for the fires, peat aplenty from the Atlantic Blanket Bogs of Donegal, Mayo, Galway, Kerry, Clare and Sligo and there was coal to be had from the Ballingarry mines in Tipperary. The Royal Irish Constabulary, though disbanded, had provided a generous pension. Combined with the income from The Glebe, the family lived well if not as well as the Murphy family across the water.

Bray waited for the pub to close at ten thirty, early closing on a Sunday. The twins, he knew, were not interested in Jo and George, just in being given instructions and being paid for the dirty work they did.

Chapter 13 - Having a Ball

The Friday following the accident, George was propping up the bar in the Rembrandt Hotel in Thurloe Place, Knightsbridge, almost opposite The Victoria and Albert Museum. He fancied himself as an Irish Cary Grant, super smooth, mixed with a smidgen of tough guy, John Wayne.

Admittedly, he was ruggedly handsome, tall with blue eyes, a highbrow and thick black hair, which gave him the vague air of a Hollywood film idol, but his ears and nose were too big for him to be truly handsome.

He was still good looking enough, in his dinner suit, to excite the interest of a fair few ladies in the bar. Some of them turned their heads and gave him approving appraisal or even a smile. His charisma came from his charm more than from his looks, but he was handsome enough to be admired from afar as a fine specimen of manhood.

There were many reasons for his happiness, He was a successful surgeon, he had a Harley Street consulting rooms and the fledgling health service paid him for his clinics at St. Mary's Paddington or St George's, Hyde Park Corner, in the morning and the Tooting hospital of the same name in the afternoon. Through that he had picked up some private patients.

His wife was beautiful, glamorous, fun and rich. She worked as well, which helped to fuel an extravagant lifestyle. They had two houses and three holidays a year, ski-ing, in winter, The Riviera, in the early summer, and Ireland in August.

Not bad for a boy from Mayo.

Dressed in black tie and patent shoes, he looked elegant and sophisticated. He still looked as fit as he did when he played rugby for Balinrobe as a teenager.

He was well-educated and, even more importantly, well-read. George could quote Shakespeare, recite poetry, his favourites were Keats, Masefield and Yeats, plus he could play the piano and sing to a certain extent, a little flat but a pleasant male voice. He was a shinning example of how good education can produce a witty and erudite individual.

"Darling," Jo said.

"My Dearest," he replied, realising both she was there, and he had been caught.

Jo had arrived at his shoulder just in time to catch him looking in the mirror, first at himself and, then, at a beautiful brunette in a dark green dress who was smoking a cigarette through a dark green cigarette holder that seemed to be an almost a foot long.

"Darling," he replied, "there's a woman over there with a blow dart pipe, watch out."

She smiled knowing he knew that she had spotted him eyeing her up as she arrived.

"Clearly, you are on watch yourself, I shall be keeping an eye on you, so you had better watch out, too."

"Darling, I only have eyes for you, my sweet," George insisted, trying to keep the nervous laughter out of his voice.

Jo wore her trademark black Balmain dress, thin at the waist and just below the knee. It was backless, a Clorinde from the 1954 collection, and had a ballerina skirt.

Her hair was coiffured, and she had removed the bandage on her sprained wrist, replacing it with a black bead bracelet made of jet.

"Sweets to my sweet, can you get me a drink, please, darling, I'm parched."

"What would you like?"

"Surprise me."

"I'm having a Bloody Mary."

"We've only been here together five minutes and you're already swearing."

"Will you have a whisky and soda?"

"I think, I prefer my B.M.s as a starter for lunch, a tomato soup, so not what you're having, and I fear whisky makes me frisky."

"Whisky and soda it is," George joked.

"Quelle Surprise, clam down, your tail is wagging. Is that the most imaginative you can be, I'll have a pastis, please, if they have it, brandy and ginger if not."

"I was hoping for the 'whiskiness' actually."

"I bet you were, you dirty dog! I'll settle for a drink right now, darling, thank you."

"I love that dress."

"The Balmain, thank you darling and you look so handsome in your penguin outfit."

"It's Chester Barrie from Harrod's," he announced proudly.

"I know, I bought it for you."

"And it fits like a glove."

"42 long and 34, 34, a mannequin's figure."

"36, 24, 34, a model figure."

"Flatterer."

"Credit where credit due, you look gorgeous tonight."

"And you are the most handsome man in the room but if I see you looking at the girl with the green proboscis again, I shall perform surgery on your nether regions."

"Forewarned is forearmed."

"There's a good boy, you will be rewarded and that, my love, is a promise."

"In that case I will behave but you cannot flirt too much either."

"As if I would," Jo replied, feigning innocence.

It was all harmless and fun in those days. A taxi took them from The Rembrandt to the Dorchester.

They were attending a charity ball in aide of the 'Bentilee Project', a housing project in the Potteries, which was the area of Stafford where the majority of ceramics and china were made in England.

In those days, quality English China graced every wealthy home. Dinner sets and tea sets had names like Burleigh, Denby, Royal Stafford, Spode and Wedgewood.

Exquisite pieces of porcelain were produced in hundreds by a wonderful workforce who were skilled craftswomen, and craftsmen, and their products were admired by people around the world. At that time, their market was relatively untouched by cheap imports.

Signs set up on easels, all over the hotel, proclaimed the December fundraiser was a dinner and dance followed by an auction and raffle all for a good cause, building low cost houses for the poor. Champagne and champagne cocktails were offered as the guests arrived in the ballroom.

ii

In the dark days of 'post-war Britain' a chance to dance and eat were always welcome but there was a frisson of excitement that night. One of London's elite cliques was meeting for some fun and it was a wonderful event to attend and a memorable sight to behold.

There was also the smell of perfume and Pommade. The rustle of silk ball gowns and dresses, the sight of the pretty women with their diamond rings, pearl necklaces and gold ear rings; the handsome men in their full 'bib and tucker': a black bow tie matched to a sombre dinner suit and crisp, starched shirt with silver or gold cufflinks and shirt studs, all added to the feeling of glamour.

It was a ball, a dinner and dance. Jo loved dancing. She told me she once walked eleven miles to a dance and eleven miles back when she was living in the house at Bromley in Ireland. She was tempted to dance that night away, so it was fortuitous that she met some of our suspects that night. It also showed these people were well connected.

Jo's father knew a police commissioner and as a result any speeding tickets Jo received, miraculously disappeared. If a publican could have that influence imagine what clout these miscreants had with the top brass in the Metropolitan Police. That was the way things worked in those days. I am not going to comment on that. I hope you know me well enough by now to know I only ever wanted to catch the villains and make them face justice.

"Who's that talking to Harold Clowes and the Fitzherberts?" asked George, raising a glass of red wine to his lips; he could not hide his curiosity.

He was a curious chap; he always wanted to know what was going on. George was charismatic and charming, but he had another darker side, that Jo knew only too well, he was fearfully jealous.

"Not a clue, darling. Why, does he have a stigmatism that needs sorting out?" Jo asked.

"He might well do," chortled George, "it's just that I recognise him, I think he was on the health committee at St Mary's."

"Lots of businessmen are, shall we find out?" Jo decided, "He might be one of the benefactors involved in Bentilee."

"What makes you think that?" George asked.

He could not hide his surprise. Jo was an expert at subterfuge and subtlety; George was a little too literal to understand. He had been spoilt as a child whereas Jo had been given her independence and as a child had watched how adults operated.

"Just a hunch, honey bunch," she replied, leading George towards the group. She had noticed even then how ill at ease Bray was, if not a friend, then a sponsor. Her powers of observation were amazing.

Where she led, he followed. 'Me and My Shadow' might have been written for her. There was no question as to who was in charge. Truly, George was like a faithful puppy, adoringly remaining at her side. He had pursued her at college, they had fallen in love with each other and yet George was so insanely jealous of any man who talked to her fearing he might take her away.

I was often the target of his jealousy and generous George could be as sharp with his tongue as he was quick at dispensing favours and they used to say hell hath no fury like a woman scorned, that was before George was born though.

Jo approached Sir Harold Clowes who had become Lord Mayor of the city of Stoke-on Trent; they had met in Grasse four years ago and he had hitched a ride in George's small 1948 MG TC Midget sports car and they had toured the Italian Riviera and the Amalfi coast together. He had joined them on subsequent trips with his girlfriend and his own car. He was just telling a couple a joke when he spotted Jo.

"How does a bull elephant find a female elephant in the long elephant grass?" he asked the wife.

She smiled before answering, Harold was known for his wit.

"I don't know how the bull elephant finds the female elephant in the long grass?" she replied, playing along with him.

"Delicious."

They both laughed genuinely enjoying the word play.

"Very good, Harold," the husband chortled, "We'll see you after dinner."

They moved off and Jo moved forward to embrace their old friend.

"Jo, darling, how are you?" Clowes enthused.

"Very well, how are you, darling?" Jo replied, smiling warmly at him.

"All the better for seeing you!" Clowes exclaimed, a smile on his face and a twinkle in his eye.

"My what big eyes you have," Jo teased. She enjoyed flirting with Harold; she knew she was safe with him.

"And here comes the big bad wolf, how are you George?" Harold quipped, smiling at George before placing his hand in George's vice like grip.

"Mad, bad and dangerous to know, you look well, how are you?" George answered, smiling broadly with a gleam in his eyes,

"Never better, must be the Cotes de Blaye they serve here."

"How is the Bentilee project coming along?" George asked.

"It's now officially the largest social housing project in Europe, we're going to be building 4,500 homes in all."

"It's going extremely well from the sound of things!"

"Fairly, well, so far, I should say, building projects are always fraught with delays and problems. How are things in the world of ophthalmic surgery?"

"I'm coping with the cut and thrust, I'm keeping a weather eye on things," George quipped.

"I see!" Harold Clowes chortled.

He pretended the joke was better than it was. George did not have as much of a sense of humour, as he thought, sadly.

"Head down, then, shoulder to the wheel, nose to the grindstone, and best foot forward, no doubt."

"You make me sound like a contortionist," George responded, it was a weak joke that had become stale from overuse on the comedy circuit.

"A magician, more like," Clowes charitably rescued the comment.

"Indeed, yes, very busy, but enjoying it all," George added seriously, he lapsed into silence.

I had the impression that people loved being in Jo's company and put up with George's presence as a penance. George could be charming, don't get me wrong, but generally it was by flirting outrageously with ladies and trying a bit too hard to be clever with men, which was trying and tiring all round. Clowes and Jo's other friends, especially the Walsh family, put up with it, but strangers were not so forgiving.

"That's good news and the pubs?"

"The Lord Rodney's Head had its best night, we've booked Tommy Trinder; you know, the music hall man."

"What's his catchphrase, 'Your lucky people'?"

"That's him; comedy is really doing well, not bad for a pub that had three customers and one light bulb when I first saw it."

"And the Black Bull?"

"I still have the glazier going in every Saturday morning to replace the windows smashed by the customers. Friday night would not be Friday night without a fight. Those boys who frequent the bar have short fuses, but they drink like fish and the takings are enormous."

"That's marvellous, let me introduce you to Bray. He's known as the pie man not because he's got the same girth as me but because he has his fingers in so many."

"Of course," George agreed readily, he enjoyed meeting people. It diluted his awkwardness.

George was a little in awe of Harold Clowes, he was so popular, naturally charming, well-connected and he always knew such interesting people. Besides, he always hoped that the people he met through Harold might have some problem with their eyes and would become one of his private patients. He was constantly on the look out for more business.

"Doctor Jo and Doctor George Fitzpatrick, let me introduce you Arthur Bray esquire, entrepreneur and philanthropist, this ball was his idea."

"A great cause," George agreed, "The Bentilee Project sounds wonderful."

The all shook hands.

"We're ahead with the foundations and I hope we can persuade you to dig deeper when we start the auction, later tonight," Bray quipped; it was an evening for levity.

Everyone laughed, politely. It was, then, that Jo recognised him. Her blood ran cold, she remembered him from the church, that Sunday, the day her car was rammed. It was unusual to see a stranger at the early mass. Then, when he spoke to George, she felt that his voice was somehow familiar. She had heard it before, perhaps on the radio.

There was something about the tone and accent that made her skin crawl. If only she could remember where she had heard it, she would know why it had such a startling effect on her, but placing it proved elusive. She felt the goose pimples rise on her arm and felt an ache growing in the very pit of her stomach.

Turning to Clowes, George started up a conversation so Jo could talk to Bray before he would later join in once she had charmed him. It was the way George operated. However, he became so engrossed in the gossip that he forgot all about Jo for those minutes while Bray spoke to her.

"So, you are both doctors, Harold tells me," Bray began.

"You are well informed."

"He was telling me about your last jaunt to Rapallo."

"And where did you go for your holiday?"

"Nowhere as glamorous, Scotland, my mother has a place near Glencoe, I like to wash away the cement with a bit of salmon fishing."

"So, you provide the cement for Bentilee."

"It's one of my business interests."

"I see."

"I believe your father was responsible for the building of the new monastery at Nunraw Abbey," he continued.

He acted as if it were common knowledge but as far a Jo knew only her family was aware of John Rickard's involvement in the building project.

"Do you know Lammermuirs?" asked Jo, wondering why he knew so much about her family.

"The architects, of course, but only through the glass company that supplied the materials for the new abbey, I haven't been there. I believe it is the first monastery built in the Great Britain since The Reformation."

"Did Harold Clowes tell you that, too?"

"No, I have done quite a bit of my own research," Bray replied.

"What on earth for?"

"Let's just say to avoid a repeat of Birmingham."

Jo was about to take a sip of her champagne cocktail when she froze. She could not believe how blatant he was being. She was in shock. She could hear the band playing.

Her mind raced: "Was that where she recognised his voice from?

"You do have your grubby paws in plenty of pies, don't you? Do I take this as a warning?" she asked.

"How are your three children, Catherina, Georgina and Patrick, is it?" Tweed asked.

"Very well thank you."

"Good, no illnesses at present, doctor?"

It was the same sarcastic tone that the lecturers at The Royal College of Surgeons used when they wanted to humiliate one of the female students. She fell back on the expected tone, bland and cold.

"None," she murmured.

"Well, let's keep it that way."

"You have been busy ferreting away," she quipped.

"Your father and mother alive and well in Ewell? What's the name of their home, Fernbank?" he continued.

"You've made your point," she hissed.

"Good, as long as we understand each other."

"Perfectly," she breathed.

"Then, all will be well."

"Will you excuse me?" Jo asked.

"Of course, it's been a pleasure."

"Oh, no," Jo hissed sarcastically, "the pressure was all mine."

"There's a good girl, I do not think any further action is needed at this stage, would you agree?"

"Agreed," she whispered, fury in her eyes.

At that precise moment, before Jo could get away, George arrived at her shoulder with his usual bad timing, blocking her escape.

"Harold has gone off to meet the great and the good. What have you two been talking about?" asked George, "What's wrong?"

He could tell Jo was upset, he could see the colour had drained from her face and her movements were stilted.

"Arthur and I were just discussing building houses for the poor; you know how incensed I get about injustice."

"Oh, yes, Jo used to visit the poor in Dublin when she was in college there and went to visit people in hospital," George announced proudly.

"I was just saying how she is a living saint," Bray lied, looking her straight in the eyes and bowing gallantly.

Jo thought his behaviour grotesque.

"More a sinner than a saint," Jo added brightly, hiding her feelings.

"A saint is a dead sinner, revised and edited, Ambrose Bierce said," George noted.

"And he is?" asked Bray.

George was delighted to inform him.

"The author of 'An Occurrence at Owl Creek Bridge', the civil war writer."

"Yes, dying with dignity," Jo added.

"Precisely," said Bray.

"Jo, shall we dance?" George suggested.

"What a splendid, idea, darling," she responded.

He had picked up on the charged atmosphere. As Jo used to say: "You could have cut the atmosphere with a knife".

George could still feel her hackles were up and she wanted to be away from the current situation, he could be incredibly intuitive when he wanted to be; George was a paradox, a dichotomy.

"Will you excuse us Arthur?" George said.

"Of course, I hope to see you after the auction," he conceded.

"I love to dance, see you later in the evening, Mr. Bray," Jo announced beaming at her husband.

"Perhaps you will honour me with a dance later?"

"I only dance with partners who are taller than me, I'm afraid, it's a rule I stick to rigidly."

With that remark she hooked her arm into George's and headed for the Dorchester dancefloor.

"What was that all about?" George asked.

"A few misogynist comments and a veiled threat to the children and my parents."

"Let's go and talk."

"Dance first and then talk."

"Your wish is my command."

George could resist everything but temptation and his temptation at that stage in his life was Jo and Jo alone. They waltzed together for almost a full hour until George could feel sweat on his forehead and Jo was feeling tired for the first time. Then, they sat down and Jo told him all she knew. Shortly after she explained, supper was served.

At the meal, Harold Clowes introduced them to Jenny Strong, the most famous, female entrepreneur, in England, and to The Lady Bargee who controlled all the barges in the Port of London. It was a working port in those days. In March 1958 a record tonnage of seventy-five million was reached. That was before the dockers got greedy and ruined it all for everyone.

"So, what do you do, Jo?" Jenny asked, as if she had not read a full dossier on Jo and her family, her Scottish accent was soft and beguiling.

"I'm a humble National Health doctor," Jo replied. "What do you do?"

"I have a haulage company, mainly trucks, seven-ton Bedford S Type RL, we paint them green because there's so much surplus paint around, which the army can't use," Jenny explained. "We're taking freight off the rails and putting it on to the roads where we can get from A to B far quicker. It's all about speed these days."

Jo stored the information, Bray was behind Birmingham and made it plain, she wondered if Jenny by labouring the point about her trucks being green was being equally candid.

Was it one of her trucks that rammed her wonderful Nash and tried to smash her to pieces?

"Well, the new roads will help, I've just been on the M1 and it is a wonderful piece of engineering," Jo noted, trying to keep the conversation going.

"Yes, it's a good road but I don't care for Birmingham, it's full of pool halls and dangerous roads," Jenny confessed.

"Have you been to the theatre or seen any exhibitions while you've been down here?" Jo asked, ignoring the comments. It was obvious to her that Bray and Strong were in cahoots.

"I don't have time for anything but work, I'm afraid. I have to go back to Scotland on Monday, I'm just here to see that a job that needs doing is completed."

"Well, we're lucky to have you here then, nothing too onerous I hope."

"Just a problem that needs ironing out."

"How was your soup?" Jo asked, knowing that it was going to be struggle keeping the conversation going. Jenny was labouring a point and steering her on to other topics was going to be an uphill battle.

"Delicious," Jenny decided.

Just as she said that Jenny's bowl was whisked away by a waiter from her right who moved swiftly and silently away. Another waiter removed Jo's soup bowl from the left-hand side. Instinctively, she realised this was not correct and because of this, she looked up at the man taking her dish away.

Their eyes locked, she recognised the face, it was the face she had seen moments before her car was crushed like a concertina and slammed into a lamppost. It was without doubt the driver of the green Bedford RL truck. Fighting her initial shock, she tore her eyes from his face and mumbled a thank you. Two shocks in one night, Jo sighed inside, thankful that she suffered from low blood pressure.

"And business," she asked, trying to normalise her conversation with Jenny as her pulse quickened and she registered that there were three people after her.

"Never better," Jenny boasted. "It takes all my time."

"Are you married?"

"Oh, yes, my husband is a physician like your husband," Jenny purred proudly.

"And like me, too," Jo responded, smiling.

"Of course," Jenny concurred condescendingly.

"What line is he in?" asked Jo.

"General surgery," Jenny informed her.

"That's hard work. You both work and very hard, then. Children?"

"Two at the moment."

"That all sounds like a hard-working household," Jo said sincerely.

"Yes."

"Are there many women in your line of work?"

"I tried to help a few but it didn't work out. Once I gave them a lift up the ladder, they tried to kick it from under me. I put one woman in a company and then she voted against me in the AGM. They're vipers the other women in my business, they know nothing of sisterhood."

"I'm sorry to hear that. It sounds terribly trying."

"That's just the politics, though. I consider business a pleasure, I like to find problems and eradicate them. It's part of the fun."

"You like a challenge, then?"

"Yes, the cut and thrust of business is the thing that keeps me interested. I try to see any bump in the road as something that needs to be flattened out."

"I'm not sure I follow," Jo said feigning ignorance, she knew that she represented the bump in the road.

"You will, you will," Jenny promised.

Jenny was being as subtle as a sledgehammer. Jo feared it was going to be a long evening but thankfully, everyone was moving around the circular table after each course, so she left George to flirt with Jenny, if he was able, she was a formidable bastion of Scottish sangfroid, rather like a castle that was impregnable, situated in the middle of an icy loch. Jo doubted whether his Irish charm would melt Jenny's icy demeanour. Anyone who had the temerity to try to break down her façade was destined to fail.

Cool, calm and calculating, Jo felt relief when she moved away from her shadow. Jenny made Jo's skin crawl. Using the movement between courses as an excuse to leave the table, Jo made her way to the telephone. Her first thought was to call me and tell me she had seen the man; the second thought was that her soup had been poisoned and she might not have time to make the call.

"Hello, is Inspector Regan there?" she asked.

"I'm afraid he's not here, I can put you through to Sergeant Stephens," the desk sergeant replied.

"Yes, please, sergeant," she whispered, hoping it would be done quickly. She did not want to be caught.

I know I should have been there, but everyone needs some time off. I was watching 'The Benny Hill Show'. It was Saturday night; I was spending some valuable time with Susie; we'd put the baby to bed, and we were relaxing. I made sure Stephens would be on duty that night. It seemed the worst events happened at weekends, so I wanted my right-hand man at his post if I was not there. I always knew I could rely on him.

"Stephens speaking, can I help?"

"It's Jo, how are you?"

"Very well, thank you, I take it you have rung to tell me something rather than enquire after my health."

"You should be the Detective Inspector," she quipped. "I think I have just been served by our killer."

"What makes you think that?"

"I looked into his eyes and my blood ran cold."

"Anything else?" he sounded unimpressed by her intuition.

"He served me from the left."

"Obviously, not a professional," he sighed, wondering where Jo was heading.

She delivered the coup de grace.

"With his left hand."

"Describe him," Stephens urged, his voice betraying his sudden excitement.

She described one of the Tweeds to the last detail, Stephens knew which one because he was left-handed; it was Derek, the dangerous one.

"Right, we'll send someone straight away."

"Thank you."

Jo returned to the table and to her horror, she was sat next to Bray.

"Jo, you're next to me, now," he announced, clearly enjoying her torment.

She put on a brave face.

"Arthur, how lovely to see you again," she simpered as she picked up her white linen napkin, which she had left on the chair, and sat down.

Bray seemed to have forgotten her earlier snub.

"I hear you are a magnificent copy artist," he began.

For her 'finals', Jo had been examined by a panel from London. As part of her examination she had been asked to draw the fissure of a hand. She used her time a Bromley to teach herself to draw. She wondered if Bray's influence stretched to stealing her medical file form the college of surgeons in Dublin. It was possible but was it probable. Perhaps, Sir Harold Clowes had mentioned something about her sketching; he had admired her drawings in Rapallo

"Harold thinks so, I did some sketches for his house, just pencil sketches of Don Quixote."

Jo felt like carrying on by saying Bray reminded her of Sancho Panza, the fat, short companion to the knight. She wondered if he shared the same appetite. It certainly looked that way. She held her tongue.

"How fascinating, a woman of many talents," he sighed, sounding insincere.

"The band are very good tonight; do you play a musical instrument?" she countered.

"Yes, the piano and I sing in a choir," Bray boasted.

"A man of many talents, too. I wonder, would you like my lamb? I had a late lunch today and I really can't face any more food, the soup filled me up."

She could not face eating anything more, she was wound up inside like a clockwork toy.

Three shocks in quick succession: Bray's confession, Jenny's threats and the waiter's apparition. That trinity had robbed her of her appetite. What was she meant to make of Jenny's cryptic remarks? What was Bray going to do? Why was the waiter there?

"Waste not; want not, that's my motto," Bray bleated, as he moved his plate towards hers.

"Oh, I agree," Jo answered, "I hate waste, I would have given it to George, but I've put him on a strict diet."

Jo moved the cutlet onto his plate using her fork. Happily, Bray cut up all his meat, preparing it for demolition, eschewing his vegetables. Just as he lifted the fork to his mouth, Jenny cried out.

"Stop, Arthur!" she ordered, screaming loudly and grabbing his arm.

Jo looked at Jenny's face, then Bray's, he stopped.

The fork was inches from his mouth, immediately he placed his fork back on the plate, flushing with embarrassment. Jenny's warning had been humiliating but worse was the feeling that he had almost eaten poison.

"What's the matter?" Jo asked, immediately taking the plate away from him and deftly wiping a dice of the lamb off with her knife and, with a sleight of the hand, she slipped the morsel into her bag.

"Arthur," Jenny scolded, "You know you cannot eat lamb!"

"Sorry, I forgot, no young animals, mutton only," Arthur mumbled, meekly looking at the tablecloth.

"Excuse me, I need to make a phone call," Jo apologised, putting her napkin on the table next to the plate.

Jo did not go back to the table but waited at reception for the police to arrive. She could guess why Arthur had not been able to eat her lamb. She was no longer in doubt as to Bray's intentions and Jenny's involvement in warning her off and her detestation of other women.

Jenny may have started off trying to help her sisters up the ladder but the treachery she encountered from those she helped had turned her against all women, it was clear. Bray was a misogynist and was so clearly her vassal.

The Scottish connection and the way Jenny spoke to him connected them.

Finally, all the dots had been joined together in her head.

Bray had to be behind all the murders or why had he warned her off that evening, why had he been at the church that Sunday and why had he so obviously referred to Birmingham? She wondered if he had been there. His voice sounded so like the ones she remembered from that night.

Jo just needed the evidence to prove he was guilty of all the murders. A piece of poisoned meat purloined from a table at a crowded banquet would not suffice; Jo would need far more than that.

After that evening, she was even more determined that Bray and Strong would face justice. By the time the police arrived, six minutes later, armed with a detailed description of Derek, he had slipped out of the kitchen and into the night. The police had arrived discreetly and interviewed Jo, taking the meat for forensic analysis. There was little else they could do during the party.

Chapter 14 - Finding the Flaws

i

Although the streets were freezing cold and frosty, it was a wonderful morning. The sun was beaming down from a blue sky. I was a little wary of the fat cumulus clouds gathering in the distance behind the church spire. Their bellies looked pregnant with rain. I was glad that I was no longer on the beat.

Sergeant Stephens was with me, sitting in the Wolseley outside No. 27 Trott Street, a Battersea two up and two down. It was a Victorian clerk's cottage, they all were. Railwaymen lived in the Shaftesbury Estate, to the east; they had lived in even smaller cottages, except for the foreman's house, which was on the corner and much bigger.

None of them had hallways; you walked straight into the lounge and they were flat fronted. The whole of Battersea had been a marsh until Lord Shaftesbury and his engineers had drained the land and built the railway lines and the junction.

Trott Street was the posh end of the area. Clerks were needed to coordinate timetables and tot up figures and fares. The pen pushers lived in the streets to the west of the railwaymen's cottages. Their houses were more substantial; they had proper hallways, bigger rooms and bay windows. Sadly, the Luftwaffe had destroyed lots of buildings in the area. That meant that, on Trott Street, even numbered houses, or most of them had been bombed to smithereens, the rest had been demolished. That meant the odd numbered row of houses had a view over wasteland bordered by Battersea High Street and the corner of Shuttleworth Road.

It was an ideal prospect for anyone on the lookout, an ideal villains lair, you had an uninterrupted view of most of the High Street and the two pubs, 'The Original Woodman' and 'The Woodman', along with the wood yard to the left of the pubs. All three establishments provided places to meet and do dodgy deals; the side roads and railway viaducts allowed for disappearing acts by the locals and loss of disorientation for anyone unfamiliar with the area.

Even we had problems second-guessing which alley any miscreants disappeared down and we knew the area. It was a warren of dead ends, side streets and railway arches.

Looking at my watch, the minute hand slid on to the hour; it was eight.

"Right Stephens, you ready to face the cold?" I asked.

"You really, think the Tweed twins are going to admit being involved in all this?" he asked, sounding wholly unconvinced.

"George identified Frank for a start. Then, either Derek or Frank was identified by the man who witnessed the truck smashing into Jo's Nash and she described Derek to a tee, at the ball, before he scarpered last night," I asserted, feeling fed up, "I thought you took her call and you said you read the full report."

"I only skimmed the parts I was not directly involved in, sir, we didn't catch them red-handed on any of those occasions. Do you really think either of them will be here?" he whined. I found his attitude infuriating at times. I know he'd had a tough war, but his glass was always half empty, never half full.

"Stephens you've been sullen since I picked you up, why the change?" I asked for wont of anything better to say. In truth, I dreaded his answer.

"I'm not at my best in the mornings, I've just finished a shift and was looking forward to going home," he complained, "Won't they think we'll be looking for them and lie low for a while?"

"I know these boys from my early days, they think they are untouchable. They haven't got caught yet, so who would blame them for fronting it out."

"As long as it's not a wild goose chase," he said cheekily, smiling at me, "You know best, sir."

I did not like the expression on his face.

"Less of the irony, Stephens, just let me do all the talking, keep your mouth firmly shut and your eyes peeled and your ears open."

"I'm not a bloomin' contortionist but I'll do my best," he quipped.

Then, he guffawed like he had heard the funniest joke ever. It was the same terrible joke that had been going around at the party where Jo had almost been poisoned. It was a poor joke from the telly.

Susie would watch the test card if it meant having the telly on, we rented ours from Radio Rentals. In all honesty, I was glad she had something to do in the evenings when I was not there.

On reflection, after doing all the chores flopping in front of the telly must have been a relief for her, cooking, cleaning the house, doing the laundry, and washing the terry-towel nappies would wear anyone out

I did not watch much telly, all tellies had small screens, in those days, and ours was no exception and I got headaches, but I knew the contortionist joke was stale, seven months stale and a bit mouldy, in fact.

I had heard it that many times. It had done the rounds, endlessly. With that piece of 'humour', we opened the doors in unison and let the chill winter wind gush into the car.

In those days, number twenty-seven had a red door, the colour of a post box, but it had faded, and the paintwork was chipped, it might not have been painted since the war. There was a small brass knocker and I rapped on that. I waited and watched for signs of life.

The small bay window offered no more information; net curtains with thick winter-weight drapes behind could not afford me a view of the premises or whether anyone was up. I heard Stephens breathing down my neck and a snatched glare forced him to step back.

I think he felt that the Tweeds would make a run for it.

The next thing I heard was shuffling, slippered feet moving slowly over bare floorboards. The door opened a little and a neck craned around the door. A blonde wig sat on a pudgy face that I recognised.

"Good morning, Mrs. Tweed," I called out cheerily, ready to jam my foot in the door if necessary.

"It's you; if I'd known, I would have pretended to be out, I thought you were the flaming milkman."

"Always a pleasure to see you madam," I soothed, smiling one of my most disarming and charming smiles. "I'm looking for…"

"If it's the boys you're looking for; neither of them are here, so you can sling your hook,"

"Mrs. Tweed, I can smell stale beer and sweat from inside the parlour, lily of the valley and cold cream in the hall, let me in, please, Mrs Tweed," I called, feeling like the big, bad wolf.

"You'll need a warrant to get inside," she insisted

"It's in my pocket, the boys haven't been nicking stuff, now, there are some serious charges against them this time,"

She held the door. She turned her back on me.

"Boys run, the Rozzers are here," she screamed like a banshee, her voice echoed in the stairwell bouncing off the bare floorboards.

Before I could prise the door open, she slammed it shut. I had officers waiting at 23 Orbel Street, the parallel street and the easiest escape route for the twins so I was not too worried.

"Open up," I shouted through the letterbox, "or I'll have you for obstructing the law."

The door opened immediately and there stood the indomitable Mrs Tweed, a red woollen dressing gown strained to keep her robust body within its confines, the cord was as tight as a violin string, trying to give shape to a body that had tasted too many chocolate éclairs and currant buns. It would take a brave man to try and barge past her. She could have squashed me against the wall like a raisin in a garibaldi biscuit. The mums who were 'protecting' their sons, they were the bane of my life. If they just let them stand on their own two feet, they would survive but not Mrs Tweed, she mollycoddled her two boys.

"Just messing about," she chortled, trying to ooze charm, "the boys are waiting in the front room."

"Thank you."

I smiled back, waiting for her to lead the way, Stephens followed. I was not expecting to be offered a cup of tea and, in that, I was not disappointed. She trotted off down the hall to the kitchen without a backward glance, so Stephens and I sauntered over the echoing floorboards and turned left into the living room at the front of the house.

The twins sat on two old armchairs that guarded the fireplace like the lifeguards guard the gates at Horseguards. There was a sofa on the opposite wall and that's where Stephens and I headed.

We stood rather than sat, Hendon fashion, this was official business not a social visit, but a cup of tea would have been welcome. There was little chance Mrs. Tweed would offer a policeman the steam from her kettle let alone a cuppa.

"Good morning, gentlemen," I began but I was interrupted by Mrs Tweed returning.

"There's two policemen in my garden, they want to know if they should come in," she announced.

"Sergeant Stephens will talk to them, any objections to my officers searching the house."

"You have a warrant, I take it?" Frank asked, sounding like someone from a 'Forties' melodrama.

"What do you think?" I replied impatiently.

I stared at him, raising an eyebrow, as if to say, why would I waste time? I took the folded paper from my pocket and handed it to him. He did not bother to open it, he recognised the cream paper and the crown watermark, and he merely placed it on the armrest of his chair and nodded.

"Of course, Inspector Regan," Derek simpered, 'we have nothing to hide."

"Thank you."

Sergeant Stephens disappeared. It was his turn to shadow her. I smelt tobacco smoke wafting in from the kitchen.

It smelt sweeter than the stench of sweat in the living room. It was time for the boys to go to the public baths at the Latchmere.

"So, what are the serious charges, Regan?" Frank asked, a sneer on his face.

"We'll get to that, all in good time. You can rest assured that it's serious though," I warned.

Derek laughed, he actually laughed.

"You've got nuffink on us," Frank insisted.

I had known these thugs for a while. I felt like shouting 'it's nothing' not 'nuffin' but I held my tongue, 'somethink' held me back. They wore their mispronunciations like a badge of honour.

"It looks like you've bitten off more than you can chew, you two," I announced ominously.

"You've never managed to make anything stick so far, Regan, what makes you think you'll manage this time?" Derek replied.

"I know one of you tried to threaten someone and the other tried to smash someone else up in their car," I explained, patiently, trying to keep the rising anger out of my voice. I detested bullies and these boys had tried to hurt Jo and harass her family.

"When was this, then?" Derek asked.

"Last Sunday morning," I said, looking pointedly at Derek, he was the driver; Frank was the fighter.

"That can't be right, can its Frank?" Derek soothed.

"No, we were working for Mr. Bray," Frank added.

"Where was that?"

"At Harold Clowes's flat, we were there all day, ask Mr. Bray," Derek insisted, trying to sound convincing.

"And who pray is this Mr. Bray?" I asked.

At the time I was proud of that remark, it sounded good to my young ears, but hearing it now, I'm embarrassed. I was an inexperienced, hungry inspector full of cliché and wordplay. Feeling disappointed about their alibi, I was at least relieved to be gathering more intelligence.

"He's our boss, has been for months, we've gone straight, Inspector, honest we have," Frank announced, not that I believed him for a second.

I thought I was smart, but the Tweed twins had outwitted me yet again. A cast iron alibi and a search that revealed nothing, led us, dare I say: 'Back to square one'. Of course, I knew who Bray was, but I did not want those two twins to tell him that. At least I knew, now that the Tweeds were working for Bray and I knew full well it wasn't as decorators or painters.

It was snakes and ladders; the warrant had been my ladder, but the snakes had seen me off.

"So Mr. Bray, how are you dealing with the good doctor; she seems to be popping up all over the place and your attempts to get rid of her have failed spectacularly." Sebastian Hepher complained, coldly.

They were in Hepher's drawing room, a typical male nest. The room was rectangular as were all the rooms in the nineteen thirties flats that overlooked George Street, Marylebone. Light flooded in through the four, square windows. It was full of antique furniture, picked for its heaviness and dark wood, a contrast to the cream walls.

He sat behind a large Victorian partner's desk on a dining room carver chair, he was wearing a three-piece suit in charcoal grey, he was always a dapper dresser, the suit jacket was double breasted becoming on a man so tall and thin.

His long neck poked out of a white shirt worn with a pale blue silk tie. His head was noble with a high forehead, a beaky Roman nose and brown eyes that blazed intelligently. His brown hair was brushed back, kept in place with the help of some Pommade.

Bray was shorter, tubby and not so well dressed. Jo was right; he looked like Sancho Panza.

He was wearing a light grey suit jacket and black trousers, a white shirt and a red nylon tie; the whole ensemble was further let down by cheap unpolished shoes. Hepher's shoes were top quality Church's and they shone so he could see his face in them.

"Just bad luck, in Birmingham, she came around for some reason, I blame the professor for not giving her enough of the cocktail. As for the car crash; the buffoon driving the truck was the wrong person for the job."

"Oh, how?"

"He drove the truck into the car that was left hand drive, if he'd hit her from the other side, she would have been crushed like a brazil nut in a nutcracker."

"I really appreciate your seasonal analogy but seriously, do you expect me to accept your feeble excuses?" Hepher hissed, his eyes locked on Bray's

"It's not my fault," Bray lied through his teeth.

"I heard you had the Tweed twins working for you. Whilst I thought these two were hardened criminals, thugs of the highest water and gangsters of the highest order, they seem incompetent beyond belief."

"They've just been unlucky," Bray mumbled apologetically.

"Really, well let's hope their luck does not run out. Besides, I was relying on you and the absent-minded professor to finish her off and he forgot to drug her sufficiently. Really, did he take his pharmacy examinations?"

"He thought she would be as high as a kite on the Benzadrine and alcohol; he toned down the dose because she was a woman. Anyone shorter and lighter would have been a complete zombie and driven straight into the wall. It was a miracle she did not crash."

"That professor of yours is an idiot, no wonder he was struck off."

"You're right, she is a giant and so he should have given her a full adult dose and she is a doctor so she can drink like a fish, plus she's Irish. He should have tripled the dose."

"She might not have been able to drive the car if he had. Normally, I would laugh at your amusing observations if the matter were not so serious. The committee wants results and they want them, now."

"The professor has learnt his lesson, a week off the laudanum was enough penance, he won't make the same mistake twice. The Tweed twins are currently reminding Jo what might happen to her father and her husband if she doesn't mind her own business. If that fails, we go for the children."

"Go for the children, now."

"Let's do it my way, for now."

"With your record so far?"

Bray felt it best to keep quiet about the poisoned lamb cutlet. If Jenny had not mentioned it to her right-hand man, it was obvious that she was as embarrassed about its failure to stop Jo as he was. It had been Jenny's idea to serve up a poisoned chop to poison Jo and she had instructed Bray to organise Derek Tweed to deliver it to the table, dressed as a waiter, it was really her fault, but she never admitted that she was wrong. She just stuck to her guns and so would he. He would gain absolutely nothing by highlighting their joint disaster. Sometimes, "the least said, the better," was the best policy.

"Look, the twins have done a good job so far, she's definitely frightened. She knows we mean business. They're the ones who will hang if things go wrong."

Bray smiled hopefully, revealing tar-stained teeth. Hepher stared back and said, "As a lawyer, I must remind you of a small matter of guilt by association," he insisted.

"They have not been caught yet," Bray argued.

"With your Doctor snooping around, the possibility is getting closer, you have to warn her off or get rid of her. I cannot understand the problem. You have got rid of people before so what's holding you back, now? Stop prevaricating and get the job done. Let's have a quick, clean kill," Hepher insisted, adjusting the cuffs of his shirt under his suit jacket. His evil eyes never left Bray's face.

"I will take care of her but without attracting too much attention. We have to let things die down a little first, there's mounting suspicion around us at the moment. Regan knows about the trip to Birmingham and they are searching for the lorry driver who smashed up her car."

"Whichever Tweed it was, he was Tweedle Dumb; let's hope that the 'D' in Tweedle Dee, does not stand for Tweedle Dunce or is the Dee merely his grade in English, at 'O' level?" quipped Hepher, chortling at his poor attempt at a joke.

"They'll keep Jo at bay, never you mind," Bray assured him, smiling like the weasel he was.

"Jo, she sounds like a friend of yours," Hepher spat angrily.

"Didn't I tell you, I met her at the ball to raise money for Harold Clowes's building project at Bentilee."

"No women in the construction industry thank God."

"Hard helmets and French waves don't go together, thankfully," Bray added, thinking he was now safe.

"Save the nineteen-forties imagery, please. Get the job done; we can't have women getting above their station."

"I agree."

"Precisely, just because a few of them flew Spits from airfield to airfield and some of them worked for Bletchley Park, it doesn't mean they should climb to the rarefied atmosphere of the boardroom. This is the 'Jet age' but we're not looking for this sort of progress."

"We'll keep them out of the stratosphere," Bray concurred, "do not worry, the Tweed twins have only just started."

"I did not ask for a start, I wanted a finish, dear boy, a finish."

iii

Meanwhile, Jo had picked me up from the police station on Lavender Hill. A couple of constables, starting their beat, gave me a second look as I climbed into the two-tone, brown Rolls, at the back of the station, in Kathleen Road. The car smelt of warm leather and Guerlain, it was fast becoming my favourite smell.

She looped around to the traffic lights that led into Elspeth Road, but she took a left, past Battersea Town Hall, and drove towards the Wandsworth Road before crossing the tail end of Cedar's Road. We both looked at each other at the junction. It reminded us both of the evening we met. We never mentioned that night.

We chatted about our respective families as we drove onto to Vauxhall and from there, to Lambeth Palace. Driving the Rolls over Lambeth Bridge, I explained about the new victim who had been taken to Horseferry Road Coroner's Court.

"Three of the same type of deaths; how did you know?" Jo asked.

"As you know Coroner's Courts investigate sudden or unexplained deaths. There are only twelve in London, so I asked them to call should any of their customers be brought in with the same symptoms, or with suspicious circumstances such as suicide," I elucidated.

"You're a veritable Sherlock Holmes," Jo admitted admiringly, steering the car around the roundabout that led into Horseferry Road, I liked to watch her drive. She was assured and competent. She enjoyed driving fast, too, if the road conditions and traffic, including the lack of pedestrians, allowed.

I never felt in danger, but she clipped along, getting to her destination as fast as she could. Buses, taxis and trucks made up the bulk of the London traffic, then, but she skilfully manoeuvred the Rolls around them all.

If there were few people on the pavement, she opened the Rolls up, if there were people around, she drove more slowly; it would have been embarrassing for a doctor to mow down anyone crossing the road.

"We're getting there. My superintendent has given me permission to follow this up, CID are aware, they should be waiting for us."

"That's progress," Jo conceded, I could tell from her voice that she was glad that we were being given leeway by the authorities.

"My superintendent put in a good word with the detective chief inspector commanding our division's CID," I boasted, pretending it was due to my efforts when it was, in fact, the need to solve the case that had inspired the top brass to let us in on the inquiry.

"It sounds terribly political, darling, the main thing is that you're on the case, again. That seems only just. After all you were the one who discovered the body and did the spade work, they seem a bit lost," she surmised, letting me know she had seen through my bragging.

"Thank you, I do think they need some help," I admitted, feeling my cheeks reddening.

"It's a strange case," Jo observed.

"We could be seeing the whole extent or just the tip of the iceberg," I continued, warming to the theme, "We could be investigating far more murders but these three hold the key. There's definitely a pattern to the modus operandi but why Battersea, Birmingham and Chelsea?"

"What links them all?"

"Precisely their conditions; their locations have no connection, we always look for patterns, but I have to admit, we have nothing."

"What was the flat like where this victim was found?" she wondered; she was looking for connections with the lovely flat where Harris was found.

"No flat, a house in Chelsea; Ben Scott-Thomas was a successful and wealthy haberdasher, but he lived in Flood Street, not Mayfair or Knightsbridge."

"That's very modern of him."

"He was apparently like that, a little bit Bohemian, he had a reputation as a maverick, but he ran a very successful firm; he had just appointed his secretary as Managing Director, so he was a controversial figure."

"Forward thinking," Jo acknowledged.

She had experienced sexism. She had seen how lecturers and other professionals had not taken her seriously because she was a woman; patients of both sexes had asked to see a male doctor, or by connotation a proper doctor.

"Very!" I conceded. I was on the same page as Jo, some coppers never saw female officers as equals, I recognised that they were not only equal, they were better in many cases. It was tough being female and having a career, there was cynicism from males and jealously from females.

"He sounds progressive," she added.

"Exactly, his company had just gone public and the shareholders were up in arms when he appointed her to the top job. He said she knew the business inside out, but it didn't placate everyone, unfortunately. I'm afraid, there was a terrible rumpus about it."

"I bet there was," Jo noted.

"Not many people were pleased," I added.

"You can please some of the people all of the time, you can please all of the people some of the time, but you can't please all of the people all of the time," she recited.

"As you and good old Abraham Lincoln would have it," I observed, letting her know I was familiar with the phrase. "A few large shareholders said he would live to regret the decision and it looks as if, in fact, they were right. He died, committed suicide."

"How sad," she said fishing a cigarette from a pocket in her fur coat and pushing in the cigar lighter on the dash.

"Particularly if he was murdered.

"Cigarette?" she asked.

"No thanks," I answered.

"Are you sure?"

I shook my head. I had smoked a few on the pavement outside 'Lavender Nick' while waiting for Jo. I was not ready for a Senior Service, yet. I watched as she parted her lips and put the tip of the cigarette in her mouth, stark white against her red lipstick.

"I did some more digging and the first two victims had only one thing in common with Scott-Thomas, they had both promoted women to prominent management positions exactly a week before they died," I concluded, looking at her profile as she concentrated on steering the beautiful car, it was a heady experience being driven by such an angel.

As she waited for the button to pop out, I wondered if I could have got used to the luxury lifestyle and decided that it would not be too difficult if I were with Jo all the time. She put the cigarette in her mouth and the cigar lighter in the dash clicked as it popped out, waiting to be taken.

"Interesting," she sighed, overtaking a taxi on a wide piece of the embankment before lighting her cigarette.

"What do you think he died of?"

"Of a Tuesday?" she joked, smiling at me before drawing on her cigarette.

I wondered when the cutting down on cigarettes would actually materialise, there seemed to be much talk about rationing cigarettes and many more excuses to have that extra one.

"From, doctor," I corrected myself.

"Carbon monoxide poisoning," she guessed.

"Absolutely right."

"Sorry for my flippancy."

"Don't worry, we use gallows humour in the Force, too."

"Tell me about these Tweed twins and how they got off," Jo continued.

"You met Arthur Bray at the ball. I never asked you what it was in aid of," I said, feeling especially guilty that I had not done more to protect Jo from the Tweed twins.

"Yes, it was a party to raise money for Bentilee."

"Bentley, the car maker?"

She laughed.

"I don't think they need money, it's a housing development of four and a half thousand houses, being built up in Stafford," Jo explained.

"Now, I remember, I read about that, Stoke City Council are building it, I remember now, not the name but the fact it's largest social housing project in Europe," I boasted.

"Precisely,' she acknowledged.

I was always trying to impress her with my knowledge; fortunately, I had read about the project in the Daily Express, "so what are you raising funds for?"

"The council are the project managers; we have to raise funds for the infrastructure and the support services amongst other things. Harold Clowes wants a community hall built there, as well," Jo informed me.

"Harold Clowes?" I asked. That was one of the names I remembered that the Tweed Twins mentioned.

"Yes, Lord Mayor of Stafford," Jo informed me.

"Does he have a flat in London?"

"Well, his paramour does, Yes, why?"

"I told you about the Tweed twins, didn't I? One of whom I am sure smashed into your car while, on the same day, the other one threatened George?"

"Yes, you remember, one of whom tried to crush me in my car and, then, poison me. It sounds like the pair of them paid a visit to my father at his office, too. You were going to arrest them once you had a warrant."

"I got the warrant all right."

"Good."

"Not so good, they have an alibi. They were with Arthur Bray all day, apparently, painting Harold Clowes's flat and Bray will vouch for them in court."

Chapter 15 - The Man in Black

ii

Sitting in the driver's seat of George's small 1948 MG TC Midget, was Mr. Dawid Olzawski, a family friend who had volunteered to help in any way he could. It was four o'clock in the afternoon and the wind made the soft canvas top of the sports car thump and it was already dark. Sergeant Stephens was sitting next to him. They both wore grey overcoats and matching trilbies, everyone dressed like a nineteen-forties gumshoe in those days. Stephens looked more like Humphrey Bogart in the Maltese Falcon and Dawid looked like James Cagney.

"That's Frank Tweed," he announced, as Frank emerged from number twenty-seven, Trott Street.

"How can you tell the difference?" Dawid asked.

"They're not identical, Frank's a bit shorter and tubbier, he used to be a boxer, 'Tweed the Tornado', Derek always wears a suit, he's in the Woodman, it's where I've just come from."

Stephens looked across the wasteland, where there had once been a whole row of houses, to The Woodman and The Original Woodman, the two local pubs. People from the flour mill on the Thames, from Price's Candle Factory, and even the mechanics from Jack Barclay, the Rolls Royce and Bentley dealership who had their service garages next to the candle factory. They all trooped in at the end of the day, foremen, apprentices and everyone in between but they never stayed long, it was the Tweed twins' second front room, they were visitors.

The 1948 MG TC Midget was British racing green, thankfully not red but it was still not the most discreet vehicle to follow a suspect. However, a police Wolseley would have been far more obvious, and the CID officers were not about to lend us one of their unmarked cars.

He wondered whether it was all a wild goose chase and that no matter how well intentioned Dawid was, he might lose Frank or Frank might spot him and shake off his tail.

All he had been asked to do was ensure that Dawid knew what the Tweed twins looked like. His mission had been accomplished.

"Our friend Frank looks like he's off to the gym to lift some weights, or off to do a bit of cat burglary," Dawid noted.

"You'll find out soon enough, here's a taxi and I'll bet it's for him, stick with him and keep the desk sergeant informed," Stephens demanded.

"Thank you, sergeant."

"Thank you, for helping us out. Jo's got some good friends."

"Actually, it was George who was so kind to me when I arrived here. He helped me out no end with advice and some money as well and Jo is my doctor. I sometimes drive the kids to school. If I'm working shifts, I can help them out."

"You're a good friend to the family, they need it, now," he said, staring out of the windscreen as Tweed walked to the corner.

"You, too, it seems."

Stephens waited until Tweed was talking to the taxi driver and slipped out of the car and walked down to the corner of road where the church was keeping the two pubs to his left, counting on Derek staying in the pub for the evening session.

The pubs were meant to close at three in the afternoon to allow the manager to get to the bank by three thirty and then restock, opening at six thirty.

Opening and closing times did not apply around there as far as the Tweed twins were concerned, they knew the publican and under his licence, friends were allowed in after hours provided no money changed hands and it was a small gathering. The Tweeds conducted their business from the pub and there was nothing the police could do about it if the landlord was happy to have him at his bar. People came and went by the side door.

Wearing a sombre trilby and a grey raincoat, like most of the office workers at that time and walking away from Tweed, Stephens would not have raised any suspicion.

Dawid started the car and pulled out, passing the taxi that had pulled up next to the kerb. He followed Trott Street around to the left, overtaking Stephens who was walking on the right-hand side of the pavement.

Dawid hesitated briefly, before turning left onto Battersea High Street, to give the taxi time to turn right into Shuttleworth Road and immediately left on to Battersea High Street. Then, he pulled out of the junction. He let the taxi pull ahead, shadowing the car at a safe distance, as they threaded their way through the side streets, heading towards Price's Candle factory.

The chase was on.

There were a few trucks and buses as the evening rush hour was about to begin in earnest. Dawid followed the taxi past York Road, the Young's Brewery and along the Upper Richmond Road, taking the left fork that led to Putney Heath. It was one of Dick Turpin's haunts; he seemed to be a spectre leaving his mark all over London.

Dawid wondered whether they would head down the A3 to Richmond. He had kept a safe distance as the taxi moved left on to the slip road by the church, leaving the A3 and heading for the roundabout where the car turned left towards Wimbledon, then turned right into the golf club.

Dawid drove past the turning, he had played golf with George there on several occasions, he knew it was a dead end, As he drove on to Wimbledon Village, he looked out for a phone box and rang Jo, not the desk sergeant as agreed with Stephens. In a few hundred yards there was a Gilbert Scott phone box on the corner. He turned into Parkside, parked and dashed across to make his phone call.

"He's gone to the Windmill near the golf club," he announced when Jo answered.

"Thank you, Dawid, I'll be finished surgery in half an hour, I'll be with you in an hour, where will you be?" she asked.

"I'll meet you in the bar at the London Scottish golf Club," he replied, "Make sure you park the Rolls out of sight."

"I was going to pop it behind the warden's stables where it won't be seen," she asserted.

"Good, thinking, see you later."

"Dziękuję Ci, Dawid," Jo said, her gratitude was obvious in her voice. She knew a smattering of Polish, just a few words like, thank you.

"Proszę bardzo," he replied but Jo doubted that giving up an evening to follow a villain was a pleasure.

Dawid hung up, replaced the receiver and slipped back into the car.

Switching on the headlamps, he started the engine and drove smoothly into the night. A silver fox, he wondered who would be at the club on a cold December night.

Chapter 16 – Moonlight Becomes You

iii

In the moonlight, Jo crept through the beech wood, the mulch of old leaves was slippery, but she was wearing her après-ski boots, black rubber boots with a thick sole and good grip. Matching ski pants and a black three-quarter length coat, which contained a map, a sharp pencil and a small rubber torch completed her outfit. She threaded her way through the tall trees, ducking for the older alders that blocked her path.

Strands of spiders' webs stuck to her hair, she ducked to avoid twigs and branches, but she was making progress, moving as silently as smoke. In front of her, there was the snap of a branch breaking. Jo could see the man in black ahead of her. She froze. Hidden by the forest, she was able to watch through a gap in the foliage.

The undergrowth seemed to pose no problems for the man she was shadowing. He strode up to a small clearing where there stood three trees, a trinity of oaks surrounded by pyres, a great mass of wood created to look like a wigwam at the base of the trunk, it was built from fallen woodland debris.

She was puzzled; it appeared at first that he intended to burn the tress to the ground. Wondering whether he had personally built these strange structures, she watched as he poured petrol over the collection of broken branches that had been piled up to look like a bonfire. He drenched the broken limbs; three branch bundles, drenched in flammable material, three victims.

Waiting until he passed up the path, she walked downhill, knowing that the lake was somewhere close by.

She crept through the undergrowth, stepping over logs; loose branches littered the forest floor like dislocated limbs, threatening to trip her.

Trails of brambles grasped at her ankles. She could see the water glinting in the weak winter moonlight. Another strand of cobweb caught in her face and latched on to her blonde hair.

Jo came out into the clearing.

In front of her, the lake was like a black mirror reflecting the light from the clear night sky above her head. There was a single paving stone, which would act as a landmark and then the rim of the lake. She walked around the circumference of the lake and headed towards Roehampton and the A3. Then, she took a fork to where the recent Roehampton War Memorial stood. The original war memorial on the site was badly damaged by bombing during the Second World War. The new memorial was erected in 1952, sited 200 metres east of Roehampton Church.

Leaning on the memorial and switching on the torch that she slipped from her jacket, she unfolded her Ordnance Survey Map, marked the approximate spot where the trinity of trees could be found with her pencil and returned to the car.

Chapter 17 - Wimbledon Woods

I stepped out of the back of a Wolsey police car. The darkness around me was absolute and the silence of the wood that lay ahead of me was eerily unsettling. I should have been able to hear something. There was not a sound. If there was the gathering that I expected, I should have heard voices. Jo had tipped me off.

She had returned to the club after her foray into the woods and Dawid had rung the desk sergeant as we had agreed. I had spoken to Jo over the telephone, in the morning, between her surgeries. We had discussed the various possibilities.

Maybe, Jo was wrong after all, I thought to myself. She had reckoned they would meet here either the next night or the night after. I was not so sure but decided to investigate anyhow.

I closed the door as quietly as I could and my driver, Sergeant Terence Stephens, followed suit. We looked across the bonnet at each other, nodding grimly and proceeded to the woods. I was glad to have him with me that night.

Moving away from where we had hidden the car, we rounded the stables block and carried on out into the open. The sails of the windmill creaked in the wind that whistled over the heathland. The sky was a midnight blue curtain, but large cumulus clouds obscured the waxing moon.

My shoes crunched noisily on the gravel as I walked to the nearside wing of the car, so when I reached the verge, I was thankful to be on the grass. When, after ten minutes walk, we reached the car park, at Wimbledon Common. It was deserted or so it seemed.

However, as we cleared the windmill, we saw three cars; there was a white Rover 75 P4, a dark blue Vauxhall, PA, Cresta and a green Morris Minor. I tried the doors; all of them were locked.

I could feel the thrill of the chase.

Sergeant Stephens followed me like a shadow. I was relieved that he seemed to be alert, and on his toes, that night, his torch flashed briefly in the night before he hid it in his tunic. I shot him an admonishing look and he smiled sweetly at me. He could be insolent at times.

Adjusting our eyes to the darkness, we moved like two spectres as we scurried along the apron of the car park, our shoes swishing through the dew coated blades of grass. At all costs we had to avoid walking over the gravel, now that we were so close to our quarry.

Stealth had to be our watchword if we were going to catch these criminals.

According to Jo's map, the ceremony should be happening nearby, just after the common sloped downwards. It should be somewhere between the car park and the lake. Sure enough, as we crested the hill that led down into dip leading to the lake, we were confronted with the ominous sight of a bizarre site.

Three bonfires burnt in front of the three trees Jo had seen. The firewood stacked up against the trunks had been moved, piled up five feet away from the trees and had been built into a funeral pyre. The wood smoke wafted towards us, the dry branches crackled, and flames leapt from the three small bonfires, burning brightly.

Three blindfolded men knelt with their hands tied behind their backs. Their suit jackets were missing, they all wore white work shirts that were lit up by the firelight. Shadows played on their faces and their identity indiscernible in the fire gleam.

Behind them stood three men, resting their hands on their victims' shoulders. All three standing figures were dressed in black and wore full-face balaclavas with two holes for the eyes and a slit for the mouth. All six men were silent; they all seemed to be focused on the burning branches in front of them.

The light from the fires guided us to the spot. We watched our footing as we picked our way through the bracken and fallen tree branches. It was dangerous and time consuming, but it looked like we had arrived just in the nick of time.

This looked to me like some ritual execution.

Distracted by the fires, I tripped twice, staggering down the slope. Stephens stumbled and slammed into a tree trunk, which broke his fall, luckily.

Our idea to sneak up on them in the darkness turned out to be flawed, the ground was too uneven and there were too many roots for us to pick our way over. We might as well have gone in with torches blazing. As we stumbled out into the clearing, six heads turned in our direction but only three pairs of eyes took a look at us. I addressed my comments to the group.

"Good evening gentlemen, my name is Detective Inspector Regan," I announced, "can you tell me what's going on here, then?"

My interruption to the ceremony was greeted with silence.

No one spoke, I, then, realised why the men in business suits would not talk because they could not; they had been gagged using silk scarves. All of the men moaned and groaned desperate to speak, to warn us I suppose, but I had not felt vulnerable, so I ignored them. Their pantomime act lasted a good few minutes until one of the men, his face hidden by a balaclava, spoke.

"Good evening, Inspector Regan," he exclaimed, it was a jovial greeting. "I think those three kneeling in their smart suit trousers are trying to warn you that your trousers are about to get a bit muddy."

The fire gleam lit up the side of his face and a smile was playing on his lips, the balaclava creased upwards. Bray's face was a mask, all leaping shadows, making him seem even more macabre.

I recognised the voice; I had interviewed him to check the Tweeds alibi about the Tweed twins painting Sir Harold Clowes's flat in London. I was not surprised to see him.

"Anthony Bray, I would recognise that weasely voice anywhere. I saw your Rover, but I wasn't sure it was you until I saw the number plate, AB 435.

"There's no need to be rude inspector, I never once made fun of your south London accent, I cooperated fully with your questions concerning the Tweed twins," Bray answered, his lips becoming a serious slit, again, his head shrouded in black apart from this gap, he was clearly more sensitive than I had given him credit.

"I presume the other two individuals with you are the aforementioned Tweed twins."

"You're a clever cop, Regan, aren't you? But even you can't see through balaclavas," Bray boasted, confirming my assumption by that comment.

He really was a bit dim, but he did not realise it.

"This is all a bit melodramatic for an upstanding accountant. Some form of Masonic ritual is it?"

"I would never associate myself with the Masons, they do far too much good for society."

"I should have known, then."

"Of course, you should. I'm no ordinary accountant, I'm a forensic accountant, specialising in stripping assets. A man like me has no affinity, not even the Rotary Club, of which I assume you are a member."

"Very funny, but why don't you tell me why we're all here?"

"What do you think?"

"It looks like a ritual execution, to me, if you must know."

"It's a rehearsal."

"For an execution?" I scoffed.

"We're putting on a new theatre production and this is realism in rehearsal, the play's called: Three Blind Mice, See How They Run."

"Very funny. You can cut the flannel," I hissed.

"It's a matter of justice," he asserted.

"And what have these three victims done to deserve Bray justice?"

"Oh, it's not what they have done," Bray replied, keeping his hand firmly on the shoulder, "it's what they were going to do. They had been warned not to promote women to key roles in their companies and they had ignored the warning, announcing appointments in The Times."

"Well, you can let them go, now, can't you?" I insisted, all swagger and bravado, believing that at that very moment a compliment of officers was speeding down the driveway towards the windmill.

"On the contrary you and your sergeant are going to join the party. That's why I led your doctor friend here, so you would swallow the bait."

"So, this is a trap?" I scoffed.

The smile on Bray's face was lit by the firelight; I knew that smirk would be wiped off his face as soon as the other officers arrived and surrounded them. I knew they should be arriving at any moment. My orders had been specific. I had told Sergeant Randall to round up some officers and bring them in a van to the spot marked on Jo's map.

"I am afraid it is you who are under arrest and you who will be imprisoned," Bray declared arrogantly.

"Oh, really?"

I could not believe Bray's gall. Of course, I did not know that he had a copper working for him, and my officers had not been contacted. I had gone into the woods expecting reinforcements. My message to Sergeant Randall had been specific but I did not know that Bray had specifically taken time to buy him off, pay him off and get him to shuffle off.

Again, Bray had thwarted me.

Chapter 18 – The Other Party - Jupiter, the Bringer of Jollity

Ray Charles had just finished singing 'Let's Go Get Stoned' and a long-playing, Calypso, record, sent from The Cayman Islands, landed on the revolving record turntable, 'Yellow Bird, yellow bird, up high..."

The only other furniture in the dining room was an ornate walnut drinks cabinet, from France, in the Empire Style, the record player, a double cane, Bergere Suite with lion claws feet, the cushions covered in red material complimenting the carpet, was pushed against the wall and there was a small dark brown table on which stood the black bakelite telephone.

The wallpaper was in the regency style, a silver and grey vertical stripe while the French windows and skirting board were cream and the deliberately, dark red carpet did not show up spilt drink stains.

Elegant couples were draped in various states of dishabille on the Bergère sofa and chairs. A Polish and Irish doctor had taken one of the two tub chairs, three couples lay back on the sofa and it was difficult to decide who they were, and each of the arm chairs were occupied, one by a doctor from Ireland and his wife who was a nurse, the other by an Irish dentist and his English wife.

The thick cushions and double cane cosseted the exhausted couples, they had been drinking and dancing solidly for three hours. There were other couples in other rooms, spilling into the surgery, waiting room and kitchen. Outside in the hall, George was acting as host. Someone closed the door of the dining room blocking out the sound and leaving behind the party

"Another, Brandy Alexander, Trevor?" George asked.

"Not for me, thank you George."

"Madge, would you like another dinky-donk?"

"Darling, I'm fine, sorry the Browns are very boring. Sadly, we need to leave, Trevor has a dull business meeting tomorrow."

"Darling?" called George, "The Browns are off."

"We've been off for years," Trevor quipped.

"I wondered what that strange smell was," Jo cried as she walked from the kitchen, "I'll get your coats, darling."

"Where are they?" Madge asked impatiently, opening the cupboard door, rifling through the coats that were hung up on hooks and hangars. She was on a mission, a mission to get home. Trevor looked sober; he had only had a few drinks. He was going to help Madge, then thought better of it and turned to thank his hosts.

"Right, Jo and George, thanks you for a lovely meal and a super party, we must go to the Alexandria, again," he announced, ignoring his wife, there was no persuading her to let him help when she was so focused.

"The only pub in London with a secret source of Irish beef," George boasted.

"And delicious it was, too," Trevor acquiesced, "thank you for the after-dinner dancing."

Suddenly, they heard a crash and a suppressed scream.

Sticking out of the cupboard door was a pair of legs attached to high heels and a prone woman lay under a pile of coats.

"Jo, Jo, I've fallen down the lift shaft," Madge mumbled from underneath.

"Madge; do get up," Trevor insisted, leaning into the coat cupboard to help her to her feet. "Jo, is that you? I can't hear you down here, I'm in the lift shaft," she complained.

"You can't hear because you've taken all the coats with you," Trevor explained patiently, stripping the coats from her body so he could find her arms and so she could see where she was.

They all laughed heartily.

Trevor helped Madge to her feet but as he did, so his waistcoat button became entangled in her long blonde hair. Poor Madge was left bending over as Trevor tried to undo and shrug off his waistcoat without pulling her hair.

When Trevor had released Madge, George escorted her to the stairs and encouraged her to sit on the third step. She held onto his arm as she sat down, giggling slightly, but relieved to be out of the lift shaft.

"Wait there, while you get your breath back," George suggested, turning around to see that Trevor had disappeared.

He was in the cupboard but at least his legs were not sticking out into the hall, so he appeared to be still upright.

If the rest of the company had not been aware of how inebriated Trevor was, they might have been sympathetic to his plight, believing that he was a martyr who looked after his wife. His behaviour betrayed his true state. The degree of his sway gave him away. Still he was convinced that, although he was not a model of sobriety, he was at least not a sloshed as his wife. He was mistaken but it made him feel better.

Trevor's disembodied voice came from inside the cupboard: "I've found them; I don't know why you don't let me look for you, especially when you're sozzled."

There was a loud bang at the front door and all four looked around. Their faces froze.

The disturbance instantly changed the mood. All feelings of frivolity dissolved. Everyone in the hall became serious, ignoring the strains of music.

Jo opened the inner front door twisting the small brass handle; the double doors beyond had two locks to secure the door and two bolts that could be rammed home if necessary.

"Who is it?" Jo asked, it was far too late for anyone to call; it was almost midnight.

"Police, Inspector Regan has sent me to collect you."

"One moment officer," she replied.

Trevor had helped Madge to her feet and George was helping them to put on their coats.

They all looked at Jo with mounting concern.

Chapter 19 - Climbing the Walls

Jo struggled to release the bonds, she knew she was tied up with her hands behind her back and she knew her face and legs were bruised. They had taken away her coat; she only wore her favourite green silk blouse and a beige camel hair and a wool skirt from Jaeger, her tan stockings meant that she was warm but that was the only comfort she had. We both shivered in the dark, cold and damp bunker, the smell of rotting leaves producing a putrid aroma that stuck in my craw. It was an icy hade, but I had to keep our spirits up. It was my fault we were there, I had to make some amends.

"Jo are you okay?" asked a gravelly voice. It took a while for me to recognise it as my own.

She had been expecting to hear George's voice if anyone's.

"Regan is that you?" she whispered.

"I'm afraid so," I replied guiltily, wishing I could see her face and wanting to comfort her.

"What are you doing here?" she asked, thinking she had been incarcerated alone.

"I'm afraid I owe you an explanation," I stammered, I knew why I was there, but I was not sure how Jo had ended up with me and I wondered what Bray had done to Stephens.

"It's not like you to be afraid, I take it something serious has happened for you to be afraid twice in two sentences," she joked, trying to make me feel better.

I snorted to show I appreciated the joke.

"It's worse than that, suffice to say, I went to your rendez-vous and the officers I had asked to be at the site never materialised, it was like being a charlatan at a séance."

"You poor, thing," Jo sympathised, she was forever thinking of others and suffered in silence herself.

"Anyway, my sergeant put up a valiant fight, but he was overpowered and knocked unconscious."

"Poor Stephens, that's terrible," Jo sympathised.

"Then, they grabbed me, there were three of them. I struggled but all I got was a twisted arm and bruised ribs as thanks for my efforts."

"I wish I could look at you."

"You shouldn't even be here."

"I wondered why you sent a car for me."

"I didn't," I complained.

"I know that, now!"

"So that's why you're here."

"You're the detective," she quipped.

"Sorry, I fouled up."

"It's not your fault. It wouldn't surprise me if Bray doesn't have contacts all over the force."

"You've got his measure, then," I noted admiringly.

"He made my flesh crawl when I met him at a fund-raising ball," she confessed, "he was threatening my family and I think he was there in Birmingham when I was drugged, he was there, or he organised it."

"You're right about him; he makes my hackles rise, too," I admitted, "and there's not many people who get to me."

"What was he doing here?"

"I know enough about Bray to suppose that this was a stunt. He likes playing the showman. I am sure he was was giving three wavering managing directors a stark warning to comply with Jenny's orders not to promote any women."

"Really?" Jo wondered.

"I'm sure of it," I lied, hoping I was right.

"When I met him that night, at the Bentilee benefit, I didn't like him one bit, he was sinister, I know he was capable of killing me, why not them?"

"A good point."

"Yet here I am."

"I have a sneaking suspicion that they want influence, not slaughter. You on the other hand, I'm afraid provided a threat and needed to be disposed of immediately."

"I'm so sorry it involved you," she apologised, and I heard her voice catch, she was very upset.

"We tried to stop him," I answered, trying to make my voice sound positive and convincing, "I think he must have got to one of my men, I had asked for one of my detective constables to organise a police raid on the common, the men never showed up, Bray must have stopped him from passing the message on somehow."

"He's got us both exactly where he wants us, out of the picture."

"Are you religious Doctor Murphy?" I wondered.

"Yes, why?"

"Better start praying now, then."

"We will get out of this alive."

"It depends on two things."

"What's that?"

"Firstly, if your prayers are good enough and secondly, if anyone in listening."

Chapter 20 - Climbing Croagh Patrick

While Jo passed out with the pain, she dreamt. She was taken back to the days when she had walked barefoot up a mountain. As her body dealt with the physical pain, her mind took her back to the last time she had truly suffered, one Lent in 1941.

Jo placed one bare foot after the other, feeling the shale lacerate her soles; she was climbing Croagh Patrick as part of her Lenten penance; she was joined by thousands of people, but George was not there, they had not met.

Ironically as she climbed, George was able to see the majestic mountain from the fields at Mile Hill House. Croagh Patrick is situated near the town of Westport in County Mayo, Ireland. The main pilgrimage route originates in the village of Murrisk.

It is 2,500 feet above sea level and no special climbing equipment is needed. You can walk up in two hours and down in one and a half hours, if you are wearing stout boots. There was an Irish expression Jo used every time I complained: "As long as you have food in your belly, a roof over your head and a stout pair of boots, you're a lucky man."

Without boots you are lost. As part of their Lenten penance a group of students had come across on the train, Dublin to Galway, and would join other pilgrims in the annual walk up the hill. They took the coach from Galway to Westport and then on to Murrisk.

From there, they walked to the base of the mountain, where they removed their shoes and wool socks or thick stockings.

Most of the people were in corduroy or wool trousers but Jo was dressed in jodhpurs and a white silk shirt that glimmered like mother-of-pearl.

It was 1941 and Jo was nineteen years old. It was the first time she had performed this penance. She had not known so much pain, her feet, after the first few steps had felt crushed by the weight of her body above them, it was infinitely worse than walking barefoot on a rocky beach or a tarmac road.

The shards of flint and slivers of stone cut into the flesh of her sole; she offered the pain up to God for the health of her soul. Jesus had suffered on the cross and on his climb to Calvary, she would suffer on her climb, too, sharing his pain, 'no cross; no crown', 'there are no gains without pains'. The irony of the clichés was not lost on her.

No Cross, No Crown was also a book written by William Penn, the founder of Pennsylvania while imprisoned in the Tower of London, Jo had found his Puritan approach unsettling, she adored beautiful things; he eschewed them.

She did not like reference to pain and gain either, she knew the phrase had been crafted by Benjamin Franklin, in his persona of Poor Richard to illustrate the axiom: 'God helps those who help themselves'. Indeed, she knew the quote off by heart: 'Industry need not wish, as Poor Richard says, and he that lives upon hope will die fasting. There are no gains, without pains.' Franklin had created Poor Richard, a country dweller, dutifully pious, who provided a rich source of prudent and witty aphorisms such as: "Early to bed and early to rise, makes a man healthy, wealthy, and wise."

There was only one path up and that was like a dried up river bed, full of smooth stones, pumice pebbles and rough rocks all of which were difficult to walk on but the centuries of landfall and landslide, rainfall and mudslide had brought the sharp stones and sharp flints and sharp shards with them, and where they had subsided, that was where the walkers stepped.

The narrow pathway was bounded by a muddy strip of grass, you could circumvent the path but only with difficulty and no one had dared do it; the quagmire you would end up in would be impossible to escape.

The grass was a slippery as an eel; bare feet were no match for that either. The path spread out halfway up and the stones were rumoured to be kinder to feet at that point. That was the incentive to complete the first section. Coincidently, halfway up the mountain was where the priest's hut was located.

As Jo passed the hut, she distinctly smelt bacon frying. Lent was a time of abstinence and meat of any kind was forbidden throughout the forty days before Easter Sunday.

Perhaps, she mused, it was just the bacon fat that they were using to cook with, which provided the strong aroma, but it made her wonder if they had been cheating, after all.

Easter was on April 13th that year and the British were fighting to take back Tobruk, The Desert Rats fighting the Afrika Korps under Rommel; Monty was doing well according to the radio reports from the BBC.

Jo, on the other hand, was having a battle of her own that day, 10th April, the day before Maundy Thursday. She was completing a physically demanding climb with nothing to eat beforehand.

It was a punishing task.

Her mental attitude, her prayers and her beliefs kept her going. It was a battle of will and determination, fighting the pain in her bare feet, the cold of the mountain and, through fasting, the hunger gnawing at her stomach.

Jo dreamt while her body tried to deal with the pain of being bound and the intense cold. Her whole body was numb, she imagined dying of starvation or hypothermia.

Suddenly, she woke with a start. She was shivering with cold, her teeth chattering. She was powerless against the cold. Sleep came slowly; she let her mind drift, accepting the stiff arms and legs, the pins and needles and the joints that ached. Inactivity and the inability to move, or get comfortable, nettled her but there was little she could do being bound hand and foot. It was the cold that bothered her most.

Chapter 21 – The Air Raid Shelter

i

"Jo, Jo," I called in the darkness when I, later, heard her cry out in pain.

"Regan, you're awake," she announced as if she had been awaiting my return to consciousness.

"How are you feeling?" I asked, my heart skipping a beat. Hearing her voice changed everything.

"Terrible, how about you?"

"I've felt better," I joked.

"Where are we? Do you know?"

"I think we're in the deep shelters on Wimbledon Common," I calmly explained.

"They weren't on the map," she argued.

"If you keep your eyes open you can see some evidence but there was only one that I saw still intact. None of them were on the map; they were designed for councillors during the war when the V2s started to come over. Their location has been kept secret. One of the park's police told me about them. Most of them have been filled in or abandoned."

"So, no one will find us here, will they?"

"We'll have to try and get out," I suggested, trying to keep the lack of hope out of my voice.

"What if they have sealed the door?" she wondered.

"It's possible they wanted us dead, but killing us would bring the whole matter out, it would bring their activities on to a different level."

"Dead and undiscovered," she whispered.

"We can't be stuck," I insisted, "We'll sort something out. There might be an emergency exit, we just have to get untied."

"How likely is that? It's like an Edgar Allen Poe story, I've always hated the thought of being buried alive," she complained.

"Don't think like that," I protested.

"Well, that's what's happened isn't it?" Jo argued.

"There's bound to be some other way out."

"I like your wishful thinking, but we have to get ourselves untied first of all, don't we?" she continued.

"I've got an idea for that," I insisted.

"Really?"

"Trust me!"

"You're meant to trust me, I'm a doctor."

We both laughed heartily, it broke the tension. We were silent after that. I wanted to work out how on earth we were going to get out of our tight bonds. I recognised the rope as dockyard grade and the knots a sailor's, they would be difficult to undo with both hands free, let alone with hands restricted and behind one's back.

Listening to each other's breathing, we fell once more into a fitful and dream-filled sleep.

When we awoke, she spoke first.

"Are you awake Dick?" she asked.

"Yes, are you okay?" I asked.

"I love a man who answers a question with a question," she quipped.

"I'm awake and alert."

"Good."

"How are you?" he asked.

I wished I could see her.

"Dying for a fag, preferably a Senior Service but I'll accept a Player's, the use of my hands would be wonderful and the removal of all my pain through a morphine drip would be bliss. What about you?"

"I'm cold, cramped, my back aches, I'm starving and thirsty, I could murder a pint and a pork pie or a ham sandwich, I feel frustrated that Bray is not where I am now, and I have a splitting headache, and yes, I wouldn't mind a fag of any description at this time."

"Why do they hate women so much?"

"Fear!"

"Fear, of us? We have to fear you!"

"How so?"

"Come on, you cannot be so naive, or maybe you are decent man and these men are far from that."

"I like to think so," I admitted.

"You must be the only one!" she snorted.

"What about George?"

"He loved my car first, my wealth second, and me last."

"Surely, not?"

"I always said we should have just been friends, he wanted to marry me, I said to him 'why spoil a wonderful relationship?' He wouldn't listen."

"You're happy, now?" I asked, wishing she would say no.

"Of course, darling, but I wanted to be a vet and have twelve daughters, life hasn't worked out quite the way I planned."

"Twelve daughters?" I gasped in awe.

"Yes, to take over the world," she joked, "boys are so beastly."

"Some," I argued.

"All of them, I met my share at medical college. We had to be wily, Jo McCann and I."

"In what way?"

"All the boys pressed forward when the consultant was examining a patient, Jo and I giggled at the back and talked loudly, after all we were too far away to hear his pearls of wisdom."

"You'd been forced out by the men, squeezing you to the back," I noted bristling with indignation.

"It worked in our favour. Of course, he would hear us and invite us to the patient's bedside, using the patronising epithet, Doctor, before asking us for our diagnosis."

"Sounds dreadful."

"It was. We used to dread his question, well doctor, what do you think? We dared not get the answer wrong."

"I suppose it was a wily way of getting to the front from the back."

"Precisely, the boys were not going to allow us at the front despite the fact that we were first there. They merely crowded us out, so we had to get ourselves back to our rightful place."

"Quite right, too."

"And the police force allows women equal rights?" she asked.

"You must remember the case of Ethel Bush," I persisted.

"Remind me," she insisted.

"In 1955, several women were attacked on Fairfield Path, in Croydon. Sergeant Bush volunteered to act as a decoy along with many of her colleagues. The assailant had seriously injured WPC Kathleen Parrott in March, and on 23rd of April, he approached Bush from behind and hit her over the head, making a wound that required eleven stitches. Bush held on to her attacker's coat and tried to hold him but fell resulting in his escape."

"She was brave."

"She certainly was. When the attacker was eventually caught, Bush was able to identify the 29-year-old labourer. In response to her actions, she received the George Medal for bravery. "

"Impressive, I remember the case, now, I would like to meet her."

"If we ever get out, I'll arrange it for you," I promised, not holding out much hope for us both.

"Promises, promises," she teased.

We spoke no more but dozed through our pain and the cold that penetrated our bones. When I woke up, again, I asked Jo to tell me a bit about herself and George.

Chapter 22 - The Cobbler's Children are the least well shod

Jo took herself off to a better place, a better time, but a more unsettling situation. It was the north side of Dublin, which was them a den of iniquity and the centre of poverty in the city. She was a young medical student in her early twenties.

She was feeling nervous as she walked towards the tenement houses. Jo passed the notorious Henrietta Street, once a wealthy enclave but it had become several tenement buildings crammed with residents; at one stage, before the First World War, over eight hundred people had been living in fifteen houses.

Jo's best friend Joanna McCann had arranged to meet her at the end of the street. They had joined a Saint Vincent de Paul drive to help the poor. They had been allocated a family each. Together they walked down the street, chatting happily until they reached the door of number 12, it was an apostolic number, in which they both took comfort.

They chatted amicably with the mother of seven children, all barefoot and thin, but not seriously undernourished. As they left, Jo slipped a note onto the mantelpiece, fastening it in place with a candleholder, which was the only ornamental piece in the house.

Their next call was Joanna's family and it was her turn to leave a bank note. The next week they returned when the mother explained that the husband had taken the money and spent it down the pub.

My Jo asked her what she needed.

"Shoes for the children, would be grand," she replied.

"Shoes you will have, shall we start with the eldest, what size is she?"

"She's never had shoes, but she'll be ten next week."

My Jo had seen children walking barefoot when she lived in the East End.

"I have a tape measure in my bag," remembered My Jo, "I'll measure her foot and the shoe shop will do the rest."

Arriving the next week with some smart blue sandals, Jo was thrilled when the daughter loved them. It was a good feeling to help others especially the poor of Dublin, they lived a hard life and anything she could do to ease their suffering was worthwhile.

The following week, she went back to visit their mother, passing by a pawnshop in the high street, she noticed a pair of the same sandals. Smiling and shaking her head at the strange coincidence, she walked on. At the house she met, the girl, barefoot again.

"What happened to your lovely shoes?" she asked.

"Pa took them to the pawnbrokers to get money for the pub," the ten-year-old replied.

My Jo's heart sank.

Chapter Twenty 23 – i - George Goes into Action

George rushed out on to the street just as the Rolls pulled up to the pavement. He had a white dog and a black dog under his arm. The nanny closed the door of the house behind him, she was unhappy at being woken so early, it was still dark outside.

"We're off to collect Regan from the station," George told his driver, Tomasz Aljoski another Polish friend.

"Clapham Junction?"

"No, Lavender Hill Police Station," George replied.

"I'll put my foot down, then."

They pulled out onto Wakehurst Road, turned into West Side, and shot along the small stretch of road to the junction where the little side road met the South Circular Road, the one way system was referred to as the race track, and the Rolls was the best car to perform on it, It was the most powerful car available at that time of day.

A heavy lorry was coming towards the crossing by the common as they approached the main road, but they managed to slip into The Avenue just before the driver because he has to break for the bend. The two dogs were lying on tartan rugs that had been placed over the brown leather seats in the back, they did not seem to notice the rush; they were curled up in comfort.

Racing from one zebra crossing to the next, they scooted around the West Side and merged with a car that was tootling along the North Side.

They braked to let it pass before slipping into the left-hand lane and turning into Elspeth Road. At the traffic lights, on the junction with Latchmere Road, they turned left into Lavender Hill and right into Kathleen Road where they parked.

The police station was a huge Victorian triple-decker, redbrick and substantial. It was reassuringly close in an area that was known for its crime. They were both pleased that it had taken them only six minutes to get there.

Within ten, they were at the sergeant's desk.

George was determined to find out what had happened to Jo and he felt sure Regan would know.

Little did he know that Regan and Jo were in the 'Air Raid' shelter together, in fact, no one except Bray and the Tweed twins knew where they were being held captive. They had no reason to reveal their whereabouts.

A dog walker might discover Sergeant Stephens's police cap in time, but they would have no idea where Stephens was being held captive or where the two other prisoners were or how long Bray would let them survive.

Eventually, he would have to dispose of them. Maybe he would just let them starve to death. It would be another mysterious disappearance in an increasingly more dangerous city.

"Good morning, sergeant," George chirped, all charm and smiles, "I've come to see Inspector Regan."

"Inspector Regan hasn't signed in."

"Is Sergeant Stephens here, then?"

"Nor has his sergeant, it's certainly unusual, they're normally very punctual."

"A policeman collected my wife last night and she hasn't come home," complained George becoming increasingly worried.

"There is another constable who's gone missing this morning, it's rare for so many officers to be absent," the desk sergeant revealed, looking increasingly puzzled. "Inspector Regan did not return from a sortie last night and nor has his sergeant."

"Sergeant, I think we might be able to find Inspector Regan," George announced.

There was optimism in his voice and a glint in his brown eyes.

"Indeed, Mr.?" he began.

"Fitzpatrick, George, I'm Doctor Murphy's husband."

"I beg your pardon, doctor," the desk sergeant's attitude changed completely when he realised it was Jo's husband. "I am so sorry about this."

"It looks like all four of them have disappeared. I do know that they were investigating some occurrence on Wimbledon Common, I'm sure that's where they are."

"Stephens did mention something about Wimbledon. I am so sorry your wife has gone missing, too, you must be very worried."

"I was until I spotted a note left by my wife: unleash the dogs of war," he explained, handing over the letter that Jo had left on her walnut veneer dressing bureau, kept in place by a marble cigarette case.

'Dearest Darling George,

Regan has asked me to Wimbledon Common, here is a copy of the map where we located the criminals. If I am not back by the morning, unleash the dogs of war. Love as ever Jo.'

George proudly handed the note over to the sergeant who gingerly accepted it like a piece of evidence that should not have his fingerprints anywhere near. Jo had drawn a wonderful sketch of the woods worthy of E. H. Shepard.

"I understand the quote sir, Julius Caesar, 'cry havoc and let slip the dogs of war,' I am a fan of Shakespeare's sonnets as well, but I fail to make the connection between that and the predicament of Doctor Murphy and Inspector Regan."

"'The dogs of war' are Ching, my wife's dog and Remus, my secretary's dog. She helps Jo out in the surgery."

"Well that is clearer, sir, I thought I was in danger of losing my mind. I'll have the dog section sent to the same location, Wimbledon Common. I take it you have something for them to sniff, or they can follow the little dogs, where are they?"

"I have two of Jo's scarves, I'll leave one for you to give to your dogs and I have the dogs in the car, yapping and waiting," George declared proudly, slipping a green, silk scarf from his inside suit pocket and handing it to the sergeant.

"I'll make the call to the sniffer section."

"Good, it appears that Jo, Regan and Stephens last whereabouts were Wimbledon Common."

"That seems a reasonable assumption."

"Do we know what happened last night? Jo was collected by another policeman, has he made a report?"

"There's where I can help you, the officer who approached Doctor Murphy to accompany him was not meant to involve her at all."

"Really?" George became more anxious.

"In fact, he was meant to arrange for some officers to surround the area, they were all standing by, but they never got the call. I only found out myself half an hour ago. You're lucky you came around so quickly."

"We came as soon as we became suspicious," George said, indicating to Tomasz with a sweep of his hand.

"I'm sure of that, sir, but I was about to come off shift and the new desk sergeant would not have been able to help you. I'll get on the blower, now."

"So, was the policeman who called to our house a bona fide policeman or an imposter?" asked George, furrowing his high forehead.

"As far as we can tell, it was an officer from Regan's section; we had a phone call from his wife shortly after one in the morning saying, he had arrived in a flashy sports car and packed a bag and left, she wanted to speak to the Inspector about it all."

"So, he was in cahoots with the kidnappers."

"If the Doctor and the Inspector were kidnapped."

"You don't mean they were murdered?"

"You have to prepare yourself for the possibility. I am afraid Doctor."

"Yes, of course but call me, George, please. I refuse to think the worst until we have exhausted every avenue."

"Same here, I admire Regan immensely and he has been very good to me," the sergeant admitted.

George smiled at that; he knew that he had someone on his side.

"Let's find him, then."

"The inspector's a meticulous man and his report was on his desk along with the action he was to undertake."

"That's marvellous," George announced happily.

"When I came on duty, I pieced everything together and sent a squad car to Wimbledon, they reported back from the police telephone box at Wimbledon Village."

"What did they say?

"There was no sign of any car except a police car, the very same vehicle Inspector Regan had signed out last night."

"That's very reassuring. At least we know where they are."

Chapter 24 - ii - Ching

As Tomasz and George drove the two dogs to Wimbledon Common, George decided to sing to lessen the tension. Fortunately, Tomasz was concentrating on driving and the dogs were so well brought up that they never complained even if someone was howling.

George could play the piano and hold a tune, but he was no Joseph Locke. Jo told me she had heard the Irish tenor singing in a cinema in Dublin before he became famous. I believed her. The famous tenor often sang before the main feature was shown, just as we had organists playing as the audience settled into their seats over here in the forties. Joseph sang to entertain the audience. George sang to keep his spirits up.

"There was an old woman who lived in the woods
weila, weila walia
There was an old woman who lived in the woods
down by the river Sawyer
She had a baby six months old
weila, weila walia
She had a baby, six months old
down by the river Sawyer
She had a pen knife three foot long
weila, weila walia
She had a pen knife three foot long
down by the river Sawyer
She stuck that knife in the baby's head
weila, weila walia."

George paused before delivering the last line.

"The more she stuck it, the more it bled
down by the river Sawyer."

George's gruesome song was such a familiar refrain, he hardly worried about the subject matter or considered Jo might be endangered.

"Three big knocks come knocking at the door
weila, weila walia
three policeman and six more
down by the river Sawyer."

Unperturbed by a lack of appreciation shown by his audience, George added the chorus.

'Are you the woman what killed the child?'
weila, weila walia."
'Are you the woman what killed the child?'
down by the river Sawyer?"

He paused and was not stopped, so he continued. The inappropriate subject did not seem to bother him one iota, as Jo would say.

"Yes, I'm the woman what killed the child!
weila, weila walia
Yes, I'm the woman what killed the child?
Down by the river Sawyer
The moral of this story is
weila, weila walia
Don't stick knives in babies heads
down by the river Sawyer."

Tomasz had managed to block out everything but the view through the windscreen and the road flooded by the light from the headlamps cutting through the morning mist, mounted on either side of the gorgeous grille. The Spirit of Ecstasy cleaved through the icy night. Sitting in the back, the dogs seemed unimpressed by the song.

Ching was a white Sealyham, a snowy version of a Welsh terrier, which was originally bred to hunt otters, foxes, and badgers.

Remus was a black toy poodle, poodles had proved to be an intelligent dog breed, second only, so Bubs claimed, to the Border collie. Neither seemed to object to George singing.

Both were trained hunters and George had thoughtfully brought along one of Jo's scarves scented with the perfume she had worn that night, Ode by Guerlain. When they arrived, they parked, and George allocated a dog each.

Before releasing them, George, left the scarf on the back seat while he and Tomasz smoked. George favoured Camel non-filters, American, Virginia tobacco but with a film star cachet. His Polish friend accepted one readily. It was chilly and the wet wind tried to find gaps in their clothing, nipping at their faces both men were relieved that they were wearing gloves and hats.

George took a black, thick, wool overcoat from the boot before collecting Jo's dog from the back. Tomasz on the other side of the car took Remus out, both dogs had to jump from the seat onto the carpet and then leap out, the fall from the seat was too daunting. Closing the aluminium alloy doors, with a reassuring clunk, Tomasz locked up while George took Ching on the lead.

Out in the dull morning, Ching looked as white as snow, he had a long, broad, powerful head, which was pointed down, his dark, deep-set eyes scanned the grass ahead, then, he looked up on the scent.

The poor dog was practically drowning in the long grass; his legs were so short, his well-muscled body straining at the leash. His ears were folded level with the top of the head and the forward edge lay close to the cheek. His tail was upright and resembled an old-fashioned shaving brush. He was on the hunt and ready to go. Remus was wagging his puppy tail and following on, he too was a hunter. They, both, seemed to be heading in the same direction.

George bent down, unclipped the lead and released Ching and Tomasz followed suit with Remus who bounded ahead. Jo's dog seemed to have recognised the scent, Remus seemed to be gallivanting around.

"There they go," George smiled, his galoshes slipping on the dewy grass as he tried to catch up with both dogs.

"I think they've found them," Tomasz exclaimed as he strode through the damp undergrowth, he seemed to be less cumbersome than George even though they were wearing the same footwear. Tomasz was a wing forward in football; George was a prop forward in rugby.

The dogs may not have been able to read a map and the dew may have diluted the scent, but they were able to track down the two victims.

On the footpath, there appeared several sets of footprints, the indentation of high heels visible in the mud. The dutiful dogs followed the tracks; Ching was sniffing excitedly and Remus enjoying smelling all the different fragrances from the forest floor.

The two men trusted the dogs implicitly; they had no choice. The sergeant was the first person they found. The dogs led them to a slight dip in the ground and, on closer inspection of the mounds of leaves piled up around and surrounding the depression in the earth, they spotted the two concrete walls that stood on either side of an iron door.

It looked like it was rusted shut.

Unperturbed by the barrier, George shoved his shoulder into the door, and it creaked open. Stephens, the poor dazed policeman was lying on his stomach, his hands tied behind his back and his feet bound.

Stephens's mouth was stuffed with a white cotton handkerchief that was tied in place by a black woollen scarf. He tried to speak when they entered but all they heard was a muffled mumbling. It sounded like he was impatient to be free and he was swearing. George and Tomasz rushed to his side to comfort and free him.

"It's all right," George said, hoping his west coast brogue would reassure him, "we've come to get you out. We're with the police. We're here to help. Tomasz and I will untie you and we'll get you to hospital in no time."

Stephens rolled his eyes in frustration but nodded his compliance. He could not move his body. His head was the only free part available to move. George noticed his missing headgear and the mud-splattered uniform. It was soaked after being immersed in damp leaves and Stephens was shivering.

Outside, the baying of dogs alerted them to the fact that the bloodhounds from the Dog Section had arrived.

Tomasz and George quickly untied the sergeant, Tomasz untying the Gordian knot at the policeman's feet while George, ever the surgeon, intended to cut through the thick rope with a scalpel that was disguised as a fountain pen, which he removed from the inside pocket of his thick, black Chester Barrie suit. Taking off the lid, he sawed through the bonds. Although, the physician cheated, the Polish man managed to untie the feet first.

Once he was free, they helped the sergeant slowly get to his knees where they let him rest for a while.

"Thank you," he sighed.

"What's your name?" George asked, putting a reassuring hand on his arm.

"Terry, Terence Stephens," replied the sergeant.

"Okay Terry, this is Tomasz, I'm George, I'm a doctor, we'll get you out of here and cleaned up, checked over and fed, how does that sound?"

"That sounds bloody marvellous, doctor," he whispered through cracked lips.

Tomasz and George hauled Stephens fully to feet and, taking an arm each, they manhandled him to the door, the dogs skipping happily behind. It was easier to leave them off the leads. They were sensible enough to sniff around the bunker and not block the doorway because the square room provided a myriad of opportunities to sniff things out.

"Close your eyes, Terry, we're going outside, we'll lead you; there's a step here, that's it, we'll have you out in no time."

"We've got you, mind the step, lift your left foot, now," Tomasz said encouragingly, "now, the right foot, that's it, nice and steady."

George and Tomasz took an arm each and escorted the dazed sergeant out of the darkness of the bunker and out into the gathering light of dawn. Terry took two deep breathes of fresh air. The wind whispered through the trees and wisps of morning mist snaked through the Wimbledon woods like lost spirits.

Two policemen arrived as the trio emerged into the clearing.

"We'll take it from here, sir," said the elder one.

"You can open your eyes now!" George assured him.

"Thank you, doctor," Stephens rasped, his throat was parched, and it was still difficult to talk but he managed open his eyes slightly.

Then, he closed his eyes, once more, blinking several times as his eyes adjusted to the light. When he opened them, properly, he still squinted, his chin was muddy, and stubble was growing all over his face. His uniform was damp from lying on the floor and it was grey with dirt and dust from the bunker.

"Get him some water, and then give him some blankets, please. I'll come and check him over as soon as I can," George ordered briskly and authoritatively as if he were back on the wards.

The dogs and the handlers found Jo and I in the next part of the shelter, the inner sanctum, a few yards away from Stephens all that time but behind a door. Our rescue was not thanks to Ching and Remus, but thanks to the police dogs that had bounded ahead of the advance party, sniffing out our scents.

Both police dogs were experienced, well-trained and well-cared for, they were expert hunters. Two big, fit and strong bloodhounds strained at their leash, scenting the Ode by Guerlain from Jo's scarf, the scent of jasmine, rose, iris, sandalwood and musk.

They also had a sweater of mine provided by my wife that had been relayed to them by a police motorcycle courier. It carried the sweet smell of Old Spice. Susie had loved the fragrance, the strong notes of sage and cinnamon that she smelt in the morning as I went to work and she also enjoyed the pleasant musk and cedar scent that remained at the end of my shift, when I finally returned home.

She missed me when I went to work. Poor Suzi would be beside herself, now, I realised, especially with the baby to cope with as well. It was fortunate that she had her mother nearby for support.

The dogs, luckily, had enough to help them locate us, distressed as we were; we hoped we would be saved. Jo's prayers or wishful thinking had worked wonders.

A gathering crowd of policeman crashed through the undergrowth, all in uniform and all wearing wellington boots. They were scouring the common.

There were twelve officers in all, two sergeants organising them. A police whistle from the officer on the right flank brought all of them to the bunker. Two of the policemen helped Terry towards the ambulance that was parked by the golf club. The other twenty-two followed the two dog handlers.

The two sergeants, who were both good friends of mine, pushed open the door to the shelter. Light flooded into the space, but it was a dull, early morning, twilight that was almost swallowed up by the darkness.

I was closest to the door on an iron bunk bed; Jo was deeper in, sitting on a bentwood chair, her arms tied behind her back. It was the first time we had actually seen each other since our incarceration.

It took us several minutes to adjust to the light that seeped into the shelter.

The dogs came in first, they were overjoyed at having found us; they were wagging their tails and sniffing around excitedly. Their handlers gave them lots of attention, a reward for a job well done. I was glad to see them too, but I was in no fit state to celebrate like them.

Hunger had ceased to be a problem by the following day, the body no longer craved food, it was a strange sensation and I was feeling weak like someone recovering from a flu fever.

"I'm here darling," George cried, rushing through the shelter towards Jo with Remus and Ching barking madly at his heals in frenzied happiness. "Tomasz, can you help Regan, please?"

Tomasz leapt into action. He was a reliable friend.

"Of course," Tomasz replied, his voice gravelly as he shouted above the noise of the barking.

"You come readily upon the hour!" Jo whispered, her mouth was dry, and her voice was cracking.

"Am I glad to see you; the girls and Patrick have been missing you! I've been desperate with worry, I knew you'd be okay, but I missed you all the same."

"Don't worry, I'm fine," she mumbled, supressing a shiver that racked her body.

"I'll be the judge of that," George insisted, checking her over.

Once he was satisfied, he moved towards me.

"Tomasz how's Regan?" George asked as he strode over to the bunk.

"His hands feel cold, but I've managed to get him untied," he replied, putting his hand on my shoulder to reassure me. I smiled weakly at him; my mouth was too dry for me to speak. I knew I would just croak.

"Thank you, Tomasz, I'll look after him." George insisted, fishing a stethoscope from his black overcoat, "Can you organise some blankets and bring the ambulance-men down here, please?"

"Of course, George," Tomasz answered, leaving George to give Regan a brief examination.

"Sorry about all this trouble, Doctor Fitzpatrick," I mumbled.

It was the first time I had met George and I looked a mess, smelt awful and felt guilty about what I had done, putting Jo in danger.

"Call me George," he insisted, "save your voice, you're both dehydrated, weak from so many hours without food, no need to apologise, if Jo has faith in you, so do I. Try not to talk, just focus on those clean sheets and warm bed and hot soup waiting for you at hospital. We'll sort everything out, the three of us."

I wished that I shared his optimism and enthusiasm. So far, I had allowed Jo to be drugged, rammed and practically poisoned. Then, one of my men had brought her here and we had almost been forgotten. It was a complete disaster.

I had promised to protect her and yet my association with her had almost finished us off. We had only just cheated death.

"What can I do for you Mr. Regan," Iris Tweed asked as she swept open the front door of number 27 Trott Street.

"Good morning Mrs. Tweed. It's not actually you that I've come to speak to, it's Derek," I replied, still feeling stiff from my incarceration in Wimbledon.

"No warrant this time?" she asked.

"Just a friendly chat, he can help us with our inquiries," I insisted, smiling at her, hoping she would understand.

"I'll put the kettle on, how do you take it?"

"Sweet and strong, like you," I replied smoothly.

She appreciated the irony and actually laughed, she knew she was strong, and she knew she was not sweet. She chortled to herself as she trotted through the hall along to the scullery at the back of the house to fill the kettle. I shut the front door and walked over the floorboard floor to the front room. Finding the door ajar, I knocked and walked in.

There, spread out on the sofa, in his smart shirt, open at the collar, and his sharply tailored trousers, was Dangerous Derek, due to his prowess in the boxing ring. It was a way of making money, back then, pugilists were well paid, the betting on fights provided fortunes for backers, fighters and gamblers. They all paid in the end.

The backers targeted by criminal gangs, the fighters beaten to a pulp or injured in some lasting way and the gamblers lost all the money they made, greedily going for more.

You never see a bookie riding a bicycle, my uncle warned me; every single one of the ones I came across had huge, expensive cars. The middlemen made the cash, the others paid. Derek never bothered to stand up, I did not expect it, and he never offered it.

"Morning, copper, you courting my mum or do you just like seeing us all, or what?" he asked, sitting up and smiling at me, I noticed he was wearing black socks, his shoes must have been out in the scullery at the back being polished by Iris.

"Where's Frank?" I asked, no sense beating about the bush.

"What's he done this time?"

"I think you know, don't you? You seemed surprised to see me. I suspect he will be, too.

"I don't know what you mean, inspector."

"Butter wouldn't melt in your mouths, would it?"

"We're looking after mum, going straight, you can't fault that, we're painting and decorating," he protested

"I admire someone who puts bread on the table," I concluded, "but your brother has crossed the line and so has Bray."

"Who?"

"Bray, your boss, the one you're working for at the flat."

"Oh, Arthur, I forgot his surname, or did Frank ever tell it to me, he got the work in the first place."

"Well, Frank won't forget him, especially when he spends a little time with him at Wandsworth prison."

"What are you on about, Regan?" he whined.

"You'll see, there's a warrant out for his arrest."

"If I see Frank, what should I say?"

"I'll do my best if he helps us to put away the rest of the gang."

"What have you got on him?"

"Apart from fingerprints, a perfect match for the boots he was wearing the night of the kidnap and an eyewitness report, not a lot," I answered nonchalantly, noticing how pale Derek went as I delivered my coup de grace.

"How did your officers get a pair of his boots?"

"Off him, of course, he thought he didn't have to be careful because Bray and his friends could make him untouchable. We went to his gym and matched the soles with a cast we had from the woods."

"So why didn't you arrest him?"

"Your brother must have been tipped off. We went from the changing rooms to the gym and he had disappeared. The fingerprints and the eye- witness means we were able to get a warrant. Let him know we're closing in and we're determined to find him."

"Looks like you've just got yourself an extra pair of hands, Inspector Regan," he announced readily.

"Thank you, Mr. Tweed, ask your brother to call in at the station at his earliest convenience, please."

"Oh, I will, inspector, I will."

Chapter 25 - Bye-bye Bray – Saturn - Bringer of Old Age

In an apartment in a Victorian apartment building that quaked every time a tube drove past on the Circle Line, was a sedate drawing room, which would have been at home in a gentleman's club or a Duke Street hotel.

There was a coal fire, smokeless of course, a green, leather sofa and two armchairs arranged around the fire and in the corner by the window there was a writing desk by the window, a carver chair where a figure sat facing someone who had turned one of the armchairs around in order to converse without craning his neck.

"Arthur, it's not like you to be afraid," the voice soothed. Sitting behind the huge desk was Bray's boss, Sebastian Hepher, "a big bully like you acting like a timid victim, I am surprised."

"I don't want to die," Bray bleated, resting his heavy hands on the arms of a red leather chesterfield armchair. "I've been a loyal servant and always did as I was told, you know that."

"But what did you say about all those you helped to their early demise? You said you were preserving society, saving the world from anarchy."

"I am."

"Yes, but we cannot afford the risk of the authorities knowing what we are up to, you're in danger of exposing us."

"Send me to Hong Kong or Africa, I don't mind, just send me away for a few years."

"I wish I could, dear boy," Hepher apologised, he shook his head slightly and pursed his lips to show regret.

"Please," Bray begged.

"You need to understand your own rhetoric. Authority is under threat from all areas, disrespect for the government, controversial documentaries, the social fabric being worn away by permissive attitudes and nosy newspapers. We need to protect the process and preserve our secrets."

"And I will; I have," Bray protested.

"Up until, now, yes. Come on, Arthur, you know the rules."

"I won't tell, I swear. They can't prove it was me; the Tweed brothers did the deeds."

Bray's face was pale, his lips looked blue. He was terrified.

"We gave you a chance; you fell at the final furlong. All you needed to do was to get rid of Doctor Murphy. It was a simple task; we even had the professor and the Tweed twins to help. You just needed to warn her off."

"I did."

"Did you?"

"Yes."

"Yet, you were meant to do it discreetly, like all the others."

"She was on to us; I did my best to be subtle."

"Not subtle enough. I'm afraid."

"You know I tried to have her disposed of by the professor and, then, by Tweed, they failed, not I."

"Yes, but now the police are investigating the disappearance of Regan as well as Jo and the one policeman that we had convinced to work with us has had to go to ground. Not a great success."

"We all make mistakes."

"What are you talking about? You have ruined all our hard work; you fool. Through knowing a police commissioner, Jenny gets to meet one of Regan's officers. She knows he is still investigating the Cedars Road suicide and she manages to bribe and extort this policeman in Regan's team, so we know exactly what is going on and then you use him to go and collect Jo, you imbecile. We had the perfect mole and then you idiotically expose him. He was arrested last night."

"I thought he was just a tame policeman."

"He was but you do not make assets like that make house calls on doctors who we want destroyed. Jo was meant to be on a slab in a morgue, instead she was bunking up in an air raid shelter with the investigating inspector."

There was a silence, then Hepher picked up the phone and dialled five, before saying: "We're ready for you, now."

The silence returned but this time Bray was listening properly, not waiting to hear from his boss but listening to the tick of the mantle clock and the roar of the jets in the gas fire.

The highly polished door of the study opened to reveal Frank Tweed. He stepped into the room and closed the door behind him.

"What's he doing here?" Bray gasped.

He went pale.

Frank Tweed stood at the doorway, dressed in black, his ski-pants, hiking boots and black submariner sweater made him look like a cat burglar but he had a black bomber jacket over the ensemble.

"Frank the Fists, what are you doing here?" Hepher asked archly, looking over at the black figure by the door.

"Well, Seb, you asked me to come in just in case Arthur here gets all funny," wheezed Frank, taking a packet of Capstan full-strength cigarettes from his pocket and hacking ostentatiously.

"Bad cough, Frank?" Seb soothed.

"You, know how it is, smokers cough, either of you gents care for a smoke, my dad used to smoke these during the war."

"Thank you, Frank but not for me," Bray replied. Hepher shook his head. "Sebastian, please, be reasonable, Tweed and I work together, you cannot turn him against me. As, I said we all make mistakes."

"Not as many as you have, Bray. Losing the policeman Jenny had in her employ; exposing the Tweeds to investigation; allowing Regan and Murphy to get so close, this is not how we operate."

"It was a small mistake."

"How many times did you try and get rid of her; was it twice? Birmingham and London, both abject failures."

"The professor was to blame for the first error, Derek for the second," Bray objected.

"You were going to let both of them take the blame and what of dear Frank, were you going to shop him to the police."

"Who told you?" asked Bray, he was looking as white as a sheet and his words came out as a gasp.

"I did," admitted Frank, smiling at him.

"Oh, yes," added Hepher, "You even failed to poison her at a dinner and dance, Frank tells me."

"You told him that?" gasped Bray, looking at Frank with genuine awe and shock.

"Oh yes, Bray," Frank announced, "no wonder you're crapping your pants."

"I haven't done anything," complained Bray.

"Mr. Hepher told me all about your plans to shop us and walk away smelling of roses, nice way to treat three loyal servants. What were you thinking, we did all the dirty work and then you toss us aside? Not very nice is it?"

"What are you going to do?" Bray whispered.

"That's up to Mr. Hepher, here, he's in charge, now. You gave the orders, now, he does. You cocked up everything and our Mr. Hepher has been brought in to clean everything up. I had a visit from Detective Inspector Reagan today, he was asking for our cooperation to bring you in. Well, we couldn't let that happen, could we? You'd snitch on us, wouldn't you?"

"You can't do this to me," complained Bray, bristling with anger, his colour had returned to his cheeks.

"I'm afraid it is out of my hands," Hepher apologised, "shrugging his shoulders, Jenny Strong has given her orders."

"Penny Pong," Arthur sighed.

"Yes, she's a stinker! It's amazing to think that the one woman who has reached the top of her industry, is now trying to stop other women from making it to the top," Hepher exclaimed in awe.

"She's a lovely lady, I'd do anything for her," announced Frank from the door, "she had a rough time, anyone she tried to help undermined her. She'd bring them on to the board and then they would turn on her, stabbed her in the front, they did. She talked to me a lot about it."

"Yes," agreed Hepher, ignoring Bray, now, "I should think you and Derek are her biggest fans. She's kept you two out of stir for long enough and she's looked after your mother, too," Hepher noted.

"God bless her," Frank added.

"Jenny or your mother?' Hepher wondered. "Never mind. If women only worked together, they could make the world a better place. They're too busy stepping on their sister's head in the swimming pool to work as a team. Imagine the force they would be if they worked together for the common good."

"It would be bloody marvellous," Frank exclaimed enthusiastically, leaning against the doorjamb.

Hepher was not sure if he had been drinking or not.

"Have you had a few?" Hepher asked.

"Not really," Frank replied

"How many?"

"A couple, down the pub for lunch, nothing wrong with that" protested Frank. "

"No," Hepher said unconvincingly.

"What about me?" Bray pleaded, "Can't you show me some mercy?"

"I'm afraid you won't receive any clemency from me," Hepher warned. "Jenny has decided that you are a liability."

"Talk to her," he pleaded.

"She's the classic case, gets to the top of the ladder and reaches down to help her sisters up and they try and pull her off or climb over her."

"You just can't trust the corporate woman," Tweed agreed, sighing dramatically.

"Well, now, she has pulled the ladder up and here we all are. Now, we have her blocking all women on any board if she can. 'Hell, hath no fury like a woman scorned', especially when it was by another woman," Hepher added, finishing his soliloquy sadly.

"I could help her get women working together," Bray offered, "We could have a new approach instead of stopping them, we could encourage them."

"Now you're being ridiculous, you do not even like women," scoffed Hepher, "That's not what Jenny wants. You've endangered all of us with your carelessness and you've almost compromised our operations. As they say, it's curtains for you."

"What's going to happen to me?" Bray mumbled.

"That's up to you, you still have your service revolver. I take it; the professor could provide you with a poison to swallow or inject."

"Neither appeal," he confessed.

"I thought not, that's why we put something in your brandy."

"But I saw you drink from the same decanter."

"A powder at the bottom of your glass."

"Of course, another mistake," Bray confessed, looking sheepish for the first time, a broken man.

He sagged back into his chair completely defeated.

"Trouble comes, not in single spies, but in battalions," Hepher said, almost sounding sympathetic.

"Funnily enough, that was what Jo Murphy said to me at the party just before she left," admitted Bray, furrowing his brow.

"Of course, I suppose she was warning you. You should have listened to her. Goodbye Arthur, you know we don't tolerate any failure."

"What will happen, next?" he asked.

"I should go to bed or at least, lie down, the professor chose a painless exit for you."

"That was good of him. What was it?"

"He choses good old hemlock; death comes in the form of paralysis, your mind will remain awake, but your body will fail to respond and eventually the respiratory system shuts down."

"It won't be painful."

"Of course not."

"Thank you."

"You're in good company, my dear boy."

"Really?"

"Indeed, you are. Socrates was executed by hemlock after being condemned to death for impiety. The professor managed to make a concentrated form of it especially for you, he wanted you to go with dignity."

"I'm sure you are here so I don't have a chance to write a confession, isn't that so?" Bray noted drily, "Or is it to ensure, I don't make any phonecalls that incriminate you or Frank, is that it?"

"Of course not," Hepher protested.

"You don't expect me to believe that?"

"I'm afraid so, you would not get far with the letter, you would need to hold a pen and I doubt whether you could dial a number. It would be beyond you, assuming you could get to the telephone."

"Is it that bad?"

"Within a few minutes you will start to perspire and, then, you will lose the ability to move shortly afterwards."

"How long have I got?"

"I would think you will be dead, within the hour."

"Hoist by my own petard!" Bray complained.

"I'll stay with you until you go, and Frank will be here, too. Think of me as Saturn, the bringer of old age. I'll keep you company. It's the least I can do."

"I'm sure you're just making sure I won't write a letter to incriminate you, I don't think you'd be here otherwise. You know I'm right. Frank's here to stop me bolting and you to ensure there is no evidence left behind."

"Another brandy?"

"Thank you, I'll have one for the road."

"That's the spirit, acceptance is the key, feeling numb yet?"

"I do feel lethargic, but I can lift a glass." he sighed, "I am finding it difficult breathing."

"Not long, now. It's just like dying of old age, slowly you'll drift away into the arms of Morpheus never to awaken again."

"I know," sighed Bray, "thank you; it's funny, I forgot how callous you could be."

"Life can be bloody, can't it?"

Hepher held his glass in one hand and the brandy decanter in the other, he smiled at Bray slumped in his chair.

iii

That Friday, my heart was heavy when I spoke to Jo. I had taken the trouble to ring between surgery hours when Jo would be writing up her notes or making medicines. In those days, doctors made up all their remedies if they could, Jo and George had set up three chemist shops, one in Trinity Road and they therefore called the company Trinity Pharmacies.

George had gone on from there to build his public house business and left Jo to run the pharmacy company. I hated calling people with bad news but at least it would be at an appropriate time.

"Hello Jo, it's Regan, I have some more bad news," I said, speaking into the receiver when she answered.

"Go on," Jo said encouragingly.

"We've found Bray's body," I replied.

"Where?'

"On a bench next to Hereford Square."

"I know it, along the road from Gloucester Road tube station," she said, "poor man."

"Poor us, he was our only lead to the others."

"Then, you'll want me to talk to some people."

"Precisely right my dear Doctor Watson."

"I'll talk to Harold Clowes and Jenny Strong," she decided.

"Good thinking, I'll talk to Tweed and Sebastian Hepher," I added.

"Who's Hepher?" she asked.

"He's one of Jenny's right hand men," I explained.

"Right, we'll talk this evening and see where we have got to," she exclaimed eagerly, dispelling my despondency immediately.

"What if I haven't made progress?"

"Then, we keep calling each other every evening until we have. Call about six, we're going out and George hates to miss the cocktail hour."

After some enquiries, I made a few discoveries, the Tweeds had absconded and Hepher was leaving town, going to see Jenny Strong in Scotland.

I managed to ascertain the train he would be travelling on by contacting the railway and persuading the British Transport Police to check the reservations lists from King's Cross Station. He was booked on the Saturday morning train.

All I needed to do was persuade Jo to be bait, which she jumped at. The plea, for her help, took place over the phone that Friday evening before Jo and George left for a party.

Early on Saturday morning, Stephens and I picked her up and gave her a mug shot of Hepher. Then, we bought her a ticket and let her board the train to find him. It was the weekend; poor George was about to lose his Saturday morning.

Jo was quite happy to leave him in charge.

Chapter 26 -The Train Trip

The sun against the train window warmed her face and she had to close her eyes from its glare. The sky above was so pale it was almost transparent, battalions of clouds massed over the sea, which was flanked by the estuary. Above the railway, on the hills, the coniferous forests provided a verdant mass above the train. Ferns and brackens lined the tracks.

A shiver ran down her spine as they went through the tunnel. Heat and light were extinguished in seconds. When light flooded back into the carriage, Hepher spoke for the first time since Jo had discovered his carriage compartment and joined him. They had, of course, introduced themselves to each other. Jo had sat down to await Hepher's reaction.

"Did you say your name was Murphy?"

"Jo Murphy."

"You don't sound Irish."

"And you don't sound like an ignorant bigot."

"Point taken and I like a lass who says it how it is. I should be talking with a plum in my mouth too, to be at a shindig like this, a conversation in a First-Class carriage."

"It's a hardly a party but I suppose with a few more passengers and some music, maybe. Besides I like your accent. It's very unusual, very distinguished."

"Thank you, I say how I see it. It's the Yorkshire way."

"What an elegant way to disguise bad manners."

"I never thought of it as bad manners, telling the truth."

"But surely making people feel uncomfortable is bad manners."

"I don't know about that, the truth's the truth."

"It's the way you tell it, that's what counts," Jo said, smiling at him sweetly. "You can be offensive with your truth. You don't have to strike someone to hurt them."

There was a long silence between them

"I believe you're right," he decided eventually after looking at her closely for a full minute "what brings you up here, lass?"

"You, my dear," she replied.

"What would anyone want with me?"

"You are Sebastian Hepher?"

"Oh, yes, though most people call me heifer, it's a common mistake, not pronouncing my name right."

"And I'm Jo Murphy," she announced confidently.

"Doctor Jo Murphy?" he asked.

"That's correct."

"I've heard a lot about you and your death-defying escapades."

"And I've heard about you and, in the interests of being truthful, I'm afraid, not all of it is good. 'By the pricking of my thumbs something wicked this way comes'."

"Oh, you're familiar with the Scottish Play; that's my boss's favourite play."

"Well, I look forward to our meeting."

"You'll meet Jenny soon enough, I'm afraid it won't go well for you."

"I relish the opportunity of proving you wrong."

"Why do you court danger?"

"Because I want to see justice done."

"How sweet and reassuring, we have a new generation of women who want a better world."

"What's wrong with that?" Jo asked.

"Nothing, nothing at all, but it's a bit difficult to achieve when men are in charge don't you think?"

"We women like a challenge."

"Some obstacles cannot be overcome."

"We're making progress. It's a slow process. Emancipation takes years look at the abolition of slavery and Irish independence. Women are winning."

"Yes, in some areas, notably medicine. Industry will never change; I'll make sure of that."

"Really, how?"

"You know."

"Yes, I do, thank you."

"But you can't prove anything."

"No, not unless we have someone to identify you as the ringleader."

"Shame."

"Of course, the only Jenny you could be referring to is Jenny Strong."

"Why would a respectable shipping entrepreneur be involved in trying to stop women from rising up the ranks like her?"

"We seem to be coming into the station; thank you for our chat, I've at least learnt that it is you who was behind all these murders."

"Where do you think you're going?"

"This is Crewe, isn't it, I'm not going all the way to Carlisle, now, I have the information I need, I'll get the train back to London."

"I'm afraid this is the end of the line for you."

Hepher produced a Webley .455, Mk VI, and pointed it at Jo.

"Really, shooting me in a station in broad daylight and running away, how far do you think you'll get?"

"This gun, the Webley service revolver is among the most powerful revolvers ever produced. I have six shots; ample I should think to execute my getaway."

"I hate the word execute."

"A sensitive soul, I take it."

"What if I were to tell you that there are armed police on this train?"

"I would laugh in your face and call you a lying scoundrel. What sort of fool do you take me for?"

The carriage door slid open.

"An old fool," I announced from the corridor, standing back to allow the armed officer to step in the carriage. "Take the gun with your free hand, take it by the barrel and pop it on the seat beside you and my officer will not have to shoot you."

Jo glanced at me briefly before fixing her eyes on Hepher's, not pleading but challenging. I stayed outside. I did not want to make him nervous. I did not, yet, know if he had released the safety catch and I was not sure if Hepher would carry out his threat. Sergeant Stephens was next to me and he levelled his Webley semi-automatic pistol.

"Bugger off copper, I'll shoot her in the heart and save the second bullet for you and the third for me if necessary."

"Don't be a fool, look out of the window, not one passenger waiting to get on, the platform has been evacuated. I've got officers swarming on to this train, give up man," I pleaded, my heart was in my mouth. I did not like the way he was staring at Jo as if this was all her fault.

"Shut up, I'm trying to think," he snapped.

His hand was steady, the gun pointed at Jo's heart. His eyes never left Jo's. I worried that she might be provoking him. She believed he would be less likely to shoot her if he could see her eyes looking into his. She was trying to connect, as a human being to a human being, making her seem more of a friend and less of a mere target. I was not sure it would make any difference if he were the cold-hearted brute, I suspected he was.

Had Hepher killed people when he was in the army? I wondered.

"You're already threatening a member of the public with that gun, you have thirty seconds before I allow my officer to shoot you. Lower the gun," I warned.

I spoke slowly, allowing him to absorb my words.

There was a loud bang that reverberated around the carriage, Jo curled her feet up and under her, instinctively rolling into a ball. Everything went into slow motion. I noticed every last detail. Smoke and cordite curled into the ceiling.

The Webley fell to the floor with a thump.

Smoke curled from Sergeant Stephens's weapon; the firearms officer's pistol was a semi-automatic Webley & Scott MP .32.

Hepher looked stunned. It was not surprising considering the fact that he had witnessed his gun being shot out of his hand. Afterwards, he held his right wrist as if it were broken. He made no move to recover the gun.

Jo uncurled her long legs and sat up. I dashed across the carriage, picked up Hepher's weapon from the floor, set the safety catch, and sat next to Jo as my favourite firearms officer trained his gun on Hepher; the barrel was still smoking, and the smell of cordite still hung in the air. My ears were ringing.

"Well, done sergeant; are you all right doctor?" I asked, putting my hand on her shoulder for the briefest moment to reassure her.

"Fine thank you," she replied as she watched me pick up the revolver by the barrel, with my handkerchief, and place it in my overcoat pocket.

"I'll send Mr. Tweed along to identify you officially, Mr Hepher, once we have you securely locked up," I promised.

"Tweed? What are you talking about?" Hepher bluffed.

"Not Frank, we have everything we need to convict him. No, you see Derek decided to be very co-operative once he realised his brother and he could be going down for a very long time."

"Really?" Hepher sighed.

"They're fond of their mother, she's a widow and they didn't want her to be too old when they get out."

"A touching story but I fail to see what it has to do with me," Hepher maintained.

"Don't you; Derek says otherwise, he's given you all up, even Jenny."

"Don't think you're won Regan; I have contacts in high places."

"I am sure you do," I sighed, trying desperately to sound calm and collected.

One of my best men had been bought by Hepher and his colleagues in crime, I was not as confident as I sounded and nor was I that sure that Hepher would be locked up for as long as I hoped.

"Would you like me to look at that hand of yours?" Jo asked.

"It's throbbing not broken," Hepher snapped back ungraciously, shielding his injured hand from Jo's gaze or from any harm.

He was like a spoilt child. Hepher might have had influence over the great and the good but he was also a sore loser.

"Good, then you won't object to handcuffs," I noted drily, "Stand up hands behind your back."

I cuffed Hepher, returned him to his seat where he sat bolt upright and offered the seat between Jo and I to Sergeant Stephens. He had done a fine job and he deserved a sit down. The three of us sat opposite Hepher who seemed anxious all of a sudden, the confidence evaporating as the enormity of his situation began to sink in. If Tweed identified him, he would be convicted as an accessory to murder on three counts and an attempted murder.

"Looks like the end of the line for you," I quipped.

At the door, there appeared two officers from Cheshire Constabulary who had searched the carriages until they discovered my uniformed sergeant, Jo and I. Already, my warrant card was attached to my raincoat and I had secured it with a safety pin. As the three of us watched Hepher, the constables entered the carriage. They immediately made an appraisal of the situation and turned to me for advice.

"Excuse me and my sergeant for not getting up," I apologised, "it will be too crowded, take a seat, gentlemen, there's room next to Mr Hepher, let me introduce you to Doctor Murphy who helped us identify and apprehend Hepher. You mentioned this train has thirty minutes until it leaves for Carlisle, how much time have we left?"

"Twenty minutes, sir."

Instinctively, I looked at my watch.

"Good work, constables, this is our murder suspect, do you mind if my sergeant accompanies you to the station?" I asked.

The policemen smiled with satisfaction; it was a fair cop.

"Not at all, sir, we have room in the black Mariah, there's three seats in the front and the suspect will be in the back. He'll need to get the handcuffs back anyhow."

"Thank you, officers."

"What are you going to do, sir?"

All eyes in the carriage were on me.

"I will keep Doctor Murphy company on the journey to… Where are we going?" I volunteered before the officers had a chance to insinuate any inappropriate behaviour.

Our prisoner greeted my remark with silence, so standing up and looming over Hepher, I opened the jacket of his dapper three-piece, charcoal grey suit. Fishing in the inside pocket, I produced a ticket. I read the destination, but Jo could not wait for me to announce it to her.

"Where are we off to Mr. Hepher?" Jo asked, smiling.

"Oxenholme," Hepher replied.

"Arthur Ransome renamed it Strickland Junction in Swallows and Amazons as far as I know," I commented, I was not particularly well read but the novels I did know, I knew plenty about.

"You're a mine of useful information, sir," Sergeant Stephens noted, a touch of irony in his voice, enough for all to suspect he was being cheeky, but not enough for an accusation of insubordination.

"Thank you, sergeant," I breathed, giving him the benefit of the doubt only because of his superb shooting, "you'd best accompany the officers and Mr. Hepher to the police station, take his gun, too, please. Make a call to the Cumbria Constabulary to let them know we are arriving and get yourself on the next train, I'll leave word with the station master when I get there, hopefully, he'll know somewhere we can stay while we coordinate our next move. If he's not there, get yourself to the local police station and they'll tell you all you need to know. Better sign out that gun for another few days as well while you're with our Cumbrian colleagues."

"Very good, sir," he replied respectfully, this time. He knew where frivolity had its place.

"We'll both be anticipating your arrival, sergeant, but, in the meantime, we'll be gathering intelligence on the gang," I informed him.

We were professionals in front of our colleagues and the man we held in custody, but I knew what Stephens was thinking and what intelligence he thought I would be collecting with Jo. He had a sordid mind that man and I could tell it was taking all his self-control to keep himself from making some crass remark and allowing himself to smirk at my discomfort.

At least Stephens had the good grace to look down at the ground so he could not catch Jo's eye or mine.

"We'll be busy, then, have a safe journey," Sergeant Stephens added, he raised an eyebrow, but I ignored it. I was not going to respond to his miming innuendo. I knew exactly what he was insinuating. Jo and I alone would find each other irresistible.

"Yourself, I may forget, your kindness, never," Jo announced.

We all smiled, including Hepher, but his smile was more grudging than all the others. The officers escorted the handcuffed Hepher to the door, then leading Sergeant Stephens on to the platform, they frogmarched their prisoner out of the station to the waiting van. He followed like a shadow. I was fond of him, he was the best sergeant in the force, I reckoned.

Later, Stephens informed me that it was he who was given the honour of closing the thick heavy metal door on Hepher. Apparently, it slammed with a reassuring, woody thud before he scurried after the officers who marched hurriedly to the front with the other officers. Of course, he had arrested villains before, but this was the first time he had put someone in the back of a black Mariah.

They were in such a rush to get Hepher to prison that they almost drove off before he had joined them, or so Stephens claimed but he was known for his tall stories and hyperbole. At least, they wanted to get Hepher behind bars as quickly as possible. Stephens has always been an affable chap as well as a good shot and the three of them got on like a house on fire according to my erstwhile sergeant's report. He always liked to exaggerate his teamwork and experience, he was hungry for promotion and, a bit of self-aggrandisement, was not beyond him.

Chapter 27 - The Lake District

"So, what's the plan, Inspector?" Jo asked, watching the raindrops trickle down the window of the carriage, as the branch line train worked its way through the rain from Carlisle to Oxenholme.

"I'm not sure doctor," I admitted honestly, "I'll pick up some Kendall Mint Cake for the wife and mother-in-law. We'll try and find out where Hepher was booked to stay and put you in a nice place nearby. I'll stay in a room at the hotel where the nest of vipers are sleeping."

I sounded brave and confident, confessional yet competent.

"You'll be at risk," she reminded me.

"Oh no, I'll book in under Stephens's name," I assured her.

"They won't know him?"

"I doubt it. He wasn't headline like you and me. You can't risk being discovered either, check in as Mrs. Fitzpatrick," I warned, "we're close, now, we'll have them soon."

"I admire your confidence. Won't it be like finding the needle in a haystack or squeezing a camel through the eye of needle, either way an impossible task?"

"Not so doctor," I asserted confidently and went into Sherlock Holmes mode, "on the contrary, it will be a piece of cake, our arrogant assassins, will use their own names, why bother with aliases so far from the influence of any police force of any size."

"I see."

"Secondly, these chaps will only stay in the finest hotels, so we merely locate the most expensive hotel in the area."

"The Lake District is a vast area."

I could feel Jo was doubting my logic.

"Ah, but our quarry tends to favour proximity to fast transport, they'll want to be close to the station so they can get to Carlisle and then on to their destination in double quick time. It's an old intelligence ploy. Stay close to your escape route."

"Clever deduction," Jo breathed.

"They're all senior executives or Managing Directors; I'll wager, that without exception, they'll all be at the best hotel in Oxenholme."

"Very convincing, Inspector."

"Thank you, doctor."

"I would have gone to the most discreet place."

"Yes, but these men are not hiding, are they? They are awaiting Hepher and his report."

The train rattled down the track inexorably, Oxenholme bound. The rain whipped against the windows and Jo gazed out at the sodden fields, wondering how she had got to where she was. One night she was pathologist on-call, the next she was helping police with their enquiries, bouncing from Birmingham to Wimbledon to Carlisle and on to Cumbria.

"Where will it all end?" she had asked me.

It was obvious that she missed her three children and George as well as her fairly uncomplicated world and the relative safety it afforded her. Who could blame her for enjoying her existence before becoming embroiled in this caper, this quagmire, this serpents' nest?

She needed to sort out the situation and get back to some semblance of normality. The life of a General Practitioner had its problems but compared to her situation at present, and all that she had endured so far, it was a safer and easier existence. I thought about my wife and young daughter, she would be too young to miss me, but I missed the missus and the newborn baby. Susie had told me she missed me even before I went away. Duty called. I felt bad about putting Jo in danger and being unable to free us from the bomb shelter, but I vowed to do all I could to protect her from now on, no matter what happened.

That was why Sergeant Stephens was armed and why unbeknownst to her, I had signed out a revolver for myself. I convinced myself that I was confident enough to deal with any eventuality but, secretly, I knew I would feel a lot better when Sergeant Stephens met us.

I could not rely on anyone being at the station when he arrived, but he was a policeman and would leave word of his arrival at the nearest police station.

Therefore, I could leave a message for him there giving him information about where we were and what work I needed him to complete, just in case he missed the stationmaster. Of course, we would need the cooperation of the local constabulary to help us haul in the culprits. Both lost in thought, we were lulled by the ostinato of the wheels on the track and by the gentle sway of the speeding train. We would arrive at teatime; we both needed the restorative effect of Assam or Darjeeling.

Chapter 28 – Waterwitch - Neptune, the Mystic

Anton Fox was at the tiller, sitting on the sailing bench, I stood on the steps that led into the cabin and Jo leant against the boards at the back of the cockpit, her green chiffon scarf saving her hair from blowing around her face. Both Anton and I wore navy sailing caps, which Anton had brought up from the cabin. There was no mistaking the graceful lines of a Thirty Square Metre, its long, lean cigar-shaped hull and lofty, slim-line, Bermudan rig.

Built by Uffa Fox, in 1937, he had set out to make a yacht with a buoyant hull and had had succeeded in producing a vessel that was both strong and seaworthy and very quick in the water. Knud Reimers had designed a boat that was forty-three-foot long and seven foot across the beam, it had a draught of four foot eleven inches, and it displaced two- and three-quarter tons.

Her sail area was an impressive 223 square foot or thirty square metres. Waterwitch was a beauty and she hit eight knots as she keeled over and the wind filled her vast sails. She was gaining on the other boat, a wooden Wayfarer designed in 1957 by Ian Proctor and manufactured by Small Craft Limited.

With a hull and deck made from plywood it was much lighter than the more beautiful Waterwitch, but she could not compete on speed and sail area with the thirty-square-metre.

John Shallow looked over his shoulder and panic was in his eyes.

His escape was being thwarted. He could not believe it. He pulled out his revolver from the webbing belt and holster that he wore over his army surplus serge trousers and serge shirt. I think he had come back from a meeting of the Combined Cadet Force or CCF at some senior school or perhaps he was part of the Territorial Army, the military reserve for the main force. It was an eccentric choice of clothing, otherwise.

It was like pursuing a World War Two infantryman who had stolen a boat. Shallow owned the boat that he was sailing, and he was desperate to escape, but even he knew he would be out sailed by Waterwitch. He was, therefore hoping to outgun us. We knew from Hepher that he was going to meet with Jenny Strong, possibly to plan the next murder.

"Sergeant Stephens, put that bucket down and come up on deck, it looks like we're going to be shot at," I shouted.

"Coming, sir, there's not much left to bring up now," he groaned through the hatch that led from the cockpit to the cabin.

I could smell the stench of fresh vomit wafting up from inside the bowels of the boat; it almost made me sick.

"Just make sure you bring your gun, I want that boat sunk before our friend gets a shot off," I continued, anxious to push home the advantage and to add to our list of detained suspects.

Someone would talk somehow.

"Easier said than done," complained Stephens, his voice was hoarse, and it sounded like he had influenza.

"We know you like a challenge, get up here double quick. Jo, Anton, both of you get down. Stephens hurry up, will you?" I shouted.

Stephens stumbled up the stairs, holding the revolver down by his side, his fingers free of the trigger; there was no round in the chamber and five shells still to be fired if he could hold down the contents of his stomach long enough to discharge the weapon.

There was a tremendous bang that echoed around the lake and all four of us, on deck, flinched automatically. The steel pole rang like a church bell as a round embedded itself in the middle of the main mast.

"No one shoots at Waterwitch," Anton complained and turned around to rummage in the cockpit cabinets.

Moments later, he emerged with a flare gun. Shallow was satisfied that the warning shot had produced the desired effect and returned to steering his craft, ignoring us and hoping he could still get away.

Jo and I were slightly shaken by being shot at, but Stephens bravely crawled towards the bow of the boat.

Meanwhile, Anton levelled the flare gun at the disappearing boat.

"Are you mad?" I cried.

"Perhaps in the American sense of the word," Anton replied, levelling the pistol at the horizon, tilting it slightly up and pulling the trigger.

The flare coursed through the air, hurtling above the water. It struck home, hitting the sail, ripping into it, snagging in the torn folds, it ignited the cloth at the same time.

The fire spread through the canvas at an alarming rate, eating up the materials and as the wind whipped the ashes around Shallow's head, he could only watch in mounting shock as his sails smouldered, turning into ash and cinders.

The boat lost its momentum and drifted impotently, now that its propulsion was broken. Waterwitch swept across the water, hauled in tight and she was sailing herself, practically, she was so tightly trimmed.

Anton still kept one hand gently on the tiller.

"Hold this," he ordered.

I grabbed the tiller, keeping it as still as I possibly could while Anton searched for another flare. The wooden bar fought with me, but I kept her steady and the sails trim, not bad for a novice.

Shallow was turning to shoot at the boat but by now Stephens had moved along the cabin roof and was sitting on the bow, using the bow frame at the front of the boat to steady his arms.

Using his right hand, leaning on the bowsprit, he lost off a round. The following loud explosion made our ears ring and sent Mr. Shallow sprawling onto the deck of his vulnerable dinghy.

He knew the chances of someone hitting him were slim even though his boat was a sitting duck now; the policeman would have to be lucky to get off an accurate shot when moving at such speed. However, he only had to be lucky once.

Our boat, the beautiful Waterwitch was running smoothly, there was no buffeting from the waves on such a calm day, so we hunters had more than luck on their side, they had the elements helping.

Shallow, raised his gun. Anton fired another flare and Stephens loosed off another shot.

Chapter 29 - Celebrating Stephens's Shooting

i

"Super shooting Stephens," I announced, lifting a glass of whiskey and soda as we sat in the cosy, warm Saloon Bar of The Commodore Inn at Grange-Over-Sands.

"Excellent effort," Jo agreed.

"I thought Anton's shooting was pretty impressive," Sergeant Stephens replied.

"Thank you," Anton inclined his head in acknowledgement, "but hitting the target at that range from where you were sitting is nothing short of miraculous; as the French say: chapeau; I take my hat off to you."

"The mutual appreciation society's annual gathering will be called to order," I quipped, lifting the tumbler to my lips.

I am partial to a bit of whiskey and soda before dinner; the Commodore had an especially well-thought-of dining room but an even friendlier and relaxing bar. We were all having an aperitif; Jo had a brandy and soda, Stephens was swigging from a pewter jug with pale ale in it and Anton, international set show-off that he was, drank Carlsberg.

It was the thin end of the wedge, buying a Swedish boat, drinking Danish beer and driving us all here in his SAAB. I always drank Watney's bitter and drove English cars, supporting English industry. He was fuelling the Swedish economy and who knew how many people would follow suit. It made no sense to me. He claimed that Anton was a Swiss name, not Scandinavian, but you would have thought our friend was from Stockholm and his name was Berthold or Sven by the way he behaved.

He wasn't even Swiss or Austrian. I never did discover his nationality.

His 1957 Saab 93 was parked outside, according to Anton it was Scandia Snow, which meant it had a bright white paint effect, whatever that was; it was gleaming, pristine and ship shape just like his yacht Waterwitch. People gawped at the trademark trapezoidal radiator grill and the beetle-like lines, it looked live a VW that had been sat on and its headlights moved closer together.

We were all a bit rattled from the shoot-out and from chugging down to Grange in Anton's cramped three-cylinder car. At least the seats were fairly comfortable.

"Three down, three to go, cheers," I toasted, smiling first at Jo and then at the rest of the supporters' club.

All of us appreciated spending time in the presence of charm and beauty. The mood in the bar was good, celebratory even. Bray had been found dead, we had Hepher in custody and Shallow was in the local nick. They were both awaiting a pick-up and transfer back to London to answer questions from my CID colleagues.

It seemed like we had finished off the trio's rule of terror. There was Jenny to bring in and the Tweed twins to deal with, but I was confident we had ended the spate of intimidation and murder.

No longer, would that unholy trinity use their bullying tactics to threaten, maim and kill.

One of the Tweed twins had also been taken into custody and was helping us with our enquiries.

Without a paymaster, the other would fade into the background but I was sure he would crawl out of the woodwork at some later stage, working for someone else and we would nab him, then.

"Confusion to our enemies," Jo added, raising her glass.

"Skol," Anton toasted in return.

I was convinced that he wished that he had been born a Scandinavian.

He was like a Norseman, tall with wide shoulders and he had blue eyes. Anyone could have mistaken him for a handsome Swede. I wanted to scream like I was in a Munch painting.

Before you say it, I know he is Norwegian.

Jo loved galleries and often we would meet there as our friendship developed, she taught me all I know about art over the years. At this stage we were not free to go to art exhibitions but as time progressed, I learnt a lot about paintings and painters. In fact, one of our capers involved a piece of art, a heavy one, too, but I digress.

Back in the bar, we were the irritating noisy ones that everyone wanted to leave; we brash Londoners were disturbing the library like calm of that provincial watering hole. Anton had a whole gambit of amusing anecdotes about sailing. I have to admit, I was jealous, I even wondered if Jo liked him more than me. He built boats; that's all I knew. I was out of my depth and awkward, repressed if you like. He was so completely confident and did not seem to have a care in the world, a Viking with charm, a Norse God.

His blue eyes and blond hair certainly helped him to look like someone from an Ingmar Bergman movie, 'The Seventh Sea' or 'Wild Strawberries'. I had read about them both, seen a trailer at a cinema; seen a few stills in the foyer. Susie loves to go to the cinema. She goes to see that sort of film with a friend of hers, the mother-in-law comes over and she goes off to the 'flicks.

"Cheers," echoed Stephens, the hero of the hour.

Stephens was a good copper; he was a superb sergeant and I would miss him when he was promoted.

His keen eye and loyalty would be hard to replace. Shooting the gun out of Hepher's hand was a masterstroke and may have saved Jo's life; Hepher might well have pulled the trigger.

His shooting on the lake was another stroke of genius. He had shot twice, holing the boat with each shot and putting the fear of god into its captain. Poor old Shallow, as he sank, he was still trying to put out the flames that had engulfed his sails. Anton's second flare had snagged in the foresail and that had caught fire, too. Canvas burns remarkably quickly. Shallow did not have a chance to return fire. He threw his gun into the water and had to swim. The fool had no life jacket.

Anton had insisted we all wore one.

At the bottom of the lake, there was a weapon and a boat, with charred sails, that had been dragged under the surface by its heavy keel.

Shallow was left treading water. Anton brought Waterwitch alongside and I attempted to fish out the slippery customer.

Somehow, Anton got the boat close enough for me to spear his jacket with a boathook and after several failed attempts to get him aboard; we decided to tow him to the jetty. Our survivor from the wreck did not struggle, the water was freezing, and we were saving him from swimming to shore and the possibility of getting hypothermia. All he wanted was to be warm and dry.

Anton sailed onto the mooring, which was an impressive feat. Stephens was put in charge of ropes, that we had to call lines. On shore, a nine, nine, nine call brought an ambulance and a blanket as well as the local police who provided him with a cold cell for him to reflect on his bad luck.

Immediately, he came out of the water, Mr. Shallow confessed to his involvement in Jenny, Hepher and Bray's shenanigans. He promised to cooperate fully with the investigation.

That was all due to Jo.

She had gone to the hotel pretending to be Hepher's mistress and luring the gang members into playing their cards.

Poor Shallow did not stand a chance against her. Jo had tracked him down at the hotel; he had not expected that; she had challenged him, he had not expected that; she had pressed Anton into making chase as he made his escape in his own boat; he had not expected that.

He confessed straight away, warning us that Jenny would skip attending the meeting, if she was not telephoned by he and Hepher and that would result in her going back to London to destroy any incriminating evidence, which I suspected she kept at her flat in Wetherby Gardens. We had some time at least; she was in the depths of the Scottish countryside and she was not due here until tomorrow evening.

Shallow made it clear that Strong would only leave when she got a call from him in the morning. The local police had already contacted the Scottish constabulary and they were going to visit Jenny in the morning before she could leave. Hopefully, they would delay her enough to give us a chance to get to London before her. If we were able to reach the flat first, she would be lost. We would all sleep better in our beds, knowing her little nest of vipers had been destroyed.

Jo was on sparkling form; she was telling funny stories, which were close to the knuckle, 'medical' jokes, she called them. The other two went puce with laughter. I could not possibly repeat them in front of my grandson so you will have to imagine what she said.

Suffice to say that we had a wonderful evening, there were several more drinks and we had some freshwater fish, bream I seem to remember. I do remember Jo ordered two bottles of Pouilly Fume to go with it, which was generous, and it was delicious. It came from the Loire and I had never tasted such a flinty dry wine.

Trying expensive wine was a revelation; my knowledge of wine at that time was minute. It was another thing Jo educated me about during our long association. We all drank beer or whiskey in South Norwood; wine was just not on the list.

Stephens drank far too much but since he had been the hero of the hour, we all turned a blind eye. It turned out his wife was Spanish, and his in-laws had educated him in the delights of wine, and he was meant to be used to it.

Used to abusing it, I would say, certainly, if his performance that night provided anything to go by. He should have known better but pulling the trigger twice in one day affects a man.

Nowadays, he would have counselling after discharging his weapon, back then, he was expected to just get on with it. I think he had killed a few people during the war and firing the gun brought that all back to him. All I know was that his officer Hugh Watts was wounded. They had been in Italy, with the infantry, when the Bren Gun Carrier that Stephens was driving had been hit by snipers.

We never ever talked about the war but most sergeants in those days who had firearms licences had seen active service in the Second World War. If they were around, now, they would be writing Blogs about the trauma of war and suing the government for all sorts. That night, we were shattered by the experience and the meal did much to lift our spirits. Stumbling to our rooms exhausted but satiated we all slept like logs, slightly sozzled logs, more Christmas pudding than Yule log.

That night we hatched a plan to race Jenny back to London. The Scottish police Obviously, she was waiting for word from Hepher and Shallow to join them. Jo suggested she fly us back to London. Jenny would be held up and had many more miles to travel and many more changes to make once she was released from 'helping the police with their enquiries'.

Stephens went pale when he realised how we were going to head south. He would not fly. Apparently, he had suffered a bad experience in a Dakota shortly after D-Day. He categorically refused and I could not force him. He offered, instead, to catch the very early morning train down to London, the milk train, as it was known. Once there he would try and expedite the issuing of a warrant to search Jenny's flat.

I decided that he was welcome to take the longer route; Jo and I did not want to risk any delays that might occur on the west coastline. If we were all able to meet up once we reached London, then so much the better but if Jo and I arrived first, it was I who would apply for the warrant.

The next morning, we set off for the airfield. Anton's Saab was quite quick for a motor with only three cylinders. I had later ascertained, he was a biker as well as sailor and he drove like he was on his flipping bike, making bends in the lanes more like chicanes.

It was like a horizontal roller coaster. Stephens sat in the front, his hands between his legs, gripping hold of his seat and Jo and I were thrown around in the back.

Jo laughed as she slipped on the leather seat and slammed into me, I kept apologising every time I slid over on a corner of the opposite line. I did not want to crush her, so I held on to the red leather strap that hung from the ceiling above the window.

Anton made us sing to keep our spirits up as we drove at breakneck speed through the winding country road.

She sat 'neath the lilacs and played her guitar,
Played her guitar, played her guitar.
She sat 'neath the lilacs and played her guitar,
Played her guitar, played her guitar.

He sat down beside her and smoked his cigar,
Smoked his cigar, smoked his cigar.
He sat down beside her and smoked his cigar,
Smoked his cigar, smoked his cigar.

He said that he loved her but oh how he lied,
Oh, how he lied, oh, how he lied.
He said that he loved her but oh how he lied,
Oh, how he lied, oh how he lied.

They were to be married but somehow, she died,
Somehow, she died, somehow, she died.
They were to be married but somehow, she died,
Somehow, she died, somehow, she died.

He went to the funeral just for the ride,
Just for the ride, just for the ride.
He went to the funeral just for the ride,
Just for the ride, just for the ride.

He sat on the tombstone and laughed till he cried,
Laughed till he cried, laughed till he cried.
He sat on the tombstone and laughed till he cried,
Laughed till he cried, laughed till he cried.

The tombstone fell on him and squish-squash he died,
Squish-squash he died, squish-squash he died.
The tombstone fell on him and squish-squash he died,
Squish-squash he died, squish-squash he died.

She went to heaven and fluttered and flied,
Fluttered and flied, fluttered and flied.
She went to heaven and fluttered and flied,
Fluttered and flied, fluttered and flied.

He went to Hades and frizzled and fried,
Frizzled and fried, frizzled and fried.
He went to Hades and frizzled and fried,
Frizzled and fried, frizzled and fried.

Now, the moral of this story is never telling lies,
Never tell lies, never tell lies.
Now, the moral of this story is never telling lies,
Never tell lies, never tell lies.

We all thoroughly enjoyed learning a new song and it only took a few rounds of the lyrics for us to know it off by heart. In fact, I sang the song in my head several times while we were flying back to London. I still sing it to my grandchildren. It's a great drinking song and I even sing it in my head on long car, train or plane, journeys to relieve the boredom

Jo was dressed for flying, a pair of baby blue Capri pants and a cream blouse topped off with a United States of America Air Force, brown leather jacket, obviously made for a small thin man. If her outfit had been a glass, you could say that she had been poured into it without saying when. Every piece of material clung to her body; the Capri pants looked like they had been sprayed on to her body and her jacket looked like it had been tailored to fit her like a glove. It certainly showed off her curves.

I dismissed all these thoughts; I was married, she was married, I was allowed to look, and I was certainly able to admire her, nothing more. She had a wonderful body, tall, lithe and strong. Jo was a slender Boudicca with curves in all the right places. If George knew I was thinking those thoughts I think he would have punched my lights out, but he was far away, and she was so close I could almost lean over and kiss her.

We were heading for White Cross Bay Airfield on the Allthwaite Road, after a few miles we turned on to the Cartmel Road; Sergeant Stephens was going on to Cark Station to start his journey to London.

With the help of our Scottish Constabulary colleagues and a fair wind, he would easily beat Jenny on her journey from the Arran Islands back down to London, especially if they dragged their feet sufficiently when she was 'helping them with their enquiries'.

Anton had graciously agreed to be chauffeur and I think he was expecting to have Jo next to him on the journey. I would not have been surprised if his hand had slipped off the gear lever and onto Jo's thigh, 'by mistake', if she had. Maybe, I as being unfair, transferring my own lustful thoughts onto him.

Whether Jo was being wise or just kind to Stephens, she insisted on sitting in the back with me.

Maybe she felt I was the safest out of the three of us.

I had noticed Stephens' lustful looks as he got more pie-eyed that night and I know Jo would have picked up on that. She was acutely aware of her sexual power as well as the fight she had to be taken seriously as a woman. Maybe, she just wanted to be close to me in the back because she enjoyed having me close.

Anton was the only unknown quantity, but he was also the only single man amongst us, so it was only Jo's wedding ring that might prevent him from making a move on her. There was just too much testosterone in one confined place and me being thrust against Jo's thighs and breathing in her Guerlain perfume did not help with my moral fortitude.

I had to fight hard to restrain the animal urge to dive on her neck and kiss her nape. Instead, I stared out of the window, hanging onto the strap and trying to prevent my thighs from sliding over to Jo's side of the seats. Ignoring Jo's giggles when her bottom slid over on to my side and her thigh brushed against mine.

She thought it was fun; I thought it was torture.

Stephens was suddenly silent, whether it was because he was hung-over or whether singing the song had given him a headache, I never learned. Anton was concentrating on his driving, enjoying setting up the SAAB for all the bends, braking before the bend and accelerating into the corners, then, opening the engine out on the straight.

Stephens, as a driver, and a police driver at that, admired Anton's driving but his stomach did not appreciate the bends and I am sure his spinning head hated the sudden acceleration and braking. I still remember the roar of the engine, Anton was keeping the revs high and the motor was working hard but I must admit he was a skilful sailor and driver, intuitive and fluid and I admired the nippy car and the man who was getting us to the airfield as fast as was humanly possible.

White Cross Bay, known locally as Cark Airfield, was home to what we know today as the RAF Mountain Rescue Unit. It arrived there in 1944 from around the corner at RAF Millom; its job was seeking out aircraft that had crashed on the Lakeland Fells.

As well, '188 Gliding School' continued to use the airfield until May 1947 when it was sold off; White Cross Bay re-opened later for private use, initially by the 'Lakes Gliding club'. In 1959, there were a few private air clubs and this one had a Piper and a Cessna for hire.

I had never flown before and the idea of a single engine plane made me uneasy. Jo had made a phone call from the hotel, the previous evening, before our celebrations began, to arrange everything and that meant that they were expecting us.

Besides that, the ground crew would have heard the howling SAAB a mile off; the white profile of the car would have stood out against the green fields and tarmac. It was by no means a subtle arrival. Remember cars were few and far between in the fifties, especially in rural areas, trucks and Land Rovers predominated.

Anton was curious about the plane's power source.

"What type of engine do these planes use?" He asked as we swept through the gates.

"A six-cylinder engine," Jo replied, nonchalantly.

One engine with only six cylinders to get airborne; I did not like the thought of that. All the planes I was willing to fly in had two engines. Plus, the engine seemed a little small for an aeroplane, the Rolls had a six-cylinder engine and that could not fly. I knew the Lancaster bombers had four twelve-cylinder engines and the Spitfire's Merlin engine was twelve, too. It seemed we were six cylinders short. I did not like flying just like some people do not like liver; I had never tried it. I later learnt to love flying and I already knew that liver cooked lightly is delicious.

The white and red Cessna 172 had a tricycle landing gear, being a variant of the tail-dragger Cessna 170 with larger elevators and a more angular tailfin. Jo turned me from train-spotter to plane-spotter that day. I looked up all about light aircraft after the caper, using my local library to find out all I could. I did not know, at that stage, that a petrol-head could be into cars and planes. Our 172 had fixed wheels on the front under the wings and the third wheel under the tail.

The only 172 I had known, up until then, was the double decker that went from Honor Oak Park to Farringdon Station via, New Cross, Elephant and Castle, Waterloo and Aldwych.

At least, the plane looked new.

That made me feel slightly less nervous, but not much. I think it was a year or two off the production line. It was American so that guaranteed reliability, I supposed. The Americans had built Boeings and Dakotas. I had heard of no accidents during the Berlin airlift.

"You three grab a tea while I go over the flight plan and complete the pre-flight checks, it will take some time," she announced as she walked off with the flight supervisor.

After forty-five minutes and two cups of tea, I visited the toilet and when I came back Anton was shaking Jo's hand and trying to kiss her cheek, the cheeky so and so.

Jo managed to turn to Stephens and shook his hand, so Anton was left pouting at a black and white photo of the airfield in the Second World War. With that Stephens and Anton left for the SAAB and the railway station.

I was feeling small and vulnerable, only Jo's confidence kept me from feeling petrified. I would have followed her to the ends of the earth in those days, so boarding a plane in a gale was nothing to me. I would have her all to myself for a few hours; a starving man will take any crumbs you throw at him.

It was freezing outside, a strong wind coming off the bay, wet and chilled, smelling of salt, of seaweed and of minerals. Climbing into the plane only took us out of the howling wind; it was not much warmer inside. On the other hand, it much was quieter once we had slammed the doors and struggled to get comfortable in our seats and strapped on the strange seat belts that just went across the lap.

She was dressed for flying; I was dressed for investigating, wearing my beige mackintosh over my grey suit and my brown trilby were my only protection from the elements, apart from my brown leather gloves and a Black Watch tartan scarf, a present from the wife, last Christmas. Then, Jo opened the window. I was just about to tell her off and tell her to shut it when the Flight Supervisor arrived at the side of the plane and I realised that it was the only way they could communicate. I would have to put up with the draught.

"Everything all right?" he shouted up at the window.

"All okay," Jo replied, smiling down at him and then watching as he made his way to the front of the aircraft clear of the propeller.

"Okay," he called as loudly as before. They started their shouting match in earnest after that.

"Mixture rich, carb heat cold, throttle open a quarter inch," Jo cried out of the window.

"Contact!" he cried.

"Clear prop!" Jo replied, raising her voice even louder so he could hear her more clearly.

The man spun the propeller before Jo engaged the gear to show that the propeller could spin. I just wanted the blooming window closed, the chill wind was crawling into the cockpit and finding every chink in my clothing and I did not like it.

She turned the ignition to start her up. Nothing happened,

"Give her another try," suggested the ground crew member.

"Roger,' she readily agreed.

I was about to quip about the fact that he had said his name was Norman, and not Roger, but I decided it against it. I knew about time and place, even then. She repeated her mantra about rich, cold and inches, turned the ignition and the engine roared into life, shaking the airframe and filling our ears with noise. I felt like a cocktail in a shaker as the plane gyrated around us. The sound of the engine was deafening, six cylinders of raw, excessive sound.

"Chocks away!" Came a disembodied voice and I assumed the supervisor had taken away the wooden blocks that kept the front wheels from rolling.

The next minute, he had headed to the tail of the aircraft.

Finally, Jo closed the window and the wind died down, she moved the throttle forward and we eased towards the runway. The propeller had vanished. It had seemed such a huge feature of the plane when I looked out at as we sat in the plane, while Jo carried out her pre-flight equipment checks but now it had become a blur of high-speed spinning.

I really did not notice it at all; it had completely disappeared swallowed up by its own speed.

I was amazed. The vibration reached fever pitch, I was being jostled about and shaken up like a milk shake in a blender.

Jo steered with her feet, this plane relied on the pilot pressing the right rudder pedal the skid pivoted to the right, creating more drag on that side of the plane and causing it to turn to the right.

My whole body shook, and I tried to look calm and composed. I thought my hat was going to be shrugged off my head, so I put one hand on the crown to keep it down. I did not want to be sprawling around the aircraft looking for my hat as we took off, that was for certain.

That was not the only thing I had to keep down that morning, we had eaten fried eggs, bacon, sausages and fried bread for breakfast at the hotel. It was a two-fold move. One to get rid of my hangover and two because I knew we would not be eating until late afternoon, a hearty breakfast, I thought was a healthy idea. We were in the northwest, after all, there were local farms with pigs and poultry, fresh food was available and barely post-rationing, we had to get out protein where we could in those days.

I regretted my choice as we trundled our way to the landing strip. I had both a nervous disposition and a sensitive stomach. It was bad enough trying to recover from the effects of the alcohol, but the greasy unctuous breakfast seemed to be bubbling away in my belly as the plane trundled over the grass to the runway. It almost proved too much for me.

Steering a plane on the ground is not easy.

There is not enough speed to bring most of the controls into action. To turn left or right, you have to increase speed on one side and decrease it on the other. By dragging one wheel you turn in that direction, which is counter intuitive. While being so much less effective than a steering wheel and wheels that steer, the drag method, also jolted us around much more, too, which did not do any favours to my queasy stomach.

This method only gave the pilot a limited control of the direction the craft was moving in while taxiing or beginning the take-off run. Once there was enough airflow over the rudder for the rudder to become effective, steering was a doddle, but we were a long way from that happy situation.

"Are you okay, Inspector?" she asked, glancing briefly up from her instruments and then returning to look out of the windscreen.

At that point, we were rumbling along over divots in the grass and Jo was manoeuvring the craft to the left at the same time.

"Fine, doctor, thank you," I replied, feeling a small amount of reflux travel up my throat.

"Dick, you look a little green about the gills," she teased. "Are you sure you are all right?"

"Just getting used to the steering method over this type of terrain," I bluffed.

I tried to muster up a smile but giving up when I realised that she was intent on getting us airborne and not establishing a rapport with me before that was achieved. On our walk from the apron, Jo had already assured me she was familiar with this method of flying and the less common 'differential braking', in which the tail-wheel is a simple, free caster mechanism, like a wheel on some furniture, and the aircraft is steered by applying brakes to one of the main wheels in order to change direction.

I failed to realise the difference between both methods no matter how many times she explained it, then and, of course, subsequently. Nowadays, this is usually integrated with the rudder pedals on the craft to allow an easy transition between wheeled and aerodynamic control.

My throat was dry, I wore a fixed grin as we rumbled along the grass towards the runway, which I could not make out, it just looked like one very narrow, very long field with hedges all around. I wondered if it was long enough for us to take off on. I was less than impressed by our speed.

It was noisy in the plane so neither of us spoke. We were strapped in and, I folded my hands in my lap, glad that I was wearing my lined brown leather gloves; coppers always invest in warm gloves, it comes from years of freezing fingers on point duty.

My head and hands were warm, but my feet and chest were frozen. My shiny shoes were no comfort in the aircraft and the soles had got damp on the walk across the airfield.

A jumper, or a 'tank-top', would have helped to keep me warm. All I had, to keep out the cold, was a nylon shirt and a woolly vest and it was, then, that it dawned on me why the pilots wore such thick sheepskin leather jackets.

After her first turn, she motored up the airfield and then after an age of rattling and rumbling across the worst terrain in England, she took a sharp right so that she could turn into the wind for take off.

She made us spin 360 degrees; and it made me dizzy; she performed the manoeuvre so quickly. The molehills and dips strewn across our path would have made a seasoned pirate feel seasick.

There was still dew on the roof of the cabin. I could feel the cold crawling under my coat and trying to sneak into my suit. Miraculously, the seats were not wet, but I guessed that Jo had wiped them down when she was completing her pre-flight checks, it would be the type of considerate thing she would do. A scrunched-up towel on the floor between us seemed to confirm my suspicions. The moment that I acknowledged its presence, we accelerated sharply.

The taxi-ing had been unpleasantly uncomfortable. The take-off was bone shaking. Scarcely, had I recovered from our about turn on the runway, I was being shaken to pieces as we rolled increasingly quickly across the field. At one stage I thought the whole airframe would shake apart. I wondered what or who would shatter first.

This was a 'rolling take off'.

Suddenly, I saw the tight grip Jo's gloved hands had on the throttle as she pushed the plane further and further and faster and faster along the runway. The shaking got worse and worse and the speed, faster and faster. It was, then, that I decided I wanted to walk to London, but I was too petrified to move and my mouth so grim set that I could not open it to speak or scream.

Everything was flying by us, the bare branches of the trees flew by, the long, lush, green grass of the airfield whizzed past the window, spongy under our wheels so we were buffeted about by the undergrowth and uneven ground. Hurtling along the runway was like being next to Jo in the Rolls when she sped along the road, only we were much higher up and the ride was a lot bumpier.

Whereas the Rolls Royce was a vehicle that was all comfort and sumptuous luxury, the plane was sparse and practical. It was all austerity and simplicity. It could have done with thicker cushions on the seats and with some sophisticated suspension on the wheels. My spine tingled and a trickle of cold sweat ran down from my armpits as we hared along the grass at breakneck speed, heading for the hedge.

I glanced over at Jo and she wore a look of grim determination. Then, it happened. We were airborne. There was no more shaking and bumping, we were floating, and it was infinitely more preferable than being on the ground.

I knew for certain because there was this incredible feeling of weightlessness. I literally felt as light as a feather. We had left the shackles of the earth and we were actually flying. Looking over at Jo, I noticed her face had relaxed and she was smiling. I was glad one of us was enjoying the experience.

From that moment onwards, I began to relax and trust in her, her abilities and the plane. The initial foreboding was replaced by this amazing feeling of freedom, we had left the confines of the earth and we were soaring above it.

A feeling of euphoria filled me, washing away my anxiety.

I decided not to worry about the landing that was about two hours and two hundred and forty nautical miles away. In no time, we were way above the ground and below the clouds but climbing.

Flying is an amazing experience; I love it thanks to that moment. I am always amazed by the take off, even to this day.

It's a miracle how bigger and bigger planes manage to take off and land safely, they just get larger and larger, longer or double-decker. Back then, only the select few flew due to the size of the aircraft and the expense.

Flying in a small plane was mindboggling. I knew how the Spitfire pilots must have felt as they took off.

Being in a light aircraft was sheer bliss. A word I had picked up from her; I was even beginning to sound like Jo, it was heaven anyway. The plane no longer vibrated, it quivered in the wind, trembling almost imperceptivity.

We were cruising at about one hundred and twenty miles per hour. I knew the plane could go faster but hurtling above the ground in a small tube made me realise how fast that actually was.

It was a strange feeling the speed felt no greater than cruising along the streets of Battersea looking for criminal activity. The noise was slightly more annoying than Sergeant Stephen's profane and inane chatter.

We were buffeted about by the wind at first, a squall coming off the Irish Sea but then Jo climbed a few hundred feet, eased back on the throttle and we settled into a wonderful motion as straight as an arrow at about two thousand feet off the ground and were travelling at about one hundred and fifty miles per hour at that stage.

It was amazing and the view was incredible.

I do not like heights, never have done but this was different, I wasn't on the sixth floor of a building, I was behind a screen in a seat and I could see fields stretching across the horizon, hedges and roads criss-crossing our path, mirror lakes like shards of broken glass reflected the grey curtain of sky above our heads.

It was blooming cold up there and Jo put on the heater, which was remarkably effective, blowing hot air from the engine into the cabin. Soon we were toasty. The six-cylinder engine kept us airborne and gave off a huge amount of heat.

We ventured a conversation, which became a shouting match as we tried to hear each other over the loud thrum of the petrol engine. It lasted long enough for me to compliment her on her flying skills and for her to explain our route. I left her to look out for landmarks and watch the dials in front of her.

We were flying on instruments, but she had the pilot habit of checking everything visually just in case the instruments malfunctioned. I was happy with that. Jo was enigmatic, she kept her thoughts to herself, but she did share the fact that she had been thinking of her sister, Moira, who had married into the Finucane family. She told me she always thought of Paddy Finucane the air ace when she flew. He had been a great hero of the Second World War.

Paddy had also been one of my sister's crushes during the same war; Juliet was eight years older than me because my mother had miscarried several times before she had me. Juliet knew him as Paddy, it was his nickname and the name the press gave him: Wing Commander Paddy Finucane. He was actually called Brendan Eamonn Fergus Finucane and he was awarded the Distinguished Service Order, DSO and The Distinguished Flying Cross, DFC. He was an RAF pilot who had been credited with five or more enemy aircraft destroyed in dogfights and that made him an ace, but he was also the youngest person ever given command of a fighter wing in the history of aerial combat.

'Paddy' Finucane was credited with twenty-eight aerial victories, five probably destroyed, six shared destroyed, one shared probable victory, and eight damaged.

On 15 July 1942, Finucane took off with his flight for a mission over France. His Spitfire was damaged by ground-fire. Finucane attempted to fly back to England but was forced to ditch into the sea and subsequently vanished.

As you know, the name was more recently associated with Brendan Finucane's nephew, the Northern Ireland solicitor, Pat Finucane. During 'The Troubles', he defended both sides of the political and religious divide in all manner of legal cases. He ended up winning human rights actions brought against the British government and he was allegedly murdered by Loyalist paramilitaries acting in collusion with the British government intelligence service, MI5, in 1989.

His uncle, 'Paddy' Finucane was a brave and successful pilot and his exploits were widely reported and I think my sister fell in love with the dashing and daring chap. She was only sixteen; impressionable and bursting with hormones like any teenager.

Finucane was a fine role model, brave, handsome and in the newspapers. What more could a girl with an open-heart want? She was devastated when he disappeared.

Fortunately, she was young.

She fell in love with a warehouse worker at the Ranks, Hovis, and McDougall, what was known as the 'Battersea Flourmills'. It was huge factory that was next to Battersea Bridge that employed hundreds of local people.

We spoke about the war briefly, when we landed.

I was twenty-seven in 1959, so I was only five when war broke out and I was eight, in forty-two, when Finucane was flying about, almost thirteen when it was all over. Jo was ten years older than me; I was born in 1932. Juliet was thirteen when the war broke out, sixteen when Finucane's face was first shown in the newspapers and twenty when she married a Canadian and moved to Lethbridge, Alberta.

Jo's war was spent in Bromley House, in Kilpedder, but she did tell me about what happened to her aunt as we travelled in the police car that I had arranged to pick us up and take us from the plane to London.

Jo's aunt was killed in a direct hit to a pub in the city. All they found of her was a hand with her wedding ring on it.

Chapter 30 - Flight of Fancy - The Ride of the Valkyries

Flying to White Waltham was a trial but soon we were approaching one of the oldest, famous, and the largest grass airfield in the country. The airfield is still situated just four miles from the A4, the road from Bristol to London between White Waltham to the south and Maidenhead to the east, if you know the area.

The important thing for us was that Central London was only thirty-five miles away. The airfield might have been the largest airfield in England but to me it looked like a green silk handkerchief, small, slippery and inadequate for the task in hand.

On our journey, the engine had become a dull drone in the background but that was because we had been lost in our thoughts. I was trying to work out how we could tie up the loose ends of the case and running through the evidence we had so far.

Jo was flying the plane. Suddenly, I was dying for the toilet and I was so relieved when the airfield appeared as we broke through the clouds.

Then, Jo, who had been sitting calmly looking at her windscreen and instruments, just as unexpectedly, leapt into action. Her hands and eyes moved over the instruments in a flurry of activity. During the flight, I had just been bouncing about in the plane, listening to the loud noise and trying to pretend I was in a car.

When we were about to land, I suddenly felt nervous. We were travelling at a rate of knots, but I could see both the altimeter and the speedometer dials were moving backwards, which was very unsettling because we were losing height quickly and unsettling because we seemed to be going too fast.

It was also unsettling because we were aiming for a narrow airstrip.

Not satisfied with the instruments, I stupidly looked out of the window and confirmed my fears. Taking off on grass had been traumatic; landing on grass was going to be worse, I felt convinced.

I was sure that we were dropping too fast and that our horizontal speed was equally alarmingly fast. The ground was coming closer and closer, the plane did not seem to be going any slower, although the rate of knots was dropping, according to the dials, but not enough in book. Our height was diminishing by the second.

Ahead of us, I could see the wooden hut and four airplanes lined up on the grass beside it. Jo flew past, dipping her wings, and circled above the airfield, a pocket of wind lifted us up and it was like being on an elevator, my stomach lurched but by now my breakfast had digested and if fear had not distracted me, I might have even been hungry.

Coming in for her approach, we lurched upward, there were pockets of air all around. Jo was an experienced pilot and as we raced towards the ground, she increased the power to push through the air currents and adjusted the trim. This was the worst part for me, and I felt my body stiffen and rubbed my clammy hands on my knees. I could feel sweat forming on the brim of my hat.

I had almost forgotten about my desire to urinate, almost. The wingtips seesawed slightly and then we were sinking like a boat, I could feel us going under. Sinking too fast, as far as I was concerned. Still we continued dropping in the sky, nearing the ground.

Rather too rapidly for my liking, the ground came up to meet us and I felt even more nervous, then. In part my anxiety was stemming from the approach of trees and shrubs, which I felt sure we would hit and would flip us over.

Then, the most enormous thump shook the whole plane, making the airframe shudder. We bounced up like a kangaroo and landed more gently, the frame rumbled, before we bounced up again, just a short hop and, finally, we made contact with the ground and stayed there.

A mere jump, skip and hop was all it needed for my heart rate to stop soaring to record levels. I felt like Roger Bannister after he had run the four-minute mile. I reckon he was less sweaty than me and his heart was not trying to jump out of his chest.

The speed at which we hit the ground shook me up, it was my first landing and the speed at which Jo decelerated shook me up even more, I felt like a Café Royal Martini by the time we had reached the apron, thoroughly shaken.

We taxied to the control tower, if you could call it that.

It was some huts with a glass conning tower on the top and a mass of aerials. Waiting in the mess, drinking his tea, was a policeman in full uniform, I noticed the three stripes on his arm. The driver introduced himself and, immediately, Jo handed her cigarettes out and Anderson acted as if it was Christmas. He had always smoked R.N, which was the NAAFI fag, the NAAFI or Navy, Army, Air Force, Institutes, being the armed forces shop at every airbase, barracks and naval docks. He had only once or twice come across Senior Service, he took one enthusiastically and, after

Jo lit it for him, using her lighter, and he had drawn on the tip hungrily before he extracted the cigarette from his mouth and blew an appreciative cloud of smoke from his nose and led us to the car, which was the standard Wolsey issue. It was waiting for us outside the 'aero-club' hut. As Anderson opened the door for us, we slid into the backseat.

I felt relieved to be back on terra firma and easing into the red leather bench seat of a Wolsey, there was something comforting about the smell and the familiar feel of the leather seats and their thick cushions. Perhaps driving was better than flying. Furthermore, the car was warm inside. Anderson had obviously kept the heating on during his trip down from west London.

After chatting briefly to the driver, Sergeant James Anderson for the record, we learned that he was ex-Royal Navy, a Leading Seaman on a destroyer doing convoy protection duties. We settled back into our seats and started our conversation about the war brought on by Anderson's proud proclamation about his previous profession. He had clearly had a good war; he came back, which was a miracle when you were trying to get across the Atlantic with all the U-boats around.

As our speed increased, the road noise and roar of the engine became louder and this meant that Anderson could not keep up with the conversation. Being in the front, too close to the noisy engine, he merely contented himself with concentrating on driving up to 'Old London Town'. The two-hour and a half hour flight had felt like eight, we were exhausted so we relaxed into our seats. That was when she told me about Finucane and her time in the Blitz. I was in Kent when the Blitz came, not a sensible place with hindsight but at that time the bombers were taking their load of bombs to London exclusively.

I was out of the firing line; Jo and her family, in the city, were not.

When the bombs started dropping in England, Jo was still at school, she was on school holiday at the outbreak of hostilities in July 1940, when the Battle of Britain was being fought; she was in the East End of London. As long as the Germans targeted the airfields Londoners were safe. She went back to school on the first day of September. Jo was just eighteen, two years older than Julie. On 4th September the Blitz started when Hitler changed the focus on raids to the civilian population. Jo was to be sent to Liverpool and across the Irish Sea to Dublin and from there she could get a bus to Bromley in Kilpedder.

The night before she left, her father sent Jo to spend the night with her aunt at the Three Jolly Weavers in Lever Street. She slept in one of the top rooms and the next day left for Liverpool from Euston. That night the pub that she had been staying in suffered a direct hit.

"What happened?" I asked.

I knew the terror of an air raid that my mother tried to hide and the jangling of my own nerves.

"My father closed all his pubs and took his men to dig for his sister," she explained.

"Did they find her?" I asked.

"They dug for four days, clearing all the rubble away. The only thing that they found, which belonged to my aunt was her hand. My father recognised the engagement ring. They never found her husband."

"That's terrible," I sighed, feeling myself about to wretch, my imagination can be too vivid sometimes. I can still see that cold pale hand in my dreams sometimes.

"There's more," Jo added, I hoped she did not see my involuntary shudder as I sat in a sombre corner of the back seat. If she had, she ignored it and just ploughed on.

"They found the nurse who had taken over my room after I left," she said.

"Where?" I asked.

"In the cellar."

"What happened to her?" I instinctively inquired, once a cop and all that, I immediately regretted it.

"They found her in the corner of the cellar with her hands blown off, she had bled to death through her wrists."

I remained silent, my lips were sealed, I tried to look sympathetic, but it was tricky when I had vomit crawling up my throat and into my mouth. I swallowed hard and fixed her gaze. Our eyes communicated our sadness and loss.

I shuddered to think that if she had been there one more night, she would not be here next to me. It was at that moment that I realised how much I was falling for her. It was corny and unrealistic, I was in love with my Susie, but I suppose I was also a little bit in love with Jo, too.

That was allowed.

I was never going to act on any of my feeling for her. I was quite prepared to love her from afar. It was going to be a story of unrequited love but a love of sorts, nonetheless.

I was doing nobody any harm.

No one was caused any pain, except for me, and that as just the ache in my heart every time I thought of her.

Chapter 31 - Getting Closer

We arrived back at '88', Jo's home on the West Side, at six, just in time to see Bubs who was there, helping put the children to bed. George was visiting the Black Lion in Kilburn High Road. I left Jo and was driven back to Penge by Anderson. We got to know each other a bit better over cigarettes that we shared on this part of the journey. I sat in the seat next to him so we could have a proper chat.

I had missed Susie and our baby boy, Brian. He was named after Susie's uncle. We both needed rest but there was no rest for the wicked in those days and the righteous had none, just for good measure. Sergeant Stephens picked me up at eight thirty, I had barely spoken to Susie, but I had managed to help settle Brian and finish my high tea. It was a moveable feast; gammon, boiled broccoli, potatoes and bread and butter. Taking the last morsel of bread and swilling the last of my tea, I heard the doorbell and rushed to answer it.

Just at the same time, Brian had got to sleep, and Susie came downstairs to the kitchen. She and I knew that it would be Stephens and that it was a call to arms. She shrugged her shoulders. Behind every good copper is an equally long-suffering and supportive wife. She has always been a real anchor for me and that's why I would never do anything to hurt her, ever.

In the car driving to central London, Stephens filled me in.

"Okay sergeant, what's going on, it better be good, I've only just got back from Cumbria," I complained.

"I know that, guv' I was with you," Stephens sighed.

Settling into my seat and buttoning up my mackintosh against the cold, I prepared for action, "Jenny's still in Scotland, I thought we'd have at least one night to recoup. You must be tired, too, aren't you?"

"I slept on the train, I'm as fresh as a daisy," he elucidated.

"I'm surprised you didn't miss your connections," I hissed with real envy, the plane trip had taken it out of me and sapped my strength. I just wanted to put my feet up.

"I got someone to wake me up at Crewe, then, I woke up just as we pulled into the station here," he boasted, smiling, he had obviously noticed I was looking tired, "I was lucky with the connections, too. I telephoned from St. Pancras and Anderson was standing by, he picked me up from Clapham South and he went on to Amen Corner by tube himself. It was so smooth, no need for flying."

"So, what's up, why are you here?" I asked, realising that I was badgering him but too tired to care, "I thought we were going to hatch a plan tomorrow. We failed to get the warrant today."

"That's all changed, sir, the police operator has contacted Jo, we're heading to 88, West Side, to pick her up, then we'll move to Wetherby Gardens," explained Stephens.

The Three Musketeers were to see action again, I thought ruefully, not for a moment thinking, at the time, that firearms would be used. I still had my gun from our trip to the Lake District. I handed it to Stephens when I discovered he had handed his own weapon back in.

"So why Wetherby Gardens?" I asked, settling into another Wolseley, the same black paintwork, and the same red leather.

"CID has been keeping the top floor flat of No. 1 under surveillance," Stephens, replied, smiling happily, he had some good news for me, I could tell by his mood.

"A bit out of our area, Stephens?" I noted, wondering why CID would include me.

"It's Jenny Strong's 'pied a terre', apparently, but she's not been there for weeks and CID told me they sent someone to Scotland to interview her so she's not coming back, soon."

"So, CID should get a warrant to search, surely?" I insisted, "Even they can't just barge in there."

"That's in the pipeline, but the sergeant contacted me to say that the surviving Tweed twin was seen sitting in a green Mini van in the same street."

"Eagle eyed, sergeant, he did well to spot Tweed," I said, looking over admiringly at Stephens who shot me a brief sideways look and a smile.

Stephens knew what I meant: good sergeants were difficult to find. He was a good man; I could not begrudge him his kip on the train. Envy is a terrible thing.

"Sergeants do all the work while our detective inspectors get all the credit," he joshed, flipping on the windscreen wipers as the rain came.

The wipers swatted away the derisory drops. I was back in my comfortable leather seats, the familiar cushions; I knew them better than my own settee.

"Well, they don't seem to lose much sleep over it, do they. Whereas inspectors get all the worry," I persisted.

"You sound war weary, sir, never mind, the doctor will be good medicine for you," he quipped.

I decided not to dignify his remark with a response.

There was a crescent moon that kept hiding behind the advancing cumulus clouds, their bellies swollen with rain. It was just a local cloudburst, but it did not put either of us in a good mood, Stephens because he had to reduce his speed in the wet and concentrate on the slippery streets in twilight.

I suppose, for myself, I was in a reflective mood, I was feeling tired and these sombre evenings reminded me of too many nights on point duty, too much time freezing to death on the beat. It always made me feel morose.

I hated working on winter nights.

Summer was a different kettle of fish. Plus, I was feeling down, down about not being with Jo anymore and depressed about my time away from being with Susie and Brian. I was torn between my feelings for all of them. I enjoy routine and certainty, not angst and turmoil.

"So why are they letting us know about it?" I asked, knowing it was not like the boys from CID to share the glory or an arrest with us mere mortals.

"Someone obviously likes your smile, sir," he quipped.

"So, we're both in the dark."

It was typical of CID; they would let you in occasionally, but you would never know why they had.

"Some things never change."

We were left to our own thoughts as we drove up the hill to Crystal Palace and down the other side to Streatham, joining the South Circular Road. Stephens raced from Cavendish Road to the racetrack, took a left into Bowood Road and then left again into Wakehurst, pulling up outside the front door.

Chapter 32 - Wetherby Gardens - Show Down

i

We collected Jo of course, on our way and of course, I jumped in the Rolls with her, leaving Stephens to lead the way. Like an addict, I needed to smell the leather and Guerlain mix and feel Jo close to me. I loved sitting so high up in the fat leather seats with walnut on the dashboard and luxuriously thick carpet at my feet.

'I suppose, I could get used to the high life,' I thought.

It was no detour to pass by her house; it was on the way to Wetherby Gardens from my home. Stephens had taken the A215, joined the South Circular and passed the front of 88, West Side, only doubling back, briefly to pick up the good doctor. She must have been waiting expectantly because she dashed out as soon as I rang the bell. I told her we had instructions to meet the CID on the corner and that they were waiting in a white Ford.

On our way, we passed an accident on Lavender Hill, at the junction of Latchmere involving a motorcyclist and a car. There was an ambulance and a police motorcyclist in attendance. We did not stop.

"That reminds me of my first R.T.A.," I exclaimed before explaining needlessly that is stood for road traffic accident. I hoped I did not sound patronising; she was a doctor after all and would have been familiar with the parlance.

"When was it?" she asked, she was an expert at getting people to talk.

"It was in fifty-four. It involved a motorcyclist, a car and a truck. After the ambulance had been, I was told to help clear up; I picked up the helmet and the rider's head was still in it," I bragged, it was a good story, though the memory of it made me shudder inside.

I hoped it would shock Jo for some unknown reason; maybe it was a story that made me look tough, tougher than I was, in fact. I could not stop the urge to impress her at all times because she impressed me so much. She was brave, tenacious and gorgeous. Also, it might have been due to my failure to protect her at Wimbledon Common that, now, I wanted to show her how manly I could be. Maybe it was in response to her story about the nurse that died in the cellar. I could not outdo her ever.

"How awful, I remember my first craniotomy, we just could not get the baby out and we couldn't perform a Caesar as the baby's head was too far engaged," she said. "She was a mother of eleven, so there was simply no other choice."

"That must have been a tough decision," I assured her.

"We had to save her. I still shiver to think of the decision I had to make but the baby was almost dead already. If I hadn't performed the operation, both of them would have died."

That shut me up. I realised, then, how similar our lives were.

We had to take tough decisions and we had to clear up the mess when things went wrong.

I sat back in my seat as Jo drove, following Stephens like a shadow.

He headed down the hill, along the rest of Latchmere Road, past the junction with Battersea Park Road and onto Battersea Bridge. We stared out of our windows at the city as it was lit up for the evening. At the traffic lights just before Chelsea Embankment, I saw Jo glance over at the beautiful Albert Bridge, glinting in the night, its bright-lit, Christmas tree, profile reflected in the mirror smooth Thames.

"Isn't it a beautiful sight," she murmured?

I saw her face in profile silhouetted against the structure and I had to agree with her.

"Yes, stunning," I replied, knowing she would be too focused on reaching our destination to notice my remark was loaded.

The only noise after that was the ticking of the clock in the centre of the walnut dashboard. I could not even her the roar of the six-cylinder as we pulled away from the lights. It was a solid piece of kit, the Rolls, comfortable and cosseting. It was wonderfully warm, and I wanted to stay sitting there for the rest of then night, just getting a bit of kip.

We were left to our own deep and dark thoughts. Memories crowded into my mind, I even remember some of them, now, but the rest of the evening is a bit of a blur especially just before I was knocked out.

That was why I needed Jo to fill in the details.

I remember us arriving at the building, noticing that there was no car there and leaving Stephens and Jo to look for the Ford around the corner. That was when I must have been hit from behind.

ii

So, there we sat in Lyons' Coffee House, our drinks getting cold as Jo reminded me of what happened that night in her own words. I had read the report, but it skimmed on most of the salient details that I knew. I wanted the inside story.

As far as I was aware, I was knocked out and woke up with Stephens standing over my hospital bed. He had taken me down the road and around the corner to St. Stephen's Hospital, a small hospital on Fulham Road; it was less than ten minutes away.

iii

Going back to that night, I was looking out for a white or black Ford Zephyr, it was a popular choice for the C.I.D, the Anglia was not glamorous or large enough for the big boys. It had been particularly warm and comfortable in the Rolls and leaving those cosy confines was a huge shock.

As I shut the aluminium alloy door carefully behind me, I felt the damp air and chill wind try to seep into my very bones. Buttoning up my mackintosh, I strolled to the corner. The operator had definitely told Stephens that the rendezvous would be on the corner opposite Wetherby Gardens.

There was no sign of any cars at the designated spot. There was only one old, pre-war, Bentley in the street. I walked to the corner; there was nothing in Bolton Gardens to the south and only a few cars in Collingham Gardens to the north.

A Standard Vanguard and a green Morris Minor were parked on one side of the street and a wine-red Rover P4 75 with a single fog lamp in the middle of the grill, the 'Cyclops Rover' and a grey Vauxhall PA Cresta on the other. I had been expecting a Bristol or Aston Martin, but I was disappointed. Then, the rain came back, spitting pathetic flecks of rain on the pavement and me.

I walked a few yards down to the Boltons and then crossed over retraced my steps but on the opposite side of the road, I looked left as I crossed into Collingham Gardens but there were no vehicles there.

My breath came out in clouds and I shuddered with the cold. My raincoat was beginning to get soaked. It was time to get back to the warmth of the car and the smell of Jo's Guerlain perfume. I crossed over to the other side of the road and I could hear my leather soled shoes slapping on the wet pavement.

Next, I heard the sound of rubber-soled boots thumping on the wet concrete. As I turned, a cosh hit me in the temple.

It felt like I had been hit with a brick.

I remember steadying myself against the garden wall. Dazed, I looked around at the hedge that marked the gardens. I dimly registered that my assailant had come from there. I staggered forward using the wall of the building for support. I wondered why he had not come at me again, but as my legs buckled underneath me, I knew why.

He knew exactly what he was doing.

I felt weakness wash over me in waves. My head ached. I had to make it to the corner and warn the others, the soul was willing, but the flesh was weak. Every step was like a huge stride up a sheer cliff. It was virtually impossible to put one foot in front of the other.

The throbbing intensified.

I wanted to talk but you have to be able to think to speak and my awareness was slipping, by the time I reached the corner, I had forgotten why I was there and even where I was. The pain in my head was so great I wanted to cry.

Stephens must have seen me. I had scaled the wall of the building and I was leaning on the stone garden wall, trying to get my breath back when I slumped to the ground. I remember Stephens putting his arms around me to try and support me and my body slipping through his fingers like water, my head still pulsated painfully.

I remember feeling the damp soak through into my clothes, the feel of the cold hard pavement against my face, the hammering in my head. I remember closing my eyes and welcoming Morpheus as his arms opened. I was lost in his embrace. I was in oblivion and it was bliss.

iv – Revelations.

Let me take you back to that night, again:

"Are you coming in?" asked the handsome, young man as the heavy main door of No. 1, Wetherby Gardens, swung open.

He was always willing to help a beautiful blonde woman, well-dressed and her hair coiffured exquisitely. If he had not been running five minutes late to meet friends for supper, he might have stayed to flirt with her, perhaps, but he was going to meet a young girl in the group. It was only down the road at the Hereford Arms, but he could not afford to be too late, making a good impression was normally a guarantee of a later date.

'A brunette in the hand was worth a blonde on the steps,' he mused.

Jo had been studying the buzzers for each flat. She smiled, her disarming smile, acknowledging his gallantry and good looks. He was fair-haired and handsome, perhaps a Guardsman, tall, elegant and thin, dressed in a light grey single-breasted suit, Jo betted it was from Gieves and Hawkes, a red and blue striped tie and white shirt hid behind a navy-blue cashmere jumper.

"Yes, please, I'm visiting the top flat, worse luck," she explained, giving him eye contact, hoping he would believe her.

"Be my guest," he announced, steeping backwards and drawing the door open.

He gave her an appreciative smile she was very good looking, stunning in fact, and the camel skirt and jacket ensemble looked reassuringly expensive. She was a bit older than his usual type but definitely attractive. With the endearing hopefulness of youth, he thought he might well see her again. Perhaps, he conjectured, he might get to know her better if things did not work out with the girl at the pub. At his age, life was full of infinite possibilities.

"Thank you," she replied, slipping past him with ease, a rush of joy ran through her, she could not believe her good fortune. A closed gate had swung open.

As Jo started to shuffle up the carpeted staircase, she heard the door slam shut behind him, which meant she could increase her pace. There was no longer any need for pretence. She wondered why Jenny Strong should buy the top floor flat, it was not for the views; the other stucco apartment buildings blocked any vista of the capital. The brass runners and wine-red carpet became a blur as she bounded up the four flights. There was no room for a lift in the stairwell.

Jenny had good legs and Jo could see why if she was trundling up and down these stairs every day. Grabbing the bannister, she hauled herself up, taking two steps at a time. Jo was tall and athletic, which stood her in good stead for the climb.

She had no idea how she would get into Jenny's apartment or what she would find there. All she knew was that Jenny Strong had secrets hidden in there. Her train was at this moment hurtling towards King's Cross St Pancras. Jo had very little time to search the flat for answers. She had to act fast.

For some strange reason, she thought of her brother at the monastery in Nunraw. Thoughts of stations triggered memories. It was from St. Pancras Station that Father Stephen had left to join the silent Cistercian order at Sancta Maria Abbey. It was a fleeting thought.

Silence was also required at Wetherby Gardens; she did not want to alert the neighbours to her presence. She rested halfway up the stairs; already she was glowing, her heart thumping in her chest. Cigarette smoking had shrunk her lung capacity, so she was panting. She was tall, a size ten, statuesque but she was not used to exercise. She 'caught her breath'.

She simply had to give up smoking, she told herself.

Taking a deep breath, she walked up the two remaining floors to the flat.

At the top, she rested. Her heart rate was returning to normal, but adrenaline kept her pulse rate racing. She wanted to remain calm and she tried her best to quell her panting. Pulling herself together on the landing at the top of the stairs, she looked down. It was a very, very long way down.

Wondering how she might pick the lock, she suddenly thought that the neighbour might have a spare key. Just as she was turning to ask, she noticed the door was ever so slightly ajar; it was not flush with the wall. 'Burglars,' she immediately thought. It appeared the lock had been forced open. She would have dismissed the scars on the white gloss paintwork as clumsiness with keys if the door had been closed.

Hesitating, only briefly, Jo determined to approach them with her charm. Perhaps, a woman might be able to talk her way out of a situation. Hopefully, her Irish charm would help to diffuse any charged atmosphere she might encounter.

On second thoughts, it would perhaps be better to call the police and let them deal with it. There were already two detectives in hospital, she remembered. She dismissed the idea. Leaving it up to the police might complicate things; the burglar might get away before they arrived. It was time for action, 'time and tide wait for no man, she intoned in her head. There was no choice; she had to go in alone. Jenny would be home soon. Jo steeled herself to open the door.

Not for the first time, in this caper, she was unaware of what lay behind the door. One thing she did know; she had to find out who was there, how they got in and what they were doing there in the first place. It was clearly not Jenny. Why would anyone break into her flat?

Her heart hammering, she pushed the door open, conscious that she should do it slowly and gently so the hinges did not creak, she stepped through the doorway and only half closed the door behind her, making sure the door would not blow shut and give her away.

She had been expecting to be greeted by a large room overlooking the street. Instead, she was confronted by a blank wall and, to her right, yet another staircase leading up from this second landing. Inwardly sighing, she tiptoed up the stairs. As Jo emerged out of the stairwell, she froze. Her head was only just visible above the last step, but she could see that the burglar had drawn the heavy claret drapes and he had turned on all the lights and lamps in the room.

It was definitely a man, big, broad and fighting fit. Her luck, it seemed, had changed. He had removed his gloves and his head was bowed as he shuffled some papers, skimming each leaf as he searched for something. His hands worked frantically through the piles of letters. Next to his pigskin gloves, was a heavy handled commando knife, which Jo immediately realised was not for letter opening.

It had a blackened steel blade and a ribbed handle. It was about a foot long, the blade being six inches. The sight of it made Jo's heart stop. Opening another draw, he took out another pile of papers and scanned each of those.

The man was wearing a balaclava, not one of those open-faced woollen ones that everyone used to wear to keep warm in winter, but a menacing black mask with two holes for the eyes and a slit for the mouth. Jo wished she had been dressed for flying; her camel Pierre Balmain skirt-suit was not ideal for fight or flight. She noticed her green silk blouse was clinging to her skin.

If there had been time, she would have taken off her jacket, it would restrict her movement, being pursued down the stairs with that drop worried her and she wanted to keep cool physically as well as mentally.

She drank in the situation.

On the desk there were piles of papers a green shaded desk lamp burning brightly and a black Bakelite telephone. The phone might be of use, the lamp might make a weapon, or the paper might offer a distraction if she showered him in it, she might be able to escape or maybe she could pretend that she could find the document for him, had been told by Jenny to help him locate it. Thoughts flooded her head.

It was as if he smelt her approach, despite her soft tread on the carpeted stairs, he sensed her presence. There was no turning back. Jo continued up the stairs.

The burglar appraised her as she entered the large drawing room. They were matched in height, he was six foot; Jo was tall, too, five foot nine. She was strong and her fencing gave her agility and stamina, but she doubted that she could match him.

Being on the fifth floor of No. 1 Wetherby Gardens meant the window could not provide escape. She could bolt down the stairs, but he would follow, hurling himself on top her, she did not doubt that for a second. Even worse, he could bundle her over the bannisters, and she would not survive the plunge to the bottom.

He put down the papers. She was ready for a fight. At first, Jo thought he was reaching for the black leather gloves. Then, she saw his left hand grasp the black, ribbed, handle of a knife. Suddenly, the odds were not so even.

She flicked, her long blonde hair away from her face, trying to see what colour her assailant's eyes were, trying to see if she recognised them. They stared at her, ice blue like her own, but his burned with anger while hers darted left and right, desperately searching the room for something with which she could defend herself. A knife-wielding thug threatened her on the other side of the desktop. Talking was not an option, yet that was her forte.

He wanted her out of the way, and she wanted to have answers. Their eyes locked over the sea of the desk. For a full minute, they held each other's gaze. He had the power; he had the strength. He was militarily fit. She was determined to stand her ground. Perhaps, he was a former soldier or a physical training instructor. He was all muscle. That was clear. She was relatively fit, and her long limbs might allow her to outrun him, but he was beefy, he could crush her easily with his strength. There had to be a way to save the situation, she reasoned, he was right, but she was right. She had to prevail.

"One of the Tweed twins?" she asked. "Breaking and entering is hardly your forte, I thought that was extortion and murder."

He was surprised to hear her posh voice, cut glass Kensington.

"Doctor Nora Josephine Murphy, I presume," the man hissed, his lips curled into a grotesque smile behind the mask.

"My friends call me Jo, but you can call me Doctor Murphy," she replied dryly, taking a step towards the desk. His mouth became a pair of pouting lips twisting into a bigger smile, he was finding all this entertaining. She heard a snort.

"I don't see any of your friends here, I dealt with Regan outside and you sent Stephens to take him to hospital. How did you get in here anyway?" he drawled in his south London accent.

Jo smiled, knowingly, provoking him.

"I recognise the voice and you're left-handed, Derek Tweed, I assume," Jo asserted proudly, taking another step, playing grandmother's footsteps. She had only met Tweed twice, but she had managed to pierce his disguise

"You should have stuck to doctoring love," he advised, the mouth forming itself into a dismissive smile that showed his teeth, "no one asked you to stick your nose in."

"Doctoring those files seems to be your purpose. What are you doing, destroying evidence?" she asked, taking another step closer to the desk.

"Mind your own business," he warned, the mouth was, now, a sneer.

"Jenny wanted some incriminating information destroyed before we could get a warrant and she sent for her tame assassin," she goaded him, moving another step towards the desk that she hoped would form a protective barrier against her attacker.

"That's my twin," he explained.

"That's what he says about you, he's pointed the finger of suspicion at you, anything to escape a life sentence, Regan tells me."

"I'm not falling for that one. I just clear up after him, normally," he said and, then, paused, "but this time I'm prepared to make an exception, on medical grounds."

"Which are?"

"I don't like doctors who think they are detectives."

He lifted up the receiver. Jo thought he was going to call someone for instructions and was about to tease him about that fact and his inability to make up his own mind, when he smashed the receiver down on the desk.

The earpiece split, the cover flew into the air and onto the floor. A silver disk fell out like a dislocated eye, the internal receiver, hanging from coloured electrical wires. He tore it off. Raising, what was left of the receiver, he smashed the mouthpiece on the tabletop. Again, the Bakelite cracked, sending the cover to join its double on the floor.

Again, he tore the shiny disk from the electrical flex. Again, he stared at her with his cold blue eyes. Again, Jo stared back at him.

Neither of them was prepared to blink.

"So, my assumptions were right," Jo beamed, hoping to rile him.

"What are you on about?" he hissed, throwing the knife from hand to hand like a juggling ball.

"You don't scare me, you're just another one of the Tweed twins at work. You've made a mess of getting rid of me so many times, what makes you think you will be successful, now?"

"This six-inch blade and boxing lessons," he assured her.

"I've seen bigger surgeon's knives, looks like you've been taking dancing lessons, more likely."

As she had hoped, the face formed into a grimace.

She had begun to anger him, already. If he was angry, he might make a mistake and if he made a mistake she might just survive. Jo looked on, as her attacker approached, moving around the table. He hunched his shoulders, preparing to pounce; his black bomber jacket made him look even bigger than he was. He was a bear of a man.

He had slipped the knife into his right hand; the other hand made a grab for her. She dodged out of the way, finding momentary sanctuary behind the desk. Jo placed her hands on the green leather top, ready to spring to the left or the right depending on the side he chose. Tweed had been disturbed before he could complete his mission.

She noticed his black backpack on the chair beside the desk and, on the leather top; she noticed his black leather gloves, which he had taken off to handle the sheaves. They would not prove useful. Wondering which of the papers she should grab before she took off, throwing the backpack at his head.

 Jo had to admit she had made a massive miscalculation and it was time for flight rather than fight. The only problem was working out the best exit strategy. Tweed had been obviously disconcerted. Jo had disturbed him while he was meant to be covering Jenny's tracks. He had no intention of leaving until his job was done.

Jo knew that he would get rid of her and then continue his search, he was not about to bolt, nor was she, although she should have done. Having her back to a blade-wielding assassin was not an option. She had no idea what exactly he was looking for, what incriminating evidence he had meant to destroy, and if he got hold of her, she would never know.

Realising, too late, that it had been a mistake to come up to the flat alone did not help her alone. Jo had expected to find the flat empty. Suddenly, survival became her only concern. She weighed up her chances, noticed how long his thighs looked in his tight-fitting trousers, she recognised them as ski-pants, he would definitely be able to run faster than her. She was wearing a skirt and all that entailed, corset, slip, stockings and high heels. Though, she could lose the heels everything else would restrict her movement.

The stirrups, which kept the pants in place, were hidden by what looked like brown Jodhpur boots. She reassessed, they were, in fact, Chelsea boots with heavy rubber soles, workmen's boots. She wondered if they might have a steel toecap and vowed to watch for any kicks he might make.

Jo knew her assailant could crush her easily with his strength. She reckoned she just might be able to outrun him, but it was a huge risk, turning her back on him and running downstairs. All her emotions screamed at her to get away before he killed her.

Desperately, she grabbed the table lamp on the desk and toyed with the idea of racing him around the bureau until they both collapsed with exhaustion, she had been a phenomenal runner at medical school. Instead, she attacked. She knew her survival depended on it.

With a furious yank she pulled the flex from the socket, leaving the plug behind, the wire whipped the back of her leg, but she ignored the pain, pulling the flex up and bunching it around the base with her free hand. She waved the lamp in his face all the while.

The lips, pouting through the slit of the balaclava, broke into a cruel closed mouth smile, yet again. It was all part of the sport. She smiled back, showing her teeth in an ironic salutation, a sarcastic smile.

She poked the table lamp at his face, deliberately provoking him. She used the stand like the handle of an epee. En garde, she aimed the lamp at his eye, pulling it away from his reach at the last second.

The lunge sent him skipping back. It was a natural reflex. Instead of following through, she bounded backwards and attacked a second time.

Cautiously, he stepped back, instinct made him avoid the lamp. He tried to swat it away like a fly but each time she withdrew, taking it from his grasp. Moving the knife into his left hand, the southpaw waved it about in front of him to intimidate Jo and block her thrust.

Jo backed into one of the rooms that led off from the drawing room, retreating into a smaller space seemed suicidal but she was hoping there might be some scissors or even a blunt object that she could use to defend herself, properly.

She had an older sister and three elder brothers, all of them had taught her to fight in their own different fashions.

He came into the bedroom and closed the door, glancing at the bed. Remembering her fencing lessons, she jabbed forward and, then, moved back quickly, in a rhythmical dance, teasing him with the prospect of being hit by the heavy brass lamp stand.

Transferring the knife from his left to his right hand, yet again, he bunched his left hand into a fist. Jo leapt forward, brandishing the lamp yet again, he opened his hand and, fed up with her theatricals, he grabbed for the lamp.

She allowed him to seize it.

Too late, he realised that he had grabbed the bulb. Quickly, she moved into action, putting both hands over his. She fastened his hand onto the hot orb, gripping his fist and wrist to keep it closed. She smelt searing flesh.

Roaring loudly, he dropped the knife from his right hand while he tried to move his other hand and wriggle free. She had trapped it securely. Jo matched all his twisting and turning, moving with him as he wriggled.

He collapsed onto his knees, head bowed to hide his face or in silent supplication.

"Take that you great Amadán," she hissed, holding his hand in place as he struggled in her grasp.

He pulled his arm away, but she just followed, the pain in his hand was overwhelming and all he wanted to do was release the burning globe that scorched his hand. His head lifted and she saw the pain etched on his face. The fire in his eyes burned even brighter. She had never seen anyone so angry before. The burning became deeper, the longer she held his hand on the bulb. There was nothing he could do but try to free his hand free, but Jo still maintained her grip, no matter how much he tried to shake her off. He twisted and turned his hand, pushed backwards and forwards yet her vice-like hold remained firm. She would not release this floundering fish no matter how much it writhed.

He was focused only on his pain, the burning sensation in his left hand. Finally, giving up on twisting free, he brought up his free hand to push her away. She had to take her empty hand from her pocket to block the trajectory with her arm. It was easy to foresee his clumsy efforts to relieve his pain. It was clear he was not thinking clearly and his pathetic attempts at escape were easily foiled.

Next, he tried to grab for the stem of the lamp using his right hand. He was not thinking straight but she was, she released her grip and gave him the lamp, kicking the knife across the floor at the same time.

The blade slipped under the closed door and the heavy handle lodged there. Holding his damaged hand above his head, to keep it away from danger the man backed away from her. For the first time, he seemed frightened, almost vulnerable.

Holding the lamp stand in his hand, not as an instrument of assault but a weapon to protect his damaged hand should she try and grab for it. He realised it was his Achilles heel.

All her instincts told her that this would be 'a fight to the death' if she were not careful. Whether he was feigning defeat, or he was actually afraid of what she might do next, did not matter a jot to her; she had to act quickly and decisively. She had to stop him getting the knife and maintain her slight advantage.

The odds were now in her favour. She had to use the advantage to prevent her attacker using the blade. If she failed, the consequences could be fatal. She rushed forward, as he edged backwards towards the knife handle, wrong footing him, as he almost tripped over the bed.

As he stumbled backwards, she easily managed to brush the lampstand and his undamaged hand away with her free hands and before he could raise either to strike her, she planted her kneecap in the soft mass in his ski pants, not twice but thrice.

Groaning in pain, he collapsed on the floor releasing the lamp and curling into a ball. He tried to kick out, but Jo had leapt over his feet already and stepped away from his arms. He was clearly not going to give up easily and nor was she.

For good measure, she stomped on the burnt hand with her high heal, which made him cry out in pain and frustration, a gurgling scream that sounded horrific.

As a doctor, inflicting pain rather than healing people baulked but she nevertheless felt he deserved punishment, he had attacked her often enough. Her brothers had bullied Jo when she was younger, so she knew how to react. She knew he would be out of action for enough time for her to grab the knife and flee.

Without hesitation, she ran over to it, bending down, she opened the door, before picking up the weapon by its blade.

Then, she slammed it shut and with her free hand, she locked the bedroom door and slipped the key into her pocket. While she hurried to the desk, she slipped the knife, handle first, into her suit jacket, the inside pocket. The blade protruded above her left shoulder a silver shard. The smashed telephone would offer her no help, so she swept all the papers into the bag Tweed had brought with him, she did not need to be as selective as he had been.

She gingerly grabbed the knife by the blade and dropped it into Tweed's swag bag, sandwiching it between Jenny's private papers, before fastening the leather thong straps. Carrying the bag in her left hand, she ran down the steps to the landing and the front door.

Seeing a man's coat hanging from one of the pegs on the back of the door, she searched the pockets and grabbed the keys from Tweed's black donkey jacket, Jo extracted them from the left-hand pocket. She made a mental note.

He had held his knife in his right hand, at first, but it was obvious that he had transferred it to the left before attempting to use it on her. That information proved invaluable, it told her, without a shadow of a doubt, which Tweed it was, Dangerous Derek.

Without meaning to, she had damaged his killing hand. It was the closest she had ever come to being stabbed so she was not going to stay around to heal him.

Wrenching open the front door, she slipped through it, slammed the door against the jamb and turning the brass key firmly in the mortise lock she fastened the door, locking it from the outside.

All was quiet on the landing.

None of the other flats had heard the struggle or if they had, they were staying firmly behind their closed doors.

She assumed many of the occupants were away for the weekend or out; no wonder Tweed had felt able to burgle the flat, the residents were few and far between on a Sunday evening. Putting the knapsack down, Jo used the longer silver key to secure the brass escutcheon lock, too, for good measure. Jo reasoned that he would not be desperate enough to throw himself from a fifth floor flat. Extracting the keys, she popped them into her left-hand pocket and slung the bag over her shoulder.

A cursory look into the stairwell, which made up the common parts, showed her the coast looked clear. Swiftly, she descended the stairs, trotting down them, her left hand on the bannister rail, her right-hand fishing for her own car keys.

Her leather shoes made no sound on the thick red carpet on the steps but clicked noisily on the marble floor as she dashed for the front door. She had signed the Hippocratic oath and yet for the first time she had hurt rather than healed a fellow human being. It bothered her. Almost being murdered bothered her more. It was the third attempt on her life in as many weeks.

Outside, the dim streetlamps showed her the way. The cold air hit her, and she realised that she was perspiring. No matter what Tweed did, now, she had a knife with his fingerprints on it and once he was threatened with prison for attempted murder, he would give up Jenny Strong's secrets soon enough. Perhaps, the papers she had taken would provide an explanation to all the mysterious events of the past few weeks.

There were three cars in the street, a green, pre-war Austin, a grey Morris Minor and a two-tone, brown and beige, 1955, Rolls Royce Silver Cloud, registration number: GPF 521.

She had left the door unlocked and, seizing the chrome handle, she pressed the button into the handle and opened the driver's door. The courtesy light flashed on.

Stepping in through the large door, she settled into the tan leather seats before shutting the aluminium alloy door, softly, behind her. Inhaling the familiar leather smell, she took a deep breath in and stilled her heart before exhaling. The silver driver's mirror and the rear-view mirror, mounted on the dashboard to accommodate the sunroof, revealed a deserted street behind her and ahead the road was clear.

There were few people venturing out on a sombre Sunday evening, just doctors who thought they were detectives and curious police inspectors who needed an arrest. Slowly, she slipped the steel key into the silver circular disc of the ignition, which was located in the walnut fascia of the dashboard to the left of the steering wheel. As she turned it to the right, the five-litre-six-cylinder engine purred into life and Jo selected drive from the black, Bakelite stalk jutting from the left-hand side of the steering column, she turned on the headlights and even indicated.

Releasing the handbrake and raising her foot from the brake pedal, she took a brief look over her right shoulder before pressing down on the accelerator, the two-tone, brown beast moved into the night, sweeping onto the main road and travelling towards Hereford Square at speed.

She snaked through the side streets that she knew so well, past Gloucester Road tube station and right on to the Cromwell Road, heading for Knightsbridge. For seven years this area had been her shopping district. Within minutes the flat was a mile away.

Jo concentrated on piloting the car through the streets, staring ahead at the road, searching the pavements, her heart pounded in her chest, but her breathing was returning to normal. Adrenaline coursed through her body. She was feeling more alert than she had ever been.

Her mind raced, processing what she had been through, the shock of the attack affected her emotions, but her logical mind was already searching for solutions.

She would need help.

There were plenty of friends to draw on. All were close by. Only she had chosen to live in the depths of south London. Most of her friends lived in Montpellier Square or Belgravia. South of the river was dodgy, then, a place of nefarious deeds and skulduggery.

Pulling up outside a public phone box, a red Gilbert Scott design, she locked the car this time and scurried to the phone box. Lifting the receiver, pushing a penny into the slot, she rapidly inserted her finger into the metal ring that danced around the figures as she dialled: 2-2-8-7-9-9-0. It took an eternity for the phone to be answered. When the call was picked up, she pressed button 'A'.

"Battersea, seven, double nine, oh, who's calling?" George announced, his west coast brogue sounding tinny in the telephone earpiece.

"George, I have a few things for you to take care of. Have I got your attention?" she asked, immediately she heard her husband's dulcet tones.

Her voice was business-like and calm.

"Of course, darling," he crooned, noticing the seriousness in her voice. That's good. Can you send an ambulance and the police to 48 Wetherby Gardens, flat number five, immediately, please?" she continued, reassured he was listening.

"I've a pen and paper handy," George answered in his soothing manner. His Irish accent helped her feel reassured. He turned over the bill from Sporthotel Hinterbrau, Ernst Reisch, Kitzbuhel, dated 6.1.58, and held his fountain poised above the paper. Jo had moved thirty-seven times since she was born, she craved souvenirs, George despite his wealth was too mean to use notepaper; he used the back of the receipts that Jo wanted to keep. Every souvenir she had was covered in George's graffiti, a fountain pen scrawl defacing them all.

Epilogue:

My head still thumped with pain when I awoke in St Stephen's the next morning. Jo had convinced Stephens to take me to the nearest hospital, saying we should call off the raid that we had been involved in because the other officers were not there. I think she had concerns about my head. Stephens knew CID and he reckoned they had made their arrests and taken the criminals off with them. Typically, he surmised, they had left one behind.

Stephen's told me what had happened next, standing at the foot of my bed, the hospital curtains were drawn around us to get some semblance of privacy. His report made my blood run cold.

I vaguely remember hearing doors slamming as the pair of them manhandled me into the car, Stephens took the top half, and Jo took my feet. He slammed the door and offered Jo a lift, but she refused, urging him to hurry to the Emergency Department where they could look at my head.

"So, she drove home, then," I quipped, feeling the bandages tight around my head and wondering if I should get Stephens to call for a nurse. I was not due to have any more painkillers for another hour, so I let it go.

"Not quite, sir," Stephens said, joining in the banter. I knew he was on the defensive, he only ever called me sir when he thought he was in trouble or there were other officers around.

I could not see any other coppers in my ward. Perhaps, I conjectured, he was being extra respectful to me, the patient; the injured party.

"Go on, Stephens," I groaned due to my condition more than my reaction to his words.

I was still groggy, and my voice was gravelly. My headache was not going to go away, but I was too riveted by Sergeant Stephens's account of that night.

"Apparently, she nipped back to number one, and, seeing a young man coming out, she marched up the stairs and said hello. She kept him talking on the top step long enough for him to think that she was resident there and had forgotten her keys to the common parts."

"Don't tell me she went in there?" I asked, trying to sound incredulous, even though I knew the answer.

"I'm afraid so, sir," he sighed grimly, pursing his lips and lowering his head slightly.

"Then what happened?" I asked.

I felt infuriation bubble up under the bandages and bedclothes.

"You'd better ask he yourself, she's here," Stephens suggested, stepping to one side to allow Jo to walk through. Approaching my bed and standing next to the pillows, she leant forward and kissed my head on the temple.

For the second time in twenty-four hours, I was floating.

"Good morning, inspector," Jo said, "I hope your head is feeling better, I managed to talk to the medical staff here and they say you should be back at your desk in a few days."

"That's good news."

"Just enough time for Stephens to finish the report, wouldn't you say," she continued.

"Absolutely, doctor," Stephens agreed, smiling indulgently at Jo. He knew what she was getting at.

"So, you can relax, we've tied up the case between us. Tweed is in custody being treated for a burnt hand; the papers incriminating Strong, Hepher and Bray are all safe with the Director of Public Prosecutions and all members of the ring have been rounded up and arrested."

"Tell me more," I pleaded, looking at Stephens to fill in the details.

"As I was saying, I saw you hit the floor like a prize fighter after a knock-out punch," he explained to Jo who was at my shoulder.

"I see."

"I didn't have time to catch him. I'd only reached the corner when you got hit."

"Where did he go?" Jo asked.

"I chased him to the gardens at the back but lost him," Stephens elucidated, "he was carrying a rubber cosh; I saw that much, and he was left-handed."

"Tweed," she whispered.

"He's still in the prison hospital, thanks to your efforts" Stephens explained, "I saw his wounds, he won't be using that hand properly for months. When he's well enough their transfer him to Wandsworth, he's not going anywhere, He'll go down for being an accessory to murder at least, or attempted murder if we can't prove he was actually involved."

Jo looked uncomfortable as he explained the damage; she had done to Tweed with the hot light bulb.

"The other Tweed, what happened to him?"

"He's left the country," Stephens insisted.

"Someone with his passport left the country. Only one Tweed is left-handed and he's the murderer, Regan got off lightly," Jo persisted.

"Well, he's inside, now, and Regan was out cold that night," my loyal sergeant reminded her, unnecessarily I thought.

"Just get on with your story, Stephens," I moaned.

Stephens took us back to the night.

"Bring the car around, St. Stephen's is the closest hospital, take him there," Jo ordered helping him to lift me.

"What are you going to do?" Stephens asked.

"I'll drive home. If I don't feel up to it, I can't get a taxi or I'll walk down to the King's Road and get a number nineteen bus to the bottom of Wakehurst Road," Jo replied. "Now hurry, we have to get Regan to hospital as quickly as possible."

Satisfied that Jo would be safe and worried about me, Stephens obeyed, collected the car and drove it around the corner to park next to me.

"What about the CID car, why wasn't it there?" I asked.

"Quite simply, Strong knew we were on the way to search her flat and Tweed was dispatched as look out. When he saw the CID, he sent them away by pretending to be you," Stephens explained.

"The little…' I began.

"Sir, ladies present," he reminded me, nodding in Jo's direction.

"Yes, he was a complete whatever you were going to say," Jo giggled.

"So, you needn't worry," Stephens soothed.

"I've brought you some Lucozade, grapes and some Planter's peanuts to build you up," Jo announced.

"I suppose, I'll have to thank you both for all your work on this one," I acknowledged grudgingly, helping myself to a grape from the brown paper bag that Jo had placed on my bedside table.

"Aren't you going to offer them around?" Stephens grumbled.

He folded his arms like a spoilt schoolboy. In my dazed state, I had forgotten my manners.

"Ladies first," I replied, offering her the bag.

"Ladies will be first, one day, mark my words," she quipped as she helped herself to a grape and popped it between her perfect white teeth.

Other Books

We hope you have enjoyed the story. You might like to consider the following books by the same author:

Gunpowder Guy or, *Remember the Fifth November,* is the truth behind the Gunpowder Plot, Robert Catesby a convert to the Church of England was apparently a Catholic zealot, Robert Cecil with a spy network second to none failed to spot the movement of 36 barrels of gunpowder, how?

The Taint Gallery is a story of desire and betrayal set against a backdrop of contemporary London and New York; this was a love affair that led to deceit and destruction.

Switch is a dark thriller, Chandler meets *'Fifty Shades of Grey'*; a nightmare comes true.

Waterwitch is a sailing adventure: two brothers sailing a boat around the Mediterranean during the Falklands War, resulting in disastrous consequences.

Major Bruton's Safari or *Uganda Palaver* is a witty account of a coronation and a safari in Uganda. As a guest of the Ugandan people, a group of disparate people experience Africa with a caustic commentator, not critical of the continent but of his own friends and family.

Innocent Proven Guilty is a thriller on the lines of *39 Steps*. A teacher discovers his brother dead in a pool of blood, he wants to find the murderer, but he has left his footprints behind

Seveny Seven is a 'Punk Portrait' The story of growing up in London during the punk era, a whimsical autobiography that explodes the myth that 'Punk' was an angry working-class movement.

The book reveals the trials and tribulations of being a teenager at the time.

Carom, named after an Indian board game, is a thriller about an art theft and drug smuggling. Finn McHugh, and his team pursue Didier Pourchaire, a vicious art thief. The action moves between London, Paris, Helsinki and St. Petersburg. Everyone wants to catch the villain resulting in a messy bagatelle. Carom is an Indian board game.

Ad Bec, a dish best eaten cold, is the story of a schoolboy who takes revenge on a bully. Stephen is a late arrival at a prep school in the depths of Shropshire. He is challenged to do a 'tunnel dare' by the school bully. When the tunnel collapses on the bully, Stephen has to solve the dilemma, tell no one and be free or rescue the bully. The story is set in a seventies progressive preparatory school.

Karoly's Hungarian Tragedy is Michael's first departure into historical biography. This is the story of Karoly Ellenbacher taken into captivity and used as a human shield by Romanian soldiers during the war, arrested during the communist era and sent down a coal mine, he escaped to England in 1956. His story of survival is barely credible.

Michael Fitzalan has written four plays:

George and the Dragon, a painter discovers a cache of bonds and sovereigns in a cellar, not knowing that it belongs to a vicious gang. Thankfully his niece's friend is a star lawyer and can help him return the money before it is too late, or can she?

Symposium for Severine is a modern version of Plato's Symposium but with women being the philosophers instead of men.

Superstar is a play that sees Thomas Dowting meeting Jesus in the Temple, travelling to Angel to meet his girlfriend Gabrielle. They convince Thomas to volunteer for work abroad. Three weeks later J C Goodman takes over Thomas's job and moves in with Gabrielle.

Michael is working on a hybrid book, a mixture between a script and a novel; *M.O.D*, Mark O'Dwyer, Master of Disguise, a private detective agency, Frances Barber Investigators, is retained to find out why a model was defenestrated from a Bond Street building.

Printed in Great Britain
by Amazon